TEMPTATION

Somewhere in the house came the sound of a door opening and closing, and Caroline found herself wondering if it was the marquis returning home. After he had ridden alongside their carriage en route to London and deposited them on the doorstep of the town house, he had gone off to the stables and Caroline had not seen him since. She gathered from various offhand remarks issued by Augusta and her aunt that his lordship kept kept irregular hours, as was only to be expected of so notable a Corinthian and one who, moreover, was of the dashing Carlton House set. "I daresay we may run into Damien from time to time at a party here and there," Augusta had said casually, "but doubtless he finds the more sedate amusements sadly flat."

Caroline thought again of the engraving she had stumbled across in one of Augusta's newspapers, which portrayed Lord Reston amongst his aristocratic cronies in a milieu of unabashed decadence, surrounded by voluptuous young women in various stages of undress. It had upset her and dismayed her. Yet despite her better judgment the engraving had intrigued her too. How *did* the marquis pass his nights, and with whom? More than once she had drifted into the most wanton imaginings, picturing herself held in the powerful arms of the marquis, against that tall athletic body, and, reveling in the sensation of her own yielding softness against his exciting masculine hardness, she luxuriously allowed her lashes to drift down as he whispered fiery words of love and lowered his mouth to hers . . .

A PERFECT ROGUE

Martine Berne

Zebra Books
Kensington Publishing Corp.
http://www.zebrabooks.com

ZEBRA BOOKS are published by

Kensington Publishing Corp.
850 Third Avenue
New York, NY 10022

First Printing: July, 2000
10 9 8 7 6 5 4 3 2 1

Printed in the United States of America

A Perfect Rogue is dedicated to my editor, Amy Garvey.

Chapter 1

Hertfordshire County, England
1812

"By Jupiter, we've beaten him!" shouted Charles High-combe, glancing triumphantly at Lord Reston as his lordship's light racing curricle hurtled into the sleepy village of Baldock amidst the deepening grayish gloom of late-December twilight.

Damien's eyes remained fixed on his sleek, powerful chestnuts, and his long-fingered hands continued to firmly grip the reins. "Not yet," he answered coolly, managing with assurance to avoid careening into a massive farm wagon laden with bristly bundles of hay, whose pugnacious-looking driver seemed determined to occupy the whole of the tiny, muddy high street. "How far behind has Essex fallen?"

Chades twisted around, squinting. "Forty—no, fifty lengths," he said cheerfully. "I *knew* that pair of his would falter eventually! How I shall laugh to see him hand over the five hundred guineas he'll owe you!"

Damien's teeth flashed white in a brief smile. "A pleasant thought," he murmured, and neatly urged his horses around an enormous puddle of water that looked likely to conceal a rut of unknowable, but possibly disastrous, depth.

"Pleasant! I should say so!" snorted Charles. "The way he's been boasting about those damned grays for weeks! If you hadn't agreed to race him to Cambridge I own I was ready to draw his cork!"

Any reply Damien might have made was stilled when suddenly a small bundle was tossed into the road ahead of them. Just as swiftly, a shrill feminine cry rent the dusk and a slight, dark-clad figure threw itself into the path of the swiftly moving curricle, arms reaching beseechingly for the bundle.

There was barely time for Charles to draw in his breath in horror; Damien, cursing savagely, instantly wrenched his chestnuts to the right, and only by sheer dint of his quick skill did the yellow-painted wheels avoid flattening the creature who instead plunged hard into the body of the curricle and fell back in a crumpled heap onto the road.

"Dear God!" Charles uttered in shock, then jerked with surprise as Damien, having pulled the horses to a stop, thrust the reins into his hands and said sharply, "Have a care! See to their mouths! I only wish I may not have bruised them too badly!"

With that he sprang from the curricle; five strides of his long legs brought him before the limp figure that lay very still amidst the mud, one small gloved hand yet clutching the little bundle wrapped in coarse frieze. A crowd had already gathered round, on their faces mingled expressions of curiosity, concern, and ghoulish fascination.

"Lord, what's in that sack?" said one elderly woman, peering down so avidly the feathers in her old-fashioned turban fairly shook. "D'you suppose it's got money in there? Maybe she stole it, and was in desperate flight from the authorities!"

"Is the lady dead, Mama?" a little girl asked quaveringly,

clutching the hand of her awestruck parent, who only goggled speechlessly at the spectacle before them.

"It ain't money in that sack!" a man dressed in the plain vestments of a shopkeeper declared firmly, craning his neck to see more clearly. "Bless me if it ain't wiggling!"

Damien pushed the shopkeeper out of his way. "Step aside!" he said in a general command, and at the peremptory note in his cultured voice the crowd obediently drew back. Damien knelt and carefully pulled at the dark woolen cloak that had been knocked askew, obscuring the victim's face.

An ugly swelling already bloomed violet on one white temple; long black lashes lay still against the high cheekbones of a young woman Damien judged to be no more than twenty, far too thin even for a naturally petite frame, and clad in shabby but genteel apparel hardly sufficient to protect her against the biting winter air. A profusion of gleaming auburn ringlets tumbled in violent disarray from underneath a faded serge bonnet, now sadly mangled, and soft, pale lips parted to reveal that indeed she breathed yet despite the tremendous blow she had sustained but a few moments before.

Relief flooded through Damien, only to be replaced by a new anxiety as he now perceived that her left arm lay twisted at an unnatural angle. He glanced up at the people arrayed in a rough circle around the girl and himself and said imperatively "Where is the nearest inn?"

"Lord help you, guv'nor. Why trouble yourself?" expostulated the shopkeeper in astonished accents. "Let the constable, when he comes, take her to the Indigents' Infirmary!"

"When I desire your opinion, my good man, I shall certainly solicit it!' " Damien said icily. "I repeat, where is the nearest inn?"

"Just down the road, guv'nor," the shopkeeper replied meekly, pointing. "The Lion and Hare. It's the best in Baldock."

Curtly Damien nodded acknowledgment, then leaned down and gently lifted the girl into his embrace. A moan was wrenched from her as her injured arm came in contact with his chest, but she remained unconscious, for which, Damien thought grimly, she would be glad of as the journey to the inn, short as it was, would no doubt have jostled her agonizingly.

A small, muffled yelp abruptly caught his attention and he looked down to see the little bundle for which the girl had crazily risked her life. As the shopkeeper had pointed out, it was indeed moving inside its frieze confinement, though with no particular energy.

"Kindly pick up that sack," Damien said to the shopkeeper, "and accompany me to the inn."

"No, guv'nor, that I won't, begging your pardon," the shopkeeper returned, shaking his head and hastily backing away. "Might be snakes in there!"

"If it's not money, why, it's probably a baby!" speculated the elderly woman in the feathered turban, in some excitement. "Why on earth did she throw her own baby into the road, d'you suppose?"

"Mama!" the little girl piped up insistently. "Is the lady *and* the baby dead?"

Tamping down his temper, Damien ignored these interpolations and rested his gaze on a bright-eyed youth of ten or so who stood watching the proceedings with interest. "Sixpence if you'll carry that sack for me," he said, and eagerly the boy came forward.

"Is it a snake or a baby, guv'nor?" he inquired, fearlessly picking up the frieze bundle which seemed to wiggle in alarm as it was hoisted into the air.

"It's a dog," Damien answered brusquely, "and given the young lady's obvious degree of attachment to it, I think it reasonable to assume she would wish us to bring it along." The boy nodded agreeably, obviously uncomprehending but pleased at the prospect of so easily earning such a generous sum, and as Damien turned away toward the inn a red-and-green-striped curricle drawn by two heaving grays flashed by him and he caught a glimpse of Lord Essex's grinning countenance and a whip raised in mocking salute.

Impassively Damien watched Essex's curricle bowl down the high street, liberally splashing mud in its wake, and then he crossed to where Charles Highcombe stood gloomily staring after their victorious rival, one hand clutching the reins of the now quiescent chestnuts, who waited with heads patiently lowered.

"The impudent bastard!" Charles growled aloud. "Vainglorious jackanapes! Flourishing his whip in such an arrogant manner, as if he wasn't going to win by bloody *default!*"

"Charles," Damien interposed quietly, and his friend twisted around with a start.

His eyes fell on the limp burden in Damien's arms and he exclaimed bitterly: "Good God, if we hadn't stopped we'd be halfway to Cambridge by now! Have you maggots in your head? Never have you let something interfere in the winning of a wager!"

An odd half-smile briefly twisted Damien's mouth and then just as quickly disappeared; imperturbably he murmured, "What a lowering opinion you have of my character, my dear Charles."

Charles flushed, then shrugged, saying sullenly, "Doubtless she would have been looked after."

"Doubtless," Damien agreed mockingly. "In your devastated state, do you feel capable of leading my poor horses to yonder inn, where I trust we may find a groom of sufficient skill to tend them?"

"Yes, of course," Charles said gruffly, then added with marked reticence, "I—I beg pardon for speaking out of turn. It was merely my—my disappointment that rendered me so."

"Don't give it another thought, I beg you," said Damien carelessly, and began striding toward the inn. "This poor wretch I now bear will doubtless live, and we shall endure Essex's uncouth swaggering with such grace and *sang-froid* it will quite take the wind out of his sails. How fare the chestnuts? Have you examined them?''

''I have,'' Charles affirmed, his features reverting to their normally cheerful cast. ''Nothing but what a few days' rest will not effect a cure. Good God, how shall we pass the time? Do you suppose this paltry inn has a wine cellar worthy of the name?'' As they passed underneath the stone archway leading to the courtyard of the Lion and Hare, he paused to dubiously eye the modestly sized red-brick structure. ''There will be fleas among the sheets,'' he predicted ominously.

A gangly white-smocked ostler came hurrying from the stables, a piece of straw dangling from his mouth, and Charles winced. ''God help us!''

''Do your best, Charles. Do your best,'' Damien said soothingly, and continued to the door of the inn where he was met by the landlord, a portly, harassed-looking individual whose reddened hands were tightly twisted together above the stained apron wrapped around his protuberant belly.

''Good evening, sir!'' he said nervously. ''I'm Phillips, at your service. I was given to understand there was an accident?''

''As you see,'' answered Damien.

''Dreadful, sir, dreadful!'' rejoined the landlord, covertly gazing at the still white face cast into sharp relief against the darkness of Damien's many-caped greatcoat. ''Is—is she alive, sir?''

''I believe so.'' Carefully Damien maneuvered the girl past the narrow entrance and stepped into the welcome warmth of the inn. ''I am Reston. I require—''

''The—the Marquis of Reston, sir?'' gasped the landlord in awe.

Damien's fine black brows drew together at the interruption. ''Yes. To continue—''

''You do my humble inn a great honor by your patronage, my lord,'' the landlord said with a servile bow.

''To continue,'' Damien said, as if the landlord had not

spoken. "I require three of your best bedchambers, and a private parlor. If you will direct me to one of the bedchambers, I will take the lady there. She will need a maidservant to attend to her, and a doctor must be sent for promptly. By the bye my friend Highcombe and I will want our dinner served in the parlor, with some decent sherry if you have it."

"Certainly, my lord," the landlord said with another low bow. "If you will be so good as to follow me upstairs . . ." With a sweeping gesture he indicated that Damien should precede him up the wide, low wooden steps. "Here, you, young Joe!" he said sharply to the boy who stood obediently behind Damien, awaiting further instructions. "What d'you mean by following his lordship into my inn? And what's in that bag?"

"The lad is fulfilling an errand for me," Damien said as he began mounting the steps. "Come along—er, young Joe. Which reminds me, Phillips. I shall also require an old blanket, and bowls of fresh milk, water, and meat scraps. *After* you have sent for the doctor." As he reached the dimly lit landing of the second floor, idly Damien wondered about the reaction of Baldock's physician when, after examining the girl, he was presented with a patient indubitably of the canine persuasion.

Oh, heavens, how her head did hurt! It throbbed, Caroline thought wonderingly, as if a spiteful demon inside her skull was relentlessly beating in time to some unholy tune, leaving her feeling weak and more than half sick to her stomach. And her arm, her left arm! It ached terribly, with a deep fiery pain unlike any she had ever felt before.

But why? What had happened to her? Was she not curled up in her narrow little bed at Denbury Manor, in her familiar attic room, the victim, perhaps, of one of her unpleasantly realistic nightmares?

A lightning bolt of pain ricocheted through her head and then, abruptly, it all came back to her, and Caroline nearly moaned aloud at the hideous recollections swamping her. Mrs. Tintham's hysterical accusations, her oldest son's sullen confession, and then her husband's more measured response which nonetheless resulted in Caroline's swift dismissal from the household. Her tedious journey from Denbury to Baldock, shivering in a drafty carriage and pressed shoulder-to-shoulder with the other passengers. Then . . . her impulsive headlong plunge into the high street, only to realize too late that a swiftly moving, high-bodied curricle drawn by a pair of beautiful chestnut horses was nearly upon her. Just before she had closed her eyes in the anguish of the certain death about to descend upon her, Caroline had caught a fleeting glimpse of a tall, straight figure clad in a fashionable greatcoat, and a stunningly handsome face and flashing dark eyes. She had heard a man's deep voice cursing, and then a staggering jolt of pain had swept her into a heavy, silent blackness.

So she was alive then! Battered and bruised, no doubt, but alive. But—how much time had elapsed since the accident? And had Mrs. Ashby given up waiting for her to come claim her position as governess?

She must get up instantly and make her way to the house on Clinton Street. She had been informed, upon her arrival by mail coach in Baldock, that Clinton Street was but a few paces from the high street, and had she not stopped when she had, doubtless she would at this moment be safely ensconced at the Ashbys' residence, teaching their two little girls the rudiments of the French tongue or displaying to them the geographic wonders of the globe. Oh, surely, surely Mrs. Ashby would understand the reason for her unfortunate delay!

If she could only summon the energy to force open her tired eyelids, Caroline thought. Once she was able to accomplish that simple act, then she could manage to—

There was a knock upon a door, and the sounds of hinges creaking, and boots upon the wooden floor.

"Good God, does she sleep still?" a man said.

"Yes, sir," respectfully answered a girl from within the chamber. A maidservant of some kind, Caroline thought muzzily, with that round country accent.

"It's been two days," the man said on a note of complaint. "I own we've managed to entertain ourselves reasonably well, Damien, but the chestnuts are fresh again and I'm promised to a house party in Kent."

"My dear Charles, I've not detained you either by force or by coercion," replied another man, his voice deeper, amused, lazy and aristocratic. Recognition blazed through Caroline's confused mind: was it not the man whom she had heard cursing, the tall figure in the racing curricle? "I believe it was you who announced his delight in the unexpected richness and diversity of the Lion and Hare's supply of aged port."

"Yes, yes, a happy surprise," the man called Charles rejoined, "for which I'm duly grateful, but what if—damn it, Damien, what if the wench *don't* awaken? We can't stay here forever, you know."

"Sleeping Beauty," said the other, pensively. "Perhaps we should try to arouse her with a kiss."

"What? Oh, I see, you're bamming me! Jawing on about nursery tales! What the devil's gotten into you? Not but what she's a taking little thing. But really, Damien, how long are we to cool our heels in this godforsaken backwater?"

"You will be relieved to know that the doctor assures me he expects her to regain consciousness at any time."

"And not a moment too soon, *I* say. By the bye, have you heard the rumor going round that she deliberately threw herself at your curricle to gain your attention?"

"No, I must confess I haven't been indulging in gossip among the *hoi polloi.*"

There was a rumble of indignation from the other man, and then that smooth, deep, indolent voice went on, "But if that was her intention, she succeeded, nearly at the cost of her life."

"Well, do you know, I'm half-inclined to believe it. Don't

you remember Lady Belgrade, who pitched herself into one of the ponds at Windemere and nearly drowned?''

"How can I fail to remember?" drawled the other. "I felt so badly for her. Milton informed me that it took no less than three of his burliest footmen to drag her to safety. And how sorry I was to be in London all the time.''

Charles laughed. "And don't forget that chit at the Templetons' ball. Elizabeth Something-or-other. The one who pretended to faint as you passed by and cracked her head open on a potted palm. Lord, what a dust-up!''

"A most fatiguing scene," agreed his friend.

"Did you see Lady Templeton's face? I thought she was going to burst from an apoplexy on the spot! And Sally Jersey, too, with that cackle of hers! It's terribly infectious, you know! I would have split my sides if it weren't for my mother casting me dagger-looks from behind her fan! Lord, I was never so glad to escape to White's!''

"I did point out to Lady Templeton that the potted palm, at least, had sustained no damage, and that her ball was sure to be animatedly discussed for some time," came that lazy murmur, "but she was curiously unassuaged.''

"She's a nit-wit, on the best of days! I say, do you care for some breakfast at the Green Man down the road? Their beefsteaks are *excellent,* and I'm famished!''

"Though I do not share your unseemly appetite at this hour of the day, I am nonetheless, my dear Charles, at your service.''

The door was shut, the sounds of footsteps receded, and Caroline lay in the bed rigid with mortification and fury.

How dare those—those two *dandies* stand there, discussing her as if she were some empty-headed society miss bent on literally throwing herself into the path of some apparently highly eligible gentleman? It was outrageous, it was offensive, it was *insupportable!*

Temper flaring hotly through her, Caroline drew a deep breath, wincing as she did so, for her ribs felt uncomfortably tender. With a supreme effort she opened her eyes at last, and perceived that she was in a bedchamber of middling size, furnished simply with the bed she lay in, a long-legged night table, an armoire, a washstand, and a high-backed chair which was at present occupied by a plump, pink-cheeked maidservant who was staring dreamily into the small fire crackling cozily in the hearth. And next to her, Caroline saw with relief, was her battered leather trunk, which housed the whole of her earthly possessions. Someone from the mail coach must have made inquiries when she had failed to come claim it by the end of the day, and had brought it to this inn. Good! At least *something* was going right. She would leave the trunk here, and as soon as she was settled ask Mrs. Ashby to send one of the servants to retrieve it.

Determinedly Caroline raised herself up on her uninjured elbow. She saw that her left arm was wrapped in linen and snugly cradled in a sling also crafted from linen, and that she was clad in a voluminous cambric nightshift far too large for her. Belonging, perhaps, to the maidservant who even now turned startled brown eyes her way.

"Oh, miss, you're finally awake!" she breathed, rising to her feet. "I'll go tell the gentleman. He'll be wanting to know!"

"No!" Caroline hissed, then managed to add, more calmly but with some force, "Please, I need you to help me! Where is my dress? My cloak? And—and my shoes and bonnet?"

"Miss, you're surely not planning to get out of bed?" The maidservant looked shocked. "Why, the doctor said you was to remain there for at least a week!"

"I *must!*" Caroline gritted her teeth and drew herself upright. The room spun dizzily around her for several sickening moments, causing her temples to pound painfully. She blinked as the form of the servant girl seemed to waver and dance in the flickering light from the fire. "What—what is your name?"

"Betty, miss, and won't you care for something to eat before you do anything else? I can bring you some lovely buttered toast and tea in a twinkling!''

It did sound tempting, but Caroline ignored the sudden rumbling from her depleted stomach. "No, no, indeed I must hurry. Please, Betty, where are my clothes?''

"Why, your dress was ruined, miss, despite all my efforts to launder it,'' came the mournful answer. "You wouldn't have believed the mud! And your bonnet had to be discarded, for no matter how I tried to restore the shape it *would* bend in the oddest ways!'' Then Betty's round, simple face brightened. "But I *did* menage to sponge your cloak nicely, miss, and the same with your shoes! They're dry as can be, and tucked away right and tight in the armoire for you!''

"Thank you, Betty,'' Caroline said, grasping the bedpost with her good hand and determinedly swinging her feet to the floor. "If you would be so good as to open that trunk, you'll find a dark blue gown in there. And—and there's another bonnet on top, wrapped in tissue.'' The latter was a flimsy thing, constructed of straw and made for summer wear, but it was all she had and would have to do. Ignoring her aching head, and retaining her grip on the bedpost, laboriously Caroline pushed herself upright. She would get dressed and out of this inn, away from those insufferable men, if it was the last thing she ever did!

"Oh, miss, you're as white as anything!'' cried Betty. "You look as if you're going to swoon dead away! Please, won't you get back into bed and let me bring you a nice vinegar compress?''

"No, Betty, you must help me with my clothes,'' Caroline answered with all the firmness she could muster. "It's very important that I go and—and meet someone who is waiting for me. Do you understand?''

Soft brown eyes gazed at her sympathetically, and with new interest. "Is it—is it an assignation, miss?''

"Yes, Betty, that's it," Caroline said baldly, deliberately permitting the maidservant to misinterpret her words.

"I've—I've a lad who cares for me too," confided Betty. "Jim, his name is, miss, he's the tanner's apprentice and he's *very* handsome and he says he loves me! I do understand why you need to go out! So of course I'll help you, miss!" Her cheeks redder than ever, Betty hurried to the armoire and flung open the doors.

It was to prove even more difficult to dress herself than Caroline had anticipated, and far more painful, but after some fifteen arduous minutes she and Betty finally succeeded. She found her brush in her trunk and managed to drag it through her tangled curls, but was unable to tie the ribbons of her bonnet herself and was forced to submit to Betty's ministrations as she formed the worn dimity into a neat bow under her chin. Then, her heart pounding with the effort of her ordeal, Caroline clutched her old brown wool cloak tightly around her and went on shaky legs to the door, where she paused with one hand on the doorknob, considering. Her two tormentors had certainly departed for the Green Man to partake of breakfast there, and so she would easily be able to slip unnoticed down the stairs to the street.

A sudden anxious thought flashed across her mind and she glanced back at Betty, who stood worriedly watching her, her plump fingers laced together at her waist.

"There—there was a little dog, Betty. At the scene of—of the accident. Do you happen to know what became of it?"

Betty's brow furrowed. "A dog, miss?"

"Yes, in a frieze sack. I was holding on to it when I—fell."

A comprehending smile broke across the broad face. "Yes, miss! I remember it now! The gentleman had it brought with him here to the inn, and had Dr. Eppleton himself look him over! Your little doggie was fine, miss, only hungry and a bit banged up, and Dr. Eppleton took such a liking to it he brought it home with him until you was well enough to take it back!"

"Oh, I am so glad!" At least her sacrifice had not been in vain. Tears of gratitude sprang to Caroline's eyes and hastily she brushed them away. "Thank you, Betty," she said softly, and resolutely turned the doorknob.

Two hours later Caroline leaned weakly against the brick facade of a tobacconist's shop, closed her eyes, and willed her mutinous knees to stop quivering. The interview with Mrs. Ashby had been short, succinct, and disastrous beyond any imagining.

Caroline had found herself excoriated as a jade, a harpy, the worst sort of loose woman, one fallen so far beneath reproach that Mrs. Ashby only wondered at herself for allowing Caroline's presence to pollute the sacred precinct of her household! To think that her benighted sister, Mrs. Charlotte Tintham, had the temerity to send to her a—a *doxy* to look after and instruct her precious girls! It was the outside of anything!

When Caroline ventured feebly to protest that her behavior at Denbury Manor had been for all her three years there impeccable, and that perhaps the letter Mrs. Tintham had sent had explained the circumstances of her untoward departure, Mrs. Ashby fixed her with a withering stare and inquired sarcastically if Miss Caroline Smythe thought her a complete booby. Didn't the entire town of Baldock know that Miss Smythe had been housed at the Lion and Hare under the *aegis* of the *beau monde*'s most notorious rake, the Marquis of Reston? It wouldn't take a simpleton to put two and two together and realize the scandalous sum!

Caroline was aghast. Her flustered attempts to correct Mrs. Ashby's mistaken understanding of the situation (much less point out that the nature of her injuries would surely have dampened the ardor of the most determined satyr) failed to even slightly pierce the armor of that lady's righteous indignation, and it was not long before Caroline found herself ushered from Mrs. Ashby's spacious, execrably decorated morning room to the front door by a supercilious majordomo who, she would have sworn, unbent his imperious mien ever so briefly to leer at her.

Distraught, she had walked back from Clinton Street onto the high street, wondering frantically what was to become of her. Her meager savings wouldn't sustain her for long; she prayed there was even enough to pay the landlord of the Lion and Hare, and the doctor for his services, and give to Betty a proper vail. It was of the utmost importance that she find employment without delay; and since she was hardly in a situation to be nice in her choice, it hardly mattered what kind of employment, as long as it was respectable and enabled her to keep a roof over her head and food in her belly.

One after another, she had gone into a milliner's shop, a modiste's, and a dry goods emporium, to inquire if there might be an opening for an assistant of some sort. The proprietors had all stared at her queerly—Caroline could not help but be miserably aware of her odd, bedraggled appearance—and had, with more speed than kindness, sent her on her way.

Suddenly a cold, feathery wetness brushed her face and dazedly Caroline opened her eyes. It had begun to snow, and a brisk wind had sprung up; the lowering gray sky was filled with the gay chaotic dance of countless whirling snowflakes. It was a sight to enchant.

Unless, Caroline thought, one was without means, or family, or friends, and was alone in a small village one had never heard of a week before, and one's arm was broken and possibly a rib or two as well. Otherwise she was sure she would be charmed at the season's first snowfall.

A giddy laugh rose in her throat. Everyone in Baldock seemed to assume she was comfortably established as the cosseted mistress of the *ton*'s most famous libertine. She was so desperate she could almost have wished it so!

Then, just as abruptly as it had come, her crazy amusement

died as the utter bleakness of her situation hit her with the force of a blow, bringing in its wake a disconcerting rush of dizziness. What on earth was she to do?

Caroline gave her head a shake, attempting to clear from it the muddling haze that seemed to be filling her brain, as if there were snowflakes dancing within her as well as without.

For now, she could but return to the inn, and pay the landlord what she could. Perhaps kindhearted Betty might know of someone in need of a maidservant. Though, Caroline reflected dismally, it was difficult to imagine an employer so philanthropic as to overlook the obvious disadvantages of hiring on a servant who was unable to tie the ribbons on her own bonnet.

Oh, God, it was hopeless. Anguished tears rose to her eyes and numbly she began trudging toward the Lion and Hare, bending her head to stare at the damp muddied ground before her. The wide straw brim of her bonnet flapped up, exposing her face to the merciless force of the cold wind swirling around her. Almost blinded by her tears and by the wind, she bumped into someone, a man, who muttered an impatient imprecation and left her to clutch in agony at her jostled arm and bite down hard on her lip to keep from crying out.

Keep going, she told herself. *You must keep going.* She put one foot in front of the other, then brought the other foot forward, and then the other again, her mind narrowed to focus on this one simple, yet so overwhelmingly difficult, task.

She passed underneath an archway, and came into a courtyard, and dimly recognized ahead of her the swaying sign of the Lion and Hare. Doggedly she pressed on, stumbling across a large stone in her path and nearly falling, conscious now only of the wind whistling in her ears. Or was it that she heard her own labored breath, rasping harshly in her throat?

Finally, after what seemed like an interminable distance, Caroline came to a narrow wood door. She bit back a thankful sob and with the last of her strength she pulled open the door and slipped inside the inn. After being buffeted by frigid, blustery gusts all along the high street, she was shocked at the warmth and quiet inside, and, heedless of how unladylike a demeanor it presented, leaned against the door and raised gloved hands to her chilled cheeks as she waited for that dismaying vertiginous sensation in her head to wane.

Suddenly a deep, aristocratic voice said thoughtfully: "Do you know, I cannot help but form the impression that you are bent on annihilating yourself."

Caroline whirled; perhaps she moved too quickly, for her senses swam sickeningly. Vaguely she perceived that tall straight figure from before, the strikingly handsome countenance and gleaming dark eyes, and it was just before the world collapsed upon itself that she felt with a curious sense of relief a pair of strong arms catch her up and hold her gently against that same tall, masculine, reassuringly solid form.

Chapter 2

Damien sat in the room's only chair, an exceedingly uncomfortable high-backed affair, crossed one elegantly booted leg over the other, and watched the girl as she slept. Charles Highcombe was right: she *was* a taking little thing, with her mane of auburn curls, strikingly dark brows and eyelashes, and delicately sculpted mouth with its soft, full lower lip. She was also clearly possessed of a considerable amount of pluck; he had been more than a little astonished when, having returned to the inn after breakfast and gone upstairs to write a letter, en route to give the completed missive to the landlord he had found the girl wilting against the wall in the entranceway, the melting snowflakes on her cloak and wet muddy slippers obvious indications that she had gone out despite her profoundly weakened state.

Yes, plainly a young lady with some steel in her backbone.

Damien sat there for he knew not how long, gazing pensively at the still form in the bed, absently admiring the play of the fire as it cast shimmering highlights in those tumbled curls.

All at once she stirred, and drew those dark winglike brows together, and still sleeping said, clearly and pathetically, "No, please do not make me leave, General! For I've nowhere to go!"

A small, strong hand clutched distressfully at the counterpane; still in the grip of some unpleasant dream, violently she shook her head back and forth against the pillow and cried out: "Oh, where is he? Can someone not tell me? I have looked—looked for him everywhere!"

Another agitated jerk of that tense frame and she was likely to jar her injured arm. Damien rose and went quietly to the bed, and lightly rested his hand on her forehead. It was warm, he noted, but not feverishly so.

"Ma'am," he said in his calm, measured voice. "Wake up. It is merely a dream."

She came awake with a start; huge forest-green eyes focused on his in bewilderment. "Oh," she murmured, "I am here—with you. I thought I was—was somewhere else."

He removed his hand and straightened. "Yes," he said. "You seemed to be searching for someone."

She blinked, and appeared to abruptly come to full cognizance of her surroundings. Coolly, and with greater composure, she said, "I suppose I ought to thank you for saving me from a painful fall to the floor downstairs."

He smiled slightly. "Only if you feel you must."

"No doubt," she went on, "you believe I purposely planted myself there in order that I might—might *gain your attention!*"

What the devil was she talking about? Gaining his attention by nearly crumpling into a cold wet heap onto the floor? Then Damien recalled his conversation with Charles the day before, conducted while they mistakenly assumed the girl had slept. His amusement grew. Prickly, as well as plucky!

"Why would I have leaped to that assumption?" he returned gravely. "Surely you must know you had already attracted my notice by propitiously flinging yourself at my curricle."

Those fine green eyes sparkled militantly. "I most certainly did not! That is, I *did* accidentally place myself in the path of your curricle—for which I am most heartily sorry!—but I am not such a ninnyhammer as to attempt to make myself noticed in such a crack-brained way, even if I *had* wished to solicit your acquaintance, which I assure you, sir, I do not!'' Her expression defiant, she drew the counterpane up to her chin and eyed him defiantly.

Good Lord, but she was charming! ''It is too late, I am afraid,'' Damien answered imperturbably. ''Circumstances have—er, thrown us together, and I fear there is nothing for it but to make ourselves known to each other. I am Reston, at your service.'' He bowed slightly.

''Yes, I know who you are, my lord,'' she said balefully.

''Indeed? Then it is I who remains in the dark. Will you not enlighten me as to your identity?''

After a moment she said grudgingly, ''I am Miss Smythe. Miss Caroline Smythe.''

''Thank you.'' Damien turned away and went to the door.

''Where—where are you going, my lord?'' she asked, her voice a little shrill. ''Will you not ask Betty to come to me?''

He glanced at her over his shoulder. ''It is Christmas Day, and Betty is home with her family. After your near mishap in the hall, you slept the rest of the day and through the night, which Dr. Eppleton—who seems a remarkably competent physician, by the bye—said was to be expected, given your exhausted condition. Pray excuse me, Miss Smythe.''

Damien returned some ten minutes later with Phillips in tow. The landlord bore in his meaty hands a wooden tray laden with a teapot, a china cup, sugar and tongs, a small chilled flagon, a damask napkin, and a plate heaped high with pastries.

''Good day, miss,'' Phillips said jovially, ''and happy Christmas to you! His lordship tells me you're feeling more the thing, and I'm glad to hear it, indeed I am! I'll just place this tray on the night table—so! Mayn't I pour you out a cup?''

''Thank you,'' Miss Smythe said, looking bemused. She had, Damien noticed, attempted in his absence to smooth her riotous curls into submission, and would doubtless be sorry to learn that her efforts were entirely for naught, though for himself he found her *déshabillé* quite fetching.

"Cream? It's fresh! Sugar?" Phillips inquired assiduously.

"No, thank you."

The landlord held out the cup, then paused. Damien went to the bed, murmured, "If you will permit me," and assisted Miss Smythe into a half-sitting position against the pillows, amusedly ignoring her palpable discomfort at both his touch and his proximity. In addition to her other admirable attributes, Damien mused, Miss Smythe was a prude. He took the steaming, fragrant cup from the landlord and passed it to her, then stepped back and nodded dismissal to Phillips, who promptly tiptoed out of the room and discreetly shut the door behind him.

"Leaving us to our little love nest," observed Damien. "A fellow of romantic sensibilities, I perceive."

Miss Smythe choked on a sip of tea, and sputtered, "How *dare* you!"

He lifted his eyebrows. "I was merely commenting on his perception of the matter, my dear Miss Smythe. Don't you find it interesting that he would cherish the notion that, having nearly dashed you to bits with my curricle, I would somehow manage to—er, make you mine while you, wracked with your various wounds, slept soundly for nearly forty-eight hours? Only a truly sentimental man could conjure up a vision of concupiscent bliss given those awkward parameters! But now that the subject has thus been raised, I must confess that I am glad that you have awakened."

"Why?" she said sharply, her fingers tightening around the handle of her cup.

"I assure you, there will be no need to hurl your tea at me in the defense of your person," Damien said dryly. In a leisurely, deliberate way he strolled to the high-backed chair which he lifted and brought next to the bed.

"Oh, don't sit!" she begged. "Do go away! It is highly improper for you to be here at all!"

"I fancy we need not worry about the proprieties at this late stage," he remarked. "Our reputations—at least as far as the village of Baldock is concerned—are in tatters, you know."

"I am all too aware of it, my lord," she retorted. "It has cost me a position as a governess!"

"Indeed?" He sat, careful of the tails of his frock coat, and once again crossed one leg over the other. His top boots, he observed, were rapidly losing their famed gloss, and their tassels had taken on a somewhat shabby cast. Bentley, his valet, was bound to be devastated. "Won't you have a pastry?" he said. "They look, happily, passable."

"Since I hardly know where my next meal may come from," Miss Smythe responded acidly, "I suppose I might as well." She put her teacup back on the night table and picked up a sugar-encrusted tart at which she nibbled morosely.

Damien watched her in polite silence, and when she had finally finished the pastry and reached again for her tea he said, "The reason I am glad you are awake, Miss Smythe, is so that we may now discuss what is to be done. I am dismayed to learn that because of your—er, unfortunate mishap you are now without employment. I suppose it is foolish to inquire if it would be helpful for me to intercede on your behalf?"

"Very foolish," Miss Smythe agreed.

"Have you family or connections to whom you can turn?"

A shadow crossed her pale face, and long black lashes shielded her eyes as she dropped them to stare down onto the counterpane. "No. There is no one."

"Pray excuse my lack of delicacy, but . . . in your sleep you spoke of someone whom you sought. May I not assist you in your search?"

"No," she said, and he thought he heard a tremor in her soft voice. Then she set her jaw and looked up at him determinedly. "You need not trouble yourself with me, my lord. I shall make do. I am sure you and your friend are weary of cooling your heels in this provincial place, and as I am given to understand your horses are fully recovered from their ordeal I have no doubt you will wish to be on your way at once.''

"I appreciate your concern for my well-being, Miss Smythe," he said with a faint smile. "I have in fact sent Charles off to London with my chestnuts. I could not help but feel that they would do better restored to their stables and the care of my grooms, and as Charles *was* anxious to proceed to Kent I permitted him to drive my horses—though not, I confess, without some measure of uneasiness. He is ham-handed, you see. Poor Charles! I do not have the heart to inform him that he shall never become a member of the Four Horse Club, no matter how ardently he may aspire to such an honor. But, Miss Smythe, I digress. Despite the admittedly profound boredom of this wretched town and a pressing obligation elsewhere I have remained in the twin hopes of seeing you awakened and, like my horses, promptly restored to your normal sphere in life. However, I now see that only my first hope is attainable.''

"I have assured you that I shall do!" she said sharply. "I pray you, my lord, make haste to fulfill the obligation of which you spoke!"

She was scowling at him with fire in those fine green eyes. "Miss Smythe," he said coolly, "I admire your independence of spirit, and trust that you do not harbor any wayward notion that I have designs on your virtue. My only desire is to assist you.''

"Why?" she responded tartly. "I do not think you are much used to assisting those in need.''

"Alas, Miss Smythe, an all too accurate reading of my character," he replied without heat. "I am a frippery fellow, you know, of no use to anyone. But," he added reflectively, "there must remain some small poor shred of conscience, for, remarkably, I cannot find it in me to go off and abandon you to your fate. More tea?''

"No, my lord, I thank you!"

He rose to his feet. "Then I shall leave you for a while, my dear Miss Smythe, for there are arrangements to be made at once.''

"Arrangements? What on earth do you mean?" she asked suspiciously.

"I shall hire a barouche and driver for you and a horse for myself, though I can only guess at the execrable quality of the horseflesh to be found! However, it is of no consequence. Now that I am fairly launched on my unwonted course of philanthropy, it would hardly do to cavil at irksome details. *You,* I am persuaded, would not!" He smiled faintly at her mistrustful expression. "You shall rest for the remainder of the day, I shall occupy myself somehow, and tomorrow we will proceed to my estate, which is, fortunately, but a few hours from here. We will go slowly, and thus minimize for you the inevitable discomforts of the journey. At Windemere you shall, I am confident, enjoy a peaceful convalescence."

"I will not go with you, my lord!" she said forcefully.

He sighed. "Come, child, don't be tedious."

"I am not a child! I would have you know I am well-used to taking care of myself! I am a full-grown woman," she informed him roundly, "of no less than three and twenty!"

"You surprise me. I had not thought you above twenty. Doubtless it is your thinness, and a generally youthful aspect, which led me astray. Did they feed you only gruel in your former situation?"

"No, of course not! That is, only for breakfast! Which hardly mattered, as I have never been accustomed to eating great quantities, nor never had the opportunity to—but that is neither here nor there! My lord, I—"

Damien interrupted her. "You know, this little village of Baldock is such a peculiarly dreadful little metropolis I cannot help but wonder if there might be another reason why you terminated your employment and came here. Besides the fact they served gruel, of course."

Miss Smythe fired up at once. "There was an elder son!" she said indignantly. "An awful toad! Pawing at me, and trying to *kiss* me in the stairwell! And when his mother came upon us she leaped to the most hideous conclusions!''

He held up a hand. ''I beg you to say no more, ma'am, and spare my blushes! An all too common tale, I understand. Perhaps you might divulge to me instead how you came to be a governess?''

''I hardly think that is your business, my lord!'' she retorted. ''And let us not stray from the point! I do not wish your charity! Pray do not importune me further! It is a preposterous idea, and I will *not* go with you!''

Unhurriedly Damien walked to the bed and stood gazing into her defiant little face. ''Very well. If you cannot help but recoil from the idea of accepting my hospitality, then you may go to Windemere for the express purpose of acting as a governess to my younger sister Augusta. There shall be no question of charity, Miss Smythe, for you shall be earning your keep. You will go with me,'' he went on pleasantly, ''if I have to forcibly drag you downstairs, stuff you into the barouche against your will, and pour a sleeping draught down your throat! (How the good people of Baldock would enjoy such a scene!) Believe me when I assure you I am capable of such an action! I trust I have made myself perfectly clear?''

He continued to look at her blandly as she glared up at him, and after several long moments she lowered her eyes and said bitterly, ''Doubtless you have done so *several* times already!''

Damien laughed outright. ''Hardly, ma'am; reluctant damsels hold no allure for me.''

''I imagine few would be,'' she muttered waspishly.

''Why, Miss Smythe, a compliment! You overwhelm me!''

She ignored that and said, still with an acerbic note in her voice, ''I am astonished, my lord, that you are so willing to take me into your home. I am, after all, virtually unknown to you. I could be a person of—of the lowest character! How can you know I will not abscond with the family plate or—or corrupt the morals of your little sister?''

Damien laughed again. "Even though our acquaintance has been but a brief one, ma'am, I somehow have no fears on that score. In fact, I am increasingly convinced of the sagacity of my scheme. It is apparent that you are just the sort of clever female Augusta will like, for I am told Augusta is herself highly intelligent."

"You are *told,* my lord?"

"Why, yes, for I do not know her very well myself," Damien replied carelessly. "But my Aunt Violet claims that Augusta is an amiable creature despite her many faults. No doubt the pair of you shall get on admirably."

"If I may inquire, my lord," Miss Smythe said narrowly, "what—what did your aunt say are Lady Augusta's faults?"

"Dear me, I seem to have forgotten," Damien drawled. "I have a wretched memory, you know."

"When the matter under discussion is of no interest to you."

He bowed slightly. "Just so."

"I vow, you are impossible, my lord!" Miss Smythe returned, and with a huff sank lower into her pillows.

"I have been wondering how to account for your old-cattishness," said Damien, "and now that I have just seen you wince I only marvel I did not think of it before! Your arm pains you, ma'am! I believe Dr. Eppleton left some laudanum for you. May I not pour you out a dose?"

She scowled awfully at him. *"Old-cattishness?"*

"It is only to be expected, after all," he said soothingly. "The invalid's pettish temperament and so forth. The laudanum?"

"No! I detest the stuff!" she snapped. 'Will you not go, my lord, and attend to your business? Surely it would be far more agreeable to you than to remain here brangling with me!"

Mockingly Damien bowed again. "I am all eagerness to obey you, Miss Smythe." He turned and walked to the door, twisted the knob, and just as he was about to exit the bedchamber he heard her say in a small, surprisingly meek voice:

"My lord?"

He half turned, and saw that her countenance had taken on an apprehensive cast. "Ma'am?"

"The dog," she said, tentatively.

Of course, Damien thought, the dog. Had he ever encountered such an original creature in his life? Alternately fierce and tender, forthright and mysterious, and altogether diverting. He was not sorry to have met her, though he could almost have regretted that once he deposited her at Windemere their short association would come to an end.

"According to Dr. Eppleton, the dog made an amazingly rapid recovery," he said, "and within hours of his arrival managed to render himself a universal favorite among the family. Dr. Eppleton pronounced him a most charming little mongrel, and quite preternaturally bright. He reports that the dog only had to be told twice not to steal Mrs. Eppleton's stockings and treat them as his exclusive playthings."

"I am glad to hear it."

"Yet you look troubled, Miss Smythe."

"The thing of it is . . . I do wonder, my lord, if . . ." She fell silent, and bit her lip. "I—I am in no position to . . . That is, do you suppose . . . ?"

"I hope you will not think it forward of me, but when the good doctor admitted to his family's immediate attachment to the dog, I ventured to suggest that you would be delighted to learn that it was welcome to become a permanent denizen of the Eppleton household."

"Oh, I *am* delighted!" A smile blazed across her face, and Damien was startled at the brilliance of it, and how the sudden happy glow in her green eyes transformed her. Good God, but thin, pale, rumpled Miss Smythe could be beautiful!

She added radiantly: *"Thank* you, my lord! I could not have hoped for a better resolution!"

"It was nothing, I assure you," he responded with studied indifference.

"How—how did you guess?" she asked. "Surely you were

not able to see that group of cruel, nasty youths snatching up the poor stray puppy and tying him up in a sack, then hurling him into the road?''

Instead of answering Damien said: ''Did it never occur to you that you yourself might have been killed?''

''There was no time to think,'' she replied impatiently. ''I *couldn't* let the poor little thing perish because of those wretched boys! Now, do tell me how you realized the truth of the situation!''

''Mere conjecture on my part, Miss Smythe. I caught an infinitesimal glimpse of those boys huddled together at the point from which their hapless missile would have been launched, saw on their faces the unmistakable expression of bloodlust, and guessed at the rest.''

''That was very perceptive of you, my lord,'' she said approvingly, then, after a moment, frowned at him. ''Yet you signally failed to disabuse your friend Charles of his abominable conviction that I had *thrown* myself into your path, like the—the Jezebel this town thinks me to be!''

''Which reminds me, ma'am,'' Damien said smoothly. ''As the future preceptoress of my sister's ethical education, do you think it quite right to have stooped to—dear me!—eaves-dropping yesterday morning?''

Two bright spots of pink becomingly adorned Miss Smythe's high cheekbones. *''Stooping!''* she uttered hotly. ''If we are to talk of stooping! To have stood there *chatting* about me as if I were—as if I were an interesting corpse on display!''

''Well, Charles for one *was* concerned that you might never awaken,'' he reminded her.

''Oh! You—you are a *devil!''* she said feelingly.

''So I have heard it remarked, upon more than one occasion. But I must add, ma'am, that although I cannot speak for Charles I myself am quite glad that you turned out not to be a corpse,'' Damien said with an odd sincerity underneath the raillery that surprised himself, and with a last look at her pink, fulminating face he quit her room.

Chapter 3

Caroline sat in the unaccustomed luxury of a commodious, well-sprung barouche as it rolled smoothly along the road to Chelmsford, the nearest town to where lay the marquis' estate of Windemere. As she leaned her head against the plush velvet squabs, a rueful smile curved her lips. Remarkably, she and the marquis had managed to depart this morning with only two quarrels breaking out between them.

First his lordship had adamantly refused to permit her to pay either the landlord or the doctor for their services (though he had shrugged and said she might give the maidservant Betty whatever she deemed was appropriate) and after they had engaged in a brief but spirited disputation he had closed the subject by high-handedly informing her that he would be sure to make a note of the sum and withhold it from her wages. With that she had had to be satisfied, as not only Mr. Phillips but also several members of the staff of the Lion and Hare were likely to be interestedly listening to their colloquy as they sat over the remains of their breakfast in the inn's private parlor, the door to which his lordship had punctiliously (and, she suspected, ironically) left open.

The second altercation had erupted when Dr. Eppleton, who had thoughtfully arrived in order to see his patient comfortably disposed in the coach, pressed into her fingers a vinaigrette, to which, he told her kindly, she might have instant recourse should she succumb to a fit of the vapors en route, and repeated his recommendation that she remain in bed for a full week upon her arrival at his lordship's estate.

"Oh, no! I must not!" she had exclaimed in dismay. "I shall have work to do!"

At which point Lord Reston had strolled up and lazily apprised the doctor that Miss Smythe would certainly stay abed for the allotted time and that he would personally ensure her compliance in the matter.

To her horror, Dr. Eppleton had blushed a vivid red, stammered something incomprehensible (she *thought* it had something to do with how fond all the young Eppletons were of the little dog, to whom they had given the distinguished sobriquet of *Wellington),* and backed confusedly away, bowing left and right.

In a wrathful undertone she had upbraided his lordship for his impertinence, whereupon he had simply raised his black eyebrows and responded in that infuriatingly silky way of his that he was merely going to obtain her solemn promise to obey the orders of the good doctor—which of course would mean he could place all his confidence in her cooperation—and whatever else did Miss Smythe believe he meant?

Then *she* had felt herself flushing hotly, whereupon she had dropped the vinaigrette and lost it amongst the folds of the toweling wrapped around the hot brick Betty had tenderly placed at her feet, and she was forced to request that his lordship extract it for her. Which he had done with such exaggerated courtesy that she had longed to box his ears, but had to content herself with *imagining* those handsome, well-shaped organs stinging smartly from a pair of crisp blows at her behest.

Heavens, but the man did provoke her! And worse still, she seemed to have rapidly developed the disconcerting habit of letting him best her whenever they crossed swords!

As the object of her ruminations chose at that moment to ride past the barouche window, to all appearances serenely unaware of both her and the biting cold without, she had the opportunity to secretly survey him for a minute or two.

The Marquis of Reston was, she mused, far more attractive a man than surely he had a right to be, having been multiply blessed with a tall, gracefully formed athlete's physique, a countenance notable for its strong and regular features (including, she was forced to admit, singularly comely dark eyes, deep-set and penetrating, and alive with an intelligence even his indolent air could not conceal), and thick, gleaming black hair that perfectly completed the image of one of Mrs. Radcliffe's dashing Gothic heroes.

Though, Caroline thought mischievously, Count Udolpho would not be likely to favor the horse the marquis now rode, for it was an uninspiring beast, rather sway-backed, that seemed stubbornly determined to move no faster than an ungainly trot. Yet his lordship sat the horse with an unassailably urbane dignity, as if mounted on one of his own magnificent, high-blooded steeds.

No, it would not do to tease his lordship about it, for without doubt he would gaze at her as one would at an importunate but insignificant gnat. And indeed, she reminded herself sternly, she would far better occupy her time by thinking of something—someone—else.

Caroline settled her injured arm more snugly amidst the nest of pillows Dr. Eppleton had created for her in a corner of the carriage, and let her breath out in a long sigh. Surely her new charge could not be more troublesome than the Misses Tintham—three young ladies who, Caroline had thought privately, if they had not been the daughters of an obscure country squire in Lincolnshire might have been amazingly well suited to a life among the indigenous savages of North America, for she doubted a more ungovernable lot of children existed on this side of the Atlantic Ocean.

She had believed herself to be long inured to life's more difficult challenges, but before her first week spent attempting to teach Miss Susan (age seven), Miss Emily (age nine), and Miss Phoebe (age ten) the rudiments of grammar, elocution, deportment, French, and singing had passed, she had come to the painful realization that before her was a formidably rocky field to hoe.

Nevertheless, she had applied herself to the task with grim determination, for what other options lay open to her? She had no connections in England or elsewhere, nor yet any character reference she might have used to seek another situation. And so her three years spent among the Tinthams could scarcely be termed pleasant ones (particularly when Mrs. Tintham had begun to require that Caroline take on some of the responsibilities of the upstairs maid, including the repairing and pressing of Mrs. Tintham's gowns and the dressing of her hair); though Caroline could hardly be glad for the brutal accident which had laid her so dismally low, she could not help but modestly anticipate an improvement in her circumstances.

Perhaps Lady Augusta *was* the bright, amiable little girl Lord Reston asserted her to be. As to the faults of which he conveniently disclaimed any memory . . . well, surely they couldn't surpass Miss Emily Tintham's habit of shrieking until her cheeks turned an alarming shade of blue whenever her will was flouted, or Miss Phoebe's tendency to consume sweetmeats to the point of virtual incapacitation and she had to be put to bed with a severe dyspepsia requiring endless hours of attendance, or Miss Susan's fondness for creeping up into the attic and setting old trunks on fire.

Caroline passed a pleasant hour optimistically imbuing Lady

Augusta with a host of winning features, then, lulled by the gentle rocking motion of the coach, she slipped into a light doze from which she swiftly awoke when the driver brought the horses to a halt. Lord Reston had dismounted and as he pulled open the door of the barouche, Caroline perceived that they had come to the outskirts of a bustling, agreeable-looking town, then shivered when the frigid winter air rushed inside.

"I beg your pardon for disturbing you," the marquis said, "but we are in Chelmsford, slightly under an hour yet from Windemere. Shall we stop at an inn to partake of luncheon?"

"No, my lord, not unless *you* wish it," Caroline answered. "I am perfectly willing to press on." She could not forbear smiling at him for his thoughtfulness.

His face seemed to harden slightly and he said abruptly, "Then let us continue," and shut the door, leaving Caroline to wonder if she had somehow offended him. A moment later he had mounted his horse again and they were riding through Chelmsford at a stately pace.

Through the barouche window she observed the high street with interest, noting that this town seemed a larger place than Baldock, and, happily, more cosmopolitan: there were a greater number and variety of shops, inns, and eating establishments crowded together amongst the tall brick and stone residences. Perhaps, she thought hopefully, there would even be a lending library.

They had soon done with the high street and were once again amidst the magnificent countryside of East Anglia, which, as she recalled from her study of geography, was originally an ancient Anglo-Saxon kingdom ruled by the Danes. They were but some miles from the North Sea, and Caroline fancied that she could just smell the brisk salt tang of the ocean. A light, powdery snow began to drift down from the sky, lending both the flat, fallow fields laced with a great many ditches and the forests which surrounded them a fantastical quality. Caroline pulled her cloak more tightly around her, hoping that his lordship was adequately protected from the elements in his dark, voluminous greatcoat and tall beaver hat.

She peeped through the window, and saw that he was riding a short distance from the coach. His elegant profile was impassive, the tip of his straight, aristocratic nose, she perceived, not the slightest bit red from the cold. Suddenly, as if he felt the weight of her gaze upon him, he turned his head and lifted his black brows at her with a faintly inquiring hauteur.

Oh! But she did not know why she bothered troubling herself about his welfare! Hastily Caroline leaned back against the squabs and looked fixedly out the other window. She was sure she did not care *how* uncomfortable he might be!

At length they turned into a large park bristling with great tall trees, traveling along a wide, winding road whose surface was, to Caroline's dismay, decidedly irregular. They passed over a trench cut sideways—for drainage from winter flooding, Caroline supposed—and she gritted her teeth and endured the jolting as best she could.

Soon they came to a handsome old stone gatehouse, which was deserted (just like one of Mrs. Radcliffe's tales! she thought half wryly, half curiously); the marquis, she saw, evinced no surprise at not being greeted by one of his retainers. They advanced slowly along the rough-hewn road and passed round a long, sweeping bend in the avenue; and there before them lay at last the full glory of Windemere's manor house.

It was a massive edifice, at once imposing and inviting, built on pleasingly symmetrical lines and constructed of a warm honey-colored stonework. Large rectangular blocks of windows dominated the tall central wing, the focal point of which was the main entrance with its lofty, ornately carved double doors; to the left and right were smaller wings, perhaps three stories high, and each topped with an airy cupola which together framed the gently sloping triangular roof of the main wing between them. Still other, lower-roofed wings fanned out for some distance to either side; they too featured a host of generously sized windows.

Caroline's first reaction was unadulterated awe. Such size, and such splendor! It was dazzling to the eye, and frankly stirring to the spirit. Then came an irrepressible thought: while it was altogether a grand and noble residence, missing were the dark-hued Gothic towers and ominously crumbling facades (and certainly the tumbledown old priory so famously beloved by ghosts) suitable for the brooding Count Udolpho. Oh, heavens, she laughed at herself, but she was absurd to even be entertaining these nonsensical meditations! Lord Reston was no Count Udolpho, and *she* had not Mrs. Radcliffe's fulsome imagination!

As the barouche drew closer, however, and she continued to study the sumptuous manor house, Caroline's appreciative half-smile faded, to be replaced by a tiny frown. There *was* something . . . odd about it, something not quite right.

Caroline puzzled this over, till finally it came to her, just as the coachman pulled up his horses on the graveled area that flanked the main entrance.

Perhaps it was because the multitude of windows seemed without the expected sparkle, or the lavishly gilded panels of the double doors were absent a certain luster, or even because the fine gravel beneath the coach wheels looked as if it had not been raked in some time . . . but for all its overarching grandeur, to Caroline the house seemed to give a poignant impression of neglect . . . of loneliness.

She barely had time to dismiss the foolishly irrelevant thought before the door of the barouche was opened by the coachman and the steps let down. Two young footmen in dark livery, with silver lace at their throats and their hair unpowdered, had come hurrying through the double doors; one rushed to take the reins of Lord Reston's horse, and the other carefully assisted her to alight from the carriage.

While Caroline nodded her thanks, a third servant, a tall,

thin, elderly man clad in the somber costume of a butler, followed hard on the heels of his inferiors and hastened to greet the marquis as he dismounted.

"My lord! We did not expect you! We had no word of your arrival!" the butler exclaimed, in tones both anxious and astonished. "There have been no preparations—none! Cook has had no chickens killed, nor begun any additional dishes for your dinner!"

"I sent no word, Milton," his lordship said calmly. "I assure you, Cook need not kill chickens on *my* behalf. I trust all is well?"

"Oh, yes, indeed yes, my lord! Things are as they have always been!" The butler's watery blue eyes widened as he registered the presence of Caroline, who timidly approached to stand near the marquis. "Will you—and—and the lady not come inside, my lord? It's bitterly cold this afternoon!"

"Is it?" said the marquis languidly, then directed the footman holding the reins of his horse to lead the coachman and his rig to the stables, and to have the grooms house them for the night before they returned to Baldock on the morrow. Then he offered Caroline his arm; shyly she slipped her gloved hand around the fine wool of his greatcoat, and could not help but feel the hard strength of the forearm it encased.

"If I may say so, my lord," said Milton, "her ladyship and Mrs. Yardley will be delighted to see you!"

"I am sure they will," responded Lord Reston, so blandly that Caroline glanced up at him and uneasily noted the flicker of unholy amusement in his dark eyes.

Her nerves tightening, she walked with him into the house. They entered into a hall of vast, soaring proportions, and she could not repress a tiny gasp of amazement. Towering fluted marble columns, classically Palladian in design, circled the hall and supported an elaborately patterned vaulted ceiling; low, broad steps of the same variegated amber and white marble led majestically to the gallery above. Romanesque busts occupied a series of shallow wall-niches, alternating with richly framed paintings of various sizes and shapes (Caroline *thought* she identified a portrait by Vermeer and a sweeping Renaissance landscape by Tintoretto). A huge fireplace, taller than was Caroline herself and guarded by fierce-looking antique jade fire dogs, held a roaring fire which lent a comfortable warmth to a considerable portion of the immense room.

Lord Reston's lazy voice startled her from her rather stunned survey. "Have you any objections to yielding your cloak to Milton, ma'am?" he asked, and Caroline realized she had been clutching his lordship's sleeve rather convulsively.

"Oh! Certainly!" she answered, flushing, and withdrew her hand from his arm, then relinquished the shabby garment to the butler who, she was relieved to perceive, had regained his composure and did not with the merest flicker of an eyelash register either disdain at handling her battered old cloak or surprise at the fact that the bedraggled damsel who accompanied his lordship was further distinguished by a broken arm cradled in a sling.

Milton handed her cloak to one of the footmen and reached out to relieve his lordship of his greatcoat, hat, and leather gloves. "The ladies are in the Little Drawing Room, my lord. Will you care to join them there?"

Before his lordship could reply, a female voice cried out from above: "You see, Aunt, I *told* you it was Damien I saw riding up the drive!"

Caroline caught a glimpse of a dark, untidy coiffure and a smiling face from the gallery overhead, and then in a swirl of nut-brown skirts a young woman came swiftly down the marble stairs. Perhaps twenty years of age, she was tall and statuesque, Caroline saw, and as did the marquis she had strikingly black hair (though perhaps not so thick and glossy as his) and dark eyes. Her features too were strong, though they did not combine to such advantage as they did in his lordship's handsome, beautifully proportioned countenance—

Caroline sucked in her breath and shot an incredulous glance at Lord Reston, who had moved forward to take the young woman's hand in his own and bow slightly over it.

"How do you do, Augusta? But there's no need to tell me: you're looking very well," he drawled, and at his careless words Caroline's deepest fears were realized. Lady Augusta was no little girl in need of a governess, but a woman old enough to be married and have children of her own!

"Oh, I never look well, Damien, there's no need to bamboozle me," answered Lady Augusta cheerfully. "I dress like a dowd, I'm far too plump, and my maid can't do a thing with my accursed hair! But whatever brings you to Windemere? I vow it's been an age since we've seen you!" As she spoke her eyes flicked curiously to Caroline, then returned to the marquis.

"Four and a half years, to be precise," said his lordship, then placed a light hand on Caroline's uninjured elbow and drew her a step forward, so that she now stood at his side. Her heart pounding unevenly in her breast, Caroline kept her eyes fixed on the marble floor (which, she noticed abstractly, was in need of a good polishing). She had been duped, perhaps cruelly, and was about to learn the true purpose of the marquis in carrying her away from Baldock. Was it to humiliate her, mock her enfeebled state and pitiful circumstances? Or were his intentions more sinister? Was this a more roundabout, Machiavellian means by which to force her to accede to a dishonorable liaison? Some men, she supposed dismally, *might* have an odd sort of preference for small, drab sparrows such as herself.

"Augusta," said his lordship, "may I present to you Miss Caroline Smythe? I have brought her to bear you company as a most worthy *dame de compagnie*. Miss Smythe, this is my sister, the Lady Augusta."

Wonderingly Caroline looked up at the marquis, then bent her knees in a brief, respectful curtsy. "Your ladyship," she murmured, hardly knowing what to think and wishing, dazedly, that she still had the marquis' powerful arm to lean on.

"How do you do, Miss Smythe?" came the civil, if bemused reply, followed by a quizzical: "A companion, Damien?"

"Call it a Christmas gift," said the marquis.

"Recompense for the carefully selected volumes of literature and poetry I send to you faithfully each year, for which your secretary dutifully thanks me and no doubt crams into a shelf in your library, there to gather dust?" Lady Augusta retorted with a loud, hearty laugh.

"Just so. Now, if you will have doubtless observed, Miss Smythe is—er, a trifle under the weather, and I fancy she has been longing to drink a dish of tea and lie down."

"She does seem quite pale," Lady Augusta agreed in quick sympathy. "Poor dear, whatever happened to your arm?"

Guardedly Caroline began, "It—it is a long story, your ladyship," but was interrupted by a high, sweet voice calling breathlessly from above.

"Augusta, I beg you, do not run through the drawing rooms and along the gallery like a zany! It is most unladylike!" Then: *"Damien!* Oh, my dearest boy!"

Dressed in flattering puce and gold, her meticulously crimped gray-blonde hair peeping out from underneath a fetching little lace cap, a middle-aged woman came rustling down the stairs toward them, a soft Norwich shawl trailing behind her. Her pink, still-pretty face wreathed in smiles, she extended white fingers, sparkling with rings, to the marquis.

"This *is* a surprise, nephew!" she exclaimed, as his lordship bowed over her hand. "A delightful one, to be sure!"

"I am glad you think so, Aunt," the marquis said. "May I present Miss Caroline Smythe? Miss Smythe, this is my aunt, Mrs. Violet Yardley."

"How do you do?" Mrs. Yardley said distractedly, as Caroline dipped her head politely. "Oh, Lord, there's so much to be done! Perhaps we can get up a little card-party for Saturday, just the neighbors, you know, though I *would* like to have a little dancing too, if some musicians can be found! And a proper dinner party, of course, to do you honor, my dear! Next week, and no more than ten or twelve couples, I daresay. As for tonight, however, I am afraid you must take pot-luck with us! But Cook *must* alter the menu at least a *trifle!* Perhaps a nice saddle of mutton, or some ham— Oh, Mrs. Dawkins, there you are!'' she said gratefully, as a stout woman dressed in black dimity, her skirts unfashionably full, trod heavily into the hall. "We've two more for dinner! You must break the news to Cook quite *gently!*''

"Certainly, ma'am. Welcome home, my lord,'' the woman said, curtsying to Lord Reston.

"Thank you, Mrs. Dawkins,'' answered the marquis. "Are any of the guest bedchambers at present made up?''

The housekeeper looked startled, as if wondering why his lordship should be troubling himself with domestic matters, then glanced at Caroline. "No, my lord,'' she said gruffly. "We wasn't expecting anyone, though *your* bedchamber is always kept in readiness.''

"Then Miss Smythe may stay there, at least for tonight. Will you be so good as to escort her? And ring for some tea, if you will, and some kind of luncheon to be brought up to her directly.''

Mrs. Dawkins' face stiffened, and Mrs. Yardley interceded, flustered and even pinker than before. "I am sure Mrs. Dawkins can have the Blue Bedchamber prepared in a trice, Damien! It is quite a handsome chamber, if you will recall! Very large and comfortable! Miss—Miss Smythe will enjoy the view of the gardens!''

"How sadly I am forever misinterpreted,'' the marquis murmured to Caroline, who stared in mortification at the floor and said nothing. "As I leave for London shortly, Aunt—which reminds me, Milton, will you send a footman to the stables to have them saddle for me a mount, and another to bring up Miss Smythe's trunk?—I thus will have no need of my bedchamber. Miss Smythe, on the other hand—''

"You cannot be serious, Damien!" interposed Mrs. Yardley in disbelief. "Do you mean to tell me you will not even stay the night at Windemere? Are you apprehensive that Cook will fail to produce for you an adequate dinner? I assure you, her abilities have much improved over the years! Why, she has *quite* a way with a Rhenish cream now!"

Lady Augusta gave a boisterous laugh. "I do not think Damien is worried about dinner, Aunt."

"As I was saying," the marquis went on, sounding bored, "Miss Smythe is not well, and I do not wish for her to be forced to wait until Mrs. Dawkins is able to have a guest bedchamber properly prepared for her. Come, Miss Smythe, let me escort you to the stairs. I am confident my aunt and sister will excuse your absence, for you plainly have ample reason for wishing to retire." He held out his arm, and once again Caroline slipped her hand around it, more thankful for his support than she would have wished him to know. She *was* rather tired, and hungry, and both her head and arm did ache, and now she felt her spirits drooping too.

She murmured a disjointed apology to Lady Augusta and Mrs. Yardley, and obediently let the marquis lead her to the foot of the magnificent staircase. "Farewell, Miss Smythe," he said. "Before I depart I shall ensure that a doctor will be sent for you upon the morrow."

Caroline resisted the craven impulse to cling to his arm and instead drew her hand away, and rested it on the cool, smooth, wide marble banister. As she gazed up at him, she wondered at the curiously intent look she saw in his dark eyes, then told herself she must have imagined it, for his countenance was set in its usual impassive lines after all.

She took a deep breath, attempting to marshal her scattered wits. Why should it matter to her if his lordship stayed or left? Whence this ridiculous feeling of abandonment, and the hurt emotions in its wake? She *ought* to say something about Lady

Augusta's age, and how little she, Caroline, was needed here . . . Oh, why did she feel so weak, so foolishly feather-brained?

She heard behind her the solid tread of the housekeeper's feet, and quickly she glanced up into Lord Reston's face once more. "Farewell, my lord," she said softly. "And—thank you." She turned from him and began walking up the stairs with the silent Mrs. Dawkins at her side, her candle their only illumination. They came onto a long, high-ceilinged gallery whose paneled walls were studded with portraits. Absently Caroline saw that here and there were haphazardly pinned sprigs of evergreen and the occasional holly wreath—tokens, she realized, of the Christmas season, although the overall effect was more scattershot than festive. Memories, at once warm and painful, flitted across her tired mind: a tiny hut, set in the hilly outskirts of Seville, filled to bursting with laughter and song; a quaint little church in Lisbon, fragrant with the scent of oranges and pomegranates lovingly clustered round a primitive Nativity scene; even a rickety cart, trundling alongside the Douro River in the Mediterranean warmth of December, rendered cozy thanks to the presence of those beloved to her . . .

"If you will step inside, miss," said Mrs. Dawkins dourly, holding open a door, and with a little shake of her head, as if to clear it, Caroline passed into a darkened bedchamber whose curtains were firmly closed against the weak gray light of a snowy winter afternoon.

"Damien, my dear, *must* you leave so swiftly?" pleaded Mrs. Yardley, pouring out a cup of tea and in her agitation spilling half of it on the saucer she inattentively passed to Augusta, who accepted the cup with a wry moue and proceeded to gulp down its contents.

They sat in the Little Drawing Room, a cheerful saloon decorated in soft shades of cream and yellow. Damien stretched his long legs before the fire, studied the plate of macaroons set on the table at his elbow, and at length selected one and bit into it meditatively. "Aunt," he said, "do you *really* believe Cook has gotten better?"

"Indeed yes! *Everyone* says so!" Mrs. Yardley handed him a cup and a tea-splashed saucer, and persisted: "Why cannot you stay?"

Augusta leaned forward and plucked a macaroon from the plate. "Oh, do not be plaguing Damien, Aunt! There is nothing for him here, and everything, I am sure, at Latham Park!"

"Oh! Of course! How remiss of me not to inquire after Miss Manderlay! And of course her dear parents the baron and Lady Calpurnia! I had a letter from Miss Manderlay—she is so scrupulously attentive, Damien, it is very good in her!—in September, in which she assured me that although her mother suffered a trifle from the rheumatism, the doctors were confident that it would not prevent the family from visiting the Duke of Clarence for the fox hunt! I am sure I have said so once if I have said it a hundred times, the duke is the very model of princely condescension! Though one *could* wish he would not talk so loudly in church! It is quite horribly distracting! But do tell me, how *are* the dear Manderlays?"

Damien sipped at his tea, drew his black brows together ever so slightly, and gently put the cup down. "I daresay I shall discover the status of their respective healths when I go to Latham Park tomorrow."

"Oh! You are to attend a house party there!" said Mrs. Yardley, nodding. "It would only be proper for you to be with them for the holiday! But why do you arrive *after* Christmas? Do not the Manderlays host an annual ball on Christmas Eve? I am sure they wanted you quite particularly for that!"

"I suppose they did." Damien looked consideringly at the plate of macaroons again, then resigned himself to waiting until he reached his town house in London early in the evening. "I was, however, delayed."

"Because of Miss Smythe?" Augusta questioned shrewdly,

leaning back against the gold brocade sofa to more comfortably sip her tea.

"Yes."

"Is she your *inamorata?*"

"Augusta!" exclaimed Mrs. Yardley in shocked accents, her teacup rattling agitatedly in her saucer. "How *dare* you employ such vulgar language? And pray," she added earnestly, "don't slump so! You will ruin your spine!"

"No, my dear Augusta, Miss Smythe is not my *inamorata,"* replied Damien composedly. "She is but a little waif whom I encountered on my travels. I hope that you will be good to her."

"Of course I will!" said Augusta indignantly. "I am sure I like her already! But Damien, I really don't know *what* to do with a companion! I fear she will intrude upon my studies!"

"Speaking of studies," cut in Mrs. Yardley, her urgency so palpable that the gray-blonde curls at her temples quivered. "Damien, I beseech you, something *must* be done about your poor sister!"

"How so?" Politely suppressing a yawn that threatened to overcome him, Damien removed a minuscule piece of lint from his buckskin trousers and flicked it to the yellow-patterned carpet. He wondered how long following his arrival it would take Hippolyte, his extraordinarily talented and even more expensive Parisian chef, to roast some Devonport fowls, accompanied, perhaps, by a dish of spinach or tender broiled mushrooms.

"She is on the verge," said Mrs. Yardley darkly, "of becoming a bluestocking!"

"Oh, pooh! I *am* one, Aunt," responded Augusta, reaching for another macaroon in an untroubled fashion. "I was born bookish, you know! But must you forever be harping about it? I am sure my brother is not the least interested, for I see him eyeing the clock!"

Mrs. Yardley drew herself up and glared at her niece. "If

you are blind to my obligations regarding yourself, Augusta, *I* am not! After your mother, my dear sister, passed on—may God keep her safe, and your poor, poor father too! *Such* a tragedy! I am sure I am not recovered from the blow!—and Damien asked me to come to Windemere, it became my sacred duty to look after you. Having not been blessed with offspring of my own, and left a widow in sadly diminished circumstances, I did not hesitate to remove from Bristol at once. A damp, moldy place it is, highly injurious to the constitution, and with those coarse sailors swaggering everywhere! Damien, it is high time Augusta was wed! She is twenty-one, and veritably on the shelf! Why, I was myself married at seventeen!''

"And much happiness it brought you!" muttered Augusta mutinously, sinking lower on the sofa.

"That is neither here nor there!" snapped Mrs. Yardley. *"My* marriage is not under discussion! If I did not find the felicity with the late Mr. Yardley for which I had hoped, it is certainly no concern of yours, miss! To be sure, he *seemed* everything that was gentlemanly, and wore the most beautifully tailored coats! And with his fair hair and blue eyes, and my own to match, we *did* make a most striking pair! How was I to have known Crayton was hopelessly addicted to the faro table? Not but what I don't enjoy a hand of whist, or piquet, or even loo from time to time—Damien! Where are you going?''

"Home," said Damien. "To London! Good-bye, Aunt! Augusta, will you be so good as to make arrangements for a doctor to look in on Miss Smythe tomorrow, and to see that she rests until her health is fully recovered? I fear you may have a struggle on your hands, for I suspect Miss Smythe will wish to assume her duties without delay.''

"Yes, I will," said Augusta, chewing on yet another macaroon. "Have no fear, Damien. Your Miss Smythe shall be properly cared for.''

"She is *your* Miss Smythe," returned Damien absently, "in

all matters save the financial. My secretary will send along the funds for her salary.''

''As you wish.'' Augusta shrugged. ''*Adieu,* my dear brother! By the bye, have you and Miss Manderlay named a date for the wedding? I'll need to get a gown made up, I suppose! What a bore!''

Damien had been enjoying a private moment imagining Miss Smythe's valiant efforts to determinedly fulfill what she perceived to be as her responsibilities, and was jolted from his pleasurable reverie by Augusta's abrupt inquiry. ''I'm afraid I don't remember the precise day,'' he said evenly. ''It is sometime in November, at Latham Park.''

''But what a long engagement!'' exclaimed Augusta. ''The betrothal was announced in the *Gazette* this past spring!''

''I had thought it long myself,'' Damien said indifferently. ''However, Miss Manderlay didn't wish to cut short the pleasures of a second season as a chief ornament of society, and who was I to gainsay her perfectly natural desire?''

Augusta stared at him. ''Good heavens, Damien! Your tone leads one to think that your affections are not a jot engaged!''

''It was merely an observation concerning Miss Manderlay's enjoyment of her status among the *ton.*''

''Damien,'' said Augusta, ''do you care for *anyone* besides yourself?''

''Augusta!'' Mrs. Yardley said shrilly. ''You are impertinent! And *will* you sit up straight? You look just like the Princess Charlotte, sprawled in that ungainly way! Lady de Clifford swore to me that the princess actually displays her *drawers* in public, and when she tactfully mentioned it to Princess Charlotte, she only declared that the Duchess of Bedford's are considerably longer, and bordered with Brussels lace. 'Oh,' Lady de Clifford said in conclusion, 'if she is to wear them, she does right to make them handsome.' ''

Augusta ignored her aunt. ''*Do* you care for anyone, Damien?''

"Of course I do," he answered coolly. "I care a great deal for my horses. Good-bye." With that rejoinder he offered a slight bow to his sister and aunt, and unhurriedly strolled from the room.

"*Well!*" ejaculated Mrs. Yardley. "I vow, your brother is positively *unnatural!*"

"Do you think so, Aunt?" Augusta murmured, unruffled. "Perhaps it is a Reston family trait." Picking up a copy of Milton's *Samson Agonistes,* she promptly lost herself among the well-worn pages, leaving Mrs. Yardley to fume in frustrated silence and pour herself another cup of tea—now, alas, decidedly lukewarm.

Chapter 4

A muted clattering noise brought Caroline drifting up from a deep sleep, and slowly she opened her eyes to see a maidservant tending to the logs she had lit in the tall, deep fireplace on the other side of the room. For a disconcerting moment Caroline had no idea where she was; then, as she took in the dark-red velvet bed curtains of the large, intricately carved oak four-poster in which she lay, the heavy, masculine oaken wardrobe, washstand, and writing desk and accompanying chair, she suddenly recalled that it was Lord Reston's bedchamber in which she resided in such unwonted comfort.

Despite the curiosity of which she was half-ashamed, she had been too fatigued yesterday to register the details of his lordship's chamber, and after consuming a rather tasteless bowl of soup and permitting one of Mrs. Dawkins' minions, a thin-faced servant girl wearing a dress with torn flounces and a cap so carelessly pinned that it looked about to topple from the wiry, carrot-colored hair it perched upon, to help her undress,

Caroline had eased gratefully between the crisp linen sheets of the bed and instantly fallen asleep.

The little maidservant tending the fire—it was, Caroline now perceived, the same redheaded girl who had assisted her before—had drawn back the elegant red velvet curtains from the two lofty windows, and soft, pearlescent morning light was suffusing the room. The ceiling was high, with whorled gilt cornices at each of the four corners; a rich green and gold paper covered the walls, and was itself decorated with handsomely framed hunting prints. A large, luxurious carpet, its muted green and yellow colors suggestive of a forest aglow with autumnal foliage, lay upon the wooden floor. It was, Caroline mused, altogether a pleasing chamber, tastefully furnished and certain to appeal to the most aesthetic sensibilities.

A sudden vision of the marquis, his long, muscular frame disposed amongst the linen sheets, his dark head resting upon the lace-trimmed pillows, flashed across her mind. Horrified, Caroline sternly dismissed the vision, but not before some secret part of her acknowledged it to be a devastatingly alluring one.

"Good morning," she hastily called out to the maidservant, who rose at once and turned to face her.

A little curtsy, then, "Good morning, miss. Mrs. Dawkins says I'm to bring you your toast and chocolate whenever you're ready."

A sense of wonder flooded Caroline. A big, soft bed and a crackling fire already lit. Toast and chocolate, served to her as she snuggled under a warm coverlet on a cold winter morning! Never in her life had she known such extravagant indulgence.

Then, as it must, hard-edged reality reasserted itself. She wasn't some cosseted high-born damsel accustomed to lying lazily abed far past the dawn, but a governess, as much a servant as was the girl who had bobbed another curtsy and obediently departed the chamber. She herself might not be set to scrubbing floors, or hauling water, but there were nonetheless chores for her to do. That she did not yet know quite what they were was immaterial; it was incumbent upon her to begin at once.

Determinedly Caroline threw back the coverlet, blankets, and sheet, swung her feet to the floor, and stood up, her simple cambric nightshift swirling about her ankles. She had just gone to her old leather trunk and lifted up the lid when there came upon the door a light tap, followed by the brisk entrance of Lady Augusta, today clad in an ill-fitting day dress of pale blue merino, the long, tight sleeves of which were noticeably too short and the high waistline looking as if it might have a lamentable tendency to pinch its wearer about the middle.

"Good morning, Miss Smythe! I came across Martha in the gallery, and she told me you were awake—but not that you had gotten out of bed! Do, pray, return there directly!"

Caroline straightened, and said, feeling more than a little awkward at finding herself in the presence of her new employer barefooted and wearing only her nightclothes, "Good morning, my lady! I assure you, after my long rest I am feeling much more the thing, and am anxious to enter upon my responsibilities without further delay."

Lady Augusta laughed heartily. "Just as Damien predicted! No, my dear, it's back to bed you go, for I am most strictly charged to keep you there until the doctor has consented to release you! I have sent for our local man, Dr. Selby, and expect him to arrive sometime this morning."

"Oh, no, my lady," Caroline protested uncomfortably, "I *must* not discommode both yourself and the staff so!"

"Nonsense! Nothing could be further from the truth! I'm extremely busy just now with a translation I want to complete, and as for the servants, they have been at loose ends for years! A bit of work will be good for them! Now, shall I assist you up, my dear Miss Smythe?"

"No, no, I am quite capable, thank you, my lady," responded Caroline, discomfited but hurriedly complying. As she tugged the pillows up so that she might sit against them and then pulled the blankets over her once more, there was another knock upon the door, and the little maidservant returned, gripping in her fingers a silver tray fragrant with the delicious sweet scent of chocolate.

"Thank you, Martha," Lady Augusta said, taking the tray and herself carrying it to the bed, there to place it next to Caroline. "You may go. Now, Miss Smythe, I've come to bear you company while you break your fast, so that we may become better acquainted. We scarcely had the opportunity to exchange two words yesterday! May I pour you a cup of chocolate?"

"Yes, thank you, my lady, but—" Caroline couldn't refrain from an appreciative sniff as the warm chocolate filled her cup; then she added firmly, "But it isn't proper for your ladyship to be waiting on *me!*"

"Good Lord, are you one of those high sticklers who insist on standing on ceremony?" Lady Augusta replaced the chocolate pot on the tray and looked at Caroline with a comical expression of dismay on her face. "If that is the case, I fear that we shall be at outs, Miss Smythe, for despite all my poor aunt's strictures to the contrary, I am a most stubbornly informal creature!"

Caroline laughed, disarmed by Lady Augusta's frank manners. "Since becoming a governess, my lady, it has been my lot to scrupulously obey the conventions! Those of my ilk may not, you know, flout them with impunity! As for myself," she went on, "I had prior to that time been much used to living a—a rather untraditional existence."

"I am so glad! I thought I was not to have been mistaken in you!" Cheerful again, Lady Augusta went to the oak chair set near the writing desk and dragged it alongside the bed, then plumped herself into it with a sigh of relief. "Now! Drink your chocolate, Miss Smythe, eat your toast before it gets cold, and tell me all about yourself!"

Caroline sipped her chocolate with considerable relish, and said, with a little restraint, "I am not a very interesting personage, my lady, I assure you. Please, will you not tell me about *you?*''

Augusta gave another of her hearty laughs. ''I can see that you are so refined you will only eat if *I* am talking, so I shall oblige you. You will doubtless wish to learn some of the particulars of the family into which you have been admitted. Has my dear brother enlightened you at all?''

''Aside from leaving me with the distinct impression that you were a child still in pinafores who required the services of a governess,'' Caroline answered dryly, ''his lordship said nothing.''

''Is *that* why you looked so stunned when you saw me?'' Lady Augusta asked, grinning. ''I thought you were taken aback by my ridiculous height, or the hair straggling—as it *will*, no matter how many pins my maid jabs into my skull!—from my topknot.''

Caroline smiled. ''In truth, I think your stature quite to be envied; I have often wished for more inches. As to the rest, I would never have presumed to judge you, my lady, being in a highly disordered state myself!''

''*You* at least had the excuse of travel, and illness,'' retorted Lady Augusta. ''Well, I must say Damien trumped you beautifully, for I never heard the least peep from you despite what I can now recognize as your astonishment at finding your prospective charge a strapping young woman of twenty-one!''

Caroline swallowed a bite of toast and dabbed at her lips with a damask napkin. Her curiosity about the lord of Windemere led her to carefully inquire, ''Has your brother always been possessed of such a—a masterful personality, my lady?''

''Do you mean has he always been so high-handed?'' Lady Augusta returned, her dark eyes twinkling. ''To own the truth, I hardly know. Damien was ten when I was born, and before I was out of leading strings he was away at school. As he never came home for the holidays, we had little opportunity to learn more of the other.''

"Never came home for the holidays?" echoed Caroline in amazement. "But whyever not?" As soon as the words were out of her mouth, she wished them returned. "I beg your pardon, my lady!" she said hastily, her cheeks burning in mortification. "Pray forgive my unseemly impertinence!"

"Oh, nonsense!" said Lady Augusta breezily. "Have I not promised to unfold to you the Reston family saga? And do call me Augusta, won't you? And I shall call you—Caroline, isn't it? *So* much less stuffy!"

Caroline hesitated, for the three years of rigid discipline she had maintained while residing in the Tintham household had fostered within her a deep sense of reserve. Yet she could not help being warmed by Lady Augusta's easygoing manners and obvious sincerity. "As you will," she murmured, her uneasiness lessening, and picked up another piece of toast. "You were saying, dear ma'am . . . ?"

"Where were we? Oh, yes! Damien never came home from school," Lady Augusta went on, "because our parents themselves were rarely here at Windemere—my father came only for the occasional hunting party—and neither preferred to be troubled with the inconvenience of having to plan for his travel, and someone to accompany him, and so on. Theirs was an arranged marriage, you see—a brilliant match, by all accounts. *She* was a diamond of the first water, and *he* was heir to one of England's oldest, richest, noblest estates. Yet apparently no one thought to inquire if the two protagonists of this farce held for each other any degree of compatibility."

"They—they did not love each other, then?" ventured Caroline.

Lady Augusta laughed again. "Far from it! They managed to produce an heir, but their interests were so diverse that they were almost never, I am told, seen in company together. I have often wondered how *I* happened to come along! If I didn't so greatly resemble Damien in our looks, I must have assumed myself to be the product of one of my mother's liaisons!"

"Oh, poor child!" Caroline uttered involuntarily.

Lady Augusta shrugged, and sank lower in her chair, comfortably crossing one ankle over the other. "I thank you for your concern, but it's hardly necessary! It mattered little enough to me. I had my books, and the local curate who was kind enough to take an interest in my schooling. He was educated at Cambridge, and, happily for me, was a considerable scholar in his own right."

"But surely yours was a—a lonely childhood?"

"I never noticed," her ladyship answered. "Having known no other life, there could be no comparisons." She added thoughtfully, "I do not remember much of her, but my mother truly *was* a remarkable beauty—like a fairy princess out of one of my storybooks!—and my father was reputedly quite the sportsman. I can only suppose that Damien and I acquired our intellects from some distant Reston progenitor. May I pour you another cup of chocolate?"

"You are most thoughtful, ma'am; thank you."

Lady Augusta promptly rose and refreshed Caroline's cup, then resumed her seat, with her feet in their scuffed dark-blue kid boots stretched out in front of her. "I am glad to see you eating and drinking with such appetite," she remarked. "You are far too thin and pale for my liking! Though Aunt Violet *did* say last night that she wished I might follow your abstemious example, so that I too might assume more delicate proportions."

Caroline did not divulge to her ladyship that both overwork and Mrs. Tintham's fondness for exercising strict principles of economy concerning the quantity and variety of food offered in the servants' hall had doubtless contributed a great deal to her present state of attenuation. Instead she could not resist turning the conversation back to the subject of the marquis, and said: "I take it his lordship enjoyed his studies?"

"Yes, I believe he did very well at Eton and at Oxford. But when he was only nineteen our father died—and my mother as well—and he assumed his titles at a rather tender age."

"*Both* your parents died?" Caroline asked. "But what a horrible coincidence!"

"Not really," Lady Augusta responded matter-of-factly. "I forgot to mention to you that their only mutual passion was gambling. I understand that from time to time they met to participate in one kind of wager or another, as long as the stakes were sufficiently high. They were killed in a curricle race en route to Brighton, competing against Lord Alvanley and his mistress. Alvanley had just ascended to the peerdom, and inherited a vast sum, and, so the tale goes, was anxious to bring himself to the notice of the prince, for the winners of the race were to be honored with a ball in their honor at the prince's Pavilion. Evidently, however, my father misjudged the distance between an oncoming mail coach and the edge of the road, and his curricle tumbled rather violently into a ditch. Interestingly enough, neither of the horses was fatally injured. I am told Damien continued to drive them for years afterward."

Caroline had been listening in horror, her cup suspended halfway to her mouth. Her mind reeled from the gruesome image of the accident her ladyship's words conjured, even as she dazedly absorbed the fact that the day she met Lord Reston *he* had been engaging in a highly perilous curricle race. Was it a ghoulish preoccupation with his parents' deaths that led him to such madness? "How—how dreadful," she whispered finally, and unsteadily lowered the cup to the tray. "I am so sorry, for both you and his lordship."

"Your sympathy, as generous as it is, is wasted, my dear Caroline. I hope you do not think me unfilial, but I scarcely knew my parents, and certainly did not care for them. How could I mourn a pair of strangers? Except for the unwelcome arrival of my aunt, their demises changed *my* life not a jot."

In truth Caroline *did* find Lady Augusta's attitude a trifle cold-blooded, but reminded herself that while her ladyship might have grown up surrounded by all the material advantages, *she* had been fortunate enough to have loved, and been loved by, her mother and father, and therefore ought not to judge someone whose circumstances had differed so greatly from her own. She drew a deep breath, and inquired, "And—and his lordship? How did he fare in the aftermath?"

"According to Aunt Violet, as soon as the funerals were over, Damien went to London, took occupancy of the family town house, and swiftly proceeded to acquire a reputation as both a brilliant Corinthian and one of the *ton*'s most dissolute young noblemen."

"Indeed?" was all Caroline could think to reply.

"Oh, yes, the gambling, the demimondaines, the Carlton House set, all that sort of thing," said Lady Augusta cheerfully. "Even a few duels, according to Aunt Violet! But as Damien is a crack marksman he emerged from them unscathed."

"How—how fortunate."

"Yes. You would think, after all his profligacy," her ladyship went on musingly, "that society would have been scandalized, and shut their doors to him! But no, for it only served to heighten his luster as one of the great catches of the *ton*."

It was not difficult for Caroline to imagine that many caps had been set for the marquis. "His lordship remains unmarried?" she asked cautiously.

"Not for much longer," Lady Augusta responded, and Caroline was both surprised at and disgusted with herself for feeling a strange constriction about the heart at her ladyship's casual words.

"He—he is betrothed, then?" she said, relieved to hear the dispassion in her own voice.

"Yes. Last spring he wrote to Aunt Violet and instructed her to come to town for the season—my dear Caroline, you can't *imagine* her transports of joy upon receiving the summons!—so that she might go about in society and assist him in his search for an eligible bride. And long before the season was ended, he and the Honorable Helen Manderlay were affianced! In my naïveté about such matters I own I had been used to thinking it a rather romantic tale—'Love is swift of foot,' as George Herbert said—but after my conversation with Damien yesterday afternoon I must confess I find myself wondering if his betrothal was transacted as coolly as was that of our parents. And indeed, why should such a notion have shocked me so? After all, Damien is patterning his career quite exactly after theirs.''

Caroline stared down into the dregs of the chocolate she had so enjoyed, then slowly lifted her eyes to her ladyship's rueful countenance. ''Do you know Miss Manderlay well, ma'am?''

''No, I have never met her, though my aunt declares her to be a paragon of beauty, good breeding, exquisite sensibility, and all that is ladylike.'' Lady Augusta shuddered visibly. ''I only pray that she doesn't wish to come to Windemere a great deal! Well, you may as well know, my dear, that I am merely biding my time until I am twenty-five: I shall then come into my inheritance, a very comfortable sum, I am happy to say, and I shall take myself off to Cambridge, where I will set up my own household.'' She added, almost defiantly, ''I shall also establish a female seminary, so that young ladies might have a *real* education! Something besides watercolor, and pianoforte, and a smattering of French! I daresay I have shocked you— Aunt Violet nearly had an apoplexy when I confided to her my plans—but it is something I have dreamed of for years, and I am determined to accomplish it!''

''It is an admirable ambition,'' Caroline rejoined, glad for the shift of topic. ''But Augusta, have you no thoughts of marriage?''

''Oh, pooh!'' said her ladyship carelessly. ''It is all very well for others, I suppose, but I assure you, *I* have no desire to entangle myself in such a way! What about yourself?'' she suddenly asked, turning her bright dark gaze upon Caroline. ''Do you long for marriage, and a family of your own?''

Feeling an odd constraint, Caroline toyed for a moment with

the dishes on her tray. "I am not in a position to aspire to it," she said quietly.

Her ladyship eyed her quizzically. "Indeed? Well, if you wish, you are very welcome to come to Cambridge with me, and teach at my seminary. I should be very glad to have you there, for you will add just the tone I will want."

Caroline only smiled, and wondered at the perplexing ache within her chest. Surely, she told herself, it was only her bruised ribs that troubled her so.

"His lordship, the Marquis of Reston," came the sonorous voice of Latham Park's majordomo as Damien stepped into a vast drawing room expensively furnished in the popular Egyptian style, complete with life-size Nubian statues of black marble, vivid green couches with legs carved to resemble those of crocodiles, and wallpaper embellished with boldly rendered lotus plants. Damien thought it all tasteless in the extreme, but allowed no trace of his revulsion to show on his countenance as he advanced toward his hostess, Baroness Manderlay, who had risen from a sofa draped with a pair of lion skins to meet him with a languidly outstretched hand.

"My dear Lord Reston," said Lady Calpurnia, managing to gaze down the exorbitant length of her nose even as she looked up at Damien while he bowed over her pale fingers. "We had your note informing us of your delay, yet could not help but wonder what could possibly have kept you from the ball."

"Nothing less than a dire emergency, I assure you," answered Damien imperturbably, and at once an image of Caroline Smythe's piquant face and fine, long-lashed eyes danced through his mind.

"But of course," rejoined the baroness majestically. "No doubt you suffered the very natural anxiety that Helen might have felt obliged to demur from opening the ball, as we had planned. You will be relieved to know that the Earl of Audley very kindly stepped into the vacancy left by your absence.''

"How thoughtful of the earl,'' Damien murmured, ''and how considerate of your ladyship to lay my concerns to rest. Won't you excuse me, ma'am? I am, of course, anxious to greet Miss Manderlay at once.'' Indolently he turned away and, raising his quizzing glass, leisurely looked about him. There was such an immense and colorful quantity of both furniture and guests crowding the room that it took him some few moments to locate his betrothed underneath a massive painting of a dashingly mustachioed Cavalier wooing a blushing damsel clad in a froth of lace and ruffles and an enormous hat as intimately they reposed on a bench amidst a brilliant spring bower laden with flowers.

Surrounded by her admirers, the Honorable Helen Manderlay sat in a low, lyre-backed chair, the hem of her diaphanous pale green day gown pooled about her spangled green kid slippers. A whisper-thin silk shawl lay negligently about her slim shoulders, leaving her sharply etched collarbone and the flesh above her low neckline exposed to the air which, thanks to the press of many bodies, was if anything too warm. She tilted her shining blonde head to meet Damien's gaze as he approached at an unhurried pace.

"Reston!'' she said civilly, and held out her hand to be kissed. ''I confess I thought we were not to see you here.''

Lightly Damien touched his lips to the soft hand he grasped in his own. ''You had my note, Helen, promising otherwise. Did you think I would fail you?''

"One hardly knew what to think, after hearing you defaulted on your race with Essex,'' Miss Manderlay replied. ''The rumors, my dear Reston, veritably flew.''

"Indeed?'' Damien said disinterestedly, watching out of the corner of his eye as a scantily dressed, tightly corseted matron stared at a voluptuous statue of the goddess Isis with palpable indignation, then snapped open her fan and began vigorously fanning herself.

"There was talk," came a smooth voice, "that you were overcome with chagrin at your ignominious defeat and languished in the country until your spirits were sufficiently restored to permit you to reenter society." The Earl of Audley, tall, slender, and elegant, parted thin lips in a slight smile. One delicate white hand rested on the back of Miss Manderlay's chair. "I, of course, discounted such a nonsensical tale."

"I am all gratitude at your incredulity, sir." Damien glanced at that hand, and then into the earl's pale blue eyes, which gleamed with malicious humor. He went on impassively: "I understand I am in your debt, for the baroness tells me you served in my stead at the ball."

"It was my pleasure," the earl answered, and sketched a mockingly deferential bow in Damien's direction. "Miss Manderlay and I have always danced so well together."

"Reston," broke in Miss Manderlay composedly, "I daresay you know everyone here? Need I introduce you to Mr. Prine at my left, or Sir John Maccabee? No? I did not think so."

"I say, Reston," said one youthful gentleman, resplendent in a yellow jacket and a violently embroidered lavender waistcoat, "what *do* you call that neckcloth of yours?"

"It's a Mathematical," put in another aspiring Corinthian scornfully. "Can't you see that triangular sort of shape amongst the folds?"

"No, it's an Oriental," said a third young man with smug certitude. "Had you memorized *Neckclothitania* as I have, Arthur, you'd have known it in an instant."

And had the young man realized the volume in question was a satirical treatise, thought Damien, he might not have made it publicly known that he had studied it. With cool detachment he watched the three friends spiritedly debate among themselves, even as he observed the earl bending low to whisper something in Miss Manderlay's shell-like ear. Miss Manderlay received his confidences with an unimpaired calm, yet the intimacy of the earl's gesture recalled to Damien his Aunt Violet's reports that he had been one of Miss Manderlay's most ardent beaux. Nevertheless, Miss Manderlay had, according to her father the baron as he and Damien sat in conference, readily agreed to receive the addresses of so notable a peer as the Marquis of Reston.

Contemplating these facts as he would methodically consider an arithmetical problem, Damien was abruptly stirred from his thoughts by a cheerful voice hailing him.

"Damien!" cried Charles Highcombe, beaming, and clapped him enthusiastically on the back. "I'm dashed glad to see you, my dear fellow!" He glanced carelessly at the circle of men surrounding Miss Manderlay, nodded at her, said by way of general greeting, " 'Servant," and taking Damien by the arm he tugged him some distance away, toward a blank-faced servant in a powdered wig and black silk waistcoat and breeches who was circulating amidst the throng holding a tray, from whom Chades accepted two tall cut-crystal glasses of champagne.

Handing one of the glasses to Damien, Charles leaned close. "I'll say this for the baroness," he whispered loudly. "Her style's on the vulgar side, but she don't scrimp on her refreshments!"

Damien took a half-step backward. "My dear Charles," he said, "need you have dragged me away in such an unseemly fashion?"

Charles grinned. "You looked mighty bored to me!"

"I suppose it is because I am nearly always bored in company," responded Damien, and sipped at the sparkling champagne. He looked thoughtfully at Charles. "You know how appalling my memory is, but I have for these several days been laboring under the impression that you had gone to Kent."

"Yes, yes, I did, but it was devilish dull there. Too cold to go out hunting, and nothing to be done but play cards and do the pretty amongst the ladies. It was so flat, in short, I almost picked up a book!''

"Good God,'' murmured Damien.

"Yes, so before I sank that low I made my excuses and traveled here posthaste, for I knew I'd find you amongst the party,'' Charles explained, then added, "And I wanted *specifically* to ensure that your head groom told you I'd managed your horses wonderfully well from that wretched little village— Billstock, wasn't it? Or, no, Banestitch!—to London!''

"Baldock,'' Damien said, bowing infinitesimally as an acquaintance meandered by. "Which reminds me, my dear Charles. You will oblige me greatly by striving to forget the entirety of that unfortunate episode.''

"Well, good Lord, what's to remember?'' rejoined Charles indignantly. "Forfeiting to that blackguard Essex, then moldering in some sordid excuse for an inn while you waited for that girl to—''

"As you say, Charles,'' interposed Damien gently, "there is nothing to remember.''

Charles' eyes widened, and then a secretive expression of comprehension settled itself across his features. "Ah! *I* see! You need not worry, old fellow! I am the soul of discretion!''

As Damien chose not to enlighten his friend as to the true outcome of his brief sojourn in Baldock, he merely replied: "To be sure you are. But tell me, Charles, how did you come to feel confident the Manderlays would welcome your impromptu arrival at Latham Park?''

Charles finished his champagne in one long swallow and leaned close again. "Why, we're cousins of a sort,'' he explained in a hushed undervoice. "On my father's side. Never told you before because my mother don't like me to mention it—because of the baron's father.''

"You refer, of course, to the fabulously wealthy mill owner in Leeds,'' said Damien.

"*Don't* shout it to the room!'' begged Charles. "It'll be

bound to get back to my mother and she'll have me deported to Australia! Or," he added gloomily, "she'll cut my allowance, which would be far worse."

"At the risk of sounding churlish, I wish to point out that I wasn't shouting," said Damien. "Nonetheless, I do beg your pardon."

"Think nothing of it," Charles replied graciously, and in one deft gesture he handed his empty glass to a manservant gliding past and plucked a filled one from the tray.

"Thank you," Damien said gravely.

"Not at all!" Suddenly Charles craned his neck to peer over Damien's shoulder. "Good Lord, do you see Darnley over there caressing that statue? It's positively indecent! Not but what that statue has a deucedly fine figure! How *shall* you like inheriting Latham Park one day, dear chap? Lovely grounds and all that, but I don't know if *I* should enjoy being saddled with a house whose best drawing room reminded me of some infidel's tomb! My mother, you know, urged me to pursue the beauteous Helen (though she don't care for the taint of trade, the Manderlay gold would have done much to repair the faltering Highcombe fortunes!) but once *you* entered the lists a paltry fellow such as myself didn't stand a chance!"

Idly Damien swirled the sparkling amber liquid in his glass. "You overwhelm me, Charles."

"It's nothing but the truth," said Charles cheerfully. "Well, to look at Helen you'd never know she comes from mill stock, would you? Sitting on that dashed peculiar chair like she's a queen on a throne! She's a bit of a cool fish for *my* taste, but there's no denying she's exceedingly handsome! Even my mother admitted to it!"

Raising his quizzing glass, Damien gazed through it at Miss Manderlay as he would at a complete stranger, noting distantly that the crowd of gallants around her had grown even larger. As if sensing his scrutiny, Miss Manderlay turned unruffled blue eyes his way, smiling slightly and raising her fan in a subtle salute.

Damien dipped his head, then slowly lowered his quizzing glass and looked to his friend. "Do you know, Charles," he drawled, "all at once I find myself possessed of a great thirst, one which I fear this champagne can't quench. Might you know where something a trifle more potent could be found?"

"Indeed I do!" Charles declared with alacrity, his face lighting up. "The baron's got some mighty fine brandy in his library, and what's more, he's invited me to partake of it whenever I choose!"

"Then," said Damien, depositing his half-empty glass on a nearby table, "I pray you, lead on."

Chapter 5

Caroline paced the long length of the gallery for perhaps the twentieth time, her soft kid slippers making no sound on the smooth wood floor. A month had passed since her arrival at Windemere, and each day had brought her closer to regained health. She had spent the initial week in bed, fretful at the enforced inactivity, yet secretly a little grateful for it too, for during those long, still hours she had come to acknowledge the bone-deep exhaustion that had been plaguing her for longer than she liked to admit, and which had only been reinforced by her injuries.

At first even reading a book had tired her, and caused her head to ache unmercifully; hearing this, Lady Augusta frequently stopped in to entertain Caroline by reading aloud from her translation of Bacon's *De Augmentis Scientarum* and the accompanying commentary she was writing. Caroline found it all frankly beyond her own scholarly abilities, but tactfully tried to fix on her countenance a look of polite interest and even managed to ask a few questions of sufficient acumen to bring a gratified smile to Lady Augusta's face. Even so, Caroline couldn't help being glad when her ladyship returned to her rooms, there to cheerfully tackle yet another complex passage of Latin.

The local doctor, one Edward Selby, proved to be a kindly, jovial man of middle age, who pronounced her broken arm masterfully set by his unknown colleague in Baldock, and whose recommendations were simple: plenty of rest and good food. After some days of this regimen (although Caroline wouldn't have deemed the food of superior quality, it was adequate, and certainly plentiful, and she found herself eating, to the doctor's satisfaction, with a considerably heightened appetite), Dr. Selby had said she might begin to take a little exercise in the gallery.

He had warned her not to overestimate her capacity, and indeed, after each of her first few slow perambulations Caroline was happy to permit young Martha, the red-haired maid, to assist her back into the beautifully canopied bed she now occupied in the Blue Bedchamber, having there removed after one night spent in the chamber of the marquis.

But now she was feeling stronger, and with renewed energy came a kind of restlessness. Lady Augusta was happily absorbed in her studies, and while she was obviously pleased to have Caroline join her and Mrs. Yardley for tea at first and then for meals, it was clear she was comfortably self-sufficient and had little use for a hired companion to help her while away the hours. If anyone was in need of such a person, it was Mrs. Yardley, who, as far as Caroline could tell, spent much of her time wistfully perusing the society sections of newspapers from town and poring over the latest editions of *La Belle Assemblée* and *Ackerman's Repository of Arts, Literature and Commerce.* Her attempts to regale Augusta with choice tidbits from these fashionable periodicals fell on deaf ears, and as she continued to treat Caroline with a kind of distant, puzzled civility Caroline had concluded that Mrs. Yardley neither expected nor desired

her to participate in her one-sided discussions about a velvet
mulberry spencer she admired, padded and augmented with a
cunning little peplum, or a fulsome description of a London
emporium called Harding, Howell and Co., detailing the contents of each of its departments from furs, fans, and articles of
haberdashery to jewelry, French clocks, and perfume.

Without any duties of her own to occupy her time (a hesitant
inquiry of Mrs. Yardley if she was in need of any kind of
assistance brought only a blank stare), Caroline found herself
vastly curious about Windemere, for she had led such a peripa-
tetic life that she was intrigued at being in a house which had
contained several generations of a single family. She was eager
to learn more of its history, but it seemed forward to set off
on explorations of her own, and as she was reluctant to either
disturb Lady Augusta or importune Mrs. Yardley she was limited to long walks in the gallery.

As she strolled now, Caroline gazed once again at the portraits she passed, trying to detect in their features the distinctively deep-set cast of Lord Reston's dark eyes, or the proud
arch of his brows or the straight, aristocratic line of his nose.
Was this coy damsel in her rigid, lace-trimmed Elizabethan ruff
and glittering, wide-skirted gown a great-great-grandmother of
the present marquis? Or, here, this stately gentleman in his
ermine-trimmed robes, long, elaborately curled wig, and high-
heeled, red-buckled shoes—was he a relative who had lived
long enough to make himself known to the present generation
of Restons?

Caroline paused in front of a large gilt-framed painting which
portrayed a strikingly handsome young couple, a dark-haired
little boy, and a trio of sleek hunting dogs. The woman reminded
Caroline of a character out of the brothers Grimm (whose
recently published volume of collected folk tales Mrs. Tintham
had been proud to point out to visitors, as an example of her
household's modernity and sophistication): with her gleaming
black hair, translucent white skin, and invitingly red mouth she

seemed the very representation of the beautiful, hapless princess Snow White who guilelessly fell victim to a poisoned apple. Yet this woman in her rubies and pearls and rich, low-cut brocade gown looked confident, arrogant, supremely self-collected. Not, Caroline mused, like someone with whom *she* would enjoy a companionable coze, nor did the good-looking, rather vacuous features of the tall, buff man at the woman's side suggest a personality compatible with her own.

But the little boy who stood so straight in his own isolated section of the painting, separated from his parents by the pack of fawning dogs—despite the look of fierce pride on his small, youthful countenance and the stiff tilt of his dark-haired head— there was something appealingly vulnerable about him, some intimation of solitude that made Caroline yearn to reach out to him. She stared into the dark eyes and compared them with a pair of brilliant, rather hard ones that remained so vivid in her memory and wondered if this aloof child had grown up to become the marquis she herself knew.

She sighed, and moved on to the next painting, which rendered in heavy dark oils the portrait of a plump little girl with untidy black hair, who was dressed in an unflattering shade of orange. In her lap she clutched a book, and at her feet the artist had included a tall, uneven stack of other volumes, which looked as if it was about to topple at any moment.

Caroline took a step nearer, in an attempt to see if she could read the titles of any of the books. *The Pilgrim's Progress. The Life and Strange Adventures of Robinson Crusoe.* And, good heavens, was that leather-bound tome Sir Thomas More's *Utopia?* Caroline inched closer, then jumped when a gruff voice suddenly spoke.

"That's her ladyship, Miss Augusta, when she was only seven."

It was Mrs. Dawkins, the housekeeper, who had approached without Caroline being aware of it. Her stolid face was expressionless as she regarded Caroline and went on, "Dr. Selby is here, miss, wanting to see how your arm is coming along. He's in the Green Saloon."

"Is he? Why, he came only the day before yesterday. Thank you for letting me know, Mrs. Dawkins," Caroline replied, and as the older woman nodded curtly and turned away, impulsively she added, "Mrs. Dawkins! If you have a free hour or two, and if it isn't too much trouble, might you—might you take me on a tour of the house, and describe to me its history?"

The housekeeper eyed her with some suspicion. "Why would you be wanting to do that, miss?"

"Because it's such a beautiful place—so old, so filled with memories! I've never been in a house like it before! Have you lived here all your life?"

Mrs. Dawkins' answer was guarded. "That I have, miss, and you won't find anyone who knows more about Windemere than me."

"I am sure I couldn't have asked a better person, then. But I wouldn't wish to be a bother." Having begun to regret her spontaneous request, Caroline was more than a little surprised when Mrs. Dawkins spoke, with a slight thawing in her reserve.

"It wouldn't be a bother. When would you be wishful of being shown around, miss?"

"After the doctor leaves, perhaps, if you've the time?"

"Certainly, miss," replied Mrs. Dawkins, and briskly Caroline made her way to the Green Saloon, filled with an agreeable sense of anticipation.

But Caroline was not to be taken on her tour that afternoon. Dr. Selby lingered so long following his cursory examination of Caroline's arm that the weak winter sun had begun fading into the gloom of dusk, and Lady Augusta poked her head into the room to inform Caroline that tea was ready and had been these fifteen minutes or more, and oh! She hadn't seen Dr. Selby at first, for his green coat blended in rather nicely against the sofa on which he sat! Would he care to join the ladies for tea?

Reddening, Dr. Selby had jumped to his feet and with a vigorous bow that sent his lank brown hair flying he thanked her ladyship and told her he would promptly take his leave; after which earnest declaration he bade farewell to Caroline, assured her that her arm was healing splendidly, turned swiftly on his heel, and knocked over an occasional table littered with a pile of Mrs. Yardley's fashion journals. Voluble in his apologies, Dr. Selby restored both the table and the journals, and, blushing fiercely now, made his way to the door and disappeared.

A few minutes later, as she handed round a cup of tea to Caroline, Lady Augusta said playfully, "How punctilious Dr. Selby is in his care of you, dear Caro! One would almost think his visits had a purpose beyond the purely medicinal!"

"Oh, do not say it!" protested Caroline, hardly knowing whether to laugh or be distressed. "Indeed, I am most grateful for his assiduousness!"

"I have it on good authority," put in Mrs. Yardley, "that Dr. Selby has been widowed for five years, and is considered in Chelmsford to be a highly eligible *parti.*"

"Oh?" Caroline said politely, uncomfortably aware of the older woman's basilisk stare.

It was at this rather unfortunate juncture that Lady Augusta suddenly said, "Oh, Caro! In the excitement of finishing my translation this morning I forgot to mention it! Damien's secretary has sent a draft for your first quarter's salary, which I shall give to you straightaway after tea."

"Surely it is a bit premature?" Mrs. Yardley said frostily. "Miss Smythe has been here but a month."

And done nothing to earn her keep, Caroline mentally added. She could hardly blame Mrs. Yardley for her disapprobation, for she felt the awkwardness of her situation keenly. As soon as her arm was free of its sling—within a few weeks' time,

Dr. Selby had promised—she could help with the sewing, at least, for it was a task neither Lady Augusta nor Mrs. Yardley showed the least inclination to attempt. Then perhaps when Lady Augusta went into Chelmsford (her ladyship being too occupied with her studies at present, and Mrs. Yardley failing to invite Caroline to accompany her on her frequent trips) she could make inquiries concerning new employment.

In the meantime, Caroline told herself, she would of course not touch the money Lord Reston had sent (though her own meager purse was nearly depleted and she *was* sadly in need of a new, warm dress or two, a bonnet, gloves, undergarments, and perhaps a pair of walking boots for when the weather turned milder).

Lady Augusta picked up a small iced cake, and said bluntly: "If it is Damien's desire to give Caro her salary a trifle early, Aunt, I don't know why it need be a concern of yours."

Mrs. Yardley sniffed audibly, and turned to Caroline. "Dr. Selby," she said, "has four young children greatly in need of a mother's tender guidance. I understand, Miss Smythe, that you are a governess by occupation?"

"Yes, ma'am," said Caroline calmly, and sipped at her tea, although inside she was writhing at Mrs. Yardley's none-too-subtle hint.

"Oh, do let us leave off talking about Dr. Selby!" Lady Augusta interposed impatiently. "I'm sure I can't think of another more utterly boring topic of conversation! Caro, would you care to hear the last two pages of *De Augmentis Scientarum?* I really do believe I've caught the flavor of Bacon's ratiocination!"

"Yes, ma'am," said Caroline, in all sincerity. "It would be a pleasure."

As winter gradually showed signs of giving way to spring, the weeks that followed were to prove interesting ones for

Caroline, though there was to be no appreciable change in what she felt to be the uncertainty of her circumstances. To her pleased surprise, Mrs. Dawkins revealed herself to be a thoroughly knowledgeable and even enthusiastic guide, and as she led Caroline along interminable corridors and through an apparently endless number of rooms, each more magnificent than the last, Caroline's sense of wonder only increased. Twelve generations of Restons had lived here, surviving the turmoils that had rocked England through the ages, from war to plague to crop failure to floods. Through it all Windemere remained, seemingly impervious to the ravages of time.

"Though things aren't as they were in Lord Reston's grandfather's day, miss!" confided Mrs. Dawkins, as they peered into what had once been a children's nursery. "I was but a girl then, and my mother an upstairs maid, but I do remember as how the house was kept in beautiful order! Many's the time I spent a whole week just wiping clean the banisters!"

Caroline shook free a clump of dust that clung to the hem of her skirt. "What changed, Mrs. Dawkins?"

"Why, the old marquis passed on, miss, and his son—that's the present marquis' father—took possession of Windemere, and I may say it meant no more to him than as if he'd been given a pair of knitted slippers!" said Mrs. Dawkins darkly.

"Lady Augusta mentioned that Lord Reston's father was much given to sporting activities."

"Aye, addicted to the hunt, he was! It was a twelve-days' wonder if we saw him here above once a year, and in the meantime the house went to wrack and ruin!" Mrs. Dawkins chuckled grimly. "No doubt you think me the poorest sort of housekeeper, miss! *I* see the dirt and the grime, let me tell you, and the draperies left unmended! But after so many years of neglect by their lord, it became well-nigh impossible to bestir the staff, and there's only so much the few of us left who know their duty can do!"

"The house is very large," Caroline agreed gently.

"That it is." Mrs. Dawkins brushed at a cobweb that dangled from the door frame, and heaved a deep sigh. "We hoped, miss, that the present marquis would be different from his father, for he was such a promising young 'un!"

"Was he?" said Caroline, fascinated, thinking of the little boy in the portrait, at once fiercely proud and terribly vulnerable.

"Oh, aye! So bright, and so affectionate! It near broke my heart when they sent him away to school! But then, when his own parents died and his lordship left university, well . . ." Mrs. Dawkins trailed off sadly.

"Your hopes did not materialize," Caroline supplied, her own heart heavy with an emotion she did not wish to analyze.

"No, miss, and what with Lady Augusta shut up with her books, and Mrs. Yardley not wishing to become involved with domestic matters, life at Windemere has remained much the same over the years." Then Mrs. Dawkins brightened somewhat. "But perhaps when his lordship has married, and brought his new bride here . . ."

"Yes," Caroline said, and stepped back into the hallway. "Did you not tell me of a suite in which Henry the Eighth stayed, ma'am? I should very much like to see it!"

Some ten or twelve days following this rather melancholy exchange, Caroline took advantage of an irresistibly mild afternoon and ventured out of doors for the first time since she had come to Windemere. Liberated at last from her sling, she spent an enjoyable hour strolling amongst the still-dormant gardens, then set out for an inviting promontory that promised an unrivaled view of Windemere's parkland. When she reached the crest, she was startled to find a solid-looking, plainly dressed, middle-aged man sitting on a carved wood bench staring dejectedly at the fallow fields that stretched out for a considerable distance until they met the forest.

"Oh! I beg your pardon!" exclaimed Caroline. "I did not mean to intrude!"

The man turned at the sound of her voice, and quickly came

to his feet. Doffing his hat, he said, "You're not intruding, miss; I'm merely wool-gathering. Miss Smythe, isn't it? They told me at the house about you."

"Yes, I'm Miss Smythe." As her role among the household had inexorably come to be more that of a guest than that of a servant, Caroline couldn't help but wonder precisely what had been said about her.

"How d'you do, miss? I'm Roger Goodsall, the bailiff." He dipped his grizzled head.

"How do you do?" Smiling, for she already liked the man's bluff, straightforward appearance, Caroline seated herself on the bench and with a gesture of her arm urged him to do the same. "Have you come to make your plans for the spring crops?"

Roger Goodsall shook his head, then sat down next to her. "Flax and mustard as usual, I suppose, miss! And too much of it," he added lugubriously, gazing toward the fields again. "New crops are badly needed, and far too many acres remain unplowed, year after year! I've said so, time and again, but . . ."

Caroline studied his troubled, weather-beaten profile, and knew the answer before she even asked the question. "Why have your recommendations not been put forward, Mr. Goodsall?"

The bailiff shrugged. "Well, miss, despite all our problems with the crops—not to mention short tenancies, outdated equipment, and the laborers' cottages badly in need of repair—the estate still manages to produce a handsome income, and I reckon his lordship, like his father before him, feels no need for improvements or alterations."

"But the laborers, Mr. Goodsall!" said Caroline concernedly. "Surely it's neither healthful nor productive for their homes to fall into disarray!"

"Eh, I do what I can, miss," said Roger Goodsall. "I suppose the situation's no worse than plenty of others," he added fatalistically. "After last year's dismal crop returns, all throughout the country, people are scared, and expect less."

"It is not right that the estate's laborers be neglected," Caroline said in a low voice.

Mr. Goodsall looked at her closely, and his bushy brows drew together. "Now, see here, miss, I oughtn't to have upset you with all my loose talk! You're not to worry about *my* problems! I'm sure everything will turn out all right, for it always does, by hook or by crook!"

Not wishing to burden the kindly bailiff further, Caroline forced a smile, and agreed with him, then changed the subject, but in her heart were mounting troubles she privately could not so lightly dismiss—troubles which swiftly came to a head but a week later, as she sat outside on the broad terrace whose stone steps led down into the gardens and magnificent fountain below. It was another beautiful early-spring day, and she had taken with her a cream-colored chair cover from the Little Drawing Room whose corner seams had loosened.

She had barely sewn up two of the seams with her tiny, meticulous stitches, rejoicing in her regained ability to use her left hand, when she was interrupted by the sound of heavy footfalls.

"Good day, Miss Smythe!" came a jovial voice, and Caroline turned to see Dr. Selby approaching, bringing with him, she perceived with dread, an enormous posy of daffodils. His visits, ostensibly to continue to monitor her progress, had only increased in frequency over the last weeks, and Caroline, doubly beset by Lady Augusta's playful remarks and Mrs. Yardley's pointed stare, was hard put to maintain the fiction that his interest in her was merely professional.

"Good day, Doctor," she returned politely, though she could have cheerfully wished him at Jericho.

"It's a fine day, isn't it? Milton told me I should find you on the terrace. To be sure, I thought you'd be basking in the sun!" he said, sitting on a *chaise longue* opposite her chair.

"And here you are, sewing away like anything! Your arm doesn't pain you, I trust? Here! These are for you, straight from my garden—and picked by little Maria herself! She's anxious to meet you, you know! As are my three other chicks, as I am wont to call them!" With a chuckle he thrust the flowers at her, and Caroline reluctantly accepted them, murmuring her thanks as she placed the bouquet on the small table at her elbow.

The doctor cleared his throat portentously. "My dear Miss Smythe," he said. "My dear, *dear* Miss Smythe."

Caroline raised her eyes to his simple, homely face, and without difficulty read there his intent. "I believe I see clouds approaching. Perhaps we should go in," she began hastily, but was forestalled from rising when suddenly Dr. Selby lowered himself creakily to his knees and, reaching into the material of the chair cover she still had in her lap, attempted to grasp one of her hands, thereby inflicting a sharp little wound from her needle in one of *his* hands.

"Oh, it's nothing, it's nothing!" he assured her, stanching the flow of blood with his handkerchief. "What is a mere prick of pain compared to the ache I suffer here!" He slapped his bandaged palm to the top of his sober waistcoat, staining it red in the process, and immediately launched into an ardent declaration of his affection and regard which, some ten minutes later, culminated with a humble request for her hand in marriage.

Her fingers limp in his own, Caroline sat numbly, her mind racing, unable to force to her lips the "yes" she knew she ought to say. She was a penniless spinster, lacking a dowry and quite alone in the world. This gentle, clumsy man wished to marry her, and though she did not love him—would never love him—perhaps in time she might come to esteem him as a dutiful wife should. For, as she surely knew all too well, she had no right to aspire to anything better, no reason to hope for a love that burned more brightly than whatever tepid flame she might at some time feel for the good doctor.

At last she opened her mouth, steeled herself to the inevitable assent, but at the final moment her courage failed her, and she murmured, "I am most deeply sensible of the honor you do me, Dr. Selby, but you must give me time—a little time in which to think." Withdrawing her hand from his, she rose, and waited while he stood too, arms hanging awkwardly at his side. "I—I shall write to you—in a week or so," she said disjointedly. *"Thank* you, Doctor!" And snatching up her sewing and the flowers, basely Caroline fled into the house.

She had just reached the safety of the Blue Bedchamber when there came a tap upon the door, and repressing a groan she opened it to find Lady Augusta, on her face an expression of the liveliest good humor.

"Caro! I was pacing round my room, pausing in the midst of a letter to Damien *(why* I write to him from time to time I'm sure I don't know, for he never troubles himself to write back! Some remnants of the obligatory sisterly affection, I suppose!), and happened to look from my window and see you on the terrace with Dr. Selby, and him on his knees in the most romantical fashion! He was *proposing,* wasn't he? Did I not predict it? I can't remember when I laughed so hard!" Grinning, her ladyship plopped herself onto a love seat dotted with blue satin pillows, then slowly her smile faded as she looked up into Caroline's face. "You do not find it amusing," she said. "But why is that? Oh, Caro! Surely you do not mean to marry Edward Selby? Why, he is a competent enough doctor, I suppose, but he's also the veriest clodpole! Not to mention that he is a widower in his forties, with numerous progeny, and hardly of a class to suit someone of *your* breeding and distinction!"

"Beggars may not be choosers," Caroline said quietly. "I might do worse than Dr. Selby."

"I did not know you wished to be married," Lady Augusta said thoughtfully. "H'm."

Caroline drew a deep breath and went on resolutely: "And I must confess, Gussie, that I am drawn to the idea of no longer burdening you here. Your aunt—"

"Hush!" her ladyship entreated, her brow deeply furrowed. "I am . . . formulating . . . an . . . idea. H'm. Yes . . . Well, why not? Yes!" Abruptly she sat bolt upright on the love seat, her dark eyes sparkling. "I own it may not work, my dear Caro, but . . . well, somehow I cannot quite picture you as the wife of a bumbling country doctor. *Nous verrons ce que nous verrons!*"

We shall see what we shall see. Caroline gazed at Lady Augusta's mischievous countenance with some misgiving, yet, if she were to be wholly honest with herself, she could not be sorry she had begged the doctor for a week's span in which to make up her disorderly, traitorous mind.

Chapter 6

"Three invitations to dine, my lord, as well as to a rout and a breakfast," Griffin Petley said. "London's still a bit thin of company, but with Easter approaching it will soon fill up again."

"Yes," said Damien, desultorily flipping through the stack of personal correspondence his secretary had just handed him. Here was a letter from Lady Melbourne, that famous Whig hostess, urging him to take his place in Parliament; here a beautifully penned epistle from Brummell, wondering when he should see his friend Reston at Watier's; here a note from the Honorable Helen Manderlay, succinctly informing him that she and her parents were just come to town, and would look forward to seeing his lordship as soon as was convenient; and here, a rare letter from Augusta, describing her latest scholarly feats— good God, a translation of Francis Bacon's *De Augmentis Scientarum;* now she was contemplating translating the other portion of his philosophical masterpiece, the *Instauratio Magna.* Then, to his surprise:

*And do you know, my dear Damien, I believe I am finally
going to succumb to Aunt Violet's blandishments and go
to London this year. There are some lectures I should
like to hear, and I believe the Concerts of Ancient Music
are going to be particularly lively. I suppose Aunt will
wish to drag me to all sorts of entertainments but I would
hope to have sufficient time to keep to my studies. Shall
you mind having us underfoot? I am sure you are well
occupied with your own pursuits and in attending to Miss
Manderlay, and will hardly notice our presence in the
town house!*

As for other news from Windemere, their aunt, Damien
learned, was suffering from a dreadful head cold (no doubt
incurred on one of her many trips to Chelmsford) but that
fortunately both Augusta herself and dear Miss Smythe had
thus far been spared. Oh! And speaking of Miss Smythe,
Augusta went on,

*. . . I am in imminent danger of losing my charming
companion, for she seems about to accept an offer of
marriage from Dr. Selby, the local physician who tended
to her injuries. Well, to be sure I wish her well, tho'
perhaps if I were to offer her some more attractive alter-
native she might be swayed to remain with me. I have
wracked my brain most diligently, but no solution has
come to me and so I am resigned to Miss Smythe leaving
us (which I expect to be sooner rather than later, as
the doctor presents the appearance of a very impatient
suitor!).*

She hoped he was well and enjoying the advent of the season,
and remained, she assured him, ever his dutiful sister, Augusta
Rebecca Julianne Reston.

Damien sat staring at Augusta's expansive, uneven handwriting, unprepared for the rush of emotions that poured through him, in a most unwelcome flood. Why the devil should he care what that silly chit Miss Smythe did? She was an onerous obligation, an unpleasant reminder of his botched race to Cambridge, and most decidedly *not* his responsibility. He had settled her handsomely at Windemere, had punctiliously instructed Griffin Petley to forward there an advance of the very generous salary he, Damien, was paying her, and now, it seemed, she had cleverly found herself a more agreeable situation. Why should it matter a whit to him if she wished to marry herself off to some provincial Romeo? It wasn't as if she needed to apply to *him* for his permission, as if she were his ward! She most certainly was not—indeed, she had been little more than a thorn in his side from the very moment they had had the misfortune to meet!

Grinding his teeth, Damien crushed Augusta's letter into a ball and let it drop onto the polished mahogany of the desk at which he sat. He wished he could so easily dispose of the disconcerting feelings provoked by this reminder of Miss Smythe's presence. He would be *delighted* when she was wed, off his hands, and out of his life!

"—so I'll write an acceptance of Lady Castlereagh's invitation to her rout a week from Thursday, my lord?" said Petley, dipping his pen in the standish and looking expectantly at Damien. "I believe you've always stopped in at her ladyship's parties."

"As you will." Abruptly Damien rose to his feet and began walking toward the door of his library. Did that impertinent girl truly believe she would waltz away as simply as that, no doubt laughing up her sleeve at him as she went? Well, he would show her who held the reins, and tightly too!

"But my lord!" Petley said, from behind him. "These other invitations! How shall I respond to them?"

Not halting in his pace, Damien snapped, "However you like!" and decisively slammed the door shut behind him.

Half an hour later he was ensconced in an abysmally decorated saloon in the Manderlays's St. James' town house, attempting to disguise his impatience as the baroness quizzed him at some length as to who among the *ton* was already established in London, and who had yet to arrive.

"Is the Princess Esterhazy come?" inquired Lady Calpurnia "Helen, you know, is a great favorite of hers. It was she who gave us our vouchers to Almack's last year, and I vow, she positively *dotes* on us!"

"I met the princess while riding in the park on Tuesday," answered Damien curtly, wondering why her ladyship had felt compelled to hang the windows with a shiny chartreuse silk while simultaneously assaulting the floors with pink and scarlet rugs.

"We must call on her directly, Helen, for she will be wondering when we have taken up residence again," Lady Calpurnia said archly. "And oh! My dear Lord Reston! Is it true Byron is in London? They say that ladies faint whenever he walks into a room!"

"Doubtless you shall see for yourself, ma'am, for I am told he is invited everywhere. As I returned to town but a few days ago it has not yet been my pleasure to encounter the famous poet."

"Yes, you were at Oatlands, weren't you?" responded the baroness knowledgeably. "How fares the so-charming Duchess of York? Does she still have about her those dozens of nasty dogs? Is *she* in London yet?"

Perhaps she was aware of the tension coiling tight within Damien, for Miss Manderlay, cool and regal in an elegant high-waisted dress of Indian mull muslin draped with ivory lace, chose at that moment to remark: "Mama, not everyone feels as you do about dogs (though I will grant you that owning a hundred of them is a trifle excessive). And as we are to attend Mrs. Jones-Layton's dinner party on Friday evening, I am sure she will be able to tell you everything you wish to know.

Reston, pray enlighten me as to the health of your sister and aunt.''

''With pleasure,'' said Damien, flashing a sardonic glance at her oblivious parent, who only smiled upon him condescendingly. ''They are well enough,'' he went on, ruthlessly consigning Mrs. Yardley to the ranks of the able-bodied, ''and are, I believe, planning to come to London.''

''Indeed, I am glad to hear it,'' said Miss Manderlay, raising limpid blue eyes to his. ''If I may be frank with you, my dear Reston, I have long thought it time that Lady Augusta took her place amongst the larger society to which she was bred, that she was married, and her mind freed of the bookish notions to which, it seems, she is morbidly attached.''

Damien said nothing, only let his eyes wander toward those astonishing curtains again.

Miss Manderlay went on, ''And surely she will enjoy partaking of the manifold pleasures of a season in town. As you know, I do myself. The country must suffice, I suppose, when there's none of the *ton* in London; but who would prefer being buried in the fens when all the world—all the world that matters, that is—is here?''

''Speaking of the world, Lord Reston,'' interposed the baroness coyly, ''I am astonished you should find us alone, for generally we are besieged with callers!''

''I approve most heartily of this plan, Reston,'' Miss Manderlay pursued, ''and would be more than happy to show little Augusta how to go on.''

''Little Augusta,'' said the marquis blandly, ''will doubtless appreciate your generous offer.''

''Of course, I do foresee some obstacles, given her advanced age.'' A slight wrinkle marred the smooth surface of Miss Manderlay's alabaster brow, then rapidly cleared. ''But with her distinguished lineage, the attractions of her fortune, and the patronage of my family, I am convinced she shall do nicely. She might not aspire to a *marquis*''—she bestowed on him her

glinting smile—"but I do know a certain viscount who is very
personable, and, I should think, not a day over fifty."

"We shall be glad to take her ladyship under our wing,"
added the baroness graciously, "regardless of the inconvenience to ourselves."

Keeping his temper firmly in check, Damien forbore to mention both the role Mrs. Yardley would play as Augusta's chaperone and the fact that the Reston family stood in no need of
patronage by anyone, least of all the upstart descendants (no
matter how wealthy) of a mill owner. Instead he rose, and
bowed slightly. "I am glad we are as one mind. I shall go to
Windemere tomorrow to fetch them."

"Them?" queried Lady Calpurnia. "Oh, I had forgotten
about your aunt, dear Mrs. Yostley."

"Yardley, Mama," Miss Manderlay corrected.

"Yes, yes," rejoined her mother impatiently. "I am sure it
is all the same to me."

"There is also," said Damien, "Augusta's *dame de compagnie.*"

Miss Manderlay raised thin, delicately arched blonde brows.
"A companion, Reston?"

"Yes," said Damien, almost savagely. "A gray little spinster, of trifling account. Good day." Another bow, and swiftly
he was gone from them, and conscious of being thankful to
have done so.

Caroline crossed the lawn that stretched, newly green, in
front of Windemere, her attention drawn, as it inevitably was,
to the majestic beauty of the house. She thought at times she
was bewitched by it, so attracted was she by its splendid lines, its
magnificence and warmth, its sense of history and indomitable
strength. She had been here nearly three months, and felt at
once as if she had lived here forever and as if there was so
much yet of its mystery to explore.

Suddenly to her ears came the faint sound of hoofbeats, and anxiously she turned to look along the length of the winding road. A week had passed since she had told Dr. Selby she would give him his answer, and still her head and her heart struggled within her for dominance. Devoutly she hoped that it was not the doctor who had come to Windemere, eager for her response.

A horse rounded the bend in the avenue, and to her relief it was not Dr. Selby's plump piebald mare, but a big, handsome, glossy black stallion . . . and its rider, she perceived with an abrupt, queer jolt within her breast, was none other than the Marquis of Reston.

It was but a matter of seconds before he rode alongside her, and pulled his high-spirited mount to a halt. She stared up into those gleaming dark eyes she remembered only too well, acutely conscious that she stood there as if transfixed. "How—how do you do, Lord Reston?" she achieved at last. "What a—a surprise to see you!"

"Good day, Miss Smythe," he returned coolly.

A weighty silence ensued, during which Caroline frantically tried to think of something else to say, and which was finally only broken by the marquis when his horse restively tossed its black-maned head. "I have no need to ask if you are well," he said then, in that same indifferent tone, "for I can see that you are."

"Yes," murmured Caroline lamely, "I am very well indeed, thank you. I trust your lordship is—is well also?"

"Oh, I thrive, Miss Smythe, I thrive," he returned with a flash of white teeth that might have been meant to be a smile. "As for yourself, I understand that I am to wish you happy."

"What? Oh! No, my lord! That is—that is to say—" Caroline could feel the fiery heat of a blush spreading across her cheeks. "Your good wishes are entirely premature," she finished, and averted her gaze from that entirely too penetrating one.

"I see," she heard him say without inflection; then, casually, "Pray excuse me, Miss Smythe," and with a little click of the tongue the marquis signaled to his horse, and rode off toward the stables without so much as a backward glance. Caroline stood watching him, her thoughts in chaos, hating herself for foolishly being glad to see him. He, a rake, a libertine, a neglectful brother and landlord, who had nearly run her down with his curricle! Then, gratefully, she remembered the enormous rent in Lady Augusta's pale blue day dress she wished to repair and the seams around the waistline which needed to be let out, and briskly she walked to the front door and, her heart pounding, whisked herself inside the house.

Damien strolled leisurely down the gallery, unmindful of the eyes of his ancestors staring out at him from within the frames of their portraits. He owned to himself that he had been astonished at the remarkable changes wrought in Miss Smythe since he had last seen her. Most obviously, of course, she no longer wore a sling and there was no longer any trace of the prominent bruise marring her temple. More subtly, however, she had lost the pallid cast of her complexion, revealing clear, olive-tinged skin which, although hardly the bone-white hue decreed by fashion, suited her admirably, heightening the brilliant green of her eyes, complementing her shining auburn curls, and providing an enticing foil for that rosy-red mouth with its full lower lip. She had gained needed weight, too, and the simple white cambric gown she wore revealed the round, feminine curves of her bust and the hint of long, supple legs beneath the light fabric. With her vivid coloring and decidedly alluring figure, she was hardly the gray little waif he had described to Miss Manderlay and her mother (though he doubted that either lady would give an obscure *dame de compagnie* a second glance): she was, in short, disturbingly pretty, and this unwonted discovery only served to heighten Damien's determination to carry her away to London and out of the arms of the local bumpkin with whom she thought to form an alliance. If Damien were truly the gentleman, Damien thought, he would doubtless let Miss Smythe slip gracefully from his grasp and settle into the dubious joys of bucolic life. Then he shrugged mentally. Instead he was a cold-hearted blackguard, and more woe to the unknowing Miss Smythe!

Unheralded by the butler Milton, whom he had greeted and dismissed to his other duties, Damien entered the Little Drawing Room, where he found Augusta supine upon a sofa in a most unladylike attitude, her tousled head propped on a pile of cushions and her legs crossed at the ankle, deeply absorbed in a newspaper.

He stood watching her in some amusement. "Cobbett's *Political Register,* Augusta?" he said. "I did not know you perused such a radical publication."

Startled, Augusta slapped together the leaves of the newspaper and lowered them so that she could peer over the edge. "Damien! There is the most shocking engraving by Cruikshank reproduced on page four, portraying yourself, the regent, Brummell, and Alvanley in the midst of a—a *harem!* With half-clad dancing girls and a—a—what is it they are called?—oh, yes! A *hookah,* for smoking opium!"

"Most shocking," agreed Damien, sitting across from her in a comfortable wingback armchair and crossing one leg over the other.

"*Do* you?" Augusta demanded, pushing herself up against the pillows.

"Do I frequent a harem and take opium? No, my dear sister, I am happy to inform you that I confine my pleasures to the more conventional dissipations."

"Drinking, gambling, and a mistress?" rejoined Augusta shrewdly.

"Just so. Does our aunt have any idea of the—er, depth of

your knowledge of worldly matters and the rank indelicacy of your mind?''

"Much I care!" Augusta folded the paper into quarters and tossed it onto the low table between them. "However," she went on, more regretfully, "I am afraid that Caro picked up the *Register* the other day, saw the engraving, and *was* greatly shocked by it. She didn't say anything, but she went white, then red, and looked as if she wished to fan herself.''

"I do not live my life to please Miss Smythe," said Damien coolly. "And might I inquire as to why you are reading a newspaper from the black-market press, one that is widely considered to be grossly seditious?''

"Oh, it's absolutely virulent," Augusta said cheerfully. "But it frequently expresses what I believe to be the views of the common people, and *that*, you know, I find to be of considerable interest. By the bye, what are your views on the Corn Laws?''

"I do not think about the Corn Laws," said Damien.

"But is it wise to protect the home market for wheat no matter how high the price rises? Such a program is beneficial only to the landowners and larger farmers; the smallholders and the farm laborers inevitably suffer, for they can't get much for their crops, and the price of bread becomes too costly.''

"Augusta," said Damien, "I did not come to Windemere to discuss wheat tariffs with you.''

"No? Why *did* you come?''

"Why, to escort you to London," he said lazily. "Did you not express a desire to join me there?''

His sister's eyes widened, and then she broke into a loud laugh. "Why, so I did!" she concurred buoyantly. "How very kind of you, my dear brother! When are we to leave?''

"As soon as possible, for I've numerous engagements in town," replied Damien. "How quickly can you and our aunt be ready?''

"Oh, I've only to toss a few things together, and pack up my books and papers. And as for Aunt, she will be so wholly transported with joy that she would be prepared to go with only the clothes on her back!''

''So that she can purchase more in London,'' murmured Damien, then added dispassionately, ''And your Miss Smythe? Does she remain here, blissfully awaiting her nuptial day?''

''Oh, no, I am confident she will wish to come with us,'' Augusta responded. ''I do believe she would only have married that lumpish doctor because she feels herself to be so useless here. But in London, she will be of incalculable benefit to me! I shall have to go to *some* parties and dinners with Aunt, and Caro must accompany me, for she has such an air of quiet distinction that I cannot help but think some of it *might* rub off on me! She is also as neat as a pin in her ways, and has very clever fingers. Why, once when I permitted her to dress my hair it looked *most* elegant, Damien, and stayed that way for hours!''

''That is impressive indeed,'' her brother said calmly, though he could not suppress an ignoble rush of triumph at witnessing the swift success of his plans. He only wished he might be there to see Miss Smythe's face when she learned she was to be parted from her unlucky swain.

''Go to London with you, Gussie?'' gasped Caroline, her brain whirling at Lady Augusta's triumphant announcement. She put down the blue dress she had been mending and gaped at her ladyship. ''I—I do not know what to say to you!''

''You need merely say yes,'' returned Lady Augusta jovially, disposing herself comfortably in the Blue Bedchamber's love seat. ''It is all arranged! You shall be able to stop complaining of your idleness once we are in London, Caro, for I shall be running you off your feet! Aunt will trot us to all sorts of tedious society gatherings, and *you* shall lend to me some of your enviable polish so that I shan't utterly disgrace the Reston name!''

"I?" exclaimed Caroline. "But Gussie, I am hardly conversant with the customs of the *haut ton!"*

Breezily Lady Augusta waved a hand in the air. "The details are immaterial; Aunt can instruct us both, for she was London-bred, you know, and was used to move among the *ton* until she married that popinjay of hers and they were forced to move to Bristol to economize. But the steadiness of your presence, your graceful good manners, your thoughtful attentiveness in conversation—all these eloquently bespeak the lady of quality, and I am sure I will be in sore need of you as we move in society's rarefied circles! You must remind me which fork to use, and not to wear my half-boots to a ball! Besides, you *know* how freely my tongue runs, Caro, and I shall rely upon you to send me quelling glances at the least suggestion of my committing a grave social solecism!"

Caroline laughed, and looked over at her ladyship affectionately. "Somehow I cannot quite picture you with knees quaking in *any* company."

"You have not seen me among the *ton,"* Lady Augusta pointed out. "They are all a veritable pack of wolves! Now, have you any other objections to raise? If so, let me hear them so that I may promptly fling them to the ground."

Caroline looked blindly down at the partially mended dress in her lap. Did she have objections? Of course she did, a whole horde of practical reasons why it would be folly for her to go to London, why she should stay here and do what was practical! And yet—and yet— She thought of a tall, broad-shouldered form, and black locks, and a handsome face with its hard dark eyes and sensuous mouth—

"I am hardly outfitted for such a venture," she said, wishing she could inject a greater note of determination into her voice.

"Well, neither am I, and I daresay Aunt will have the time of her life dragging the both of us round to the shops and the modistes! Next you are going to say it will be horribly expensive, and I am sure it will be, but not a penny of it is coming from *your* purse, my dear, for these are costs you did not know you would incur when you very kindly agreed to be my companion.''

''But Gussie—''

''My own allowance is sufficiently large, if you are worrying that I will have to deprive myself of either gowns or books. Next I am certain you will say that Aunt Violet will not approve of your rejecting Dr. Selby's suit and instead remaining with me. Is that not so?''

Dumbly Caroline nodded.

''Believe me, Caro, you will be such a credit to Aunt Violet you will only add to her consequence, and *that* she will not fail to recognize! Mark my words, within a matter of days she will be *preening* over you!'' Her ladyship gave a bark of laughter.

''Of that I am not wholly convinced,'' said Caroline ruefully. ''Mrs. Yardley does not at present regard me with any noticeable approbation.''

''Pooh! She doesn't look benignly on me, either!''

''Neither am I convinced,'' Caroline said, ''that you would have proposed such an expedition were it not for the silly tangle I've gotten myself into with Dr. Selby.''

''I am sure I shall enjoy myself a great deal,'' came the airy reply. ''The gadding about with my aunt will be a trifle dull, of course, but there will be an abundance of other more worthwhile activities to occupy my attention—libraries, lectures, galleries, and so on.'' Lady Augusta's jolly expression suddenly sobered, and she said, quite seriously: ''Caro, you don't *really* wish to marry Edward Selby, do you?''

Caroline met her friend's eyes frankly. ''N-no,'' she admitted. ''But—''

''Well, here's the thing,'' her ladyship went on ingenuously. ''You will come to London and while you are acting as my support, you may look about you, to see if you can find anybody else you'd rather marry.''

At these words Caroline looked away, then, putting aside her mending, rose to go stand by the window which overlooked the gardens below. Perhaps Augusta was right. There might be some other gentleman—blue-eyed and fair-haired, for example, and of a middling stature with shoulders that were not intimidatingly broad, who was quite unattached—whom she would find agreeable. A deep sigh escaped her. If not, she could use her time constructively to hunt for new employment where she could feel less like a luxuriously sheltered object of charity and more like someone who was legitimately earning her keep. Yes, that was the right thing to do. After some few weeks had passed, she could tactfully ask Augusta, without fear of hurting her feelings, to give her a character reference so that she might begin her search.

Resolutely Caroline drew up her chin, and turned to face Augusta once again. "Yes," she said quietly. "I will go to London."

Chapter 7

Caroline lay awake in the predawn dimness of her bedchamber, savoring the opportunity for a few minutes of quiet reflection. Since their arrival in the Restons' Grosvenor Square town house a fortnight ago she and Augusta had been subjected to a dizzying whirlwind of activity, and it seemed that their days were filled from morning to night.

Declaring both young ladies unfit to see and be seen by society until their wardrobes were suitably refurbished, replenished, augmented, and supplied, Mrs. Yardley, a martial light in her eye, conducted them on such a massively acquisitive expedition of Piccadilly's fashionable shops, warehouses, modistes, milliners, and bootmakers that Caroline felt obliged to protest, and was swiftly silenced by both Mrs. Yardley and Augusta, with the latter adding firmly, ''If we are going to do this thing, Caro, we may as well do it right. By the bye, that pale green sarcenet Madame Huppert is showing you will suit you wonderfully well. We shall take it, *madame, merci,* and do include some of that handsome lace to go with it!''

Their afternoons were spent with dancing masters, and in extended colloquy with Mrs. Yardley, who lectured them at length about society's elaborately codified rituals and strictures.

A lady's day followed an invariable routine. For those who were so inclined, a ride in Hyde Park was *de rigueur* early in the morning, followed by breakfast at home. Next one shopped and made calls on those with whom one was on intimate terms. Then came lunch, and another round of calls, either to stop for a brief visit or to leave cards; a leisurely promenade in Hyde Park between five and six was considered highly *à la mode*. Dinner was served at seven, and in the evening there were soirees or excursions to the opera or to the theater, and then balls or dances which began at ten o'clock and could continue until well past three in the morning.

The rules of conduct for a lady, Mrs. Yardley told her pupils, were inviolable.

Only a lady who wished to be thought fast would dare show herself abroad without a corset, or would be so bold as to dampen her petticoat.

Diamonds and pearls were never worn in the morning.

No lady could participate in the waltz at Almack's unless she had received the approval of one of its patronesses, and she would never dance more than three dances with the same partner in any given evening.

A lady should confine her conversation to light, innocuous civilities, such as inquiries as to someone's health, remarks about the weather, or a genteel discussion of the arts, such as an opera one had attended or a painting viewed at the Royal Academy.

An unmarried lady under the age of thirty was never to be in the company of a gentleman without a chaperone. She must never go about unescorted, unless she was taking an early walk in the park or was on her way to church, and it was unmitigated social ruin to be seen walking or driving down St. James' Street.

No matter the weather, heavy, concealing pelisses or shawls were to be avoided at all costs—

"Egad!" burst out Augusta, and shot up from her seat. "Enough, Aunt! One more of these draconian dictums and I shall go straight back to Windemere!" She clutched at her hair, sending pins flying, and declared dramatically: "O! that this too too solid flesh would melt, thaw, and resolve itself into a dew; or that the Everlasting had not fixed His canon 'gainst self-slaughter! O God! O God! How weary, stale, flat, and unprofitable seem to me all the uses of this world. Fie on't! O fie! 'Tis an unweeded garden that grows to seed; things rank and gross in nature possess it merely."

Mrs. Yardley stared at her niece in blank astonishment. "I *beg* your pardon?"

" 'These are but wild and whirling words,' " Caroline quoted, smiling.

More mildly Augusta said: "Oh, do you like *Hamlet* too? I understand Kemble is playing in the current production at Covent Garden. Shall we go to see it?"

"I should like that, for I have never seen *Hamlet* performed," Caroline replied eagerly, then, mindful of her duty, turned to Mrs. Yardley and added, "If you think it unexceptionable, ma'am."

"I shall have to consult *The Family Shakespeare,*" the older woman said doubtfully. "Mr. Bowdler may think it too vulgar and blasphemous for such tender ears as ours."

"Aunt," said Augusta, scowling awfully, "do you really have such a pestilent volume in this house? Do you have any idea of how that man desecrated Gibbons' *History of the Decline and Fall of the Roman Empire*?"

"The Society for the Suppression of Vice thinks very highly of Mr. Bowdler's works," retorted Mrs. Yardley piously.

"That tears it!" Augusta said rudely, her voice an exasperated growl, and marched to the door where she turned and announced: "I am going to soothe my lacerated nerves with a few hours of Plato! Disturb me at your peril!"

After she had gone Caroline and Mrs. Yardley looked at each other in silence.

Finally Mrs. Yardley said in an anxious tone, "I do wish Augusta would refrain from using those low, slang expressions of hers. People will be sure to remark upon it."

"She really is doing very well," Caroline said gently. "She has stood still for innumerable fittings, has done her best to master all the dances, and in general has listened to you very patiently, ma'am."

"Yes, but I fear she will never be what is termed a graceful dancer," Mrs. Yardley said gloomily, then brightened. "However, Monsieur Rubideaux says *you* are doing very well indeed, Miss Smythe! That is of *some* comfort to me, at least."

Thinking now of her surprise at Mrs. Yardley's unexpected compliment, Caroline turned onto her side and smiled. Augusta had been right: her aunt's frosty attitude had indeed warmed slightly over the past days. As little as Caroline felt the need to curry the older woman's favor, it nevertheless made for a more pleasant environment.

Somewhere in the house came the sound of a door opening and closing, and Caroline found herself wondering if it was the marquis returning home. After he had ridden alongside their carriage en route to London and deposited them on the doorstep of the town house, he had gone off to the stables and Caroline had not seen him since. She gathered from various offhand remarks issued by Augusta and her aunt that his lordship kept irregular hours, as was only to be expected of so notable a Corinthian and one who, moreover, was of the dashing Carlton House set. "I daresay we may run into Damien from time to time at a party here and there," Augusta had said casually, "but doubtless he finds the more sedate amusements sadly flat."

Caroline thought again of the engraving she had stumbled

across in one of Augusta's newspapers, which portrayed Lord
Reston amongst his aristocratic cronies in a milieu of unabashed
decadence, surrounded by voluptuous young women in various
stages of undress. It had upset her and dismayed her. Yet despite
her better judgment the engraving had intrigued her too. How
did the marquis pass his nights, and with whom? More than
once she had drifted into the most wanton imaginings, picturing
herself held in the powerful arms of the marquis, against that
tall athletic body, and, reveling in the sensation of her own
yielding softness against his exciting masculine hardness, she
luxuriously allowed her lashes to drift down as he whispered
fiery words of love and lowered his mouth to hers . . .

Caroline jerked her eyes open, sat up in bed, and flung off
the sheets. Good heavens, she was doing it again, letting her
willful mind stray to places it shouldn't! Whatever was the
matter with her? Despite the idiosyncratic circumstances of her
youth she had been strictly raised, and it was impossible for
her to condone the relaxed morality the *haut ton* permitted its
members; it followed, then, that she should take a dim view
of the marquis and his sybaritic ways. But Caroline could not
find it in her heart to wholly condemn Lord Reston, for more
than once in his dealings with her he had shown himself to be
capable of thoughtfulness and generosity.

The accident in Baldock, for example, had certainly not been
his fault, and rather than leave her half-dead in the road, as
many another gentleman might have done who counted winning
his wager of greater importance, he had stopped, forfeiting the
race, and seen to it that she was well cared for. Then, when
he had learned that because of her mishap she had lost her
position (and that one painful exchange with the redoubtable
Mrs. Ashby had served to convince her that she would have
found in her yet another Mrs. Tintham!), he had gone out of
his way to establish her in another situation, one that was
infinitely more comfortable, and to settle on her an extravagant

salary. No, he was not utterly the cynical, frivolous reprobate he painted himself to be; she had firsthand knowledge of that.

A little stab of pain pierced her breast, and restlessly Caroline climbed out of bed, to go to the window and peep past the curtains to the still-quiet street below. What an absurd fancy it was, to pass these idle minutes in thoughts of the marquis, when he was well and fully betrothed; even were he not, his station was so far above her own that simply to contemplate such a union was akin to foolishly wishing to scale the towering heights of Olympus.

Besides, she thought wryly, letting the curtain fall back into place, she never even *saw* Lord Reston, which made her wistful reveries all the more ridiculous, for doubtless he had forgotten about her entirely.

Yet to her surprise she did encounter the marquis but a few days later, when, having awoken very early in the morning from an unpleasant dream, she dressed and slipped downstairs, intent on a solitary stroll in the park. She pulled open the front door and let out a soft cry, so astonished was she to unexpectedly meet his lordship on the step.

For the merest second she thought he, too, looked startled, and then a slight smile curled his lips as he raised his dark brows and said calmly, ''Good morning, Miss Smythe.''

He was clad in formal evening dress, the black satin knee breeches, white waistcoat, and black long-tailed coat exquisitely tailored and of the finest materials. His neckcloth, tied in intricate folds, was still crisp and dazzlingly white. Were it not for the tiniest trace of redness evident in his deep-set eyes Caroline might have imagined him to have just risen from his dressing table, ready to call for his carriage and set off for the night. And here it was, barely past dawn!

''You stare, Miss Smythe,'' drawled the marquis. ''Do I displease you?''

Thus recalled to herself, Caroline blinked, and stammered, ''N-no, my lord! That is, I—I do beg your pardon! Pray excuse

me for blocking your entrance!" She hurried outside, leaving
the door open for him to proceed on his way.

Instead he merely looked at her inscrutably for several seconds, then remarked: "You are going to walk in the park, I
take it?"

"Yes, my lord."

"I've a better idea. Do you ride? How should you care for
a forbidden gallop along the track, before the rest of the world
arrives to frown upon us?"

Feeling her face light up, impulsively Caroline said, "I
should like it above all things, my lord! It has been three years
and more since I've last been on a horse, but I do dearly love
to ride!"

"Good. Have you a riding costume?" At her nod he went
on, "I'll send word to the stables for two mounts. Do return
to your room to change, Miss Smythe, and I shall shortly do
the same and meet you back here within—shall we say, half
an hour?"

Demurely Caroline answered, *"I* need but fifteen minutes,
my lord, but I am more than happy to accommodate *you.*"

He laughed. "You are a refreshingly expeditious female, I
perceive. Fifteen minutes it is, Miss Smythe."

They thundered along Hyde Park's soft, sandy track, and
Caroline laughed to feel the absolute freedom of the moment,
urging her horse to gallop even faster and thrilling to feel
the responsive creature beneath her comply, as if sharing her
unfettered exhilaration. Her first minutes in the saddle had been
awkward ones, and she had worried that she was no longer the
horsewoman she had once been; but before long her confidence
had rapidly returned, aided in large part by the horse the marquis
had chosen for her, a sleek, sweet-tempered beauty named
Dorca, with soft intelligent eyes. Never had she been so fortunate as to ride such a steed as this! Oh, how glorious it was to

be riding again! She hadn't realized until now how much she had greatly missed it. Caroline glanced over at the marquis, easily keeping pace on his own mount, and saw his countenance more relaxed than she had yet witnessed it. The only sound was that of the horses' hooves, and as the park was nearly empty of people, it was if they two were sequestered somehow, enveloped in a magical kind of privacy.

Privacy! Oh, dear! Caroline suddenly recalled one of Mrs. Yardley's many admonitions. Here she was, alone with a gentleman—and galloping *ventre à terre,* too, which evidently was *also* improper. How Mrs. Yardley would scold! Well then, she must never find out, Caroline thought wickedly, and laughed again.

She couldn't have said how much time had flown by before she felt her hat loosen atop her curls as a playful breeze rushed past, and quickly she called out to his lordship, signaling that she desired to slow down. He complied, and shortly their horses were walking side by side and she was able to secure the pins in her hair with one gloved hand comfortably holding the reins.

"See how their sides are barely heaving!" Caroline said to the marquis. "I do believe they enjoyed the gallop as much as I did!"

The marquis smiled. "Here, I perceive, is another refreshing facet of your personality, Miss Smythe: you are unafraid to express your pleasure in something so simple as a ride in the park."

"Dear me, is *enthusiasm* prohibited as well?" said Caroline with exaggerated dismay. "I shall have to inquire of Mrs. Yardley. If it is, do forgive me for the gross *faux pas,* my lord."

He shot her a quizzical look "I take it my aunt has undertaken your education in the ways of the *ton?*"

"Indeed yes, my lord! With considerable vigor!" Caroline said with a laugh, then added jokingly: "As well as the Herculean task of transforming a poor country mouse into the polished sophisticate you see before you!"

"I am at a loss to account for your self-deprecation," responded Lord Reston. "The habit you wear is charming—the military style becomes you admirably, as does that smart plumed shako!—and I observe that you are dressing your hair in a new and equally fetching fashion."

Caroline peeped at his lordship uncertainly beneath her lashes. Was he serious? His tone was neither teasing nor ironic; he seemed for once quite sincere. Thrown off-guard, and feeling a revealing blush crawling hotly up her throat, Caroline said at random, "Thank you, my lord! The—the modiste thought the rage for the military cut would not look too—too severe on me, and—and Mrs. Yardley had a hairdresser come to the house just yesterday! I own I did not like to part with *quite* so much of my hair, but—but it *was* very long, and Mrs. Yardley assures me the shorter style is all the crack!" She gave a breathless little laugh. "I vow, I feel quite like little Cinderashes of the storybook, all dressed up for the ball!"

"Waiting for the prince?" said the marquis.

The sudden edge in his voice discomfited Caroline still further. Gathering her scattered wits about her, with an effort she lightly returned, "Well, I do not know that we should be discussing Cinder-ashes at all, my lord, for I understand that in certain circles it is a taboo subject! It is said to be a tale which encourages all sorts of immorality from which children should be shielded, including envy, narcissism, and excessive interest in clothing! Not to mention arrant dislike of stepmothers!"

"Good God, do not tell me you are a proponent of Evangelicalism," the marquis said dryly, "convinced that the calamities afflicting England are brought on by divine displeasure as a scourge for our collective sins, chief among them suspect literature for children."

"I cannot speak for those who espouse that view," answered Caroline, "but do you not think there is something of value in what Mrs. Hannah More says?"

"Her followers must believe so, when at Methodist sermons they shriek and bellow and roll upon the ground, gasping and choking until their faces turn black."

Earnestly Caroline said: "I do not refer to the hysterical outbursts of an easily swayed crowd, my lord, but to Mrs. More's precepts concerning charity and helping others in need."

The marquis shrugged. "I am afraid I do not find the saintly life at all appealing, my dear Miss Smythe. I am cut from a very different sort of cloth."

"Not so different as you would like to believe, my lord," Caroline retorted daringly, "for you have more than once come to *my* aid! And let us not forget that wretched little dog you saved in Baldock!"

Lord Reston's handsome face was bland as he said lazily, "Anomalies, Miss Smythe, merely that and nothing more."

Feeling chastened, Caroline fell silent, and fixed her gaze on the sandy path in front of them.

After some time the marquis said: "You disapprove of me, Miss Smythe, do you not?"

Caroline glanced at his lordship, and saw that his eyes were hard again, and gleaming with some dark emotion she could not fathom. "I would not presume to pass any sort of judgment on you, my lord," she said quietly.

"Yet you do!" he returned harshly. "Do not attempt to deny it, for I can see it in the very tilt of your head and the compression of your lips!"

Stiffening, Caroline lifted her chin. "Perhaps I *am* perplexed, my lord," she said, aware of the tension vibrating in her own voice. "I am told that fields at Windemere lie uncultivated, or are sown with outdated crops; that the dwellings of your tenants are sadly neglected; and I have seen with my own eyes the torn curtains within the house that is your birthright, the once-beautiful furniture covered with dust and the servants so demoralized they can't be bothered to properly set the caps on their own heads! I do not understand it, and I tell you, my lord, it nearly breaks my heart!''

"How kind of you to interest yourself in my affairs, Miss Smythe," the marquis said icily. "Are there any other areas of my life into which you wish to intrude? If so, you must not let something so trivial as common civility or your own ignorance keep you from enlightening me at once!"

Hot tears flooded her eyes. Attempting to blink them away, hastily Caroline averted her gaze and murmured shakily, "I— I am so sorry, my lord! You are right, and it was unconscionable of me to have blurted out the things I did! I wish my unmannerly words quite unsaid! Pray let us make our way home at once!"

With a curt nod the marquis guided his horse from the track; dashing the back of her hand across her eyes, Caroline followed suit, and in uncomfortable silence they proceeded toward Grosvenor Square. She could have cheerfully bitten off her tongue for having spoken so rashly. All her earlier happiness had fled, and it was with depressed spirits that she accompanied his lordship from the park and into the streets leading toward his town house.

While they had been riding, the sleepy somnolence of early morning had given way to the bustle of brisk commerce; around them now were white-aproned bakers, ringing their tinny bells and calling out, "Hot loaves!" as well as buxom milkmaids carrying brimming chums on shoulder yokes. A bandbox seller trudged alongside them, his wares toted on a long pole, and everywhere were vendors hawking sand, live rabbits, baked apples, rat traps, fish, ice, muffins, jellied eels, lavender, door mats, and tripe cuttings.

An enticing scent of freshly baked buns from a pastrycook shop tickled at Caroline's nostrils, and she turned her head to locate its source, only to see some short distance ahead of them a burly brick-dust seller, whipping his overladen donkey with a stick, as the skinny creature only stood stock-still, its head pathetically lowered, and refused to move.

"Oh, we must stop!" cried Caroline, sliding quickly to the ground and thrusting Dorca's reins at the marquis. Approaching the stocky, scowling man she said urgently, "Please! Don't beat the poor thing! Can you not see there are far too many sacks for her to carry?"

The donkey's owner paused with his arm upraised, and turned his beetle-browed scowl upon Caroline. "Who the 'ell are *you,* to be tellin' me 'ow to treat me own property?" he returned belligerently.

"Only look how much weight she has to bear!" Caroline said, placatingly. "If you were to give her fewer sacks, perhaps—"

"And 'ow am I to make me livin'?" demanded the man. "At a penny per quart, it's 'ard enough as it is, thank you!"

"And how will you make your living when that poor decimated beast drops dead from exhaustion?" Caroline retorted, indignant now.

" 'Ere now! I'll not take interference from the likes o' *you!*" Threateningly he took a step forward and raised a hamlike fist.

"That's quite enough," came the quietly authoritative voice of the marquis, and the man's eyes turned wonderingly to that tall, broad-shouldered figure as his lordship, having dismounted as well, came to stand next to Caroline, who felt a reassuring rush of relief at having the solid strength of his presence beside her.

"Why, I didn't see you, guv'nor," the brick-dust vendor said fawningly, lowering his clenched fist to tug at the soiled brim of the hat on his head. "Are you with *'er* then?"

"Yes," said the marquis, and Caroline, risking a glance up into his face, was surprised to see the masklike expression of frozen anger replaced by a hint of a rueful smile. His dark eyes looked down into her own, and he said in his deep, lazy drawl, "I feel sure you will have a solution to the seemingly intractable problem of this scoundrel's hardened brutality toward his animal, Miss Smythe."

Caroline drew a deep breath, and felt on her own countenance the flicker of an answering smile. "I do, but I fear it is a crude one, my lord."

"Fire away," he murmured. "I have every confidence in your ability to masterfully spike his guns."

More relieved than she would have liked to admit at having the dreadful antagonism between them dissolved, Caroline turned confidently to the burly brick-dust seller. "We wish to purchase your donkey," she said. "How much do you want for her?"

The man's eyes widened for a moment, then narrowed consideringly. "Oh, no, miss, I'm sure I couldn't part with Dolly 'ere!" he declared affectingly. "You see, she and me 'as been together since she was just a tiny thing!"

"I'm certain you have," Caroline said dryly. "How much?"

"Why, it'd be like sellin' me own mother! I *couldn't,* miss!"

Caroline shrugged. "As you will," she said, and began to turn away, when the man cried out.

"Wait!"

She turned back. "Yes?" she said coolly.

"Well, miss . . . seein' as 'ow you're so determined-like . . ." A grimy finger reached under his hat to scratch at what was probably an equally dirty scalp. "It'd be a sacrifice, but . . . I suppose I'd take a quid for 'er."

"A pound!" said Caroline disdainfully. "You originally paid a half crown, if that, and now you demand eight times that for a broken-down beast?"

Piqued, the man replied, "I'll 'ave you know I gave a full *bull* for her!"

"Very well then. You paid a crown; we shall pay you twice that, a half sovereign. Kindly remove those sacks from her back, and give me her leading rope."

"Give me the blunt first!" said the man greedily, clearly well pleased with the bargain, and extended a dusty hand, palm up.

Shyly Caroline looked up at his lordship, and still with that same slight smile he reached into the pocket of his coat and withdrew from it a small purse, extracting a coin which he tossed to the donkey's owner, who caught it neatly and, calling for an acquaintance to come assist him, began unloading the sacks.

"*Thank* you, my lord!" Caroline whispered gratefully. "I forgot that I had not brought my reticule. I will reimburse you the moment we return home!"

"That will not be necessary," answered the marquis. "I shall instruct my secretary—"

"To do nothing," interrupted Caroline mischievously. "Did you think I had failed to notice the oversight concerning my expenses in Baldock, my lord? It is a matter I have been wishing to discuss with you for the longest time!"

"I do not know why I keep Petley on," the marquis said in a mournful tone. "He is the most careless fellow."

Caroline only laughed, and reached out to take the rope the brick-dust vendor offered.

"Have a care, Miss Smythe!" Lord Reston said warningly. "She may bite, or attempt to kick you."

"Not she!" said Caroline, drawing close to the emaciated little donkey and tenderly stroking her neck. "Look how docile she is, my lord. Oh, the poor thing! Only see the sores on her back!"

"My grooms will know what to do," said the marquis. "Keep hold of that leading rope while I assist you to mount again, Miss Smythe—so! Very good," and gracefully resuming his own seat, he held out a long-fingered hand. "Give me her rope, if you please."

"I do not please, my lord," said Caroline firmly. "I do not think it at all suitable for the Marquis of Reston to be seen with a donkey in tow."

"But you must see how uneasy Dorca is with—er, Dolly

alongside her,'' he pointed out. ''My Heracles will be, I assure you, unmoved.''

Caroline was forced to own that her pretty Dorca *was* nervous at having the little donkey trail so closely next to her. ''Well then,'' she said brightly to the marquis, ''I shall wait here while you go on ahead, my lord, and if you would be so good as to send a footman to escort me back—''

''I shall do nothing of the sort. Give me the rope,'' Lord Reston repeated, and reluctantly Caroline complied. As his lordship had promised, Heracles accepted the proximity of the little newcomer uncomplainingly, and they continued without further incident. His cool urbanity so utterly unassailed that one might have thought he frequently rode through the streets of fashionable London with a donkey on a rope, the marquis commented: ''My compliments, Miss Smythe, on your shrewdness in conducting that transaction.''

''Oh, in Spain and Portugal it is to be expected that one haggles, you know!'' replied Caroline unthinkingly. ''Otherwise the shopkeepers would steal one blind!''

Black brows went up. ''You have been in Spain and Portugal? Surely not during the period of the war?''

Caroline cursed herself for having been lulled into an unwitting admission about her past. ''Y-yes,'' she said hesitantly.

''Good God!'' the marquis said. ''You cannot have traveled there for pleasure!''

She looked at Lord Reston, and what she saw in his face encouraged her sufficiently to tell him, ''My father was a soldier, my lord, and my mother and I—we followed behind as best we could.''

''Yours was no doubt an extraordinary childhood,'' said the marquis. ''Yet you gaze at me as if you anticipate a scornful response.''

''I suppose I do,'' Caroline said quietly. ''The few to whom I have thus far confided my circumstances were scandalized.''

''It would take a great deal more than that to shock me, I

assure you. It is just as well, I daresay, that most people are too greatly concerned with themselves to inquire about *you*.''

Caroline smiled a little at that. ''Just so. I ought to confess, my lord, that neither your sister nor your aunt know the truth of my background. Not,'' she added hastily, ''that there has been any need for me to prevaricate, for I would not, had the topic arisen, but—but it hasn't.''

''My theory proved,'' answered Lord Reston dryly. Then he looked at her and said with unwonted gentleness: ''Your parents are dead, Miss Smythe?''

For the second time that day, tears flooded her eyes. Fighting them back, she said, with only the tiniest tremor in her voice, ''Yes, my lord. Pray excuse me, but—but it is rather a difficult topic. Might we—might we speak of something else?''

''But of course,'' he said, still gently, and she rushed on.

''It—it is about Dolly. I am so thankful to you, my lord! But—but now that we have rescued her, I cannot help but wonder what is to become of her. I do not imagine your grooms would welcome her as a permanent addition to your stables!''

''No,'' Lord Reston replied. ''They are likely to feel that the tone of the place would suffer considerably. Never fear, Miss Smythe, I am contemplating a possibility for Dolly's future—one that does not, I assure you, include hauling sacks of brick dust.''

''Oh, what is it?'' Caroline asked him eagerly.

He smiled, and Caroline's heart leaped to see the unmistakable warmth in those dark, intense eyes. ''I shall say no more,'' he returned, ''until I have witnessed the fruition of my plans. In the meantime, you may be certain that Dolly will be admirably looked after in my stables.''

Impulsively Caroline leaned across the distance between them and, hardly able to believe her own boldness, briefly laid her gloved hand on his forearm. ''You are very good,'' she said softly.

''I am afraid I cannot agree with you, Miss Smythe; however, we shall not quarrel on that point again," he replied, but with that same warm light in his gaze, and then, as they rounded a corner and approached Grosvenor Square, the marquis said thoughtfully: "Have you observed the stares we are attracting? I should not be at all surprised if we were to set London on its ears: before long it will be all the rage to be seen riding with one's own donkey trailing alongside."

All too cognizant of her rapid pulse and the breath coming more quickly between parted lips, Caroline laughed, a trifle self-consciously, and said: "I only hope that may be so, and that more poor creatures like Dolly are saved from unkind owners!"

"I am speaking of fashion, Miss Smythe, and you persist in speaking of altruism," he said in mock reproof. "Really, I do not know how you shall get along amongst the *ton.* I shall have to mention it to my aunt, so that she may redouble her educational efforts."

"Oh, do not, my lord, for I fear Lady Augusta will be at wit's end should she be forced to endure still more lectures," rejoined Caroline playfully, then said: "Oh! I see a carriage coming to a halt before your town house. I very much hope I haven't detained you from meeting your visitors! And pray," she begged, "do give me Dolly's rope, my lord!"

"Nonsense," he said, then, as they came closer to the carriage, he went on, in his voice once again his customary silky detachment: "I perceive, Miss Smythe, that you are to meet this morning my betrothed and her mother."

Her stomach twisting, Caroline gripped Dorca's reins more tightly and watched with an impending sense of doom as two elegantly dressed ladies—one young and slim and blonde, the other older and distinguished by a purple turban ornamented with a towering spray of ostrich feathers—turned on the step to greet them.

Dear God, Caroline thought wildly, but she was a fool! For a fleeting hour or two, she had managed to forget about Lord

Reston's fiancée, forget about the impassable gulf stretching between herself and him, forget everything but the acute pleasure she found in his company and the way she felt when she was with him. Oh, she was a thousand times a fool—and here, it seemed, was her jolting return to reality, in the slender, regal form of the Honorable Helen Manderlay, whose cool blue eyes, as they met Caroline's, were wholly devoid of interest, curiosity, or jealousy.

His lordship dispassionately tendered the introductions, describing her only as his sister's *dame de compagnie,* and as soon as Miss Manderlay and her mother the baroness had nodded distantly in her direction, the marquis bade them all a general farewell and continued on toward the stables, Dolly still obediently following in his wake. As Caroline herself followed the butler, Uxley, and the Manderlays up the stairs to the drawing room, were her heart not so leaden within her, Caroline might have smiled to think that neither his fiancée nor his future mother-in-law had deigned to remark to his lordship that they found the sight of him with a bedraggled little donkey at all out of the ordinary.

Uxley announced the presence of Lady Calpurnia and her daughter, who then trod in a stately manner into the room. Caroline, hesitating on the threshold and unsure whether she properly was to stay or to go (especially given that she was clad in her riding habit), caught from Augusta a wild-eyed look and interpreted it as a frantic signal for support, for her ladyship had been in the throes of composition and wore an old ink-stained apron over her day dress; her dark hair had been carelessly caught up in a knot on her head, and there was a conspicuous smudge of ink on one cheek. Mrs. Yardley, still in her nightdress and lacy wrapper, had clearly been nodding over the *Gazette,* but was now galvanized into action, jumping to her feet and wringing her hands as she spoke with considerable agitation.

"Lady Calpurnia! Miss Manderlay! We did not expect you!

Indeed, we are expecting no one just yet, for dear Augusta and—oh, there you are, Miss Smythe! We have been wondering where you have been! The wardrobes of Augusta and Miss Smythe aren't quite ready—though Madame Huppert did very well with your riding costume, Miss Smythe, very well indeed!—and we aren't receiving visitors at present! However, I daresay Uxley forgot we were not at home and—well, it isn't of the slightest consequence! *You,* of course, dear ma'am, dear Miss Manderlay, will always be welcome here! Will you not be seated? Anywhere you like! Augusta, do clear the sofa of your books, please, and empty that chair of papers. And *here* is a pile of my journals: permit me to simply whisk them away—oh, thank you, Miss Smythe!''

As she carried the armful of periodicals toward a side-table, Caroline discreetly slipped her handkerchief to Augusta and brushed her fingers across her left cheekbone. Augusta nodded slightly, and, turning away to straighten a stack of papers, managed to expunge most of the ink she had smeared there, so that a few moments later she was able to introduce herself to the baroness and Miss Manderlay with tolerable composure, Mrs. Yardley still too flustered, as she flitted about the drawing room restoring order, to remember that her niece had never met their two visitors.

Next the baroness, having lowered herself into the room's most comfortable chair, smiled benignly upon her hostess and said, "We have come to see how you go on, Mrs. Yardley, and to offer our guidance as you prepare Lady Augusta for her *début.*"

"Oh, it's not really a *début.*" Augusta put in, only to be overriden by her aunt who said, bristling slightly, "You are very kind, ma'am, but you must know that I am sure I am more than capable of—"

"I shall be glad to introduce you to the Princess Esterhazy," the baroness went on graciously, "for you will be wishing admission to Almack's, of course."

"I am already acquainted with the princess," Mrs. Yardley said stiffly.

"Indeed? Then I will be happy to assist you in the renewal of your acquaintance," came the unruffled reply.

" 'Advice to Julia,' " announced Augusta blandly, and went on in a facetiously oracular manner:

> *All on that magic list depends;*
> *Fame, fortune, fashion, lovers, friends:*
> *'Tis that which gratifies or vexes*
> *All ranks, all ages, and both sexes.*
> *If once to Almack's you do belong,*
> *Like monarchs, you can do no wrong;*
> *But banished thence on Wednesday night,*
> *By Jove, you can do nothing right.*

"Just so," approved Lady Calpurnia, "though the meter strikes me as rather uneven. One of *your* verses, Lady Augusta?"

"No," Augusta said tightly, "it's by Henry Luttrell."

A magnanimous nod, setting the ostrich feathers swaying. "We know him."

"Do you, ma'am?" responded Augusta, now with some eagerness. "I should very much like to meet him."

"Yes, he showed a good deal of interest in Helen last year. I discouraged him at once, for although he is considered very charming and amusing, he has no claim to birth, wealth, position, or influence. I do not think it would be suitable for you to know him."

Augusta's dark brows drew together ominously. "Well, as to *that*—"

"As for your Miss Steele, Lady Augusta—"

"I believe it is Miss *Smythe,* Mama," said Miss Manderlay, without bothering to glance at Caroline.

"—having looked Miss Smythe over, Lady Augusta, I must

say that she seems presentable enough, though her complexion *is* rather brown. Perhaps Denmark Lotion might help. You may feel free to bring her with you to small assemblies and the occasional supper party, but I do not think I shall be able to secure a voucher to Almack's for her, and of course she must not dance.''

"Whyever not?" Augusta burst out indignantly. "She dances beautifully! *Much* better than I do!''

Miss Manderlay graced her ladyship with a pitying smile. "You have much to learn about the ways of society, my dear Augusta—if I may be allowed to address you so! I am only too delighted, as your sister-to-be, to place myself quite at your disposal.''

Caroline could see by the blaze in Augusta's eyes that she was on the verge of a furious retort, and so she secretively nudged her friend's foot with the toe of her riding boot, hoping that in her own eyes Augusta would see the plea for prudence there.

Apparently she did, for she said nothing, and instead stared toward the window in sullen silence for the remainder of the Manderlays' call, while Caroline, listening to the rather stilted conversation that ensued amongst the other three ladies, told herself that the baroness was quite right: it was hardly proper that a mere companion should join in the dance. Instead she would wisely use her time mingling amongst the elderly dowagers who sat against the wall, discreetly inquiring after further employment. It was a sensible plan. It was the practical thing to do. It made Caroline wish she were dead.

Chapter 8

"Your carriage awaits, my lord," said Uxley, and had just put his hand on the doorknob to usher his master outside, when Damien heard Augusta speak from the top of the stairs.

"My dear brother! Well met! You are just in time to see us off for our first ball!"

Damien turned, and what he saw made him ignobly wish he had more carefully timed his exit. More than a week had passed since his early-morning ride with Caroline Smythe, during which interval he had attempted to forget it as best as he could. As little as he liked to admit it, he had enjoyed their interlude together with a dangerous intensity. With her lively intelligence, her warm heart, her compellingly piquant looks she aroused in him thoughts and feelings he desired profoundly to discourage. To his own chagrin he saw now how willingly he had deceived himself in playing an instrumental part in bringing her to London. He had done it less out of an angry determination to exert control over her destiny than a furtive longing to have her near—a longing which he exerted his utmost to subvert by throwing himself into his usual pursuits with a reckless energy. He had rarely been home: for a few hours of sleep, a bath, a change of attire, and the occasional, brief conference with his secretary Petley. To his relief he hadn't once encountered Miss Smythe, while, at the same time, for reasons he did not intend to examine, neither had he sought out Miss Manderlay, though he had on more than one occasion been waggishly informed by his friends that she serenely went about her business, accompanied by her ever-present court of admirers and to all appearances unmoved by the neglect of her fiancé. Damien had told himself he should be troubled by the *on-dits,* but found instead that he was more preoccupied with a vision of a lithe little form, brilliant green eyes, and rosy, tempting lips . . .

And here was Miss Caroline Smythe in the flesh, shyly descending the staircase wearing a pale green evening robe with tiny puff sleeves and a delicate lace overdress fastened down the front with buttons of sparkling paste emeralds. Her auburn curls were drawn high on her head in a classical Psyche knot, with a few burnished ringlets coaxed free to dangle charmingly about her ears. Around her shoulders was draped a soft, sheer silk shawl; long white gloves and green satin sandals completed her toilette. She looked elegant, distinguished, and devastatingly feminine, and Damien was hard put not to stare at her. Instead he forced his eyes toward Augusta as she came briskly down the stairs, looking surprisingly *comme il faut* in ivory satin and a length of spangled silver net dangling negligently from her elbows. Her black hair was twisted into a thick, unadorned coil, the simplicity of which became her well and set off to striking advantage her white skin.

And behind his sister was Mrs. Yardley, resplendent in a lilac crêpe gown trimmed at its wide hem with shiny silk floss, and caught about the waist with a gold cord and tassels. Pearls hung from her ears and around her neck; in her gloved hands she carried a richly embroidered shawl and a handsome chicken-skin fan.

"Well, Damien, do we not look fine?" challenged his aunt playfully. "And do but consider Augusta and Miss Smythe! I believe I may without false modesty congratulate myself on the success of my efforts, and *you* need not fear that we shall put you to the blush!"

Damien bowed, murmured, "I did not for a moment consider the possibility of your failing, ma'am," and found his eyes drawn inexorably again to Caroline Smythe, who stood watching him with such an unguardedly wistful expression that his blood heated violently—so violently he actually took a step away from her. "You all look very well," he said to his aunt in a deliberately bland tone, and went on: "Whose ball are you gracing with your presence this evening?"

"The Stanhopes'," replied Mrs. Yardley. "I do not suppose there will be above two or three hundred there, which I thought would do nicely for our first outing of the season. I am certain Diana Stanhope sent you a card nephew; would you not like to join us?"

Repressing an unexpectedly fierce inclination to say yes, Damien only said: "Thank you, no. I am on my way to White's."

"What, and forgo the opportunity to see Miss Manderlay?" Augusta inquired with patent insincerity. "For we are given to understand that she and the baroness will be attending as well."

Damien put up his brows; what was his sister getting at? "Do I detect a faint note of hostility in your voice, my dear Augusta?"

"Well, since you asked—" Augusta began, ignoring warning glances from both her aunt and Miss Smythe. "I take leave to inform you, Damien, that Miss Manderlay has treated us with such patronizing hauteur that I have been *yearning* this entire week to give her a vicious set-down! Not two days pass but she and her mother come to call, full of advice we neither require nor wish for! Oh, and as for the baroness! Never have

I encountered such rudeness! And Aunt Violet was used to say she *liked* her!''

Mrs. Yardley faltered, ''I own I *did* think her ladyship's manner altered since the spring, before Damien—that is—but—but doubtless I am only imagining it!''

''Before Damien came up to scratch, you mean?'' suggested Augusta bluntly.

''Augusta!'' Mrs. Yardley gasped. ''That is *quite* enough!''

''And what's more,'' Augusta went on hotly, ''when Aunt told Lady Calpurnia we had accepted the Stanhopes' invitation, she *forbade* us to bring Caro along! If it weren't for Caro sidling up to me and pinching me smartly, I do not know *what* I would have said to that woman!''

''Indeed, it was very well done of Miss Smythe,'' interposed Mrs. Yardley hastily, ''for she administered the pinch *quite* surreptitiously! As to the matter of Miss Smythe's accompanying us—'' Here she broke off to toy for a moment with her fan, then raised troubled blue eyes to meet his. ''Far, far be it from me to issue a complaint,'' she said, ''for we are *very* grateful that you have opened your house and hearth to us, my dear nephew! But—but I am quite at a loss to understand how the Manderlays have apparently arrived at the conclusion that we are to move in society under their *aegis!*''

Under other circumstances Damien might have laughed, for it was a tangle which appealed mightily to his keen appreciation of the ridiculous. But this ran a little too close to the bone, and he was starting to feel trapped by the unwelcome emotions crowding in on him. ''I am sure I do not know,'' he said coldly, suppressing a pang of guilt at his own culpability. ''I am not the Manderlays' keeper. And now, if you will excuse me, I must go.'' He bowed, and left the house, indifferent to the realization that Uxley had been frozen in his post by the door, with only the slight bulge to his eyes attesting to the fact that he had been privy to a most titillating conversation.

* * *

Feeling more than a little drained by their encounter with the marquis prior to their own departure for the Stanhopes' ball, Caroline was glad for the chance to stand quietly in a corner of the magnificent ballroom and collect her thoughts. She had, she admitted, been shaken to see Lord Reston so unexpectedly. After their eventful ride in the park, she had spent some sleepless nights, schooling herself to accept the situation as it was, rather than hopelessly pining for what could not be. Perhaps, she had reasoned, she and the marquis could be friends? Surely a dismal enough compromise, when compared against the dazzling glory of her dreams, but was that not better than trying to utterly close off her heart to him? *As if I could!* ran through her mind, like an electrifying bolt of lightning, when as she was coming down the staircase she perceived him at the door, tall and magnificently handsome in his somber evening dress, with his black hair gleaming in the soft light of the hall's chandelier.

Oh, she *was* a fool, she now thought despairingly, and, anxious to be distracted, gazed more attentively around the crowded, rather oppressively warm room. With breathtaking speed following their arrival, Augusta had been helplessly whisked off to dance a quadrille and Mrs. Yardley was plunged into an animated group of acquaintances she had not seen since the season before; and Caroline, left to her own devices, had made her way to this relatively sheltered nook not far from where the orchestra sat. At that moment Augusta caught her eye, pausing in the middle of one of the figures, and made a little moue eloquent of disgust. Her partner was a sallow youth half a head shorter than she, with a countenance notable only for its chinless aspect and an expression of narrow determination.

Caroline smiled sympathetically, then was suddenly assailed by a mysterious sinking sensation. She turned, and found that the Baroness Manderlay was bearing down on her, the puce demitrain of her lavishly figured gown trailing behind in an undulating ripple.

"Why, Miss Smythe!" the baroness said in chilly accents. "I am sure I did not think to see you here."

Caroline dipped a little curtsy. "How do you do, ma'am?" she murmured politely.

The baroness frowned. "To be sure, I am shocked, Miss Smythe, and disappointed. I believed I had made myself clear to both Mrs. Yardley and to Lady Augusta as to what was correct procedure."

"I am merely a companion, ma'am," answered Caroline, torn between anger and amusement. "I do as I am bid."

"What you are," pronounced Lady Calpurnia coldly, "is impertinent. I had thought you seemed like a creature of some moderate understanding. I am baffled, therefore, as to why you were so forward as to thrust yourself into a situation of such impropriety."

"A companion, ma'am, accompanies," returned Caroline, tilting her chin and unflinchingly meeting the older woman's censuring gaze. "And since I am not *your* employee, but that of Lady Augusta, I do not think I need answer to you."

"Well!" uttered the baroness, her puce-covered bosom heaving with such force that the long, opulent necklace of diamonds she wore glittered even more brightly. "Such rank insubordination! You may be sure, Miss Smythe, that I will be addressing both Mrs. Yardley *and* Lord Reston concerning your appalling behavior!" And, with all the ominous portent of a modern-day Cassandra, Lady Calpurnia swept away from Caroline, her demitrain rippling frenziedly in her wake.

Go ahead, you—you old bat! thought Caroline unrepentantly. Her knees shaking a little with the fury she had struggled so hard to conceal, she looked around her for a vacant chair, and spied one tucked next to a waist-high pedestal on which sat an enormous vase of hothouse flowers. She had just taken a step toward the chair when she felt the light touch of a gloved hand on her arm. Startled, she found herself next to a slim, exquisitely dressed lady some years older than herself, who smilingly spoke.

"How do you do? How *beautifully* you handled the baroness! I could not hear what was said between you, but it was plain to see she was stalking away in a *towering* rage! I had thought this ball was going to be thoroughly *dull,* but you have quite *enlivened* it for me! Oh, I cannot *wait* to tell Emily Cowper! She will think it so *droll,* for she despises all *mushrooms,* you know!" Then, apparently perceiving that Caroline was regarding her with blank astonishment, the lady gave a tinkling laugh and went on with unabated gaiety, "Poor girl, you must be thinking me quite *mad!* Or at the very least *stricken* in my manners! But you must forgive me: I simply *had* to come up and congratulate you on so thoroughly *trouncing* the odious Baroness Manderlay! We none of us wished to admit her— all, alas, save for the Princess Esterhazy, who in a moment of *weakness* gave way, for she thought the baroness' daughter too beautiful, and too *wealthy,* to be turned away! Oh, she regrets it *now,* of course, for she cannot refuse to acknowledge the acquaintance, and now the baroness quite *hangs* on her! I would *pity* the princess, but you must admit it's rather *comical!*" Another tinkling laugh, then, carelessly: "I'm Sally Jersey, you know! And you are—?"

Feeling a little dazed, Caroline said with all the composure she could muster: "I am Caroline Smythe, ma'am, companion to the Lady Augusta Reston."

Lady Jersey smiled at her in the friendliest fashion. "I *thought* I saw Violet Yardley come in! I believe she and I have been *introduced,* but I do not know her at all, though I am *rather* more familiar with her nephew Lord Reston! He and the regent and his set, you know—and the regent and myself— well, *that* is a tale from long ago! And so that tall handsome girl attempting the quadrille is Mrs. Yardley's niece, Reston's younger sister?" At Caroline's murmured "Yes, ma'am," she nodded decisively. "It will do! It will do! You are staying at

Reston's town house? Yes? Then I shall shortly call upon you all, my dear, and you may expect vouchers for Almack's—for all *three* of you! Ah, there is Emily now! I must go and *regale* her with my anecdote! *How* she will laugh! *Adieu,* Miss Smythe!'' And Lady Jersey tripped off toward her friend, whom she hailed with lavish expressions of delight. Caroline watched for a moment, hardly able to believe what had just transpired, then walked to the chair she had spotted before and sank gratefully into it.

Vouchers for Almack's! She thought of the baroness' certain fury upon learning that the obscure Miss Smythe was to be admitted past those hallowed portals, and could not repress a tiny smile of amused triumph.

With a flourish the orchestra brought the quadrille to a close, and Caroline looked toward the dancers to see Augusta, an expression of grim forbearance on her face, nod at her partner and stride unescorted toward the refreshment tables, only to be neatly intercepted by Mrs. Yardley, who presented to her another young man just as the musicians swung into a galop. A mulish thrust of her lower lip, and back into the dance went Augusta with her new partner, and appearing well pleased, Mrs. Yardley turned to rejoin her clique. Her own passage was checked when a round-faced, pleasant-looking gentleman of some thirty years of age came up to her and bowed. Mrs. Yardley evidently recognized him, for she smiled and nodded, then, when the gentleman glanced directly at Caroline, she seemed a trifle nonplused and said something which caused him merely to shrug good-naturedly. Caroline watched, rather baffled, as Mrs. Yardley and the gentleman together came her way, then rose to her feet and curtsied slightly as Mrs. Yardley introduced to her one Mr. Charles Highcombe, adding, ''Mr. Highcombe is a dear friend of Damien's, Miss Smythe! They were bosom-bows at school, you know, and so to this day they remain! He wished to meet you, and to solicit your hand for the country dance which follows the galop! But I was obliged to inform him that, regrettably, you do not dance! I am sure, however, that *no one*—'' Here she flashed Caroline a significant glance, which Caroline had no difficulty in comprehending as a veiled reference to Baroness Manderlay. ''—*no one* might object to conversation between you, for I regard Mr. Highcombe as one of the family! And you, too, my dear! Oh, good heavens, Augusta just trod on Mr. Swinton's shoes! And judging by that terribly unattractive scowl on her face one might be tempted to think she did it deliberately! Oh! I have just this instant seen your dear mama, Mr. Highcombe! How well she looks! I must go and say hello to her!''

Caroline gazed warily up into Mr. Highcombe's cheerful gray eyes. This was, no doubt, Lord Reston's accomplice on his ill-fated race to Cambridge. Could he have some sinister purpose in seeking her out? It was difficult to believe so, for Mr. Highcombe grinned at her, and, as soon as Mrs. Yardley was out of earshot, he said with the innocent air of a schoolboy bent on mischief: ''You *do* seem familiar, Miss Smythe! Might we have met before? In the country somewhere, perhaps?''

''No, Mr. Highcombe, I do not think so,'' said Caroline, trying, and failing, to maintain the proper note of severity in her voice. ''Pray, sir, do behave and be discreet!'' she begged him. ''I am certain Lord Reston would wish you to do so!''

''To be sure he would,'' agreed Mr. Highcombe, ''for he swore me to secrecy as to our mutual adventures in Bowlstack!''

''Baldock,'' Caroline reminded him, her lips quivering as she tried not to laugh.

''Yes, yes, that's it! But you see,'' he confided engagingly, ''having noticed you a few minutes ago, I could not resist coming over to you to tell you how greatly you have improved since our last meeting! Females like compliments,'' he added by way of explanation.

Now she did laugh. ''Thank you, Mr. Highcombe! It is true that we weak women cannot resist the blandishments of your sex! But,'' she added firmly, ''I cannot think it right for you to approach me so, Mr. Highcombe, for tongues are bound to wag! I am merely a companion, you know—''

"*Are* you?" he exclaimed in evident surprise. "I am sure Damien never told me so, the dog!"

"—to Lady Augusta," Caroline went on, undeterred, "and am therefore a social nonentity!"

"Well, if you're worried I'm going to dangle after you, don't!" he replied frankly. "Not but what I wouldn't *wish* to, for you've turned out to be quite a diamond of the first water! Thought you was a pretty little wench when first I saw you, but you were so knocked up it was difficult to *really* tell! The thing of it is, my mother dragged me here so that we might cast about us for a suitably well-heeled girl. The Highcombes have a distinguished lineage, but we're as poor as church mice! I say, you *aren't* swimming in lard by any chance, are you?" he appended hopefully.

It was impossible, Caroline thought, to be offended by this jovial, easygoing rattle. "No, Mr. Highcombe," she said gently, "I am afraid not."

"Pity," he said, then brightened. "Shall we go and have a look at the comestibles?" he suggested. "Mrs. Stanhope's ices are always very good! Though you'll want to avoid the negus at all costs!" He offered Caroline his arm, and with a smile she took it, and began walking with him across the room.

"It *is* warm in here," she said, "and an ice sounds so refreshing—" All at once she felt an odd chill shimmy down her spine, and broke off. "Mr. Highcombe!" she whispered. "Do you know the identity of the tall gentleman to our left, standing next to Miss Manderlay?"

"Oh, that's the Earl of Audley," he answered. "Supercilious fellow, ain't he? Why do you ask?"

"He's—he's staring at us," Caroline responded in a low, uneasy voice. "Quite pointedly!"

"Is he? No doubt he's admiring you, Miss Smythe," said Mr. Highcombe gallantly.

"I doubt that, when he has Miss Manderlay by his side!" retorted Caroline, and could not resist adding: "They seem— they seem quite comfortable together, do they not?"

"Oh, yes, very cozy!" answered Mr. Highcombe casually. "The odds in all the betting books were good that he'd win the fair Helen's hand, but then Damien nipped in and surprised us all! May I offer you an ice?"

"Yes, thank you," Caroline said, unsettled, and was glad to turn her back on the pale blue eyes that had been directed her way with such overt, calculating curiosity.

Augusta settled herself against the rich, soft squabs of the carriage with a loud sigh, and eased her slippers from her feet. "I did not rest once the entire night," she complained. "And there *you* were, Caro, eating ices and sipping champagne, looking so cool and at ease that if you were not my friend I vow I would have *hated* you!"

"Did you have *no* refreshments at all, poor Gussie?" said Caroline remorsefully.

"No! None! All I did was dance!" said Augusta bitterly. "And be bored to death!"

" 'Twas a good evening's work," Mrs. Yardley said complacently. "*All* of the *ton*'s most eligible young men sought to partner you, Augusta! There were not enough dances to go around! You were a veritable belle of the ball!"

"Aunt," said Augusta, "let us not deceive ourselves! I am considered a prize on the Marriage Mart because I am rich, and from a good family! It is not because of my beauty or my grace—hah!—that I was pursued with such vigor, like a fox before the hounds!"

Airily Mrs. Yardley waved a gloved hand. "Pish! What does it matter? You outshone all the other girls!"

"Not Miss Manderlay," rejoined Augusta dryly. "Good heavens, Aunt, she behaves as if she were quite unattached!

And her mother permits such coquettishness with every sign of complacent approval!''

"Yes, so I observed," admitted Mrs. Yardley. "I own I would not wish *you* to conduct yourself in such a manner, but—but—well, this is how the *ton* is! Husbands and wives don't hang about in each other's pockets, you know! Indeed, it would be considered shocking if they did! And Miss Manderlay has been much used to being the cynosure of all eyes! I am sure Damien knows what he is doing," she concluded loyally, then yawned widely behind cupped fingers. "Oh! Do excuse me! I am eager for my bed, my dears! I vow it is nigh on four o'clock in the morning!" Her eyelids drifted shut, and soon she was nodding gently in time to the swaying of the carriage.

Augusta gave a quiet snort. "Society!" she whispered scathingly. "Did I not tell you they were all a pack of wolves, Caro?"

Caroline leaned forward and placed a hand on Augusta's knee. "You must be sorry you contrived to bring us to London," she whispered back. "Why should we not return to Windemere at once?"

"What, before I've had a chance to enjoy myself? Which reminds me, on Thursday afternoon there's a lecture on geology which I *will* attend, even if I must incur the wrath of my aunt! Did you meet anyone you liked, Caro?" Augusta asked, in a quick change of subject.

Caroline shook her head, and into her mind came irresistibly an image of the marquis. "No," she said softly.

"I daresay not," murmured Augusta, "for while I was being pushed and pulled about the dance floor I could not help but see that Aunt was too busy amongst her own set to take you about a bit."

"She is not my chaperone," Caroline reminded her ladyship. "Indeed, I would not expect her to act in such a capacity."

"Well, *I* am now acquainted with a number of gentlemen, and perhaps one of them, my dear Caro, shall catch your fancy.

Though in all honesty I must warn you that I have never encountered such a clutch of sapskulls! I am now more convinced than ever that I shall *never* marry! Are you *certain* you wish to?''

Caroline only smiled and said nothing, and wondered, a little forlornly, where the marquis might be.

''Reston!'' said the Prince Regent, a trifle peevishly. ''*Will* you stop beating me at faro? You already have my vowels from White's, not three hours past!''

''Your highness knows he may redeem them whenever it is convenient,'' Damien said, and ignored Brummell's sardonic glance from across the table. They both knew from past experience that the prince, at once extravagantly self-indulgent and vociferous in his contention that his income was insufficient to his exalted status, was unlikely to pay his debts, which yearly mounted ever higher.

''Mighty gracious of you!'' said the prince testily, adding: ''Don't think I didn't see that look on your face, George, for I did! Thought I was too deep in my cups to notice, eh? I tell you, I'm as sharp-eyed as ever!''

''Indeed, sir, you verge on the omniscient,'' murmured Brummell blandly.

For a moment the prince's fleshy, still-handsome face contracted into a fierce scowl; then he burst into a great shout of laughter and pounded hilariously on the felt of the table. ''There are times, George,'' he declared, ''when I would dearly love to have you clapped in irons!''

Brummell's gaze was almost feline in its cool equanimity as he said, ''But then who would advise you as to the cut of your coat?''

''Just so!'' said the regent, seeming much struck. ''Then I *shan't* have you hauled off to Newgate just yet!''

Brummell inclined his head with mock humility. "You are too good, sir."

"That I am!" boisterously agreed his highness, and imperiously called for more wine. "And George," he advised with a meaningful edge to his voice, "I recommend that you not forget it!"

"Shall we play another round, sir?" inquired Damien of the prince, accepting the fresh wineglass a uniformed manservant proffered to him.

The regent quaffed his wine in one gulp, swallowed, then abruptly threw the glass into the fireplace near which he had tenderly seated himself an hour before (for he had an obsessive fear of draughts), shattering the delicate crystal into a multitude of luminescent shards. "No, by Jove, I'm sick to death of cards!" he said, petulant again. "I've lost at White's, now I've lost at—what's the name of this hell, Mildmay?" he demanded of another member of their party.

"*Le—le Jardin d'Eden,* sir," replied Sir Henry unsteadily, weaving a little in his seat.

"The Garden of Eden for *some.*" The regent cast a sour look around him. "Is there a snake among us, I wonder? Or more than one?" Then he poked roughly at Henry Pierrepoint, who lolled in the chair next to his own. "What's to do, eh? What's to do?"

Sipping at his wine and dispassionately watching the prince, Damien wondered if his highness realized, even dimly, that at that moment he sounded precisely like the father he despised, the old mad king, who was wont to hold a hand to his ear and say plaintively, "What? Eh? What?"

Pierrepoint was frowning into his empty glass, in a prodigious effort of concentration. Then his brow cleared; he looked up and said simply, "Women!"

"Why, that's it!" averred the prince, brightening. "We've played cards, we've drunk our fill, now it's time for some wenching! Pierrepoint, I salute you! I would, that is," he added loudly, *"if* I had a glass to do it with!" A servant scurried to obey, and with wine in hand the prince smiled broadly. "You're a damned genius, Pierrepoint!"

"I know," said the other modestly.

"Your health!" The prince drank deeply of his wine, then lumbered to his feet, his corset creaking loudly as he did so. "Mildmay! What was that nunnery to which you conducted us t'other night? I liked it very well! I had a fine bit o' muslin there, as I recall—very soft and plump! I do like a chit with some meat on her bones! Let's go back!"

There were some enthusiastic utterances of assent from various members of the group assembled round the faro table. George Brummell only smiled in his catlike fashion at Damien, who too was silent as he stood up and helped Sir Henry Mildmay to do so as well. An odd sense of unreality was overtaking Damien, as if this familiar scene, one that had been repeated many times over in more or less the same way, had transmogrified from the known, the pleasurable, into something disturbingly alien.

In fits and starts the regent's party made its slow way to the door of the exclusive *Jardin d'Eden,* and thence down the steps to where their carriages stood waiting for them amidst the heavy dark pall of deepest night.

"May I ride with you, Reston?" murmured Brummell. "Prinny's coach is bound to reek dreadfully of spirits."

"You may have my coach," Damien replied. "I'm walking home."

Brummell looked at him with sudden intentness. "What's this? Guilty thoughts of your betrothed? My dear fellow, the shackles aren't even clasped about your leg yet."

"A peculiarly apt expression," said Damien. "Have John Coachman take you to your lodgings as well. I can't imagine Prinny's carriage will smell any better after his visit to Mildmay's brothel. Good night." Without bothering to bid farewell to his other companions, Damien strode off in the direction of Grosvenor Square.

As the voices behind him faded, it was with a sense of relief that he breathed in the cool evening air. Perhaps it would serve to clear the curious befuddlement he was experiencing—not the blurry haze of too much wine, but a new and different sensation instead. This night, he mused, had been no different from a score of others. Always before he had participated without much thought; there had been nothing else to do, so he had done it. Why, then, did he now feel as if he were in some kind of waking nightmare, one in which all the rules that had been used to make sense no longer did so?

With an almost desperate ache he wished there was someone with whom he could talk—could *truly* talk—and at once he thought of Caroline Smythe. She of all people might be the one who could understand him.

But then his heart wrenched painfully within him, for though they might *talk* together, there could be no further intimacy between them, no matter how ardently he might desire a greater closeness: he was as plainly separated from her as if an actual stone fence had been constructed between them. He was not free, he could offer her nothing but *carte blanche,* and he would not so dishonor her.

Damien shook his head in bewilderment. Whence these scruples? Whence a concern for another person that was stronger than his own for himself?

"God damn it to *hell!*" he muttered viciously between his teeth, and half-wished he had gone on with the regent and his friends, for then he would not be plagued with these tormenting thoughts.

As he walked on, he was startled to see a shadow crouched in the gutter shift toward him. A moment later, in the dim light of the street lamp, he perceived it to be a child, of no more than eight or nine years, wrapped in a dirty cloak far too big for him.

A skinny arm was extended past the folds of the cloak, and a small voice croaked supplicatingly: "Can ye spare a little sumpin', guv'nor?"

As was his habit, Damien continued past the beggar. Then, unbidden, came an image of Caroline Smythe throwing herself into the road for the sake of a miserable puppy nobody cared about. With a grimace, Damien suddenly wheeled about, thrust a hand into the pocket of his coat, and produced a guinea which he tossed to the astonished child.

"Guv'nor! Oh, bless ye, sir! *Thank* ye, sir!"

"You're welcome," Damien muttered over his shoulder, and continued on his way, trying to focus his attention only on the sound of his rapid footsteps. But it was to no avail; he could not avoid the harsh truth of his own dilemma.

God help me, he groaned to himself. *God help me . . . for I no longer know who I am.*

Chapter 9

Mrs. Yardley surveyed the crowded drawing room with transparent gratification. It was the afternoon following the Stanhopes' ball, and such a horde of callers had descended upon them that there was scarcely space in which to move about and greet their guests. No hostess could hope for a greater success.

Watching Mrs. Yardley from the corner in which she quietly sat, Caroline could not but smile at the wholehearted relish with which the older woman was enjoying herself. Augusta, on the other hand, was ensconced upon a sofa surrounded by gentlemen of various ages, several of whom were talking at once; on her ladyship's face was an expression of barely concealed irritation as she occasionally made monosyllabic replies. Lady Jersey had come and gone, bestowing on a radiant Mrs. Yardley the promised vouchers; other of Almack's patronesses had visited as well: the beautiful, sweet-mannered Lady Cowper, the cool and reserved Mrs. Drummond Burrell, the voluble Countess Lieven, and finally the Princess Esterhazy, who was dogged by the Baroness Manderlay with such single-minded tenacity that Caroline regarded the harassed patroness with deep sympathy. Then, to her surprise, a few of the gentlemen drifted *her* way, with only a smile and a bow to Miss Manderlay, who gracefully occupied a seat in the center of the drawing room, clad in a clinging pale blue day dress that highlighted her golden, sylphlike loveliness to perfection.

" 'Servant, Miss Smythe!'' said Charles Highcombe, with his infectious grin. ''What a crush! My mother brought me over to ogle the newest heiress! As if I *would* make up to Damien's little sister! However, I don't wish to dash my mother's hopes just yet, for she'll be bound to find *some* brutal way in which to punish me! I say! It's beastly hot in here, ain't it? Wouldn't you like me to open this window?''

''Yes, thank you, Mr. Highcombe,'' replied Caroline, smiling gratefully up at him.

''There! A dashed sight better with a bit of breeze coming in!'' he pronounced, then jumped as one of his companions nudged him sharply with his elbow. ''Good God, there's no need to *impale* me with that bony limb of yours, Max! Miss Smythe, may I present Sir Maxwell Gage? And Mr. Francis Chester? Sir Maxwell, Mr. Chester—Miss Smythe!''

The young men bowed. ''How do you do?'' they said, and politely Caroline returned their salutations. The conversation that ensued among them was rendered lively both by Caroline's tact in encouraging the gentlemen to speak about themselves and by Mr. Highcombe's relaxed banter. Caroline had just raised the diverting topic of an upcoming balloon ascension sponsored by the Royal Aeronautical Society, when it seemed to her the breeze from the window was supplanted by a colder, considerably less pleasant current in the room.

''Mr. Highcombe!'' came a smooth voice. ''Once again I find you *tête-à-tête* with this young lady. How charming to think that you have ingratiated yourself with such dispatch.'' The Earl of Audley, tall, slender, impeccably dressed, stepped into view and smiled suavely at Charles Highcombe. "Pray, will you not introduce me to her?"

Seeming none too pleased, Mr. Highcombe obeyed, and Caroline, murmuring, "How do you do, my lord," shot a nervous glance at him as the earl bowed low over her hand.

"I am delighted to make your acquaintance, Miss Smythe. Mr. Highcombe, I spy a suddenly vacant chair behind you: might I trouble you to bring it here?" When Mr. Highcombe returned with the chair and placed it opposite Caroline, the earl disposed himself in it and said serenely, "You are very kind. There is no help for it, I fear; youth, you know, must give way to age."

"I daresay you are not so much older than I, sir," said Mr. Highcombe stiffly.

"Not in age, perhaps," rejoined the earl gently, "but in experience. And that, my dear boy, is what truly matters."

Mr. Highcombe glared, opened his mouth, then looked down at Caroline before bowing abruptly and walking away. The earl maintained a composed silence and Caroline an apprehensive one until Mr. Chester and Sir Maxwell, daunted, reluctantly meandered away.

"Now we may enjoy a comfortable chat, Miss Smythe, without those callow youths about us," said the earl. "Or have I chased away prospective swains?"

Caroline felt herself gripping her fingers together with a tension she would rather not reveal, and forced herself to relax her hands. She did not know what sort of game the Earl of Audley was playing; she was best served, she thought, by retreating into the opaque mask of a servant. "You must know, my lord, that I am but a paid companion to the Lady Augusta," she said. "If one or two of the gentlemen present wish to while away a few moments with me, then that is by their choice."

"You underrate your own charms, Miss Smythe. Indeed, I observed your little coterie to be taking a very obvious pleasure in your company."

Caroline inclined her head and said nothing.

"Do you know, Miss Smythe," the earl went on in his caressing fashion, "you interest me extraordinarily."

"I am sure I cannot think why."

"Can you not? Why, you are a woman of mystery, Miss Smythe. Helen—that is, Miss Manderlay—was unable to divulge anything about you, save that you have suddenly appeared on the scene as Lady Augusta's companion. Out of nowhere, as it were."

"I am also sure," Caroline responded, "that I can be of equally little interest to Miss Manderlay."

The earl gazed at her with those pale blue eyes, and Caroline was abruptly struck by a certain kind of familiarity he bore to Lord Reston. Oh, not so much physically, for to her his thin, fair good looks were but a pale contrast to the muscular vitality of the marquis with his gleaming black hair and sensuous, strongly marked features. There was, rather, an urbane elegance they both shared, in mannerism as well as in dress: a sophistication and a kind of infinite world-weariness. Yet ultimately she found them as different as light and darkness, as different as good and evil.

"You seem to be on intimate terms with Charles Highcombe," remarked his lordship.

"He stands on so little ceremony I suppose one might think so," she replied evenly, then added: "Interestingly enough, my lord, I made the same observation to Mr. Highcombe about you and Miss Manderlay."

The earl's bloodless lips curved into a smile. "Oh, so you have claws, do you, Miss Smythe?"

Caroline's own smile was false as she said, 'Why, I cannot think what you mean, my lord," and rose to her feet. 'Will you excuse me? I see that her ladyship is gesturing to me." This was a lie, but she could not find it in her to feel the slightest twinge of conscience as she moved past the earl's chair and swiftly made good her escape.

* * *

A few days had passed since he had walked home from *Le Jardin d'Eden,* and greatly to his consternation Damien remained haunted by his disquieting thoughts. No amount of port or wine or brandy could still them for long, nor any number of sessions boxing at Jackson's Saloon, shooting at Manton's Galleries, or fencing at Angelo's. They were temporary distractions only, and in the end failed utterly to obliterate his torment.

One morning, having risen unusually early and surprised his valet, Bentley, by being already half-dressed and pacing restlessly about his bedchamber when that worthy arrived with warm water for the shaving bowl, he permitted Bentley to shave him and rapidly finished dressing, tying his neckcloth with such speed and unconcern that Bentley was moved to protest.

"My lord! Surely you are not satisfied with *that?* Why, the ruffles are not quite symmetrical! Allow me to give you a fresh cloth!"

"Oh, never mind, man, the sun will still rise in the east and set in the west," said Damien impatiently, and quit the chamber. Within minutes he was in his town curricle and driving his chestnuts toward St. James' Place, conscious of a sensation uncomfortably close to desperation. Shortly he reached the Manderlays' town house and was promptly admitted, ushered inside by a butler who responded to his brusque inquiry with a perplexed look.

"Yes indeed, my lord, Miss Manderlay *is* in, but—but I am not sure if she is *at home!*"

"Ask her and see," said Damien, and waited for what seemed like an interminable amount of time while the butler conveyed his message to the upper regions of the house. At length the butler returned, and invited Damien to follow him to a saloon upstairs. Miss Manderlay awaited him there, bedecked in a voluminous rose-colored *peignoir* rendered demure by a dizzying profusion of ribbons and lace. Her blonde locks were con-

fined only by a matching rose ribbon tied in a bow at the crown
of her head, and on her narrow feet were a pair of soft velvet
slippers. She half lay on a long, low-backed sofa, leaning against
the elaborately scrolled end-piece; behind her stood a hatchet-
faced, straight-spined woman of indeterminate years who was
dressed severely in black.

"Reston!" Miss Manderlay said with her glinting smile.
"You have caught me unready for the day. But Grymes said
you appeared to have come on an errand of some urgency, and
so I thought it best not to keep you tarrying downstairs for *too*
long. You must forgive my mother's absence: she has not yet
risen from her bed, and so I have asked my maid Eugénie to
lend me countenance."

"Send her away," said Damien impetuously.

Blonde brows arched high. "My dear Reston, I do not
think—"

"Do as I say, Helen." He stared hard at her, until finally
her blue eyes dropped and she spoke.

"Eugénie, his lordship wishes for a private conversation.
You may leave us."

The maid bobbed a stiff curtsy, said, "Yes, *mademoiselle,*"
and walked from the room. When the door had closed behind
her, Miss Manderlay gave a little laugh.

"You are very demanding this morning, Reston," she commented archly. "Pray, will you not sit down?" She indicated
a chair set perpendicularly to the sofa on which she reclined.

"I thank you, no," he said curtly, and felt a muscle leap
involuntarily in his jaw. It was only then he realized he had
been clenching his teeth tightly together.

She shrugged. "As you will." Her voice was calm as she
went on: "I have not seen you in some time, and have been
looking forward to the opportunity of informing you as to
Augusta's progress. I am pleased to tell you she does very well
indeed. She did not lack for partners at the Stanhopes' ball,
and on the day following the ball she entertained numerous

callers and received quite a multitude of posies.'' Miss Manderlay laughed again. ''Indeed, Mama later confessed to me her
anxiety that *I* would feel outshone by Augusta's attainments,
and when I was able to assure her with the greatest sincerity
in the world that I was not, she remarked upon what she termed
my *magnanimity.* But I was obliged to disabuse her of that
notion, for only a person afflicted by rampant insecurity would
feel threatened by another's accomplishments—and that, I
fancy, has never been one of my besetting sins.'' When Damien
did not respond, and simply continued to gaze at her, Miss
Manderlay said with a new hint of impatience in her voice:
''Reston, whatever is the matter with you? I wish you will not
keep standing there like a block.''

''Very well,'' answered Damien, and with rapid steps he
came to sit beside her, and took her soft white hand in his.

Miss Manderlay acceded to this intimacy, and said, more
tolerantly, ''What brings you here, Reston? Is there something
you desire to discuss with me?''

''No, Helen, I do not *desire* to discuss anything,'' returned
Damien, and resolutely drew her close to him. One of his hands
went round her back, and the other moved to slowly, lingeringly,
slide from her shoulder the gossamer material of her *peignoir.*
He pressed his lips to the cool, pale flesh he had revealed, and
proceeded with a leisurely deliberation along her collarbone,
and higher to the slender column of her throat, nipping gently
as he went; then, when she neither moved nor spoke, he raised
his head to kiss her, slanting his mouth across hers and with
the subtle, heated play of his tongue urging her to open herself
to him. Still she remained unyielding; Damien groaned, feeling
the desperation rise more fiercely within him, and with a light,
skillful touch he caressed through her gown a small, soft-rippled
breast.

It was then, with a gasp, that Miss Manderlay wrenched
herself away from him. ''Reston!'' she said coldly, restoring

to her shoulder the sleeve he had displaced. *"Must* you enact the role of lover? I vow it is too, too quaint."

His breath rasping loudly in his own ears, Damien pushed back and looked at her across the distance they had created between them on the sofa. "Quaint?" he echoed.

She gestured carelessly. *"You* know—the overeager fiancé wooing his intended and so forth, so amusingly prevalent among stage comedies. To be quite candid with you, Reston, I do not know why you would suddenly attempt to—to assault me so. For us there has never been any pretense of what the lower classes are vulgarly fond of characterizing as *love,* and I assure you I believed us to be going along just as we should."

"Have you, Helen?" said Damien. "And do you intend to deny me your bed once we are married?"

"Of course not," Miss Manderlay replied, in the indulgent tone of one addressing a backward child. "We will want an heir, of course. Beyond that, you need not worry that I shall attempt to restrict you in your habits, Reston. I should not wish you to feel you need dance attendance on me, and indeed, I daresay I would find such unconventional behavior rather confining. After all, though we have many acquaintances in common, we do not share the same groups of friends; I see no reason why either of us should abandon the circles in which we have been used to move merely because we are married."

"I see," Damien said slowly. The almost frantic desperation that had been driving him was now giving way to a heavy, leaden coldness that seemed to seep into his very bones. He looked at the pale, precise oval that was her face, at her cool, immaculate beauty. Her composure, he thought with a kind of despair, was such that she could have been carved from marble. He tried to imagine her on their wedding night, what she would feel like in his arms; he could only picture an exquisite statue. "Thank you for enlightening me, Helen," he said, and rose to his feet. "Pray accept my apologies for disturbing you."

She smiled and held out her hand. "Not at all," she said

kindly. "I am glad we have had our talk, Reston, and that we have cleared the air between us. Do give my compliments to your sister and aunt, won't you? Good day."

"Good day," said Damien, and having bowed over her extended fingers, he turned and left the saloon. As he drove aimlessly about town, having no particular destination in mind, for the first time in his memory he found himself contemplating his future as it stretched out ahead of him. After he and Miss Manderlay were wed, his life would go on much as it had before. He would gamble, drink, race his curricle, keep and discard mistresses, visit at various country houses where he would hunt and shoot and fish, go to Newmarket to bet upon the horses and Brighton to be entertained at the Pavilion. Once in a great while he might stop in at Windemere. There would be a child, perhaps, or two, who would be bundled off to school as he himself had been. Eventually he would grow old alongside the prince, Brummell, and the others of his set, unless illness, accident, or other misfortune intervened sooner. In the meantime, he would be occupied; he would be diverted; he would be . . . alone.

This last thought seemed to hit him with the force of an unexpected blow, and as he abruptly pulled his chestnuts to a halt, it echoed cruelly within his mind.

Alone . . . alone . . . you have lived alone, and you shall die alone.

Then Damien was aware only of a blind need to escape—to escape from himself—to get away, now, before everything he had ever believed in, everything he had always relied upon, crumbled into dust before his very eyes.

"Go on!" he said harshly to his horses, and obediently they plunged forward into a rapid trot.

To Caroline their days and nights seemed to blend into a single unified flurry of calls, dinner parties, assemblies, balls, and excursions. More than two weeks had passed since the Stanhopes' ball, and she felt as if she had hardly had the time to pause and draw breath. To be sure, it was upon the unwilling Augusta that all of the attention was initially heaped; Caroline would have been happy to remain unobtrusively in the background, yet as time went by she was surprised to find that gradually more people came to nod and smile at her, and even to stop and converse with her. As Lord Reston had cynically foretold, they were pleased to accept her at face value—as a quiet, self-assured, well-mannered companion who had been accepted into the noble Reston family—and to her relief they did not trouble to delve more deeply into the particulars of her circumstances or of her past. Nevertheless it *was* agreeable to feel that she had become, perhaps, a very tiny star amongst the large, glittering constellation that was the *ton*. She was not in danger of losing her head because of her petty triumphs, however: she had lived too long amidst hardship and discomfort to regard her new luxury and glamour as anything other than temporary pleasures. It was also impossible to take seriously Augusta's entreaties that she try and encourage the gentlemen she met to consider her as another eligible miss on the Marriage Mart. For one thing, she could offer, aside from what she considered to be the meager attractions of her own person, none of the worldly attributes that were considered necessary to render a candidate valuable. For another, she had yet to encounter a gentleman who had in any way stirred her mind, or roused her emotions, or made her heart pound with swift deep strokes in her chest. There was only one gentlemen she knew who could do that . . .

Yet once again Lord Reston had disappeared—this time, she gathered from a puzzled report tendered by Mrs. Yardley, in a very real sense. Griffin Petley, his lordship's secretary, had ventured to inquire of Mrs. Yardley if she were aware of any plans the marquis had fomented regarding travel away from town. Mrs. Yardley had not, and though she was hardly concerned for her nephew's safety, she *did* wonder where he had gone, and for how long.

"I cannot think where Damien could have vanished to, my dears," she told Augusta and Caroline at breakfast one morning. "Everyone is *here* in London; there can be no reason for him to be elsewhere! Oh, dear, I do hope no one will ask us where he is, for it would give a terribly *odd* appearance."

Caroline pushed a half-eaten muffin about her plate, and said: "Do—do you suppose he is all right, ma'am? I gather such behavior on his lordship's part is unusual."

"Oh, Damien is well able to take care of himself," put in Augusta comfortably, and bit into another pastry.

"Yes, of course, but—" Caroline hesitated. "Ought inquiries to be made? For how long has his lordship been away, ma'am? Did his secretary know?"

"About a week, according to Mr. Petley," answered Mrs. Yardley. "The head groom said that Damien went out one morning in his curricle, and never returned."

A *frisson* of alarm danced up Caroline's spine. "I do not know a great deal about such matters, ma'am, but—but ought we to be anxious? There are, for example, the Bow Street Runners who—"

Mrs. Yardley surprised her by chuckling. "My dear! Your worry for Damien is commendable, but not, I am convinced, in the least bit necessary! He will turn up, you will see, right as rain and astonished that we would have troubled ourselves to fret about him!" She reached for the urn to replenish her teacup, and at this amiable chastisement Caroline fell silent, though the apprehension persisting within her could not, she knew, be so easily dismissed.

How long he had stood staring at the barren fields of Windemere, Damien could not have said. His mood was bleak; his temper, black. He felt as though he was waiting for something, although what that might be, he did not know, and this humiliating sense of his own ignorance only deepened his frustration.

Far in the distance, Damien caught sight of a doe and her tiny fawn, the former nibbling on the long, tender grass that grew abundantly on the edge of a copse of trees. Spring, he thought, was a subtle, subdued event in the city, having more to do with changes in weather and temperature than anything else; here in the country, however, it announced itself boldly and exuberantly: the forests were bursting with new, green growth, the air was mild and fragrant with the faint scent of wildflowers, birds chirped and sang, and the sky above him was a deep crystalline blue. It would have taken a man with senses far more dulled than were his own to have failed to acknowledge the beauty which surrounded him, yet the gnawing disquiet which ate at him made it all seem more of an impenetrable mystery than a simple pastoral scene to be viewed, admired, and forgotten.

"Good day, my lord," came a quiet voice, and with a start Damien turned to see his bailiff walking up the hill to come stand beside him at a respectful distance.

"Good day, Goodsall," returned Damien shortly. He braced himself for the certain outpouring of remonstrances and recommendations that was to follow. He had successfully avoided his bailiff for years, both in person and by ignoring his periodic letters.

Instead Goodsall said only: " 'Twas a surprise to learn you were come home, my lord. One of the lads in the stables told me of your arrival a few hours ago. Neither Milton nor Mrs. Dawkins having seen you in the house, I reckoned I would find you somewhere on the grounds."

"Your conjecture," Damien said, "was correct."

"It's quite a sight from here, isn't it, my lord?" Roger Goodsall lifted a brown, work-hardened palm to shield his eyes from the brightness of the sun. "So clear a day you feel as though you could see the whole world from here!"

Surprised at such a poetical flight from his bailiff, Damien glanced at him quickly, then just as rapidly regretted it, for it was then that Goodsall turned to face him directly. *Here it comes,* he thought sourly, and felt his countenance hardening.

"Are you planning a long stay, my lord?" Goodsall asked in his mild way.

More than a little taken aback, Damien said: "I hardly know."

Goodsall nodded equably. "Well, I hope you'll enjoy your time here, my lord. I won't be disturbing your solitude any longer then," he went on, and touched his fingers to the brim of his cap. "I only wanted to bid you welcome. Good day, my lord."

"Good day," repeated Damien, and watched in some bewilderment as the sturdy bailiff turned and began trudging down the slope.

Late one rainy afternoon Caroline was enjoying a rare moment of leisure in a small, cheerful saloon at the back of the town house, deep in a novel she had just taken from Hookham's Library—Miss Austen's *Sense and Sensibility*—when into the room burst Augusta, looking half-drowned but sparkling with good humor, with a wrapped package under her arm.

"My dear Caro," she cried, *"such* news!"

Swiftly Caroline put aside her novel, urgently wishing to inquire if Augusta brought tidings of Lord Reston's return. But, chary of too transparently revealing her feelings, she only smiled and said: "What is it, Gussie?"

"I have been to a *book auction!* At *Christie's!*"

A little doubtfully Caroline said, "Have you, Gussie? But—but—I had thought such things to be patronized only by gentlemen."

"Oh, yes, I suppose so," responded Augusta ebulliently, "but I had read a notice of its being held today in the *Morning Post,* and I was determined to attend! Aside from a few odd looks, no one paid me the least attention! And what do you think? I successfully bid on a first edition of Mary Wollstonecraft's *Vindication of the Rights of Women!* Not," she added scornfully, "that there was a great deal of competition for it! But it is mine now, and oh, what a prize, Caro! 'Why should women be kept in ignorance under the specious name of innocence? How grossly do they insult us who thus advise us only to render ourselves gentle domestic brutes?' Of course Mrs. Wollstonecraft *did* succumb to the pressures of society, and ended by marrying William Godwin and living a most conventional life, but what an inspiration her works have been to me! At first I couldn't believe how fine a copy was offered for sale, with the pages still uncut! I daren't unwrap it to show it to you just now, for I am dripping with rain and I do not wish for it to be damaged. Isn't it nearly time for tea? I'll go change my gown for a dry one, and meet you in the drawing room in a trice! Lord, what an absolutely *splendid* afternoon!" At the threshold Augusta paused, and said casually: "Oh, and by the bye, I met a young man there with whom I had the most *intelligent* conversation! Quite gentlemanly, and he seemed to know a great deal about books, though he didn't try to bid for any."

With that, Augusta disappeared, leaving Caroline to digest the implications of that last remark before she, too, rose to prepare for tea.

Chapter 10

Augusta halted on the threshold, and surveyed the room critically. "Why, it is nothing remarkable," she observed. "It is spacious enough, I suppose, but I would hardly call it one of the Seven Wonders of the World!"

"Augusta, pray lower your voice," begged Mrs. Yardley, urging her niece and Caroline further inside. "People don't come to Almack's for the *ambience,* but for—for the *cachet!* It is the dress, the jewels, the magnificence of the attendees themselves which makes it such an extraordinary place! And," she added proudly, "I fancy we may go amongst them with considerable assurance, my dears!" She gazed with approval at Augusta's stylish gown of shimmering jonquil sarcenet and at Caroline's white satin slip and crêpe overdress, which featured tiny leaves of the palest green embroidered around the low neckline, edging the short plaited sleeves, and circling the hem which seemed to float around her as she moved.

Caroline herself could not but be glad for the confidence lent to her by wearing such a splendid dress, and knowing she was looking at her best, for Mrs. Yardley had built up to such a crescendo of excitement about their first visit to Almack's that she had grown increasingly nervous as the hour approached. But here was Lady Jersey to greet them in the most amiable fashion, and Lady Cowper too, and then Charles Highcombe came strolling over to engage her in amusing badinage while Augusta, promptly importuned by half a dozen gentlemen, resignedly went off to dance, and Mrs. Yardley to investigate the card rooms.

"Dull as dishwater, ain't it?" said Mr. Highcombe, looking about him discontentedly. "A second-rate orchestra, and a few tables of lemonade and old cakes!" He caught Caroline's smothered laugh, and grinned sheepishly. "Yes, Miss Smythe, we both know why I'm here! Valiantly attempting to rescue the family fortunes and all that! Which reminds me, would you care to be introduced to my mother?"

"Mr. Highcombe, you terrify me," answered Caroline, only half in jest. "Would that not be a sad waste of her time, when there are heiresses to be interviewed?"

"Well, she's giving me the gimlet eye as we speak! You see," Mr. Highcombe confided, "she feels I ought rather to be bowing and scraping and in general making a cake of myself with the other young ladies, instead of standing here and enjoying myself with you! And rather than abandoning you like a churl, I thought I might conduct you to her, so that you could sit and converse!"

"Alas, caught between Scylla and Charybdis," murmured Caroline, then, when she perceived Mr. Highcombe to be looking at her in puzzlement, she went on, "You are very kind, sir! I should be glad to meet Mrs. Highcombe!"

Mr. Highcombe's mother proved to be an emaciated dame of some fifty years whose mien was, to say the least, glacial. Her reception of Caroline could not have been termed welcoming, and as she offered a few clipped, desultory remarks while keeping her eyes fixed firmly on her son's dilatory progress about the room, Caroline found herself pitying the poor maiden who was sooner or later to be brought into the Highcombe family fold. All at once she was surprised to see a girlish smile distend Mrs. Highcombe's withered cheeks, and that lady's fan spread wide and fluttered erratically.

"Why, Lord Byron! How *do* you do?" she said obsequiously, coyly stretching out clawlike fingers to be saluted, and Caroline looked up to see before them a man stepped straight out of classical antiquity, so finely chiseled were his features, so gracefully did his fringe of soft dark curls frame his astonishingly handsome face. His full red lips were parted slightly, and beneath heavy, provocatively lowered lids he stared at Caroline in a smoldering manner that seemed to her more than a little forward. So *this*, she thought, feeling rather more that she wanted to laugh than to faint, was the famous poet!

He ignored Mrs. Highcombe and said commandingly to Caroline, "They are playing a waltz! I wish to dance with you!"

"Thank you, my lord, but I do not dance."

"No?" His large brown eyes were stormy, and then he demanded abruptly: "Have you had any refreshments?"

It was an odd way to invite a lady to partake of a claret cup, thought Caroline; aloud she merely said politely, "No, my lord."

"Good! I do not like to see women eating, unless, perhaps, it is lobster or champagne. Come and talk with me then!" He held out a white, rather delicate hand, and Caroline, only too glad to depart from Mrs. Highcombe's side and confident her relief was shared by her, rose, and following a murmured farewell she permitted Lord Byron to take her to a nearby window, which was open to admit the refreshing night breezes.

"You are very beautiful!" his lordship told her, fixing his burning gaze upon her. "With those eyes—that hair! You are like a mysterious nymph of the woods! Why have I not seen you before? I have been longing to worship at such an altar of loveliness!"

Unmoved, Caroline said prosaically, "I am but newly come to London, my lord. I daresay that explains why we have not previously encountered each other."

"Every lost minute a tragedy! Tell me your name this instant! But only your Christian name; surnames are so rarely pleasing to the ear!"

"Caroline, my lord."

"Caroline!" he echoed, his white brow furrowing in a manner highly suggestive of a pout. "An unfortunate misnomer! I shall strive to forget it! *You,*" he pronounced dramatically, "are different from all the rest! I knew it from the moment I walked into the room tonight and saw you! I had been sad, and weary, but you have revived me, like a draught from a sacred mountain stream! You, sweet goddess, are a *woman!* No foolish airs, no simpering blushes!" He leaned closer and said in a low, thrilling voice:

> " 'Tis true, your budding Miss is very charming,
> But shy and awkward at first coming out,
> So much alarmed, that she is quite alarming,
> All giggles, blue; half pertness and half pout;
> And glancing at Mamma, for fear there's harm in
> What you, she, it, or they may be about,
> The nursery still lisps out in all they utter—
> Besides, they always smell of bread and butter."

He looked at her expectantly, and Caroline said solemnly, "Yours, my lord?"

"Yes," he returned carelessly, "I've just today tossed it off. Do you like it?"

"It is very cynical, my lord," she said.

"It is, isn't it?" he rejoined, sounding pleased with himself. Then, without warning, he added, "Well, good-bye!" and went off, and was soon absorbed into a slavish crowd of admirers.

Caroline watched appreciatively, and had barely mastered

the impulse to yield to a hearty peal of laughter when she was confronted by a short, slight, pretty young woman whose brown curls were cropped boyishly close to her head, and whose enormous eyes seemed far too large for her thin, sensitive face.

"He is mine, you know," she announced matter-of-factly.

"Is he?" said Caroline, fascinated.

"Yes. He is Paolo to my Francesca."

Recalling the famous line from Dante, Caroline could not resist quoting: *"Quel giorno più no vi leggemo avante!"*

"That day we did not read any further," repeated the young lady, and favored Caroline with a smile so blindingly luminescent that it verged on the irrational. "They think they are going to carry me off to Ireland, and that I shall forget him there! I shall never forget him! Never! Do you know what I wrote about him in my journal?" she asked suddenly.

Growing less intrigued and more uncomfortable by the moment, Caroline only shook her head.

"Mad, bad, and dangerous to know." She laughed shrilly. "Yet we were meant to be together! And if he should approach you again, you may tell him that Caroline Lamb *knows* what he is about!" With a swirl of her skirts she spun on her heel, and stalked away, conspicuously avoiding Lord Byron and his knot of followers.

Good heavens, thought Caroline wryly, *what a tiresome pair! How greatly they each deserve the other!* She moved back into the room and soon found herself in conversation with one of Mrs. Yardley's friends, who after wishing to know every syllable of her conversations with both Lord Byron and Lady Caroline Lamb (which Caroline discreetly described only as the merest exchange of civilities) next launched into an avid monologue concerning the Prince Regent's appalling treatment of both his wife and daughter, whom he kept sternly separated from each other, only permitting them to visit once a week.

"They may dine together, Miss Smythe, at the same table," said Mrs. Russell indignantly, "but never alone! Always in carefully selected company! Have you ever heard of such callousness toward one's own flesh and blood?''

Thinking of Lord Reston and his parents, Caroline made a sympathetic noise, and asked if Mrs. Russell had yet been to see the exhibition of Mr. Turner's paintings at the Royal Academy.

"Oh, to be sure I have!" replied Mrs. Russell. "Indeed, they are very handsome! Have you heard the latest *on-dit,* Miss Smythe, concerning Princess Sophia? They are saying she has given birth to an illegitimate child, and that its father is a *dwarf* some thirty years her senior! No one dares tell her father the king, for he positively dotes on all his daughters, and says they are all Cordelias! From the play by—by Sheridan, you know," she added informatively. "Of course, it would hardly matter if anyone *did* attempt to tell him, for they say he sits by the hour speaking with the spirits of the long dead, oblivious to any attempts to talk sensibly with him!"

"Indeed?" said Caroline. "Shall you be attending the queen's Drawing Room next week, ma'am? I am given to understand by Mrs. Yardley that it is one of the chief events of the season."

"Oh, yes, I always go! Did you hear that Mary Cole continues to plead her cause before the Committee of Privileges on behalf of her illegitimate son, so that he might inherit his father's title and estates? Oh, 'twas a romantic tale, Miss Smythe! She, a butcher's daughter, carried off by Lord Berkeley, only to be lured into a sham marriage, after which he proceeded to live with her as man and wife for twenty-five years! It is said he was unfaithful to her, and from time to time threatened to have her thrown off the property, but that despite all he loved her till the end! Once, when the butler spoke improperly to Mrs. Cole, Lord Berkeley had him fired upon the instant!"

"Very romantic," said Caroline, and excused herself. She had but taken a few steps when a slender gentleman, exquisitely dressed in sober black and white, his chestnut locks brushed into precise disarray *à la Brutus,* came up to her and bowed, saying in a pleasantly modulated voice, "For this past hour I have been desirous of making your acquaintance, ma'am, and thanking you for what I hope will be your salutary influence upon the fashionable world!"

"I, sir?" said Caroline, astonished.

"Indeed," he said with a small, friendly smile. "The simplicity of your gown, the charming mode in which you have dressed your hair, the utter lack of ostentation about your person, all combine to delightful effect. I can only pray that others will notice, and duly follow your example. To illustrate: do you not perceive Lady Mornington, the rotund female adjacent to that wilting potted palm? Lace, ribbons, tassels, a spangled scarf, *and* feathers, not to mention rubies, diamonds, *and* half a dozen cameos pinned here and there for good measure! Why does she not plant a British flag in her coiffure and have done with it?"

Privately Caroline was in complete agreement with his assessment of that lady's toilette, but only said aloud: "Sir, you are severe."

"Of course I am! As the arbiter of fashion I *must* be! I'm Brummell," he explained. "You must forgive my brashness for so boldly importuning you, but I have searched in vain for a lady who seemed to be your cicerone, and the patronesses yet remain occupied in greeting newcomers."

"How do you do, Mr. Brummell?" responded Caroline, thinking he well and truly earned his famous sobriquet of *Beau,* for the neat elegance of his appearance could not but solicit admiration. "I am Miss Smythe."

"Believe me when I say that it is a pleasure, Miss Smythe," rejoined Mr. Brummell with another of his congenial smiles. "Am I correct in thinking you are making your *début* at Almack's? I am certain I would have noticed you before."

"Yes indeed, it is my first time here."

"And what are your impressions thus far?"

Quickly Caroline reviewed in her mind what had transpired, and for the fourth time that evening she stifled an irreverent laugh. "It has been . . . interesting, sir."

"There is a wealth of meaning in that single word, Miss Smythe."

"Perhaps," said Caroline, returning his smile, and deftly turned the subject of the conversation to less potentially controversial areas.

They had been talking easily for some quarter of an hour on a variety of topics, when Mr. Brummell said suddenly: "I must leave you, Miss Smythe, for I have just seen a long-lost friend enter the room. May I say how greatly I have enjoyed our exchange?"

"I also, sir," Caroline said. He bowed gracefully and walked away; idly she watched him go, until abruptly her eye was caught by an iridescent flash of peach silk, and she saw Miss Manderlay, ethereal in a gown of sheer *mousseline de soi,* sweep past her into the dance, accompanied by one of her many satellites, this one a brawny gentleman sporting a luxurious mustache that drooped dashingly past his chin.

Naturally it was a waltz! Caroline thought, and was hard put not to enviously stare as Miss Manderlay glided about the floor, her skirts whirling fluidly about her and looking so lovely that Caroline might *almost* have wished to see her mustachioed companion tread disastrously on a flounce.

Damien had barely said "Good evening" to Lady Jersey before George Brummell strolled up and chided him for having lately made himself so scarce. Damien opened his mouth to reply but Brummell smilingly interceded.

"My dear Reston, do not attempt to fob me off with Banbury tales of urgent business! Prinny, you must know, is wholly convinced you have found a lady-love so monumentally captivating you have locked yourself in a boudoir somewhere, emerging only for the occasional meal.''

''Where *prowess* is limited, *imagination* must suffice!'' put in Lady Jersey roguishly, giggling.

Brummell laughed, and went on, ''But seriously! *Where* have you been, dear boy?''

''Elsewhere,'' said Damien. ''Sally, do you not think poor Miss Smythe ought to dance the waltz? See her there, with the toe of her slipper tapping with such poignant longing!''

''I *do* see her,'' Lady Jersey said. ''But I do not *know*, Damien, I do not *know* . . .'' She thought for a moment, then, her eyes sparkling with mischief, declared gaily: ''Yes, why *not?* I shall *tweak* a few noses by granting my permission, I suppose, but what care *I* for that? Go, then, for the orchestra has played through *half* the piece!''

''Thank you,'' said Damien, and with a nod to his friend Brummell he walked toward Caroline Smythe, who, as she stood watching the dancers, was not yet aware of his presence.

She was, he thought, even more enchanting than he had permitted himself to remember during his self-imposed exile. Her large, fine green eyes, thickly lashed, seemed yet more brilliant, her complexion more translucent, her slender, feminine form more lushly alluring. The prince might have been more right than he knew, for Damien *had* found a woman monumentally captivating—

No, he reminded himself firmly: he had come here tonight (having returned to his town house earlier in the evening and been apprised by Uxley as to the ladies' whereabouts) to test his resolve, to prove to himself that his feelings for Caroline Smythe sprang from a ludicrous infatuation, and that they would quickly fade were he to know her better. For, he had realized, he was barely acquainted with Miss Smythe; as with so many other things, he thought, with familiarity inevitably came disillusionment, and then the death-knell, boredom. Then, and only then, would he be free again, and himself again.

He drew near to Miss Smythe and, as if sensing his presence, she turned. He was not prepared for the dazzling smile which lit up her face and blazed from her eyes, but having steeled himself to confront his private demons, he responded with a more reserved smile and a small, elegant bow.

"How do you do, Miss Smythe?" he said.

"Lord Reston!" she said, sounding a little breathless. "You have come back! I was—that is, *we*—or rather, your sister and aunt—were—were so anxious about you! Are you well, my lord?"

"Quite well. I trust you are the same?" He looked into her upturned face, into eyes which glowed like living emeralds. This was going to be difficult, but surely, he told himself, it *would* get easier.

"Oh, yes! I am very well, thank you!"

"Lady Jersey has decreed that I might present myself to you as a desirable partner. Would you care to dance?"

Rosy lips parted in surprise. "Dance? With you, my lord? Oh, indeed! But—"

"Come, Miss Smythe, surely you would not wish to contravene Lady Jersey? It would be tantamount to refusing obeisance to the king." He was pleased at the light, teasing tone he had achieved.

At his words Miss Smythe dissolved into charming confusion, as warm pink color spread across her cheeks. "Oh, no, I should not want to—she has been so kind to me—very well then, my lord! Thank you! I should like to dance with you very much!"

"You do me great honor," he said, and held out his arm to escort her onto the floor. Moments later she had stepped shyly into his embrace, and a shock of fiery desire, hot and liquid all at once, ran through his body as he laid his hand upon her waist, and she placed her fingers into his own. Damien struggled to regain mastery of himself as they began moving together in time to the lilting rhythms of the waltz, as effortlessly as if they had danced together many times before.

Nothing was said between them for some time. On Miss Smythe's face was now a small, rapt smile, and Damien himself was too caught up with his own unruly emotions, and his ungovernable reaction to holding her so closely to him. Finally he said, in an effort to distract himself and so dispense with his turmoil, "You dance very well, Miss Smythe." A mere platitude, but it would suffice.

"Thank you, my lord," she replied, and added ingenuously: "I am enjoying it so much!"

"I am glad," he returned, with a semblance of his normal composure. "And are you equally enjoying your first visit to Almack's?"

A dimple peeped irrepressibly in one soft cheek, and demurely she said, "As to that, you must know, my lord, that tonight I have had my paeans sung by none other than Lord Byron himself!"

An answering twinkle of humor rose within him and he said gravely: "Lionized, Miss Smythe?"

"Indeed! As an altar of loveliness, a woodland nymph, *and* a sacred mountain spring! All this in the space of five minutes! *And* had a poem recited to me!"

With her face alight with humor, her white pearl-like teeth flashing as she laughed, Damien had never thought her more comely, and could hardly blame the poet for his extravagant praise. Aloud he said: "Why, I am all amazement, Miss Smythe, that having been raised to such celestial heights you lowered yourself to dance with a poor mortal like myself."

"Yes, after being showered with Lord Byron's encomiums I had thought to preen myself about a bit, but was brought sharply back to earth by Lady Caroline Lamb, who warned me that she was awake on all suits and would tolerate no interlopers. Good Lord! I wish them the joy of each other!"

"You do seem to be enjoying yourself, Miss Smythe, though

not in what I would believe to be the usual way,'' he commented dryly.

She laughed again. ''Well, my lord, after a painful interlude sitting next to Mr. Highcombe's mama, all else must by comparison send me into transports!''

''I perceive from that remark that you have renewed your acquaintance with poor ham-handed Charles.''

''Yes, and I assure you, my lord, throughout these weeks he has been the very soul of discretion!''

''Has he?'' Damien said, though he was careful not to let his own skepticism manifest itself in his tone. ''And so you have met the dragon-lady, as Charles and I were disrespectfully wont to refer to her as boys! Did she offer to bite off your head, Miss Smythe?''

Another peal of laughter. ''Why, no, my lord! Mostly she ignored me!''

''You were more fortunate than you know,'' he said, unable to repress an amused smile, and felt his heart jolt to see the responsive sparkle in those vivid green eyes. For a moment he forgot why he had sought her out tonight, and his fingers tightened urgently on her waist. Then, half to his relief, the music came to a close; they stopped, and the contact between them was broken.

''Thank you, Miss Smythe,'' he said formally, and, locating his aunt sitting amidst a dense, colorful cluster of middle-aged ladies chatting volubly, he there conducted Miss Smythe, and with another bow he left her.

As he walked away, Damien congratulated himself on the success of his endeavor. Despite a few missteps, he thought, he had not done too badly. He was almost looking forward to his next encounter with Caroline Smythe, which was sure to harden his heart even further. Nonetheless, he didn't wish to rush his fences: it was best to take his leave now, while he remained on firm ground.

''Reston,'' came a composed voice behind him, and he turned

to see Miss Manderlay, looking cool and elegant in softly draped silk, her shining blonde hair confined high on her head in a sleek topknot, coming toward him. At her side was the Earl of Audley, slim and debonair in the requisite knee-breeches and white cravat.

"Good evening, Helen," he said, and nodded at Audley. "Sir."

"How do you do, Reston?" came the earl's affable reply. "As I made mention to Miss Manderlay, I was not a little shocked to see you here! For you do not usually frequent Almack's, do you?"

Damien looked into Audley's pale blue eyes, and saw the lazy malice gleaming there; instinct warned him to tread warily. "No," he said without inflection, as he absorbed the fact that the earl was choosing, however covertly, to cross swords with him.

"I am sure it is very thoughtful in Reston to come see how Augusta does tonight," said Miss Manderlay.

"Yes, very brotherly," agreed the earl. "Might I compliment you on how well you dance the waltz, Reston?"

"It is not to be marveled at," interposed Miss Manderlay serenely, "for Reston is widely known to be a skilled sportsman and athlete, and these diverse talents would certainly foster in him the ability to be equally as accomplished in the art of dancing."

"Thank you, Helen," Damien said.

She smiled regally upon him. "It is only the truth, my dear Reston. We have rarely danced together, nor ever ridden together (for you know I do not care to expose my complexion to the brutality of the sun), but the tales of your Corinthian exploits, which the gentlemen assure me are much to your credit, are frequently circulated."

Damien only bowed, and the earl said: "Indeed, it is quite fatiguing merely to listen to a catalogue of your achievements,

Reston! I must confess I do not share your enthusiasm for the violent activity to which, apparently, you are addicted.''

"To each," said Damien coolly, "his own."

"Yes, there is no accounting for the peculiarities of taste," rejoined Audley, in his silky voice an undercurrent which set Damien's nerves prickling edgily.

"I had heard," said Miss Manderlay, "that you have been out of town, Reston."

"That is so."

"Business matters?" inquired the earl blandly.

"Matters requiring my attention," was all Damien said.

"To be sure! You need not worry that Miss Manderlay was repining in your absence, my dear fellow. I was but one of many who attempted in my small, modest fashion to help beguile the time until you should return."

"I suppose I ought to thank you."

At Damien's gently uttered words, Miss Manderlay's porcelain countenance betrayed the faintest trace of consternation, as her blue eyes moved from the earl to the marquis. "It is true, Reston, that I have seldom had an hour that has not been pleasantly filled, in one way or another," she said, in her tone a subtle note of placation. "My mother and I have been racketing about town (if you will forgive the cant expression!), for our calendars are quite filled, and we have thus had the opportunity to enjoy the company of many of our friends and acquaintances."

"But of course you have," said Damien imperturbably, and as he looked down into her crystalline blue eyes, he allowed the latent speculation that had long been lingering at the back of his mind to now come to the fore. Once she was the Marchioness of Reston, did Helen intend to take the Earl of Audley as her lover? She was too conventional a young lady to contemplate such an action while yet unmarried, but it was clear that she derived a particular pleasure from her relations with the urbane earl. Damien asked himself if he would care if she did embark on such a liaison—which, if discreetly conducted, would hardly be behavior worthy of comment among the dashing matrons of the *haut ton*. Instead of an answer emerging, however, he found that his gaze was inexorably drawn to Caroline Smythe, who sat far across the room amongst his aunt and her intimates, politely listening, her hands folded quiescently in her lap, her head attentively tilted. All at once her eyes found his, and Damien could not but be achingly aware of the sudden pulse that beat strongly at his throat.

"My dear Reston, I fear you are not attending," said the earl dulcetly, and Damien abruptly returned his attention to the other man.

"My pardon," he said.

"I merely observed that the orchestra has commenced the polka. Prior to your arrival, I had engaged Miss Manderlay for it, but I would be happy to relinquish my claims should you wish it."

"That will not be necessary," Damien answered, and after a brief bow he did not stay to watch them proceed into the dance, but turned away and, after exchanging the usual banalities with a handful of people whom he knew, leisurely he strolled out of Almack's, wondering, as he went, if Caroline Smythe had watched him go.

Chapter 11

Some days following that first visit to Almack's Caroline was awoken by a light persistent tapping on her door. Groggily she stirred in the darkness of her bedchamber, and called out:

"Come in."

The door opened and one of the maids entered, and with a little curtsy on the threshold she said rapidly, "Begging your pardon, miss, but Lord Reston is downstairs, waiting for you. He wants to know if you've forgotten that you'd made plans to go visit an old friend in the country today, and please could you make haste, for his horses are waiting?" She let out her breath in a rush, obviously relieved to have discharged such a long and complicated message.

Dazedly Caroline sat up, and pushed tumbled curls off her brow. "But we made no such—" Abruptly she broke off, and said instead: "What time is it, Meg?"

"Just past five-thirty, miss."

Caroline swung her feet to the floor and padded to the window, where she pulled back one of the heavy draperies. Sure enough, there was a curricle in the street below, with his lord-ship's handsome pair of chestnuts waiting patiently in the traces and a groom at their heads. She glanced at the sky. The soft gray of night was giving way to morning's blue; there was not a cloud to be seen anywhere, and it promised to be a beautiful day.

Her spirits lifting, Caroline let go of the drapery and said, "Some warm water, Meg, please, and quickly too!" As the maid bustled to obey, with eager steps Caroline went to her armoire and began contemplating the gowns that hung therein. She did not know what the marquis had meant by referring to plans to visit an old friend, but she wasn't about to let slip the intriguing opportunity which had so surprisingly presented itself. Still fresh in her mind was her memory of their waltz, and how it had felt to be guided with such grace and leashed power as together they moved in time to the music. It required no effort at all to relive the sensation of his strong hand settled intimately upon her waist, to recall the subtle scent of him, clean and faintly spicy and wholly masculine, to remember how it had felt to be held so close to him, almost as if within his embrace, against that tall muscular body—

A kind of languorous heat seemed to gather low in her belly, and spread sinuously to her lower limbs, pooling between her legs in molten, aching waves that were half pleasure, half pain, and left her feeling curiously empty, hungry, yearning for . . . for something she was certain only Lord Reston could give her. As if in a dream, Caroline slowly turned and looked at herself in the tall cheval glass that stood next to the armoire, and saw that her cheeks were flushed, her eyes sparkling and heavy-lidded, her lips as red as if she had dipped into the paint-pot. Wonderingly she raised her fingers to her breasts, to cover the tingling of nipples that had hardened beneath the thin cam-bric of her nightdress. The soft, rounded flesh she cupped seemed heavy to her, like some kind of succulent exotic fruit, and fever-warm. Would the marquis find her desirable? she wondered, feeling the throbbing staccato beat of her heart inside her. Would he like to stroke her breasts, and hold them in his own long-fingered hands? She stood very still and gazed into the mirror as if she could divine a reply from within its mysterious silver depths.

There was another tap on the door, and Caroline jerked her hands away, calling "Come in, Meg," and, feeling herself redden in embarrassment, she reached almost at random into the armoire and pulled from it a mint-green carriage dress as the maid reentered the room, carrying a basin which she carefully placed atop the washstand.

"Thank you," Caroline said, hearing in her voice a little betraying tremor which, thankfully, Meg seemed not to notice as she took from Caroline the gown and laid it out upon the bed.

"Will you be wanting your kid half-boots, miss, and that pretty parasol?" she asked.

"Yes, Meg, that would be lovely, and the straw bonnet with the green ribbons, please," answered Caroline, and bent over to gratefully splash water on her overheated face.

A third tap sounded, and a second maidservant entered with a tray. "Tea, miss, and a muffin," she announced. "The master said you'd likely wish for it before you left the house."

"Yes—how kind—" murmured Caroline, and hurried through her ablutions, then sipped at her tea and ate half the muffin after she slipped into the gown with its cascading white ruffles at the throat and cuffs and Meg methodically fastened the innumerable little buttons at the back. Swiftly Caroline brushed and dressed her hair, placed her bonnet atop her curls at a saucy angle, and slipped on the dainty half-boots; as she hastened down the stairs to the hall, carrying the long-handled parasol, a tiny reticule, a shawl, and her gloves, she thought to herself that no more than twenty minutes could have elapsed since she had received his lordship's discreetly couched invitation.

"You remain wonderfully prompt, Miss Smythe," came Lord Reston's deep, cultured voice, and as Caroline descended the final step she perceived him to be leaning casually against the door jamb that separated the hall from his library. His lordship was dressed in an exquisitely cut coat of dark blue superfine; his long athlete's legs were sheathed in tight, pale yellow pantaloons, with shining black Hessian boots pulled over them. On his handsome face was an expression Caroline was hard put to decipher: his customary mask of polite, slightly bored civility was in place, but his dark eyes held a hard, hot gleam that struck her as one of reckless challenge. It was, she realized suddenly, not unlike the stormy light that had sometimes seemed to glitter in his eyes that night at Almack's.

She did not speculate further on what his odd mood betokened; instead she said, "Good morning, my lord," and offered him a little smile. "Thank you for the breakfast which you thoughtfully had sent up to me."

He did not move from the door jamb, but only dipped his dark head in acknowledgment of her words. "I take it you are free to join me upon an expedition of some few hours? My sister and aunt can spare you this once from your daily round?"

"Yes, indeed," Caroline replied. "Lady Augusta is to be presented tonight at the queen's Drawing Room, you know, and Mrs. Yardley wishes for her to rest quietly throughout the day, and is even to release her from the duty of receiving callers." She added punctiliously, "I have left a note for her ladyship, and have promised to return far in advance of the time when I shall be needed to help her dress."

"So you shall," said his lordship, and pushed himself upright. "Then let us be off, Miss Smythe, for I do not like to keep my horses standing for too long."

Caroline assented, and within a very few minutes they were on their way, clattering briskly along still-somnolent streets. She glanced over at the marquis, who sat easily handling the reins of his lively, high-spirited pair, and said, "Pray enlighten me, my lord, as to the identity of the 'old friend' whom we are to visit!''

''As to that, Miss Smythe, I prefer to wait until the moment of reunion has arrived,'' replied his lordship. ''Have you ever been to Wimbledon?''

''No, my lord, but I understand it is quite a pleasant suburb.''

''Yes. I own some property there. My grandmother, who apparently believed my father would promptly sell it off to pay his gambling debts, instead left it to me. I am told he made a rather ugly scene at the reading of the will.''

''Did—did you know your grandmother well, my lord?'' Caroline ventured to inquire.

''No, she was bedridden in her later years, and was able to travel only once to Windemere during my own sojourn there,'' said Lord Reston. ''She was a handsome, formidable old lady, as I recall, and very imperious: but we liked each other.''

Caroline looked at him sympathetically. ''It was a pity she passed away while you were so young.''

''I daresay she would have grown less fond of me the older I became,'' he answered dispassionately. ''She lived in fear of seeing me grow up to become like my father.''

Caroline hardly knew how to respond to this frank statement, and fell silent. They traveled for some distance without speaking, until finally, as they passed the outermost boundaries of the city, she said, a little shyly, ''Mrs. Yardley asked me, my lord, if you had divulged to me during our conversation at Almack's your location during your recent absence from town. I was unable to satisfy her curiosity.''

''Or your own, Miss Smythe?'' he said.

''Or my own, my lord,'' she acknowledged quietly. ''I confess that I was—I was anxious for your safety, for no one seemed to know where you had gone.''

He shot her an enigmatic glance as they drew abreast of a lumbering cart filled with barrels of various sizes, and then he had skillfully passed the cart and they had the narrow road to themselves once more.

"Poor Miss Smythe! Did you picture me dead in a ditch somewhere, slain at the hands of a murderous cutpurse?"

"Indeed, I did not know what to think," she said, wondering at his ironic tone, for she was not at all sure that its mockery was directed at herself.

"Allow me, then, to relieve your mind of its ghastly imaginings." His countenance was unreadable as he went on: "I was at Windemere."

"Windemere!" Caroline exclaimed, unable to conceal her astonishment. It was the last place she would have guessed him to be.

"Yes, the ancestral home," the marquis replied dryly. "No doubt you are wondering how I managed to occupy myself, Miss Smythe. I rode a great deal, and spent many hours in the library reacquainting myself with its contents."

If he had not volunteered this surprising piece of information, Caroline might well have wondered how he had passed the time; she also wondered as to the significance of his visit—if any. What else had his lordship done while he was there? "Did—did you enjoy yourself, my lord?"

"Enjoy myself? Well, I like to ride, and I like to read, Miss Smythe, and I did discover some excellent bottles of vintage port, overlooked all these years, in a dusty corner of the wine cellar. If you mean did I tramp round the fields with my bailiff and rouse the servants into an orgy of cleaning and polishing, I am afraid you will be very much disappointed in me."

He spoke in that same strangely ironic fashion, and for a crazy moment Caroline thought she sensed in him a wild, deep unhappiness. She did not know how to comfort him, however, and afraid of his rejection, she said nothing, despising herself for her inarticulate timidity.

He, too, lapsed again into silence, and broke it only when they had traversed some very pretty countryside, and eventually turned into a gently winding lane lined on either side with blossoming apple trees. "This is Landsdowne, my grandmother's estate."

"But how charming!" Caroline said, with unforced enthusiasm. At the end of the rambling lane was a tall, rather narrow brick house whose outline was softened by the presence of two detached pavilions. Each of the three buildings featured row upon row of white-trimmed dormer windows and a cheerfully informal assortment of chimneys. The overall effect was unpretentious and inviting, and was heightened by the beds of bright flowers which surrounded the lower-lying pavilions.

"As you can see, my grandmother favored the Dutch style," remarked Lord Reston. "Evidently my grandfather, a relic of the Augustan age which preceded our own, wished to have it torn down and assign the great Adam to build a house upon more classical, statuesque lines. My grandmother protested strongly, and so Landsdowne was left unmolested. After my grandfather died, she came here, leaving, very properly as she thought, Windemere to the tender mercies of her son and his bride."

"Is the house tenanted, my lord?" asked Caroline, careful to avoid taking up the potentially tendentious subject of Windemere.

"No," said his lordship. "I cannot think my grandmother would have wished it to be occupied by strangers."

Caroline realized she must have been looking at him inquiringly, for he gave a short laugh and said: "Even a hardened reprobate, Miss Smythe, may cherish a faint trace of sentimentality. The farms, however, are let to the same family which managed them during my grandmother's day. It is to one of these farms that I intend to conduct you—if you think you can endure a rather rougher track."

"Certainly!" she replied stoutly, and some ten minutes later, after they had driven alongside the house and continued past prosperous-looking orchards and fields, they pulled up in front of a small, meticulously maintained cottage, half of which was draped in a delightful profusion of trailing roses, scarlet and white and pink.

Caroline was tightening the ribbons on her bonnet, which had been shifted awry at the jolting of the curricle, when from the cottage came a short, plump woman clad in simple blue dimity and a white apron which covered her from her collarbone to her ankles.

Smilingly she said: "Welcome, my lord, and you, too, miss! We had your note and have made the preparations you asked for, my lord. And here's Timothy, to take care of your lordship's horses!"

A man who was as lean as that lady was portly hurried round the side of the house to take the reins of the chestnuts, saying affably as he did so, "Good day, my lord! I'll give them water, and some hay if they want it!"

The marquis assisted Caroline to alight, and introduced to her Mr. and Mrs. Mills. The latter said courteously as her husband led the horses away, "The day's warm already, and you've traveled far, I know! May I not offer you some lemonade, or beer if his lordship prefers?"

"Miss Smythe?" said the marquis.

Caroline looked up at him and replied, "I confess I am so anxious to see our—our friend, my lord, that I would gladly postpone the partaking of refreshments! However, if *you*—"

"No, let us proceed at once," he said. "Mrs. Mills, if you will excuse us?"

"Of course, my lord! I'll be in my kitchen when you should have need of me."

Lord Reston held out his arm to Caroline and willingly she accepted it. Together they walked along a little tree-shaded path, past a flourishing garden and a handful of whitewashed outbuildings, and came next to a large fenced pasture of rich green grass in which some half a dozen horses of various sizes grazed. His lordship stopped, and so too did Caroline, reluctantly withdrawing her hand from his arm.

"My lord?" she said, mystified.

"Miss Smythe," he responded gravely, "do you forget your friends so soon?" He looked out into the pasture, and Caroline followed his gaze with her own. After a few moments, comprehension swiftly dawned, and she broke into delighted laughter.

"My lord!" she cried. "It is *Dolly!*"

So it was. Gone was the skinny, sore-infested creature of weeks past: in its place was a robust little donkey whose brown coat now gleamed with obvious good health, and whose brown eyes, inquisitively turned their way, were no longer dulled by hunger and frequent applications of the lash.

Caroline joyfully clapped her hands. "Oh, see what a beauty she has become! My lord, *what* a good thing you have done!" Beaming, she looked up into his face, and was surprised to see a flicker of emotions play there, yielding so rapidly to his usual reserve that she thought she might almost have imagined it.

"One of the few good things I have done, Miss Smythe," the marquis said, and for the second time that day she seemed to instinctively feel a stark unhappiness that tormented him.

"You have displayed toward *me* nothing but goodness," she said softly.

"Have I?" he said. "Of that I am not so sure."

"I do not understand you, my lord. In Baldock, you—"

"Pray do not launch into another catalogue of my heroic deeds," he interrupted. "Then you approve of the manner in which I have settled Dolly's future? The Mills have pronounced themselves very glad to have her, and tell me that she is an amiable companion to their other livestock."

Caroline tamped down a rush of hurt feelings at what struck her as a rebuff. After a moment she was able to say with tolerable equanimity: "Yes indeed, my lord. It is plain to see that she is perfectly happy here."

"Good," he said; then, after an uncharacteristic hesitation

he went on, "I had thought that before we return to town we might take a picnic to a pleasant bluff I know. It is but an easy stroll from here, and I believe Mrs. Mills has packed a basket for us."

Caroline's dampened frame of mind at once gave way to elation at the prospect of another few hours alone with his lordship. Too, she thought, perhaps she might come to learn what it was that seemed to trouble him so greatly. "I should like that very much, my lord!"

"Good," he said again, and in short order they were walking up a gentle hill that led, after some ten minutes, to a high grassy point which was enclosed by a rough semicircle of trees which lent both an agreeable canopy of shade and a natural seclusion. His lordship spread a blanket upon the grass and gratefully Caroline sank down upon it, then removed her bonnet and drew off her gloves.

"Mrs. Mills was right; the day *has* grown warm," she commented, and with a smile she took from the marquis the glass of cool lemonade he held out to her. "Thank you, my lord! It is—it is very beautiful here!" she went on, trying to not stare as the marquis pulled off his blue coat and laid it alongside her bonnet and gloves. She had never seen him without his coat, and now there was merely his fine lawn shirt and neckcloth to cover the bare flesh of his broad shoulders and what she was sure would be a tapered, magnificently muscled chest. Feeling her face flush hotly, deliberately Caroline fixed her eyes upon the view. "Do—do you come to stay at Landsdowne often, my lord? It must be a welcome respite from the city."

"No, I have never yet done so," replied the marquis. "Would you care for some cold chicken, Miss Smythe? Some salad? And here is bread, still warm, and a little pot of butter that Mrs. Mills informed me she had just this morning churned."

"It all looks wonderful," said Caroline appreciatively, accepting the filled plate he extended. Then, as he uncorked a bottle of red wine and tilted a long-stemmed glass her way,

"No, I thank you, my lord. I am content with this delicious lemonade."

"As you will." He served himself from the cloth-covered dishes, then poured a glass of the ruby-red wine. They ate in a silence which seemed to Caroline half companionable, half strained. She found herself staring at the colorful vista of fields and orchards that lay below them, when she would have much preferred to look at the marquis, who sat next to her in the Indian style, with his long booted legs comfortably crossed. At length they both finished, and set aside their plates; the marquis poured himself another glass of wine.

"That," Caroline said with a contented sigh, "was quite the nicest meal I've had in ages. I must remember to tender my compliments to Mrs. Mills!" Feeling satiated, and a little drowsy, daringly she uncurled her legs, careful to tuck her skirt around her ankles, and leaned back upon her elbows. Dreamily she admired the lone few puffs of white cloud slowly drifting across the blue sky, and thought how very like a lion one looked. Or was it a dog? And the other, next to it—did those curling puffs not resemble a smiling face, round and jolly? "How delightful it is here," she murmured, only dimly registering that her eyelids were becoming steadily heavier. "I shall be sorry when we must go. I do believe I could stay here forever . . ."

As Miss Smythe's soft voice trailed off, Damien turned his head to look at her. She had fallen asleep, and lay relaxed upon the blanket, with one hand resting upon the high waistline of her gown, the other loose at her side. Her lips, the color of a luxuriant rose in bloom, had parted slightly, and she breathed as lightly and as easily as a child.

But she *wasn't* a child, thought Damien, half-ashamed to find himself hungrily staring at her. She was utterly a woman, slender and ripe all at once, with her round, perfect breasts, tiny waist, and gently flaring hips all tantalizingly hinted at beneath the light, gauzy material of her dress. Desire, fiery

Take 4 FREE Books!

We created our convenient Home Subscription Service so you'll be sure to have the hottest new romances delivered each month right to your doorstep — usually before they are available in book stores. Just to show you how convenient Zebra Home Subscription Service is, we would like to send you 4 Kensington Choice Historical Romances as a FREE gift. You receive a gift worth up to $24.96 — absolutely FREE. There's no extra charge for shipping and handling. There's no obligation to buy anything - ever!

Save Up To 32% On Home Delivery!

Accept your FREE gift and each month we'll deliver 4 brand new titles as soon as they are published. They'll be yours to examine FREE for 10 days. Then if you decide to keep the books, you'll pay the preferred subscriber's price of just $4.20 per title. That's $16.80 for all 4 books for a savings of up to 32% off the publisher's price! Just add $1.50 to offset the cost of shipping and handling. Remember, you are under no obligation to buy any of these books at any time! If you are not delighted with them, simply return them and owe nothing. But if you enjoy Kensington Choice Historical Romances as much as we think you will, pay the special preferred subscriber rate of only $16.80 each month and save over $8.00 off the bookstore price!

We have 4 FREE BOOKS for you as your introduction to
KENSINGTON CHOICE!

**To get your FREE BOOKS,
worth up to $24.96, mail the card below
or call TOLL-FREE 1-888-345-BOOK
Visit our website at www.kensingtonbooks.com.**

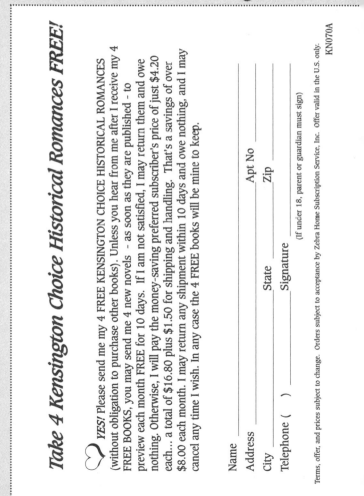

Take 4 Kensington Choice Historical Romances FREE!

YES! Please send me my 4 FREE KENSINGTON CHOICE HISTORICAL ROMANCES (without obligation to purchase other books). Unless you hear from me after I receive my 4 FREE BOOKS, you may send me 4 new novels – as soon as they are published – to preview each month FREE for 10 days. If I am not satisfied, I may return them and owe nothing. Otherwise, I will pay the money-saving preferred subscriber's price of just $4.20 each... a total of $16.80 plus $1.50 for shipping and handling. That's a savings of over $8.00 each month. I may return any shipment within 10 days and owe nothing, and I may cancel any time I wish. In any case the 4 FREE books will be mine to keep.

Name _____

Address _____ Apt No _____

City _____ State _____ Zip _____

Telephone ( ) _____ Signature _____

(If under 18, parent or guardian must sign)

KN070A

Terms, offer, and prices subject to change. Orders subject to acceptance by Zebra Home Subscription Service, Inc. Offer valid in the U.S. only.

PLACE
STAMP
HERE

ԼԼդ.ԼԼԼԼլԼԼ.ԼԼԼ.ԼԼ.ԼԼԼ.ԼԼդ.ԼԼԼ.Լ.ԼԼ.Լ

KENSINGTON CHOICE
Zebra Home Subscription Service, Inc.
P.O. Box 5214
Clifton NJ 07015-5214

and impetuous, coiled within him, tightening his stomach and making him feel as if his very bones and sinew were alight with urgent need. He drank half of his glass of wine, and wondered if she had noticed he had only told her that he'd never *yet* come to visit Landsdowne.

Once he had thought he could never offer her *carte blanche*. Today he had found his resolution wavering. Why should he not set her up as his mistress, install her at this cozy estate, and come to her whenever he wished? It would be a felicitous arrangement for them both. It was not an arduous journey from London, and she would like to live here. She as much as said so—

With a bitter smile he finished the last of his wine. What a fool he was to think that Caroline Smythe would so dishonorably give herself to him—and what a fool he had been to believe that he could so rashly spend time in her company and remain coolly aloof. It seemed that where Miss Smythe was concerned, his self-delusion knew no bounds. Clamping his teeth against a groan, Damien closed his own eyes, surrendering to the flood of loss and chagrin that threatened to swamp him in its dismal tidal flow.

"Oh, no, please!" Caroline Smythe muttered, and rapidly Damien opened his eyes and turned to look down on her. She still slept, but was dreaming now, and surely of nothing very gratifying, for her delicate, winglike brows were drawn tightly together and fingers which had before lain open had begun to clench spasmodically.

"Where is he? Oh, dear God, can no one tell me where he is gone to?" One of her hands lifted as if in appeal, then dropped again to her side. "General, I beg of you, do not make me go back! I have nowhere to go—nowhere at all!"

Without thought, wishing only to ease her distress, Damien reached out and rested his palm on the side of her face. "Caroline," he said quietly, "wake up. It is only a dream."

With a gasp she did awaken, and gazed up at him with wide

green eyes. "I—I am so sorry," she whispered disjointedly. "A—a nightmare—forgive me—it was nothing—"

"Hush," Damien said, "you are safe now," and he leaned down to softly press his mouth against hers, in a kiss that held everything of tenderness in it, and nothing of raw, selfish lust. It was meant to comfort, and to reassure, and to be the briefest of butterfly caresses. Only ... only Caroline Smythe's arms crept about his neck, tentatively at first, and her lips parted with an unmistakable alacrity beneath his own. Then, somehow, his tongue was lapping in teasing, provocative little strokes at her teeth and lips and tongue, and she gave a low moan, in so doing yielding to him even more of the intimate access he craved, and her fingers entwined themselves in his hair and were gripping it fiercely.

Damien's groan echoed her own cry of pleasure, and with almost desperate eagerness he lowered himself to the blanket so that his body was pressed against hers, chest to chest, hips to hips, legs to legs. She half-turned to meet him, supple within the arms he slid about her and seeming almost to purr when he again ravenously sought out her mouth with his own.

This kiss *was* raw, and blatantly needful, and this time her tongue, warm, wet, shyly questing, met his, then parried the deep thrust of his tongue with a sensual slide along his lower lip. A shudder of excitement ran down Damien's spine, and the hand that was splayed upon her back pulled her even more firmly against him. Through the fragile lawn of his shirt he felt the pliant delectable weight of her breasts, and at their tips the nipples as hard and erect as pebbles. His own manhood was equally as hard, and he knew she could not fail to be aware of its length pressed demandingly against her, at the tempting juncture between her thighs.

Her fingers had gone again to grasp at his hair, and to pull his head to her so that he might kiss her still more deeply. He groaned again, and complied, slanting his mouth hard against hers, and blindly he wished that he might bury himself completely within her. As if acceding to his unspoken yearning, she murmured incoherently, and he slid his hand around her back and along her rib cage, intending to catch in his palm the round fullness of a breast, and to avidly taste a nipple with his tongue and suckle at it through the hot, wetted material of her bodice until she cried out for mercy, then begged him for yet more. She did not resist as his hand curved along one smooth globe, and Damien knew then that nor would she resist were he to slide up her skirt and take her here, now, upon this grassy bluff.

This realization, though welcome in its way, acted as a kind of shock that sent his senses reeling. Just as he knew with absolute certainty that she would this afternoon give herself to him, freely and with an ardor that would match his own, he understood that she would do so because she wanted him. No, by God, more than that: because Caroline Smythe would only open her heart and her body to a man she loved.

His breath rasping harshly in his ears, Damien withdrew from her to murmur ''My sweet Caroline,'' and smooth back a tumbled auburn curl that had escaped from her coiffure. His hands, he perceived, were not quite steady as he sat up, and raked his fingers through his own hair. She would have offered to him a woman's ultimate gift because she loved him. It was a gift he had to refuse, for he . . . he loved her too much to accept it.

The full force of his own emotions burst upon him, like a long pent-up dam giving way, and irrevocably he let go the deceitful illusion that what he harbored for Caroline Smythe was akin to a mere calfling's infatuation. This was not, as he had arrogantly attempted to assure himself, a single instrument plucking out a reedy tune of fleeting lust; no, this was an entire orchestra playing rich and sweet and loud: this was a man's full complement of feelings for a woman he liked and respected and desired and cherished . . . and *loved,* body and mind and soul.

Joy and despair fought wildly within him for dominance. Joy, at the ecstasy of knowing that he loved and was loved. Despair, for no matter how passionately he might wish it were otherwise, he could never have her.

"My lord?" came her soft, puzzled voice. "D-Damien?"

He turned his head and saw that she too had sat up, and that in her huge green eyes were glistening unshed tears. He reached for her hand, then pulled away, too afraid of his own reaction were he to touch her again. "Ah, God, I have made you cry," he said, hearing in his voice the painful ache of remorse.

Carelessly she brushed at her eyes, and whispered tremulously, "Not because of—of what just happened. I can only— only be glad for it, I swear to you! I am so sad because I can see your unhappiness—can feel it as if it were my own!"

He looked at her in amazement. No self-pity from this magnificent woman, no missish reproaches, no hysterical accusations of seduction. Instead her concern was for him, only for him. *Christ!* Damien thought, his chest agonizingly tight. *The unbearable irony of it!* To find in one instant that your heart was for the first time in your life alive, and whole, and beating in unison with another's, and in the next moment to have that heart so completely, utterly broken. Again he stretched out his hand to her; then, overcome with hopelessness, he let it drop once more to the blanket.

"I can offer you nothing," he said hoarsely. "The immutable circumstances of my situation—"

"We need not speak of them," she interposed quietly. "You are not free, and may not with honor release yourself from your—your commitment. I understand that; I have always understood that. You have never attempted to mislead me in any way, and must not feel—culpable for what has transpired between us." She lowered her eyes, and said, very low, "I wished, very badly, for—for it to happen."

"I too," he said, and could not repress a heady flicker of pleasure to see the answering jubilation that blazed on her face at his words. He went on slowly: "Perhaps for as long as I have known you, though I hardly knew myself well enough to recognize that I was falling in love with you."

"Oh, my dear," she whispered brokenly, and now the tears did fall. Swiftly Damien gathered her to him, and held her as she wept, and gave her his handkerchief to dry her face, as he did so promising himself over and over again that it would be—*must* be, for the sake of his own sanity—the last time he ever held Caroline in his arms.

Chapter 12

Caroline nodded briefly at Uxley and would have hurried up the stairs to her bedchamber, all too conscious of her flushed face and red-rimmed eyes, but halted when the butler cleared his throat and spoke portentously.

"Mrs. Yardley has asked to see you, miss, as soon as you returned to the house."

"I—I am feeling a trifle unwell," Caroline said, keeping her head lowered so that the wide brim of her straw bonnet might help to shield her countenance, "and thought to lie down in my room. Pray, will you not so inform Mrs. Yardley?"

"Mrs. Yardley apprised me it is a matter of considerable urgency, miss," said Uxley. "You will find her in the Young Ladies' Drawing Room."

"Yes, very well," returned Caroline. "I shall need but a few minutes to—to change my gown; it is—it is soiled."

"According to Mrs. Yardley," intoned Uxley solemnly, "the matter is in the nature of an emergency, miss."

"An emergency?" repeated Caroline in some surprise. "But

what on earth could have happened since this morning? Has someone fallen ill, or suffered an injury?"

"I believe Mrs. Yardley's anxiety pertains to Lady Augusta," said Uxley, adding conscientiously: "As to her ladyship's health, miss, I could not tell you."

"Why can you not tell me, Uxley?" Caroline asked, for the first time feeling alarm rise within her. She was well aware of the fact that although the butler was colorless in both manner and appearance, little that went on in the household escaped his notice.

"Because, miss, her ladyship is not here."

"Not here? But I thought she was to—well, never mind that! I shall go at once to Mrs. Yardley. Thank you, Uxley!" Quickly Caroline went up the stairs and to the Young Ladies' Drawing Room, where she saw that Mrs. Yardley, rather than indulging in a comfortable nap upon the sofa, as was her afternoon habit, was pacing in obvious agitation about the small saloon.

"Mrs. Yardley, what has happened?" said Caroline, hastily unfastening the ribbons of her bonnet and casting it onto a small side-table.

"Oh, my dear Caroline!" cried Mrs. Yardley, and rushed to her, taking both Caroline's hands in her own. "It is Augusta! She has *gone!*"

"Gone?" Caroline was beginning to stupidly feel not unlike a parrot. "Do you mean that she has returned to Windemere, ma'am?"

"No! That is to say, I do not know!" wailed the older woman. "She could be anywhere! And tonight is the queen's Drawing Room! We shall all be *disgraced* by her absence!"

"Come, ma'am, let us sit on the sofa, and there discuss this at our ease," said Caroline soothingly, and drew Mrs. Yardley down next to her. "May I not ring for some tea for you?"

"No, for I am sure I could not drink a drop!" was the tragic reply.

"Very well. If you please, will you not divulge to me the entirety of the story?"

"Only that Augusta left the house sometime late this morning, without a word to anyone! Not to her maid, not to Uxley, much less to myself! In searching her room we found *your* note, my dear—did you have a pleasant drive with Damien? How kind of him to take you about, for it has proved to be quite a lovely day!—but no clue that might yield the slightest hint as to her destination! It is past two now, and the hairdresser is to come at four, and Madame Huppert at five to check all the seams of Augusta's gown and ensure that the hoops fall correctly, and the carriage is to come at seven, for there is bound to be the most dreadful crush, you know! It shall take us *hours* to make our way through the procession to St. James' before we are able to alight from the carriage, much less leave our wraps and push on to take our places in line! If she is not back within the hour I do not know what we shall do! Oh, Lord, do you suppose it is because of the hoops, Caroline? She protested so vigorously against wearing them! But one *must*, as I told her! I could not but agree with her that they are cumbersome, and sadly outdated, and so awkward to move about in, but there is nothing to be done for it! Perhaps she did not diligently practice her curtsy as I requested, and now, upon the eve of her presentation, she fears failure and has fled in mortification! Oh, my poor Augusta! I have pushed her too hard, and she has tumbled over the brink! This is *dreadful!*" Then Mrs. Yardley turned wide, horrified eyes to Caroline. "You do not suppose—oh, it is too wretched a thought!—you do not suppose Augusta might have cast herself into the Thames, as I have heard of other desperate young women doing when they believe life holds no other recourse for them?"

"No, indeed, I am quite sure she has not," replied Caroline consolingly, patting Mrs. Yardley's hand, though privately she could not but wonder what sort of odd start had taken possession of her friend.

* * *

"Well! I do not know when I have enjoyed a walk so much!"
said Augusta cheerfully. "It is one thing to stroll about and
abstractly enjoy the beauty of nature, but to have such-and-
such a tree pointed out to one as an elm, and such-and-such a
one as a beech, and to be enlightened as to the names of the
resident birds and have classified the clouds that float overhead—why, it is *considerably* more interesting!"

Thomas Culpepper modestly ducked his head and returned
her beaming smile with a shy one of his own. "As to that,
Lady Augusta, I have long considered myself to be a naturalist
of sorts—the merest amateur, of course, but my studies of the
natural world have never seemed to me to be *work,* but pleasure
only."

" 'Beauty is Nature's brag,' " quoted Augusta, " 'and must
be shown / in courts, at feasts, and high solemnities.' "

"Milton," said Mr. Culpepper instantly, and went on:

> "All nature is but art, unknown to thee;
> All chance, direction which thou canst not see;
> All discord, harmony not understood;
> All partial evil, universal good;
> And, spite of pride, in erring reason's spite,
> One truth is clear, Whatever is, is right."

Augusta wrinkled her brow for a few moments, thinking
hard. Then, triumphantly: "It is Alexander Pope!"

"You are right, my lady," said Mr. Culpepper, smilingly.

"The verse is very pretty, but I fear I cannot condone Pope's
sentiments," she said thoughtfully. "To say that 'Whatever is,
is right' suggests a profound complacency. There are far too
many problems in the world, and to remain immune to them
seems to me nothing less than a crime!" She took a deep breath
and went on, almost defiantly, "For example! Concerning the

education of women! It is my *strong* belief that a great deal needs to be accomplished!'' She looked into Mr. Culpepper's face—heavens, how pleasant it was to be able to look *up* into a gentleman's eyes, and especially into ones such an appealing shade of greenish blue!—and was more than a little relieved to see that he was nodding his head emphatically.

''I am in complete agreement with you, my lady.''

''Oh?'' responded Augusta hopefully, and listened happily as Mr. Culpepper shared his views on the subject. Remarkably, they were quite aligned with her own, and he expressed himself, she thought approvingly, with a nice mixture of temperance and zeal. Emboldened, she told him of her desire to someday establish a female seminary—a plan he entered into with gratifying enthusiasm—and they passed an agreeable interlude discussing the ideal curriculum for such an establishment. However, while they both concurred that mathematics, philosophy, Latin, Greek, and French were naturally to be included—as well as the usual instruction in reading, writing, composition, history, and geography—Mr. Culpepper pushed eloquently for courses in logic, metaphysics, and astronomy, while Augusta was more concerned with the range and depth of literature that was to be studied, from the ancient writers to the contemporary.

''There are only so many hours in the day, my lady,'' argued Mr. Culpepper, ''and one must be careful not to press forward too rapidly with tender young minds. Would it not be preferable to simply make available to the pupils a variety of books and periodicals—carefully selected as to suitability, of course— and permit them to be read during times of leisure?''

''Of course! There shall be an extensive library! But one cannot effectively learn about and grow to love literature in isolation, you know! *That* would be akin to giving someone who knows nothing about plants a handful of seeds and instructing them to cultivate a garden!''

''Your point is well taken,'' admitted Mr. Culpepper, and added with a boyish grin, ''Are we then, perhaps, creating far too demanding a schedule for our poor young ladies? Within a week they shall be pleading for classes in lace-spinning, deportment, and cooking!''

Quick to note his use of *we* and *our,* Augusta was conscious of feeling a warm glow of camaraderie. She gave the gloves she held in one hand (for it was such a warm and pretty spring day that it seemed a shame to be stifled in kid gloves that only made one's palms perspire) an exuberant little twirl and said, laughing, ''As for cooking, sir, I am not so sure that would not be a splendid addition to our curriculum! I have often thought that were I better informed on the subject I might have on more than one occasion dropped a useful hint in Cook's ear, for she burns both fish and fowl with equal disregard!''

Although Mr. Culpepper smiled at her light rejoinder, and said, ''Indeed, a burnt roast set before one does little to stimulate the appetite!'' Augusta perceived a new constraint in his manner, and asked bluntly: ''Sir, what is it I have said to offend you?''

''Nothing, my lady, I assure you,'' came the swift, courteous reply.

''No, pray do not fob me off with polite reassurances! Though we have known each other but a brief time, you cannot fail to have observed that I am a proponent of plain speaking! Moreover, I realize that I am all too capable of saying disastrously *gauche* things, and I should be wretched to think that I had in some wise given insult.''

''By no means! It is *I* who should be begging *your* pardon, my lady!'' Mr. Culpepper exclaimed. ''It is only my own foolish sensitivity which rendered me so Friday-faced! It is just that—''

He broke off awkwardly, and earnestly Augusta said: ''Just what?''

Mr. Culpepper came to a halt on the path on which they had been ambling, turned to her, and said haltingly, ''Your chance comment regarding your cook, my lady, must only remind me of the immense difference between our respective stations in life, and make me question the propriety of permitting myself to indulge in this opportunity to converse with you.''

"Propriety!'' said Augusta scornfully, and snapped her fingers. "Pooh! I care *that* for it, sir!''

"As much as I sincerely admire your liberal turn of mind, Lady Augusta, I myself am not in a position to disregard the social niceties.'' He squared his shoulders and continued determinedly: "I will not dissemble, my lady, regarding my own background. I am but the third son of a country parson, raised in circumstances which, though perfectly respectable, were, I shall not scruple to tell you, humble! In my youth my schooling was inferior, and as my father's duties were onerous I was largely self-taught. Happily for me, one of the passions of the local squire was collecting books, and he generously allowed me to quite haunt his library! I was able to attend Cambridge only by dint of the strictest economy on the part of my family, and by the occasional assistance from one of my uncles, who prospered in the Norwich cloth trade; and, of course, I sought employment as a tutor during the holidays. Now that my studies are complete I am presently attached to the family of Sir Everard Richmont, helping one of his sons prepare for admittance to Eton. His mother being excessively fond of young Humphrey, she has brought him—us—to London so that she might oversee his care while she and her husband participate in the season's activities. My charge, however, being of what Lady Georgianna is convinced is a sickly disposition, I am frequently released from my duties and am free to amuse myself as I see fit. I hope to take orders in the fall, assuming that I am able in the meantime to secure a curateship for myself.'' Mr. Culpepper concluded this speech with a stiff little bow, his hazel eyes at once proud and anxious as he looked down into Augusta's face.

"Well, that is quite a lot of information to digest,'' said Augusta, "but if it was intended to put me off, I am afraid it sadly missed its mark! You are to be congratulated on your enterprise, Mr. Culpepper, for it is abundantly clear that you have worked harder than *I* ever have in my life, and you make me feel quite ashamed of the little I have accomplished!''

''It was not my intention to compare my accomplishments with yours, my lady,'' he returned gravely. ''I only wished to lay the truth before you, so that there might never be a question of false pretenses between us.''

''As the old English song goes, it is good to be honest and true,'' said Augusta, smiling, then all at once she found her gaze locked with Thomas Culpepper's, and she became aware of an odd fluttering in her insides. *Heavens,* she thought vaguely, *it must be the rumblings of an empty stomach, for I do believe I've missed my lunch. Oh, good God! Lunch!* ''What time is it?'' she blurted out, then fortuitously had her answer when a church somewhere in the vicinity tolled once, twice, thrice.

Augusta clapped a hand to her cheek in dismay. ''Oh, Mr. Culpepper, I fear I have lost track of the time, and am now *exceedingly* late! My aunt has probably gone off into apoplexy by now! I must return home at once!''

His expression was concerned as he said promptly: ''Then may I not walk you home, Lady Augusta?''

''You are very kind, sir, but in the interest of expediency I believe I had best find a hackney!''

''Let us go straightaway,'' he said, and within a very few minutes he had efficiently hailed for her a hackney cab. Augusta hastily gave directions to the driver, and Mr. Culpepper handed her up. ''Thank you!'' she said, and then found herself strangely reluctant to withdraw her bare hand from his when he did not immediately release it.

''I do not know if it is right to ask it of you, my lady,'' he said, ''but I should very much like to see you again,'' and once more Augusta felt that curiously unsettling sensation tickling inside her.

''Yes, I should like that too!'' she said. ''But—''

"I know that I may not call at your house," he interrupted. "However, might we not meet somewhere about town?"

Augusta thought fleetingly of Aunt Violet, and how wholly reprehensible she would consider her niece's behavior this day. Then she focused again on Thomas Culpepper's earnest blue-green eyes, now on a level with her own, and after a moment she answered decisively.

"Thursday next! I am to have tea with Mrs. Bulwer, and as Aunt does not care for her modern views she will not come with me. I shall stay but briefly: will you wait for me at the steps of her house?"

"With great pleasure," replied Mr. Culpepper, and tightened his hand over hers.

Suddenly feeling the heat of the day quite particularly, Augusta told him Mrs. Bulwer's address; he released her, said, "Until Thursday, my lady," and shut the door of the cab. "Good-bye," called Augusta, and then they were rattling briskly down the street.

She leaned against the squabs and energetically fanned herself with her gloves. Good heavens, but it felt like summer already! And oh, how Aunt was going to scold! Then there was to be the tedium of dressing for the queen's Drawing Room, and the long, drawn-out vapidity of the event itself— but then only a few days until she was to take tea with Mrs. Bulwer . . . How pleasant it was, Augusta thought, to have something to look forward to! And she hummed a gay little tune as the hackney rolled toward Grosvenor Square.

After much persuasion, Caroline finally succeeded in coaxing Mrs. Yardley to take a few sips of tea and nibble on some toast, and then to lie back on the sofa and permit a cool cloth to be laid on her forehead.

"Oh, that does feel refreshing, my dear," Mrs. Yardley murmured feebly. "My temples are positively *pounding*. Might you shift the cloth to the left a trifle? There! That is just right; thank you. I am sure I do not know when I was last laid so low, for in general I would consider my constitution to be quite robust. Of course, there *was* that little episode with dyspepsia last week, but the blame for that may safely be heaped upon Lady Donleavy's head! It was the turtle soup, I am convinced of it! Or, possibly, the turbot. Did you partake of either, Caroline? No? How wise of you, for I can remember thinking to myself that there was something the least bit *off* about those dishes, and the pickles, too! However, the chamomile tea you brewed worked wonderfully well, and I was on my feet again in a trice, as good as new!'' She paused thoughtfully. ''Now I am thinking of it, I *did* have a cough earlier in the month, as I am sure you will recall, but 'twas the merest trifle, and *not* pleurisy, as I at first feared. However, that rash I suffered prior to the cough gave us all a scare, did it not? I vow I was only *waiting* for the fever and the delirium to arrive, announcing itself as typhus! Napoleon, you know, is said to have lost many thousands of his men to it last winter during their retreat from Russia. I am sure I feel dreadfully sorry for them, even though they *are* our enemy. Only think how their wives and children must have felt! No, typhus is not to wished upon anyone, and I can only be glad at how narrowly I evaded it. It was a most peculiar rash, wasn't it? I declare I had *welts* everywhere, and oh, the agonies I endured at their itching! I cannot think, as Augusta insisted, that it was due to that lilac-scented powder I purchased at the apothecary's. Nonetheless I refrained from subsequent use and the rash did, thankfully, subside, and my Clara seems content to have ownership of it now. Do you like the new way in which she dressed my hair? I own I thought it a trifle *jejune* at first, but I have received so many compliments on it that I am quite overborne!'' Suddenly Mrs. Yardley's eyes popped open, and she sat bolt upright on the sofa. ''Hark! I hear the door! And there—do you not hear the pounding on the stairs? Only Augusta would be so unladylike as to tear up them in that hurry-burly fashion!''

Sure enough, Augusta herself burst into the room and ripped off her bonnet, crying ''Hello, Aunt! Hello, Caro!'' It was a penitent niece who leaned down in order that she might be enveloped in her aunt's embrace, dutifully submitting to both remonstrations and tearful expressions of anxiety as to her welfare.

''Yes, I know, I am *hideously* sorry to have been so late!'' she said, patting Mrs. Yardley's shoulder. ''I only stepped out to hear a lecture on mnemonics, fully intending to be back by luncheon, but—well, I regret giving you cause for alarm, Aunt! When is the hairdresser to arrive, and Madame Huppert? Have I time to eat? For I swear I'm famished!''

The remainder of the afternoon passed in a frenzy of activity as Augusta and Mrs. Yardley, surrounded by various attendants, readied themselves for the queen's Drawing Room, and it was only as Augusta was about to follow her aunt out the door that she stopped at Caroline's side and whispered, her dark eyes sparkling, ''I cannot *wait* to divulge to you the whole of my adventure, Caro!'' Aloud she said, ''Oh, *blast* these hoops!'' and negotiated the doorway with such impatience that she nearly exposed the whole of her white silk petticoat to public view.

''Augusta!'' came Mrs. Yardley's anguished bleat, and shortly there followed the sound of the Reston carriage moving slowly through the street, already crowded with other fashionable vehicles bound for their respective destinations.

Caroline spent the evening in her bedchamber, attempting to finish *Sense and Sensibility,* but found that the words on the pages refused to be translated into meaningful sentences. Instead, vivid memories of her day with Lord Reston continued to willfully intrude, and with them emotions that made her feel both exalted and desolate. He was in love with her, he had said it in a slow, wondering voice that could leave her in no doubt of his sincerity! And the kisses they had shared, the fiery, magnificent kisses that exceeded even her wildest imaginings: she knew they branded her heart as forever belonging to him. And yet—

There was no future for them, and no hope. Worse, the present held nothing but heartache, for even the most superficial of exchanges between them would remind them of how utterly they were bound to travel on separate paths, would painfully remind them of what could never be.

Tears trickled down Caroline's face, and dripped unheeded onto the pages of her book, as she faced again the relentless truth of her situation. In a few months the marquis would marry Miss Manderlay, and she would be alone.

Again.

At last she swiped a handkerchief across her damp face and blew her nose. *You have become a veritable watering-pot, my girl!* she chided herself, and dabbed with her sleeve at the wetted *Sense and Sensibility* still open in her lap. *Try to act less like Miss Austen's poor overwrought Marianne, and more like sensible, prudent Elinor!*

Despite this bracing recommendation, a troubled, nearly sleepless night ensued, and it was with heavy, dark-circled eyes and a pale face that Caroline made her way downstairs to breakfast the following morning. There she found Augusta already seated at table, a plate heaped high set before her.

"Good morning, Caro!" said Augusta cheerfully. "You *must* try the apricot tarts; they are divine!" And suiting action to words, she sank her teeth into a flaky crust and rolled her eyes ecstatically.

"Good morning, Gussie," Caroline replied, hoping she did not seem too obviously wan as she took her place opposite Augusta and poured herself a cup of tea. "How did you fare at the Drawing Room?"

"Oh, it was very dull, as I expected! I met the queen—who was very kind, but seemed rather distracted—and some of the princesses, and then Aunt and I milled about in our finery until

I thought I should drop from the heat! Of course we couldn't sit down, because of our dratted hoops, and there was such a crush we could never make our way to one of the rooms where we might secure a cool drink for ourselves, and as everyone was chattering away at the top of their lungs the din, my dear Caro, was truly indescribable! Of course Aunt had a wonderful time,'' she added in closing, and finished the apricot tart.

"Well, you have done your duty, Gussie,'' said Caroline, summoning up a smile.

Augusta laughed. "Indeed I have! Even Aunt said so! And *now,* Caro, should you care to learn why I was so awfully late yesterday?''

"Very much so.''

"Do you recall the book auction at Christie's I attended, where I purchased a copy of *Vindication of the Rights of Women*? I believe I mentioned that I had encountered quite a pleasant young gentleman there? Well, what do you think? He was at the mnemonics lecture! I could not help but notice him afterwards as we all stood up to leave, for he is quite splendidly tall, you see, and somehow we happened to spot each other at precisely the same moment! And then it seemed the most natural thing in the world to find ourselves crossing through the doorway at the same time, and nearly bumping into each other, and by then it was silly not to introduce ourselves! His name is Thomas Culpepper, and he is impressively well informed on a *vast* number of topics. We walked through Hyde Park, and you would be amazed, Caro, to see how much he knows about trees and plants and birds and insects! I know *I* was! At any rate, we had the most delightful conversation, and before I knew it the clock had struck three!''

"Indeed, Gussie, he sounds a most interesting young man,'' was all Caroline said. While she was pleased to hear that Augusta had enjoyed herself, there was no denying that Mrs. Yardley would vehemently disapprove of Augusta's unconventional conduct, and Caroline could not but question whether it was her responsibility to make mention of the fact. She was forestalled, however, when Augusta rejoined good-humoredly.

"You are thinking, dear Caro, that I have acted the complete hoyden! I suppose I have, but I cannot regret it, for I liked Mr. Culpepper enormously! Though not of the Upper Ten Thousand, his family is perfectly respectable, I assure you, and he is as much the gentleman I had thought him to be at our first meeting! And," she added, "I am to meet him again, on Thursday afternoon!"

Caroline regarded her friend across the tabletop. There was that pretty sparkle in her eyes again, and she spoke with an ebullient determination that made it clear she would brook no objections to her plan. Hesitantly Caroline said: "How are you to meet your friend, Gussie? Mrs. Yardley—"

"Oh, Aunt is to know nothing about it," replied Augusta carelessly, "for I am to take tea with Mrs. Bulwer—do you recall meeting her at the Thornboroughs' levee? She is the widow of General Bulwer, and the most delightful woman! She is a painter and a poet, and terribly learned! You are welcome to come with me, you know, for she specifically included you in her invitation! Aunt will not join us, as she does not approve of Mrs. Bulwer's 'free and easy ways,' as she terms it—I believe she heard a rumor that Mrs. Bulwer has been known to publicly wear *drawers* and was scandalized. She cannot cut the acquaintance, however: Mrs. Bulwer's circumstances are unexceptionable, and though Aunt will not *like* for me to go to her house, she will not *forbid* it! Mr. Culpepper is to wait for me at the steps of Mrs. Bulwer's house. It is unfortunate that he may not come here, but it does not matter in the slightest!" She picked up a buttered muffin half, bit into it, and after a pause said thoughtfully, "Do you know, Caro, it occurred to me this morning as I was dressing that there is something to be said for wearing gowns that are tailored to fit one's form. It is very strange, but I never used to care about such things before we came to London."

Augusta went on to vivaciously describe the high points of yesterday afternoon's mnemonics lecture, and Caroline quietly sipped at her tea, wondering if Augusta realized how her seemingly irrelevant remark about clothing revealed quite a great deal about the current state of her mind—and also, perhaps, her heart.

Chapter 13

A pleasant silence filled the drawing room. Mrs. Yardley was happily engaged in reading the numerous cards of invitation that had just arrived; Augusta sat on one of the sofas, immersed in a massive volume of *The London Flora*. Her wicker workbasket set on the carpet near her feet, Caroline was setting small, neat stitches into the hem of one of Mrs. Yardley's day dresses, which had been torn on a recent expedition to the Picture Gallery in Pall Mall.

"Carnations and auriculas—h'm!" murmured Augusta absently, and flicked the page over with her forefinger.

Caroline glanced at her, then bent her head again to her sewing. It was Thursday morning, the day upon which they were to go to Mrs. Bulwer's house. It was with considerable interest that she observed that Augusta had come downstairs wearing a pale pink walking dress of fine French cambric, trimmed with wide, delicate frills of lace, which previously she had scornfully rejected as schoolgirlish. It became her tall, statuesque figure admirably, and gave a soft glow to her white skin. Caroline had refrained from comment, however, and had silently continued to debate with herself as to whether she ought to plead with Augusta to refrain from participating in a clandestine tryst. On the one hand, Augusta was a grown woman who was more than capable of making her own decisions. On the other hand, Caroline was, at least nominally, Augusta's companion, and should she not, therefore, make a push to ensure that her charge did not knowingly precipitate herself into some kind of dreadful scrape?

Her preoccupied reverie was broken when Mrs. Yardley uttered a triumphant "At *last!*"

Augusta looked up from her book. "What is it, Aunt?"

Her face wreathed in smiles, Mrs. Yardley waved a stiff, gold-bordered card in the air. "We have finally been invited to Carlton House, my dears! I had been wondering if we were to be summoned to one of the prince's soirees, but did not like to mention the possibility to you for fear we should not be. Of course, as Damien is one of the prince's intimates, I should have thought it wonderful if we were *not*, but—well, one never knows, after all, and we may now consider this invitation to be the final jewel in our crown!"

"A florid metaphor," commented Augusta dryly.

Mrs. Yardley paid her no heed, only continuing rapturously: "You and Caroline both must have new gowns, of course. We shall have to pay Madame Huppert a ruinous fee to make them so quickly, I daresay, but you cannot be seen at Carlton House in dresses you have worn before! I suppose *I* shall have to have a new one as well, although there *is* my new burgundy silk which *might* suffice. If I had some beads sewn onto it, perhaps . . ." She trailed off meditatively, and only then did Caroline speak.

"My dear ma'am, surely you do not mean to include me in your party? You have been more than magnanimous in taking me about with you, but I cannot think it would be appropriate for me to join you at such an illustrious fete."

"Oh, but you are invited too!" Mrs. Yardley informed her.

"I?" said Caroline, shocked. "But—" She broke off. Had Lord Reston dropped a word in someone's ear at Carlton House? And if so, why? Such an encounter would bring neither of them joy, save for the brief, bittersweet pleasure of glancing into one another's face. She shook her head slightly, as if to clear it of her confusion. It was useless to speculate precisely how her name had appeared on the coveted list of invited guests.

"Well, my dears, shall we repair to Piccadilly?" said Mrs. Yardley briskly. "I should like to see Madame Huppert's fabrics immediately. New gloves will be in order, and perhaps stockings as well, so there are a few shops and warehouses we should visit while we are in the area."

At that, Augusta, whose attention had returned to *The London Flora*, again looked up. "I cannot, Aunt," she answered. "As you know, I am shortly to take tea with Mrs. Bulwer—and Caro, too, if she wishes it."

Mrs. Yardley sighed impatiently. "That wretched Mrs. Bulwer! Can you not go another time, Augusta? We must commission your new gowns at once, you know, for the soiree is but a week away."

"I am sorry, Aunt, but I could not be so discourteous; she is expecting me," said Augusta, so firmly that Mrs. Yardley sighed again, and rose to her feet, saying resignedly:

"Very well! I shall go myself, then, and inform *madame* as to what shall be required. However, you *will* accompany me tomorrow?"

"Oh, yes, to be sure, whenever you like," came the airy reply, and then Augusta was lost once more in her book.

Mrs. Yardley exchanged a speaking glance with Caroline, who smiled and gave a little shrug, and picked up her sewing. After Mrs. Yardley departed in a flurry of kerseymere and carelessly dangling shawl, it was silent again in the drawing room. Caroline's thoughts flew as fast her needle, until finally her mind was made up and she said:

"Gussie."

"M'm."

"Gussie, I need to speak with you."

"M'm."

"Gussie!"

At last Augusta lifted her head. "Whyever are you shouting at me, Caro?" she asked reproachfully.

Caroline could not repress a smile of rueful amusement, which quickly faded as she began, "I hope you will not be angry with me, Gussie, but—but I do not wish to go with you to Mrs. Bulwer's. As much as I am sure I would enjoy the company and the discussion, I would not want to be a party to any subsequent subterfuge or—or deceit." She drew a deep breath and went on, "How, for example, are we to coordinate our return to the house? How, if there were to be a miscalculation, would I explain to your aunt the discrepancy if she should get wind of it?"

To Caroline's surprise Augusta said warmly, "Oh, my dearest Caro!" and, putting aside the heavy volume, jumped to her feet and came to the chair in which Caroline sat to embrace her affectionately. "Why on earth should I be angry with you? I can but admire your scruples, and be grateful that you do not offer to scold me for behavior which I know is *risqué!* Though I am sorry you will not come with me to tea, I should be unhappy to have you do so knowing that *you* were unhappy. You are a *true* friend, and I thank you equally for your concern and your tacit support!"

"I confess that I am not so comfortable with the tacit support, Gussie," responded Caroline with a faint smile, "but I *am* concerned and I *am* your friend, and can only trust that you know what you are about!"

"Pooh! You need not worry in the slightest!" said Augusta breezily. "I daresay we shall stroll again in the park, and talk about horticulture, and that will be that! Indeed, Caro, I am not at all sure that I will wish to see the gentleman again, for

I imagine it would soon grow tedious to be forever sneaking about merely to enjoy a convivial chat with someone!''

To a certain extent, Augusta was to be proved right: she and Mr. Culpepper *did* walk through Hyde Park for the second time, and animatedly discourse upon some of the more intriguing aspects of *The London Flora* (with which, Augusta was pleased to learn, Mr. Culpepper was entirely conversant). More unexpectedly, however, when a light, inconsequential drizzle abruptly gave way to a torrential downpour, they were forced to seek refuge in a small pavilion set near a pretty little lake, though by the time they reached its welcome shelter they were both dripping with rain.

''Well, so much for *this* silly bonnet!'' said Augusta, pulling it from her head and regarding the drooping pair of peacock feathers with disgust. ''The poor bird, to have been so needlessly deprived of its plumage!'' She looked about her with interest and went on: ''We are the only wayfarers here, I perceive! Look how the rivulets of rain have formed a sort of curtain around us! If we had only a cup of tea and some macaroons, I should think it quite cozy!''

''Are you chilled, my lady?'' asked Mr. Culpepper anxiously. ''May I not give you my coat to drape about your shoulders? Though it, too, has gotten rather wet, I am afraid!''

''It is only a little water!'' returned Augusta bracingly. ''I shall not melt, sir, I assure you!''

''You must let me know the moment you feel cold,'' he answered. ''The warmth of my coat, damp though it is, would surely be helpful. I would not wish you to catch cold.''

Augusta could only smile at being treated with such solicitousness, for she was not some fragile, die-away miss who slathered herself in liniment and wrapped a woolen cloth about her throat the moment the temperature dropped by a few degrees. Why, at Windemere she was accustomed to sleeping with a window open in her bedchamber all the year round!

She was on the verge of saying as much to Mr. Culpepper,

when suddenly she realized that it was not unpleasant, after all, to be fussed over a trifle, or to have oneself tenderly led to a bench and assisted to sit on it, as if one were the most precious being on earth and—good heavens! There was that giddy, fluttery feeling inside her again! And *this* time she could not attribute it to an empty stomach, for she had eaten quite heartily of gingerbread and Neapolitan cakes at Mrs. Bulwer's!

"Thank you, sir," Augusta said, for the first time feeling a little self-conscious in his presence, and busied herself with the arrangement of her skirt, watching out of the corner of her eye as Mr. Culpepper seated himself next to her. It struck her, with far more import than when she had at first casually remarked upon it, that they were for all practical purposes alone in this deserted pavilion, shielded from the view of any hurrying passersby by the rain sluicing heavily over the eaves.

"I do hope this storm passes quickly!" she said brightly. "I should very much like to resume our walk!"

"I cannot be sorry for it," Mr. Culpepper said in a low, earnest voice, and half-turned on the bench so that he might face her. "I have been wanting all the afternoon, my lady, to tell you how greatly I have been looking forward to our rendezvous today."

Augusta dropped her gaze to her cambric-covered knees, and began tracing with her forefinger a random pattern. "Oh?" was all she could think of to say, for all at once her heart was hammering away in a most disconcerting fashion.

"Yes, Lady Augusta," he said earnestly. "I can think of nothing but you! You have enchanted me! With your lively intellect, your refreshing frankness of speech, your beauty and charm—"

"I am not beautiful," objected Augusta, feeling herself to be on solid ground once again, though she wasn't quite able to bring herself to lift her eyes to his. "Indeed, I am far too tall, my hair will never obey me, and I am *decidedly* plump!"

"You are beautiful and charming," Mr. Culpepper said,

reaching out and taking possession of the hand which had stilled in its pattern-tracing, "with hair I long to caress, a figure which fills me with profound admiration, and a height which is *perfect* for me!"

At these ardent words Augusta did shyly look up. "Do you mean it?" she asked, in a small voice she scarcely recognized as her own.

"Yes!" declared Mr. Culpepper, so vehemently that Augusta could not but be convinced. "I have never meant anything more in my life!"

"You see," she confided, "most of the gentlemen I've met look at me as if I'm some sort of—of talking giraffe! Oh, they try to conceal it, of course, but it is painfully obvious when we have nothing to say to each other and I am looming half a head above them!"

"They are *idiots!*" he said savagely, and the next thing she knew she was clasped tightly in his arms and he was kissing her passionately.

Augusta thought to resist, for it was horribly improper, after all, and they had only known each other for a few hours and had not even been formally introduced, and someone might at any moment step into the pavilion, and really she could hardly breathe, and she had never wished to be held so closely against a man, had never aspired to fall in love and marry, and . . . Augusta closed her eyes, and tilted her head back so that he might angle his mouth just a little more completely over her own, and after that all conscious thought faded quietly away.

At length Mr. Culpepper lifted his head and smiled down at her, his green-blue eyes shining. "You," he said simply, "are divine."

"I do not know about that," returned Augusta dreamily, "but I must say that this kissing business is inadequately described in books! Why did I never know how wonderful it could be?"

Thomas Culpepper only laughed, and leaned down to do it again.

* * *

As the Reston carriage slowly inched its way toward the torchlit portico of Carlton House, both Caroline and Augusta were markedly quiet. Mrs. Yardley, no doubt assuming that they were properly overawed by the honor about to be bestowed upon them, contented herself with an occasional exclamation of glee, and otherwise left them each to her own private thoughts.

Caroline could only guess at what was preoccupying Augusta: her ladyship had said nothing regarding her second encounter with Mr. Culpepper, but her conspicuously bright eyes and pink cheeks, as well as her unwonted silence, had eloquently betrayed her. Caroline had not attempted to press her into speech, on the assumption that had Augusta wished to confide in her she certainly would have found the opportunity to do so. Moreover, and despite her best efforts, Caroline had found herself increasingly subject to fits of despondency—a lowering depression of her spirits which had been exacerbated by restless nights in her bedchamber and frantically hectic days filled with activity as the season's already rapid pace only continued to increase.

She had not seen the marquis since their momentous drive into the country a week ago. Evidently he still came to the house, but on a schedule so contrary to that of the ladies that his presence was no more substantial than a ghost's, though Caroline secretly felt as achingly haunted by his absence. The piercing joy she had experienced in his arms, the dizzying pleasure of his kisses and his caresses, the blissful knowledge that he cared for her—all this had inexorably begun to give way, even that first troubled night after their drive, to the hard, cold reality of her situation, until what had briefly flared into such hot, forgetful hope had flickered intermittently as the days went by, then was finally extinguished into irrevocable blackness.

It was this very bleakness of her soul which had made her

even less inclined to pry into Augusta's affairs, despite the fact that Augusta was obviously bubbling with suppressed happiness. Even Mrs. Yardley had commented on her niece's complaisance in being dragged about to the shops to purchase the goods necessary for their Carlton House toilette. "Have I shown myself *so* abysmally reluctant before, Aunt?" was Augusta's blithe reply, and more than once Caroline had caught her with a book open before her but her dark eyes fixed unseeingly on some distant object, in their depths an unmistakably soft, tender expression.

It was impossible not to wonder what the outcome of this covert liaison would be, and cravenly Caroline hoped the Reston wrath would not fall on her too harshly for the knowledge she had failed to volunteer. She castigated herself for what was perhaps a dreadful moral lapse on her part, but she seemed to be floating through her days in a kind of surreal paralysis. At times, she admitted desolately, it was impossible even to contemplate the idea of the future, for she felt hopelessly entangled in the all-encompassing present, like some poor trapped insect caught in a luxurious spider's web.

The carriage slowed to a halt, jolting Caroline from her unhappy reverie, and she looked out the window to see an opulently dressed footman reaching out an immaculately gloved hand for the handle of the door.

"Here we are, my dears!" sang Mrs. Yardley. "How *beautiful* you both look! I should not be at all surprised if the prince himself favors you with a few minutes' conversation!"

As she carefully stepped onto the ground, assisted by one of the footmen, Caroline glanced indifferently at the delicate white silk of her gown. It *was* lovely, and so was Augusta's dazzling pale yellow slip and gold overdress, but somehow she could not dredge up anything resembling Mrs. Yardley's fervid enthusiasm.

As they approached the portico, Mrs. Yardley told them importantly, "The prince and his architects, you know, have labored for many years to renovate Carlton House and bring it up to the prince's exacting standards. Indeed, many have declared it to be the equal of Versailles!''

''It *is* grand,'' agreed Augusta, craning her neck to eye the high ceiling of the massive entrance hall, which was lined with towering columns of gleaming porphyry marble. ''Although I feel rather like we have come into a cathedral, Aunt!''

''Only wait until you have seen the Blue Velvet Room, where the prince holds audience!'' promised Mrs. Yardley. *''This* shall seem as nothing!''

They made a crawling progress through the ever more magnificent suite of rooms that led from the entrance hall, for it was as crowded here as had been the streets they had traversed in the carriage. Caroline made frequent use of her fan as sluggishly they moved forward amongst their brilliantly attired fellow guests, from time to time being forced to hook her arm through Augusta's so that they might not be separated from each other, so closely packed together was the throng.

At length they came to the Blue Velvet Room. Feeling a little dazed by its overpowering splendor (not to mention the stifling warmth of the room itself), Caroline registered only a scattered impression of thick blue carpets, ornate blue velvet settees, and an enormous triple-tiered chandelier whose sparkling crystal drops caught and reflected the blue shades that dominated the gargantuan chamber.

''What do you think, my dears?'' inquired Mrs. Yardley proudly. ''Does it not far surpass the entrance hall?''

''Well,'' said Augusta, ''it is very *blue.''*

Mrs. Yardley only begged her niece to keep such irreverent observations to herself, and when she finally had done with her lavish expressions of praise, their little group moved on.

At the same snail's pace they passed through the Throne Room, classically Romanesque in design and decorated in stately red brocade, and moved on to the Circular Dining Room, which contained a bewildering quantity of silver-framed mir-

rors, and thence to the Rose-Satin Drawing Room, whose walls
were painted a soft pink (''Which reminds me unpleasantly of
uncooked meat!'' Augusta mischievously whispered to Caroline).

As her gaze touched upon the Gobelins tapestries, the Sèvres
vases, the exquisite marquetry of the furniture, Caroline was
suddenly conscious of a niggling sensation of being watched.
As discreetly as she could, she turned her head to look around
her, but could not discover who might be staring at her—if,
indeed, she reminded herself, there *was* such a person. What
a goose she was! She turned back to Augusta and Mrs. Yardley,
but discovered to her alarm they had in the interval while she
was distracted somehow drifted away from her.

Her heart beating uncomfortably fast, she began to ease her
way through the crowd, searching for a glimpse of Augusta's
shining black coil of hair with its handsome aigrette of diamonds, or Mrs. Yardley's bead-encrusted turban of burgundy
silk. Never had she wished so devoutly to be taller!

There! Was that not Augusta, standing next to the high doorway trimmed in shimmering gold leaf? Eagerly Caroline
pressed forward, only to be disappointed as she crossed the
threshold and found herself in a ballroom so vast it seemed to
stretch on forever, with neither Augusta nor her aunt anywhere
in sight. No one was dancing, for there was no room for it,
but somewhere there was an orchestra, whose musicians were
playing as loudly as they could to be heard over the resounding
cacophony of what must have been hundreds of voices.

As she stood and looked around her, vigorously manipulating
her fan and attempting to maintain on her countenance a mask
of polite interest, inwardly Caroline felt as if she had stepped
into one of own nightmares. How was she ever to locate Augusta
or Mrs. Yardley amidst this multitude? Thinking she heard a
male voice calling her name, she twisted about, and believed
she spied Charles Highcombe's round, affable face nodding at
her from a distance, but then the phalanx of people around her

shifted and he disappeared from view. She turned again, and saw Miss Manderlay—at least she *thought* it was she—but a few arm's lengths away, and at the same time the peculiar feeling that she was being scrutinized did not diminish, but only continued to grow. The back of her neck prickled, and rapidly she plied her fan, welcoming the rush of air, even if it *was* warm. Good God, was there not an open window somewhere, so that she might draw near it and breathe deeply for a few minutes? An urgent longing to escape took hold of her, and blindly she began working her way through the crowd, though she did not at all know where she was going. She only knew that she must move, go somewhere, *anywhere* but here—

"Miss Smythe." It was a calm, male voice, reassuringly familiar; a hand, beautifully gloved, rested lightly on her arm to check her flight. "Are you quite well?"

Caroline looked up into the serene, attractive face of Mr. Brummell, and felt herself relax infinitesimally. "Yes, Mr. Brummell, I thank you," she replied. "I—I trust *you* are well, sir?"

"Oh, yes, Miss Smythe, tolerably so," he said, "though I've been brushed against and bumped into so many times tonight that I fear the clothes I'm wearing will have to be consigned to the fire in the morning!" Fondly he stroked a hand along the sleeve of his fine blue long-tailed frock coat. "Well, if that is the price one must pay to make one's appearance at Carlton House, so be it." He smiled faintly at her, and went on: "I am pleased to see you, Miss Smythe. It was I who ensured that your name was included among the Reston party—Prinny, you know, always asks me to review the guest lists for his gatherings—but I was not sure whether we should meet amidst the crush."

"It was very kind of you to think of me, sir," answered Caroline, conscious of a foolish disappointment that it had not been the marquis, after all, who was responsible for her name appearing on the family invitation.

"By no means! However, now that we have encountered one another, I am not at all confident that you are enjoying yourself as I had hoped." His eyes were keen, and kind, as he looked down into her countenance which was, she feared, either very pale or horribly flushed.

Flustered, she murmured, "It is—it is only that it seems rather stuffy in here, Mr. Brummell."

"Yes, I know! Prinny and his terror of fresh air! Not to mention the fact that there are three times as many people here as there should be! I have tried, I assure you, to convince Prinny to limit the number of guests to whom he opens his doors, but he is not to be persuaded! He is so delighted with his achievements in the remaking of the place that he wishes all the world to see it. I daresay you have heard of the disaster that followed his first ball here as Prince Regent, some two years ago?"

"No, Mr. Brummell."

"On the day after the ball, anyone with the means to purchase a ticket was admitted to Carlton House, where the flowers, the plate, even the dining table with its absurd artificial stream remained in place. Instead of the hundreds that were expected to come, many thousands arrived, and the scene soon degenerated into a vulgar melee. Rather than waiting their turn to go in by the front door, people crawled in through the windows; women fainted, and men were trampled underfoot, until finally, on the last day, the Duke of Clarence climbed up onto the outer wall and shouted that the exhibition was curtailed, on account of the danger to the public. It was feared there might be a riot."

"Was there?"

"No, there were many Yeomen of the Guard present, with arms prominently displayed."

"Good Lord! Was it not a sad debacle, sir?"

"Indeed! Instead of generating goodwill among the populace, Prinny's gesture only inspired hostility and anger among them. Poor fellow." Mr. Brummell's smile was both pitying and sardonic. "Alas, it does seem to be the leitmotiv of his regency.'' Then, without missing a beat, smoothly he said: ''I perceive you are to be singularly honored tonight, Miss Smythe, for the prince himself descends upon us.''

Caroline gave a little panicky gasp, and felt the light touch of Mr. Brummell's hand on her elbow as he turned to the splendidly dressed, rather corpulent gentleman approaching them. At some fifty years of age, Prince George retained a boyish quality that not all his years of dissolute living could quite vanquish. He was still good-looking, although in a somewhat florid fashion, with a magnificent head of thick, light brown hair that waved artistically about his face. His nose was sharp, his complexion only a little sallow, his eyes a vivid blue. About him hung the subtle, cloying scents of both perfume and brandy.

''Well, well, well! Monopolizing yet another of our pretty women, are you, George?'' the regent said jovially. ''Introduce me!''

Suavely Mr. Brummell obeyed. Caroline bent her knees in as deep a curtsy as she could manage within the confines of her narrow skirt and murmured, ''How do you do, sir?''

''You *are* a beauty, Miss Smythe, and not in the common way, either!'' remarked the prince, placing fleshy fingers under her chin so that he might better study her. ''Your curls are quite lovely. Is that unusual shade of auburn wholly yours?''

Caroline flashed a startled look at Mr. Brummell, who only rolled his eyes ever so slightly. She answered bemusedly: ''Why, yes, sir, indeed it is my own.''

''Not a wig?'' he inquired.

''No, sir.''

''Lovely,'' he repeated, and allowed his fingers to slide down the length of her bare throat before he drew his hand away.

Repressing a shudder of distaste, Caroline murmured, ''Thank you, sir.''

''Well! Is this your first visit to Carlton House, Miss Smythe? What do you think of my humble residence?''

"It is—it is amazing, sir," she replied with perfect sincerity.

The prince chuckled, evidently well pleased by her answer. "Yes, it is! I am glad you think so, my dear! I do like having beautiful things about me! I am sure you have observed that I am quite the connoisseur of art?" At her nod, he continued: "However, I daresay you did not know that I have assembled one of the finest collections of paintings in all of Europe?"

"I—I am not at all surprised to hear it, sir."

"Oh, yes, it is universally acknowledged. As a matter of fact, I've only recently added to my collection Rembrandt's *Shipbuilder and His Wife*. It cost me five thousand guineas, too, but it was well worth it! Would you care to see it, Miss Smythe?"

Uncertainly Caroline said: "I would not wish to keep you from your other guests, sir."

"Not a bit, not a bit! It's just downstairs, in my library, where I think the morning light casts just the right illumination upon it. *We* must rely upon candles, but we shan't let that disturb us, shall we? If you will excuse us, George!"

Horrified, Caroline cast a mute glance of appeal to Mr. Brummell, who promptly said, "I am sorry, sir, but just prior to your arrival Miss Smythe was complaining of the headache and of chills, as well. As I mentioned to her, I should not wonder if she was coming down with a violent bout of the ague. I was on the verge of escorting her to the ladies' retiring room so that she might sit, and ask one of the attendants for a vinegar cloth."

The prince recoiled, an expression of frightened dread on his doughy face, and hastily said, "You must not let me stop you! Another time, Miss Smythe, another time! Farewell!" And he hurried off, as quickly as his bulk and the press of the crowd would permit.

Relief washing over her, gratefully Caroline smiled at Mr. Brummell. "*Thank* you, sir! An outrageous fabrication, but one I am by no means inclined to chide you for!"

"Perhaps not so outrageous, Miss Smythe," he replied, "for—forgive me!—you *are* looking a trifle wan!"

"You are very good," Caroline said, shaken to realize that the toll of the last week was more apparent than she would have liked, "but truly, sir, it is the heat which has made me so!" Rallying, she continued: "However, if it would not too greatly inconvenience you, I *should* like to repair to the ladies' retiring room, for I see that the hem of my gown is in dire need of a pin or two!" Having uttered two untruths of her own, she was again relieved when Mr. Brummell did not contradict her, but only offered her his arm, murmuring, "It would be my pleasure, Miss Smythe," and with a dexterity that was marvelous to witness he led her amongst the glittering horde back to the entrance hall and then to a considerably smaller hallway off it.

"Do you perceive that door with the astonishingly ugly Grecian head upon it? There is your destination. Shall I wait for you?"

"Oh, no, sir, for you have graciously spent too much time with me already," Caroline protested. "I should not wish to detain you further."

"I do not think it would be possible to spend too much time with you, Miss Smythe," he surprised her by commenting, with a small, gallant bow. "May I say that I hope to see you resumed to your usual bloom very soon?"

"Thank you, sir!" Caroline said, and, feeling more than a little overcome by his kindness, offered him a heartfelt smile before turning and with rapid steps making her way into the retiring room. To her dismay, this chamber too was filled to overflowing with volubly chattering ladies, offering her little of the respite she craved. Careful of her gown and her coiffure, she splashed tepid water from a basin onto her overheated cheeks and patted them dry with a soft linen towel given her by one of the attendants. Next she looked in vain for a vacant chair or an opened window.

Well, she thought resignedly, there was nothing to be done for it. Back she must go, and continue her search for Augusta and Mrs. Yardley. If only her head *hadn't* begun to ache, as if foolishly conforming to Mr. Brummell's chivalrous prevarication! She pressed her fingers to her forehead, took a deep breath of the stale, sweet-scented air, and went back into the hallway and joined the swirling mass of people eddying about the entrance hall. No sooner had she done so than she was assailed again by an uneasy prickling at the back of her neck. A shudder quivered down her spine, and for a brief, startling moment she felt cold, deathly cold, before once again the suffocating warmth of the hall enveloped her.

I must find them soon, Caroline thought with a kind of hazy desperation, and was just about to cross the threshold into the Blue Velvet Room when a sudden, unsettling premonition forestalled her and abruptly she paused.

"Why, Miss Smythe," came a silky voice, and she whirled around, to find without astonishment that the Earl of Audley stood before her, his tall, slim form clad in a sumptuously rich frock coat of lavender satin embellished with jeweled buttons, knee breeches of the same regal hue, and a white satin waistcoat embroidered in gleaming silver thread. "How delightful to see you here this evening!"

"How do you do, my lord," she said colorlessly. "Forgive me, but I must not tarry, for—"

"Do not, I beg, deny me this rare opportunity to speak with you," he interrupted smilingly. "For I have long been desirous of finishing the conversation we began these many weeks past, in Mrs. Yardley's drawing room. Come, there is a cozy saloon but a few paces from here, where we might converse in comfort."

"My lord, I do not think . . ." Caroline began, then trailed off weakly as the earl drew her hand firmly into the crook of his arm and escorted her to a room gaudily decorated in overwhelmingly elaborate chinoiserie. The shiny blacks and bright scarlets seemed almost to throb before her eyes, and wearily Caroline sank onto a scrolled jade bench, wondering dismally why on earth *this* saloon—apparently alone among the entirety of Carlton House—was unoccupied.

Leisurely the earl seated himself on a bench opposite her. "Do you not feel as if we have been magically transported to China, Miss Smythe? Or, if not quite that far, at least to the prince's Pavilion in Brighton?"

"I have never been to the Pavilion, my lord."

"Have you not? I am sure that you will visit it someday, my dear. Perhaps the Lady Augusta and Mrs. Yardley will take you there this summer."

"Perhaps, my lord," was Caroline's vague, guarded response.

"Which reminds me: you never did tell me how you came to be an intimate of the Reston *ménage.*"

The earl's swift, unsubtle segue summoned to Caroline's mind the image of a snake baring its fangs as it prepared to strike. "I cannot think why such a subject would be of interest to you, my lord," she answered, and attempted to rise, only to discover that her legs were curiously rubbery.

"You must not underrate your ability to fascinate, Miss Smythe," he replied in what she considered to be his odiously caressing fashion. "Indeed, I have on more than one occasion observed how compelling an influence you exert."

"I am not at all sure that that is a compliment," responded Caroline bluntly.

"But it is, my dear, I assure you! Now, I pray you, will you not tell me all about yourself?"

The earl's thin face, with its intent pale blue eyes, seemed to swim hazily in the uncertain light of the room, and Caroline felt a rush of clammy heat sweep over her. Urgently she willed her legs to obey her, but to no avail. "My lord!" she said, wishing, for the first time in her life, she had tucked a vinaigrette into her reticule. "Will you—will you not go and procure for me a glass of lemonade? I should be most grateful to you!"

"Shortly, I promise you," he replied coolly. "When you have told me what I should very much like to know."

In that moment, as she only gazed mutely at the earl, Caroline could not but think him the cruelest man she had ever encountered.

Ignoring the cries of greeting that bombarded him, Damien pushed his way through the densely packed entrance hall. He had arrived at Carlton House late, only to glimpse a sight that sent his heart racing both with pleasure and with alarm: Caroline, pale and fragile-looking and breathtakingly beautiful in a simple white gown, about to be led down a side corridor by the Earl of Audley.

Did the man mean to make love to her? Damien thought, and felt his fists clench ominously at his sides. If so, the earl would greet tomorrow's dawn as his last. Never mind the scandal attached nowadays to the practice of dueling; what cared he for something so trivial when Caroline—his light, his love—was so grossly endangered?

A richly dressed couple lurched in front of him, plainly in the hilarious throes of inebriation. The woman, plump and pink, whose arms and earlobes and décolleté sparkled with gemstones, squealed with laughter when her companion embraced her as if in a waltz and attempted to swing her about, causing them to crash into the people standing nearby.

Damien cast them a glance of disgust and rapidly moved past. Good God, he thought, had there truly been a time when he had found the prince's soirees amusing?

At last he entered the side corridor, which, thankfully, was less congested, and looked about him. There were six closed doors on either side, all painted a bright, garish red. There was no way to tell behind which one were Caroline and the earl.

Muttering an imprecation under his breath, Damien wasted no time and brusquely opened the first door, and there surprised a gentleman and a young woman on a red and gold brocade sofa, who were each but half-dressed, frozen with limbs intertwined as they stared at their unexpected intruder. Without a word of apology Damien slammed the door shut, and proceeded to methodically make his way along the corridor. The second, third, fourth, and fifth doors all opened to reveal similar scenes, but finally, at the sixth chamber, he pulled open the heavy red door to find Caroline sitting on an Oriental bench, her spine not as straight as was her usual wont, her face a ghastly white and her green eyes curiously glassy. Across from her was the earl, staring at her with a focused concentration that surprised Damien with its naked exigency. It was not the expression of a man bent on amorous conquest, but of someone who wished for some other thing quite powerfully.

They both turned upon hearing the creaking of the door.

"Damien—my lord!" uttered Caroline in obvious amazement and relief. She stretched out a hand to him; exerting his utmost to reveal nothing of the strong emotions under which he was laboring, without haste Damien moved into the room and pretended not to see the fingers extended beseechingly, then slowly lowered. Already she had unwittingly betrayed herself—and him—by the use of his first name.

"Miss Smythe," he said lazily. "Audley."

Anger at being interrupted and a blatant speculation had revealed themselves on the earl's face before being replaced by his usual mien of languid hauteur. "Reston," he responded, with a nod of acknowledgment. "What brings you to this rather obscure area of Carlton House, I wonder?"

"Why, I was to meet someone here," Damien said. "But it seems the lady has failed to make the assignation." He ignored the look of painful hurt in Caroline's eyes, and continued in a tone of profound indifference: "Since you are here this evening, Miss Smythe, I assume that so too are my aunt and sister. I must say I quite wonder at you for wandering off unchaperoned; it is not behavior to be condoned.''

"Yes—I—I am sorry, my lord,'' she murmured submissively, lowering her head.

"Have you any particular excuse to offer, Miss Smythe?''

"No, my lord,'' she said, so dully that he felt a stab of anguish for so deliberately misleading her. But with the earl observing, he dared not go to her, take her in his arms, and kiss away her distress until once again she smiled at him.

He glanced as if bored at the earl. "I cannot trouble you with the duty of restoring Miss Smythe to my aunt, sir, so I suppose there is nothing to be done for it but to perform the deed myself.'' In reality he intended to take her as expeditiously as possible to his carriage and see her home, for she did not appear at all well. "Come, Miss Smythe,'' he said imperiously. "I am sorry to have broken off your colloquy with Audley, but I cannot think *that* quite proper either.''

"No, my lord,'' Caroline said, and as he watched her slowly rise to her feet Damien prayed that her will would not fail her, for should she falter, and threaten to crumple to the floor, he knew he couldn't stand idly by, but would rush to support her no matter the consequences.

"I am ready,'' she told him, and with an admiration no less fervent for its being concealed he watched her hold herself defiantly upright and turn his way.

"Let us go, then. Farewell, sir,'' he said to Audley, who, to Damien's displeasure, stood and spoke smilingly.

"I will accompany you.''

To this Damien was forced to civilly accede, and together the three of them walked from the saloon into the corridor. He was utterly, achingly aware of Caroline at his side, but steeled himself to portray only cool disinterest, a facade he need only maintain until they were safely away in his carriage.

When, after some five minutes of proceeding away from, not toward the entrance hall because of the earl's unwelcome presence, Damien's covert rancor toward the earl only increased when that gentleman showed no signs of detaching himself from their little party, and, indeed, maintained a flow of urbane small talk that scraped across Damien's nerves like a saw against metal.

It was with unabashed gladness, therefore, that he next heard a familiar voice cry out above the clamor.

"Damien! Caro!"

Moments later, Augusta sailed toward them, cutting through the assemblage like some queenly figurehead come to life, authoritatively parting the ocean's waves. In her wake, quite literally, came his aunt and, Damien was startled to see, Miss Manderlay, slim and radiant in silver satin and matching lace.

"Oh, Caro!" said Augusta, affectionately grasping Caroline's hand in her own. "Where in heaven's name did you go off to? We have been searching for you everywhere!"

"I—I am so sorry, my lady," murmured Caroline. "I fear I must have quite spoiled your pleasure in the soiree."

"You cannot be serious," Augusta said, looking more closely at the pale countenance of her companion. "As you must surely know, I have been wishing us gone this past hour and more!"

"Hello, Damien," interposed Mrs. Yardley. "How do you do, your lordship? As you see, we have brought Miss Manderlay with us, for when we encountered her in the ballroom and she realized that Caroline had gone missing, she expressed an ardent desire to assist us in our search."

"How kind of you, Helen," Damien said. "No doubt you have found more than you expected."

Miss Manderlay offered him her sweet, glinting smile. "I do not know that that is quite so, my dear Reston."

Augusta's dark brows went up as she glanced between her brother and his fiancée. She did not comment despite her evident puzzlement but only said: "Aunt, I am ready to go home, and I believe Caro is as well."

Disappointedly his aunt began, "But my dear Augusta—"

"Aunt," Augusta rejoined firmly, "I am fagged to death, and hot and thirsty and hungry as well! If you wish to remain you may do so, and I daresay Damien will escort us to our carriage in your stead. Is that not so, brother?"

Damien was surprised at the warm affection he felt for Augusta; it was clear to him that she too was anxious to have Caroline, who was growing paler by the minute, whisked away. He bowed, and smiled faintly at Augusta, saying, "Indeed yes, sister."

"Oh, very well!" Mrs. Yardley capitulated. "Let no one say that I have failed in my responsibilities! Though I *was* hoping to see the regent this evening! It *would* be odd to spend half the night at a party and fail to even catch sight of one's host, even if he *is* a prince of the realm! Too, there is an *on-dit* circulating that Mrs. Fitzherbert is here! *She* who broke with *him* a decade ago, because he placed her lower down the table at a dinner party in Carlton House itself! I am most heartily sorry we were not able to peek into the Gothic Dining Room, for it is reputed to be the height of splendor! At all events, it would certainly have been interesting to witness an encounter between the prince and his former mistress, would it not? They say she retired with a pension of six thousand a year, and that the prince continues to wear round his neck a portrait of her! Well! I do not know why we are all simply standing about! Let us waste no more time! Come, Augusta! Come, Caroline! Farewell, Miss Manderlay! Damien! My lord!"

With an air of virtuous dignity Mrs. Yardley began walking toward the end of the entrance hall which led to the portico, and, murmuring their adieus, meekly Caroline and Augusta followed, the latter flashing at Damien a quick, mischievous smile. It took all of his considerable self-control not to trail behind them; instead, conscious of an urgent desire to himself leave Carlton House as soon as humanly possible, he bowed to both Miss Manderlay and the earl, expressed his entirely false pleasure in seeing them this night, and strolled away, ostensibly toward the interior suite of rooms and there to mingle amongst the other guests. His true destination, however, was a flight of back stairs, known only to a few of the prince's intimates, that would take him to the kitchens and thence directly to the street, where he might summon his own carriage in more or less rapid order. An ignominious departure, to be sure, but what of that?

In one swift, harsh stroke, he had administered a great hurt to Caroline; it had occurred to him in the interval since then that perhaps he had unintentionally done her a great kindness in leaving her to think that his affections were not deeply engaged. She might emerge from this woefully star-crossed affair with her heart intact, and go on to find someone else to love. As she should, he told himself. *As she should.*

Yet this rational, considered decision of the intellect brought him nothing but cold, cold comfort, and as he emerged onto the street and into the mild evening air of spring, bleakly Damien thought he had never felt so utterly chilled in all his life.

Chapter 14

Augusta tied the satin ribbons of her bonnet in a neat bow under her chin and looked worriedly at Caroline, who was drawing on her gloves. "My dear Caro," she said, "are you certain you feel capable of a walk in the park this morning? You were so white and listless as we left Carlton House last night I quite feared you would be laid low with an illness of some kind."

"Oh, no, Gussie, I believe a walk is precisely what I need," answered Caroline stoutly. "I slept very well"—this was a gross exaggeration of the truth, but no matter—"and partook of an excellent breakfast"—she had made herself eat heartily in order to assuage Augusta's obvious concern—"and now lack nothing but a little exercise to bring me nicely about."

"If you say so," responded Augusta dubiously. "You remain a little too pale for my liking."

"*Interestingly* pale!" retorted Caroline. "I have long thought my complexion to be disastrously brown!"

"You mean the Baroness Manderlay considered you so,"

was Augusta's dry reply. " 'Perhaps Denmark Lotion might help,' " she went on, lifting her nose in the air and mimicking with remarkable accuracy that lady's distinctively haughty manner. "It is to her credit, I suppose, that she did not recommend that you take lead or drink vinegar! *Ugh!*"

Caroline could not repress a smile, but reverted to their original topic and said: "It is very sweet of you to offer to go with me on my walk, Gussie."

"Well, do you know, I don't feel in the least inclined to do any translating today," Augusta confessed. "It is too beautiful a morning to remain closeted in my rooms with only my books to keep me company!"

Caroline made note of what was for her friend an astonishing statement but once again discreetly remained silent. They nodded at Uxley, standing at his post by the front door, and stepped out into the pleasant sunshine. Soon they had reached the outskirts of Hyde Park, and were strolling along one of its broad, shaded footpaths.

"Speaking of the Baroness Manderlay," said Augusta, "I daresay you thought it more than a little odd to meet us last night with her redoubtable offspring, the Honorable Miss Manderlay, in tow?"

"I own I did think Mrs. Yardley's explanation surprising," admitted Caroline. "Whyever should Miss Manderlay concern herself with *my* whereabouts? She has barely even acknowledged my existence."

"I wondered as well. But no sooner had Aunt divulged to her that we had lost you somewhere in the Rose-Satin Drawing Room than she declared her unshakable determination to assist us in our search. For my part, Caro, I was surprised to see you in the company of the Earl of Audley! I would not have thought you to find him at all congenial."

As Caroline did not care to divulge to Augusta the strange circumstances of having been nearly dragged off for a private disquisition with the earl, she only shrugged and murmured, "A chance encounter only."

Augusta accepted this explanation without demur and continued: "And Damien! When we first met up with you it struck me that I have never seen him appear so grim and cold! Had you said something to displease him, Caro?"

A fresh wave of despair washed over Caroline. Summoning all of her resolve, she answered as lightly as she could, "As to that, Gussie, I could not tell you, for his lordship did not confide in me!"

"Well, he did seem to cheer up a bit when I made known my intention to depart—for I would not have subjected you to ten minutes more of that—that *bedlam* which apparently passes for a party at Carlton House, even if it meant having to callously desert my aunt! Good heavens, what a charming shrub that is! I must ask Thomas—that is, I must consult *The London Flora* upon our return home. Do you not see those pretty pink blossoms, Caro? I wonder if they possess a fragrance?"

Her own cheeks becomingly pink, Augusta went to the shrub and sniffed at one of its flowers. "The faintest trace of a scent," she announced, taking again her place at Caroline's side, and as they resumed walking went on to cheerfully call to Caroline's attention other points of botanical interest.

Only too glad to quietly listen to Augusta's lively exposition, Caroline nodded and smiled, while secretly she wished she could give vent to the acute misery pervading her, body and soul, though it seemed impossible that she could ever cry enough tears to help heal the rift in her heart.

Last night the marquis *had* been grim and cold; his dark eyes had been like ice when he came into the saloon in which she sat with the Earl of Audley. And then to hear him say he had arrived, not to rescue her from the supercilious clutches of the earl as she had hoped, but to meet a lady by prearrangement!

It had been nothing short of a terrible blow. Caroline would have been hard-pressed to say which was worse: sharing with the marquis a love which could only be unrequited, or loving him steadfastly and discovering that his attachment to her had been but a capricious one.

Her eyes filled with tears and she blinked hard to keep them at bay, nodding politely as Augusta spoke.

"As for grass, it is a far more complex plant than one might think! There are numerous varieties, each with its own idiosyncrasies and subject to a range of blights, and—oh, look, Caro, there is Damien, riding along that track over there, though I am not sure that he sees us! Do let us wave at him! And—and—why, I do believe another gentleman is riding toward us, and if I am not mistaken, he is an acquaintance of yours!"

Forcing her gaze away from the distant figure of the marquis, Caroline turned to see a red-haired man on a bay horse rapidly approaching them. That compact, muscular form, that flame-colored hair and easy grin . . . Her brows creased: could it be . . . ?

"Caroline! Caroline Smythe!" he called out exuberantly. "Of all the dashed good luck!"

"Captain Prescott!" Caroline exclaimed in joyful disbelief, as the gentleman pulled up his horse, dismounted, and came to her, taking the hand she eagerly held out and grasping it tightly in his free one.

"Good God, to think of meeting you here in London! How the devil *are* you, my girl?" he said, warm affection evident in his voice, then added hastily, "I do beg your pardon, ladies! Too many years in the military!" he explained to Augusta, releasing Caroline's hand to courteously lift his black high-crowned hat to her ladyship.

Augusta only smiled, saying, "Believe me, sir, I have said worse things in my life, and all too frequently!"

Captain Prescott grinned back at her, and quickly Caroline performed the introductions. "Captain Prescott has for a long time been a great friend of my family," she explained, "only we had lost touch with each other these past few years."

"I wrote to General Gage, inquiring after you, as soon as I

sold out and returned home to Devon in March, but he was unable to provide me with much information,'' Captain Prescott said to Caroline. ''I didn't want to give you up for lost, my girl, but there wasn't much I could do at the moment! So after having a look round the estate and ascertaining that everything was in reasonably good order, I betook myself to London to conduct a little business, and, wonder of wonders, here you are!''

''Yes,'' she said, smiling back at him, ''here I am indeed.'' Impulsively she stretched out her hand to him again. ''Oh, Harry, it is wonderful to see you!''

''It's wonderful to see *you,* my girl,'' he replied simply, his freckled face beaming as he again gripped her fingers in his own.

Augusta observed them benignly. ''Were you in the Americas, Captain, or in the Peninsular Wars?''

''In the Peninsula, my lady, for some ten years.''

''That *is* a long time!'' she commented. ''I hope you were not injured?''

''Oh, once or twice. Nothing serious, I'm happy to say.''

''Captain Prescott on more than one occasion sustained injuries of quite a serious nature,'' Caroline intervened. ''I am sorry to contradict you, Harry, but I will not permit you to hide your light under a bushel! Once, Gussie, we came terribly close to losing the captain, when a bullet had lodged in his shoulder, in one of the battles near Oporto. He had risked his own life to save two of his wounded men, dragging them across enemy lines to the safety of the British encampment, and had gone back to look for more of his men, only to be cut down by a French sharpshooter. He was not found until the next day, having bled nearly to death. But he had given his brandy flask to a fellow soldier whose injuries were even worse than his own; it cannot be said with any certainty, but I do believe it was the captain's generosity and his own encouragement to the wounded soldier that kept him alive throughout the night, until help could safely come for them both.''

"Now, Caroline—" said the captain, uncomfortably.

"Do not attempt to deny it, Harry, for you know it is the truth!"

"Well, if we are to boast, then, I will have you know, my lady, that it was Caroline herself who nursed me back to health, though I daresay she didn't catch more than an hour of sleep in the week it took me to recover from the fever I contracted!"

"You, Caro?" Augusta turned wide, fascinated eyes to Caroline. "But what on *earth* were you doing in Portugal during the war?"

Now it was Caroline's turn to be uncomfortable. "My father was a soldier, Gussie, and my mother and I—well, for some years we were with him in Portugal and in Spain. Captain Prescott was kind enough to befriend my father, and to look after my mother and me as we followed along behind the army."

"But what an extraordinary tale!" Augusta exclaimed. "I perceive that I am in the company of *two* heroes! Why have you never told me of this, Caro?"

Hesitantly Caroline replied: "The circumstances were unusual ones, to say the least, and hardly comprised the background of a lady aspiring to the position of governess to a genteel family—or—or of a companion. I am most heartily sorry for maintaining silence on the subject, Gussie, and—and hope that you can forgive me for my duplicity.''

"Duplicity? Pooh!" cried Augusta. "Rather say that I have taken you too much for granted to learn more about you, my dear Caro! It is *I* who should be begging *your* pardon! You are the noblest girl I know, worth any dozen of hothouse ladies spouting nonsense about pianofortes and watercolors and the steps of a quadrille! Why, I can only begin to imagine the horrors you encountered, and the discomforts you suffered!"

"And never once did I hear a word of complaint, either, my

lady," put in Captain Prescott. "There was one time, in Coimbra, when our rations ran low, and we went for almost a fortnight living off corn foraged from fields which had already been harvested. For every ten cobs she found, Caroline gave nine to a family of Portuguese whose children were starving. If I hadn't forced her to retain one for herself, she likely would have given that one away as well."

"Oh, pray let us speak no more of it, Harry," begged Caroline, feeling an embarrassed heat suffuse her face. "These are events of the distant past, and—and in any case, I am anxious to hear how you are spending your time in the metropolis!"

The captain glanced wryly at Augusta. "And she's modest to a fault, too, my lady."

"That, Captain, I have already discovered for myself," rejoined Augusta, slipping her arm around Caroline's waist and giving her an affectionate squeeze.

"You two have put me to the blush long enough!" said Caroline firmly. "Harry, enlighten us as to your activities at once!"

"Well, as to that, my girl, I've come to visit Tattersall's, and procure for myself a horse or two, and a carriage suitable for tooling round the countryside in high style." The captain grinned. "I've been away for so long that I must reestablish myself among the locals, you see, as a gentleman of the first stare! Then, too, I've come to confer with my bankers and, of course, to purchase some clothes in which to parade about, for I've only worn uniforms for the past decade, and the fashions have changed a bit since then!"

"Do you miss the military life, Captain?" inquired Augusta.

"I thought I would, your ladyship, for I had vowed long ago to keep fighting until Napoleon was well and thoroughly defeated, and I was reluctant to leave the army until old Boney was a threat to us no more. But by last year, you know, Wellington had already defeated Boney's best marshals, and my father was urging me to come home and take over the running of the estate. So between these two compelling factors I finally agreed to sell out; I am of the opinion that it won't be too long before we are at peace again, with the French wholly trounced.''

"I pray that day may soon come,'' Augusta said soberly.

"Aye, so do we all,'' agreed the captain.

"Your parents must be delighted to have you home again, Harry,'' said Caroline. "I hope they are in good health?''

"Oh, yes, they are as hale as ever,'' he returned, cheerful once more. "I had feared that upon my return I would find my father in a decrepit state—for he is nigh on seventy now!—but despite a slight feebleness of his limbs he is quite his old self, bullying my poor mother and sisters at every opportunity, and badgering *me* to marry and produce for him as soon as humanly possible a brood of some nine or ten children!''

Caroline laughed. "Why not an even dozen?''

The captain's infectious grin flashed again. "I do not doubt that he is building up to that number! And he is cantankerous enough, bless his crusty old soul, to live long enough to see that I fulfill my duty!''

They all laughed. Then, hearing the sound of horse's hooves growing closer, they turned together toward the sound.

"Hello, Damien!'' Augusta called amiably. "I had hoped you had seen us, for I waved to you in a most unladylike fashion! Whatever took you so long to join us? The most wonderful thing has occurred! This is Captain Harry Prescott, an old friend of Caro's, who just happened to come across us as we strolled! Is it not a piece of remarkable good fortune? Captain Prescott, may I introduce to you my brother, the Marquis of Reston?''

The captain swept off his hat and bowed. "It is a pleasure to meet you, my lord.''

Damien dipped his head in acknowledgment. "Sir.'' He stared down at the trim, red-haired gentleman, a fiery jealousy burning within him. He had observed them from a distance: had seen Caroline's enthusiastic greeting and their fond clasping of hands, not once but twice. Now that he was in closer proximity, the intimate rapport between them was easily apparent, for they stood almost shoulder to shoulder, so nearly of the same height that Caroline need not stretch herself up on tiptoes should she wish to kiss the gentleman, as she might with himself who was considerably taller—

Damien's hands clenched tightly on the reins and his horse gave a little nervous sidestep. At once he relaxed his grip and schooled himself to listen more closely to Augusta's enthusiastic chatter.

"—Captain Prescott was in the Peninsular Wars for some ten years, Damien, and has only recently sold his commission and returned home. His estate is in Devon, but he has come to London on business. We must invite him to take potluck with us one night soon, for I am longing to hear more about his experiences during the war! Damien, were you aware of the fact that *Caro* was in the Peninsula?"

"Yes," Damien said, glancing at Caroline, and observing that her gaze was politely fixed on Augusta. Was there any reason why he should be startled to find that she was apparently avoiding his own eyes, after the abominable way he had treated her last night? No, he could not blame her, only—only he had not thought, in his arrogance, that she would find someone else so swiftly!

"And to think," Augusta continued, in a marveling tone, "that she and Captain Prescott had lost touch with each other, and were it not for their chance encounter this morning, who knows if they would ever have met again?"

"Indeed," was Damien's cool, brusque response. Suddenly a memory stirred, and flew at him with a kind of winged vengeance, like an evil bird of prey: Caroline sleeping on the bluff that afternoon at Landsdowne, crying out in the midst of her nightmare. *"Where is he? Oh, dear God, can no one tell me where he is gone to?"*

And again, in the inn at Baldock: *"Oh, where is he? Can*

*someone not tell me? I have looked—looked for him every-
where!''*

Damien knew he was glaring down at the captain, but was
powerless to mask the resentment and envy blazing through
him. No doubt *this* was the man for whom Caroline still
searched in her dreams; *this* was the man to whom she had
given her heart and, perhaps, her body.

An angry red mist seemed to float across Damien's vision,
and for a brief, crazy moment he wanted nothing more than to
settle his fingers about the captain's sturdy throat and slowly
choke the life from him.

He shook his head, and the mist dissolved, leaving him once
again staring clearly into the mocking face of reality. *He* could
offer Caroline nothing: not his name, his life, his fortune, not
even the dubious honor of his protection. In fairness he could
not even offer her his heart, for she deserved more than that
paltry offering.

She deserved love, and marriage, a home of her own and a
family to cherish.

And here, suddenly, was the stalwart Captain Prescott, looking to be a most eminent candidate to supply her with all those
things and more.

He should be glad, Damien told himself.

Should be.

Instead he was consumed with bitterness, and a raging jealousy, and a self-loathing so strong he felt his muscles tighten
from the violence of it.

''—do you not think that would be delightful, Damien?
Damien! Are you attending to me?''

With a start Damien realized that Augusta was addressing
him; on her face was a puzzled expression as she looked up at
him.

''What is it?'' he snapped.

''Why, I only said that since it is such a warm day, we might
all go to Gunter's for some ices.''

"I thank you, no," he said curtly. "I must go." And with that terse rejoinder he swung his horse's head around and cantered away. As he went he heard a church bell toll. It lacked two hours to noon, but Christ, he desperately wanted some brandy, or port, or even a few glasses of Blue Ruin—gin not ordinarily being a beverage in which he indulged—to soothe, soften, then finally extinguish the emotions roaring hotly within him.

Rapidly he rode to a certain house he knew in Mayfair, narrow and elegant and fronted with expensive brick tiles. There an unctuous lackey took his horse, and a neatly dressed butler admitted him with only the faintest look of surprise on his otherwise impassive countenance. Damien waited briefly in the sunny, high-ceilinged drawing room, and then the butler returned, informed him that the lady was at home, and let him make his own way up the stairs, along a richly carpeted hallway, and into a boudoir he had not so long ago known very well indeed.

"Hello, Jenny," he said.

Clad in a sheer, lacy *robe de chambre,* trimmed in swansdown and loosely belted, and under which her low-cut, amethyst silk nightdress was plainly visible, Jenny White came forward to welcome him with both hands outstretched. "Damien, my dear!" she said warmly. "I could not believe it when Thurber told me you had come, for you have not been to visit me in some months now!" A charming pout formed itself on her round, rouged, extremely pretty face. "I suppose I should be scolding you for neglecting me so shamefully, instead of being so congenial to you!" she went on sternly, then burst into a girlish peal of laughter. "But I never *could* stay angry with you for long!" Still grasping his hands, she led him to a long, low *chaise longue* covered in soft lavender velvet and placed near the fireplace. He sat, and leaned against its fancifully curlicued back, carelessly stretching his booted legs out before him.

Jenny remained standing, and gestured to the bell pull next to the mantelpiece. "A drink, my dear? I have only to ring for it."

"Yes—no—" muttered Damien, and raked his fingers through his hair. A few minutes ago he had been certain that he would have sold his soul to the devil himself for a brimming snifter full of brandy, yet now, oddly, he found himself vacillating. "I don't know."

"You needn't decide right now," Jenny said, her delicately penciled eyebrows lifting high at his unusual indecision. She sank down next to him in a swirl of fluttering swansdown and lace, and swept a long fall of crimped black hair over her shoulder. "Well, my sweet, what has brought you here so unexpectedly?" she asked. "Is this a social call, or do you intend for our visit to be rather more *intime?* I ought to tell you that I have not been *too* lonely these past months—for a lady in my occupation must not be idle for very long, you know!—but I have no objection to renewing our *arrangement personnel,* if you should wish it, for I have always found you to be very satisfactory . . . in every way." She smiled, and laid a soft hand on his knee.

As if for the first time, Damien found himself looking at Jenny White, studying her black eyes with their carefully tinted lashes, her full cheeks and lips painted an inviting red. Through the negligent draping of her nightdress and robe he had no difficulty discerning the curving outlines of her plump, languorous figure with its large breasts and voluptuously flaring hips, and rounded thighs enticingly slanted apart.

Once he had found Jenny very desirable. Even now he could view her as if from afar and abstractly conclude that her charms were fulsome and ample. But today . . .

In his maddened state of mind he had come here impulsively, hoping to slake his wicked thirst and to subsume his turmoil in the familiar comfort of her practiced body. Both appetites she had straightforwardly offered to satisfy.

He could reach out and stroke his fingers around a heavy breast, could lean closer and kiss that red, smiling mouth, could unfasten his trousers and guide her black-haired head between his legs, then take her later to the massive canopied bed that stood center stage in the bedchamber adjoining this room and have her as many times as it took to deaden the anguish that throbbed relentlessly along his veins.

Instead he sat very still, one arm flung along the back of the *chaise longue,* the other resting on a soft velvet cushion, and thought of auburn curls, green eyes, a tender, eager mouth pliant beneath his own, and a few illicit moments of unbridled passion and joy on a secluded bluff.

Jenny removed her hand from his knee, folded it in her lap with its mate, and gazed at him inquisitively. "What is it, my dear?"

"Nothing."

"A bouncer if ever I heard one," she said. "Something is wrong, Damien. There was a time when we were very close, and I have learned to read you quite well! Will you not speak to me of your troubles?"

"You are astute, Jenny."

"In my profession one must be," she answered. "Perhaps you might begin by telling me why you have come today. You stayed away for a long time—which," she added, "I cannot complain of, for you ever treated with me generously, and there were, after all, no agreements between us! But I *was* a little surprised to see you here no more. Perhaps your fiancée insinuated herself a little too closely into your affairs, and insisted that you curtail your . . . accustomed way of life?"

A bitter smile twisted his lips. "Hardly."

"Then I can only conclude you have found another *petite amie* with whom to pass your nights."

"No."

Penciled brows again rose high. "No? I confess I cannot picture you living like a celibate monk, my dear."

"It is the truth."

"Now you have begun to alarm me, my dear Damien! Have you suffered financial losses that inhibit your expenditures? Or perhaps it is one of those particular illnesses . . . that afflict gentlemen?"

"No."

"I am glad to hear it, but I remain utterly baffled!"

He looked into her pretty face, and knew that his own countenance was hard. "I came here today to use you, Jenny," he said.

"Of course you did." Her voice was calm.

"You do not seem particularly taken aback, or affronted."

"Why should I? All the gentlemen who visit use me, just as I use them." She waved a white hand, indicating the luxurious surroundings of her boudoir. "Because of your patronage, and that of others of my clientele, I go along very well indeed. I own this little town house, you know, and have a carriage and two horses, four discreet servants whose handsome wages I comfortably pay on time, and several dozen gowns straight from Paris." She giggled. "Hardly a shabby accomplishment for a gamekeeper's daughter from Hereford!"

"Are you, Jenny?" he said, momentarily distracted from his cold, hard misery. "One wouldn't guess it from your deportment or your speech."

"No, I worked hard at that," she replied. "I came to London hoping to be a maid of some kind, but couldn't find employment, so I ended up where many a country girl like me does: *en un bordel.* Fortunately for me, the proprietress wasn't a bad sort of woman, and her tolerance enabled me to both learn my trade well and to study what gentlemen—the nobs, the nobility like yourself—liked. So when eventually I set out on my own, I hired all sorts of tutors to instruct me in the higher graces, then strove to provide for my visitors a bit of refinement along with their fun. And, as you can see, my plan has succeeded brilliantly."

"Yes," he agreed. "Am I correct in thinking you do not divulge this information to many of your—er, visitors?"

"Good heavens, no!" she said. "I am telling *you* this, Damien, because . . . well, I have always liked you rather better than the rest, for you paid your bill without the ridiculous haggling so many of the gentlemen tediously indulge in, and were a superb lover."

He smiled faintly. "I observe that you place in the first order of importance the matter of the bill."

"Naturally! I am a woman of business, after all!"

"Of course. Thank you for being so candid with me." Then Damien's smile faded, and after a time, in which she regarded him in sympathetic silence, he said with difficulty: "Jenny, I have fallen in love."

With a little cry she clasped one of his hands between her own. "But that is *good* news, my dear! I am so happy for you!"

"Do not be," he said. "I do not refer to my betrothed."

"So? Among the members of your set, it is to be expected that husbands and wives find fulfillment in the beds of others."

"It is not like that, Jenny," he said heavily. "She is a genteel young woman, unmarried, and raised in a stricter moral code than my own."

"Does she love you?"

A band of iron seemed to constrict about his chest. "I do not know. Once I thought she did, but now . . ."

Jenny's black eyes were keen and warm as she nodded wisely and said: "I see how it is, my dear. It is this young lady you wish to court, and win, and marry; you do not desire to wed the one to whom you are engaged."

"Yes. You are right." With these few simple words of admission, Damien irrationally felt a little of the crushing burden he carried drop from him.

"Well then, you must break off your engagement," Jenny said calmly, "and pursue the young lady whom you love."

Abruptly Damien stood up, and felt his hands clench into frustrated fists at his sides. "You know I cannot, no matter how ardently I might long to."

"Why? Because according to the arbitrary dictates of society, a man may not end a betrothal, and only the woman may do so?"

"Because my honor is at stake," Damien said between gritted teeth. "Because it is all I have left." He opened his hands, palms up, as if to emphasize the futile emptiness of which he spoke, then dropped them again to his sides.

Jenny rose to her feet, and came to him. "I do not pretend to understand you," she said softly, "but I can understand the pain you are feeling. There is nothing else I might say to you, but . . ." She placed a hand on his sleeve. "Would you take some comfort in *my* bed? No charge," she added. "Just . . . between former friends."

Briefly Damien covered her hand with his own. "The spirit in which you tender your offer is greatly appreciated, Jenny, but—"

"But no," she said. "It is clear that there is only one woman you wish to hold in your arms." She sighed, then her red mouth curled in a smile that was more than a little wistful. "She is a lucky woman, did she but know it."

"Good-bye, Jenny," said Damien. "And . . . thank you."

"Good-bye." With that same sad half smile she watched him go to the door, and leave; both of them knew that this time it was forever.

Chapter 15

Augusta paced for what must have been the hundredth time around the flowered border of the big, oval-shaped carpet laid perpendicular to the foot of her bed. Her conscience, which for some time now had been comfortably dormant amidst the excitement and happiness she had experienced in meeting and coming to know Thomas Culpepper, had, slowly but surely, begun to trouble her.

Before she had come to realize the full extent of her feelings for Thomas, she might have dismissed the clandestine meetings, the snatched kisses, as foolish pranks to be lightly committed and then as easily forgotten.

But when a lark unexpectedly developed into something deeper and more serious . . .

When it was no longer an overgrown schoolgirl's game . . .

Augusta paused, and absently toyed with the tassel looped round one of the damask bed hangings. Now it no longer seemed appropriate to comport herself in such a surreptitious fashion. Caroline had tactfully expressed her reservations about such behavior, and now her gentle words had come back to haunt Augusta.

She must do the right thing. She would speak to Damien, and confess all, and request that Thomas be admitted to the house so that Damien might make his acquaintance, and see for himself how worthy a gentleman Thomas was. She could do no less: *that* would not be worthy of her, or do honor to the tremendous esteem in which she held Thomas.

With a sigh, Augusta sat down on the end of her bed. The task might have been a less daunting one but for that odd encounter yesterday with Damien in the park. Prior to that episode, she had begun to feel the glimmerings of a new rapprochement between herself and him: a subtle, surprising, but very welcome warmth. Yesterday, however, he had been forbiddingly cold and remote, once more the unapproachable older brother keeping her effectively at a distance.

Although . . . it had not been *her* at whom his barely veiled hostility was directed. Rather, the focus of it had seemed to be Captain Prescott.

Indeed, Augusta mused as she reviewed the episode again in her mind, if she had not known better, she might have thought that Damien was—well, *jealous* of Captain Prescott! But—

But Damien was betrothed; the captain, on the other hand, was an extremely eligible gentleman, one with whom Caroline (who had not, to Augusta's knowledge, formed a *tendre* for any of the other men she had met in London) was already on more than friendly terms.

It had in fact occurred to her that Caroline and Captain Prescott, so fortuitously and romantically reunited, might make a match of it, so well suited did they seem for each other.

That would make two marriages, then: Damien and Miss Manderlay's, and Caroline and the captain's.

Augusta's brows drew together. It was an equation that should have sorted itself out neatly enough, but somehow the elements refused to fall into place.

How confusing.

"H'm," she muttered aloud. There was only the one solution that she could see; why then did it still seem curiously unsettled?

She shook her head, and summoned her attention back to the problem at hand. Yesterday's odd encounter notwithstanding, she owed it to Damien to make a clean breast of her situation. How to arrange a meeting with him, however? He seemed to be so rarely in the house.

She thought for a few moments, and then her brow cleared. Of course: she would write a note to him, and leave it on the desk in his library.

Augusta rose, and went to her own desk, and within two or three minutes had scrawled a message requesting an interview with Damien at his earliest opportunity. She waved the piece of hot-pressed paper back and forth to speed the drying of the ink, then, without bothering to seal the note, left her bedchamber to make her way downstairs to the library.

She had just reached the bottom step when, to her surprise, Uxley opened the door to admit Damien himself, dressed in elegant riding gear. His boots and trousers were liberally spattered with mud; he clearly had ridden hard.

"Damien!" she said, with, it was to be hoped, any trepidation she might be feeling wholly masked. "Can you spare half an hour for me? I should like very much to talk with you!"

He looked at her frowningly. "As you can perceive, I am in no state in which to conduct a conversation. Will you not wait until I have bathed, and attired myself properly?"

Augusta took a deep breath. It would be entirely too easy to accede to Damien's request, and then, perhaps, let this precious opportunity slip away as her courage ebbed. "I do not mind your dirt," she replied, attempting for a teasing note.

"I do," he said, then he eyed her more sharply. "Is it a matter of such urgency that it may not be briefly postponed?"

"Well, it is not urgent, precisely . . ." Augusta fidgeted with the note she held in her hand, to her dismay feeling her resolve wavering. "It is only—that is to say—I should not wish you to be uncomfortable while we converse, and longing to be done . . ." Then, cravenly, she smiled brightly and said: "I am being silly! Of course it can wait!"

"If you are sure," Damien said.

"Yes! Certainly!"

"Very well." He had but taken a step toward the stairs when there was a firm knock upon the door. Uxley opened it, and briskly Captain Prescott crossed the threshold into the hall.

"My lady! My lord!" he said, taking off his hat and courteously dipping his head. "Good day to you both!"

"How do you do, Captain Prescott?" said Augusta. She glanced at Damien and saw that his face had frozen into harsh, uncompromising lines. Quickly she hurried across the hall, her hand extended, and placed it into the captain's so that he might bow over it. "It is a pleasure to see you this morning!" She saw his gaze flick to Damien.

He said, a note of anxiety in his voice: "I fear I have arrived too early, my lady! Please forgive me! The bumbling of an old soldier unused to fashionable ways, I am sorry to say! Will you not excuse me? I shall return again at a later time!"

"Nonsense, Captain!" Augusta said bracingly. "I do not know if my aunt is yet abroad, but Caro and I have been up for hours, having breakfasted quite early! She is at her needlework in the drawing room; I am sure she will be happy to see you!"

"If you are positive that I do not intrude . . . ," said the captain hesitatingly.

"Not at all!" Augusta turned to lead the captain up the stairs, and caught upon Damien's countenance a fleeting expression of such raw agony that she paused, perplexed and more than a little concerned. Then it was gone, and with his usual cool deliberation he had moved aside to let them pass.

It was at that moment, however, that the door to Damien's library opened, and his secretary Mr. Petley emerged. Looking a little surprised, doubtless at seeing so many people arrayed about the hall, he bowed deeply, encompassing them all, and said, "I beg your pardon for intruding, my lord, but I thought I had detected your voice! I have just received a third message from Miss Manderlay, marked for immediate delivery, and assumed that you would naturally wish to see it without delay." He trod across the marble floor and handed the sealed missive to Damien, then bowed again and retreated once more into the library, shutting the door gently behind him.

Augusta watched as Damien without haste broke the wafer and unfolded the note from Miss Manderlay. Then, realizing abruptly her rudeness in standing about while her brother perused his correspondence, she gestured to the captain. "Will you not follow me, sir?" Uncertainly she added, not knowing whether she was throwing highly incendiary fat into the fire: "Will—will you care to join us when you have changed your raiment, Damien?"

After a moment Damien looked up. "No, you must excuse me," he said coolly. "I am summoned to the side of my betrothed, for apparently she wishes to discuss wedding plans." He folded the note, then stood impassively waiting for her and their guest to precede him up the stairs.

"Oh! I see!" Augusta's tone was falsely bright, for she was conscious of feeling acutely uncomfortable, without knowing precisely why. "Well, do give my regards to Miss Manderlay, won't you? Uxley! Will you have some refreshments brought up to the drawing room? Thank you! Come along, Captain!" And while politely the captain followed her up the staircase, Augusta could not refrain from darting a quick peep over her shoulder at Damien, who remained where he was, staring fixedly at the note in his hand. So might one of Medusa's victims have appeared, thought Augusta, after unwarily looking into those accursed eyes!

Oh, but what a nonsensical notion! she chastised herself, and continued up the stairs, the captain behind her at a respectful distance. Shortly they entered the drawing room, where Caroline sat near the window, her head bent over a fine lawn handkerchief she was hemming and the sunlight catching the vivid red highlights in her simply arranged curls.

She looked up as they entered, and Augusta watched as her expression changed from what seemed like somber preoccupation to a welcoming smile.

"Gussie! And Harry! I did not dare hope to see you so soon, *mon ami,*" Caroline said warmly, putting aside her sewing and rising to meet them.

Captain Prescott clasped her hand and said with mock gruffness: "Did you think I would stay away long, my girl, when we have so much catching up to do?"

"Indeed we do!" Caroline agreed. "I am so glad you have come!"

Still narrowly observing Caroline for any signs of being in love with the captain, but seeing only a friendly affection, Augusta suggested that they all sit and dispose themselves comfortably for a chat. "While we can," she added. "Before the usual flood of callers swamps us and we may discuss only the merest trivialities!"

"Then I *am* early," the captain said remorsefully. "You ought to have sent me away, my lady!"

"What, and miss this golden opportunity?" retorted Augusta. "I may as well tell you at the outset, sir, that I am not one for ceremonious folderol!"

"In that case . . . ," said Captain Prescott thoughtfully, and paused for a few moments before going on, obviously choosing his words with care, "I hope you will excuse my plain speaking on such short acquaintance, my lady, but are you quite sure it is convenient for me to be here? I have on the two times I've encountered your brother the marquis received the distinct impression that I am *persona non grata,* and I should not wish to trespass on any mandates he might have laid down."

For once Augusta was disinclined to speak frankly, for she did not desire to share with either Caroline or the captain her own puzzlement on this very subject. So she said, taking refuge in the literal, "No, Captain, I assure you, my brother has issued no ultimatums regarding you. You may rest easy on that score."

The captain's pleasant, freckled face relaxed. "I am relieved to hear you say so, my lady."

"You have seen Lord Reston twice, Harry?" inquired Caroline, her gaze fixed on the handkerchief she had resumed hemming.

"Aye, just now," he replied. "In the hall. His lordship seemed more than a little perturbed by something, and I could not help but think it might have been something to do with the intrusion of my clumsy self."

Caroline glanced briefly at the captain, and Augusta was surprised to see in her green eyes a flicker of what might have been hope, before her eyelashes dropped and the needle she held flashed again, moving rapidly in and out of the lawn material in her hand. She said nothing, however, and there was a short interlude of silence that seemed curiously awkward to Augusta, who then volunteered: "Well, as to divining the cause of my brother's peculiar mood, Captain Prescott, he might very well have been rendered out of sorts at being the recipient of that dictum from his fiancée, Miss Manderlay, requesting that he repair to St. James' Place to confer about preparations for their wedding."

The captain nodded easily. "That would certainly explain it! A man doesn't like to be bothered with such things, I daresay!"

"Yes, I am sure you are right, sir," affirmed Augusta cheerfully, though secretly, she felt as though she had begun to dimly realize that the lives of those around her were more darkly tangled than she had ever even suspected.

* * *

"My dear Lord Reston," said the Baroness Manderlay, "whatever has kept you so long away from us? I understand from Helen that she had written to you twice already, before her third note went off early this morning!"

It was with an effort that Damien tore his gaze from the plasterwork ceiling, so elaborate in its execution of what seemed like hundreds of dimpled cherubs cavorting amidst a panoply of frothy clouds, so fantastically painted in discordant yellows and blues, that it could not fail to hypnotically attract the eye. He looked instead at the baroness, and at once found himself almost transfixed by the large, three-tiered ruff of stiff white lace with which that lady had chosen to cap off her ensemble, which consisted of a Guinevere-styled gown of coral-hued jaconet (replete with long, full sleeves, bound with golden cords spiraling down the arm), flimsy kid sandals whose gold straps were studded with replicas of old Roman coins, pink lace stockings, and a tiny beaded reticule of a remarkably loud shade of violet.

"What?" Damien said blankly.

Lady Calpurnia smiled indulgently, and her fingers went to pat the ruff around her skinny throat. "You are admiring my *betsy,* I perceive! It is the very latest in fashion, you must know!"

Damien blinked, and tried to shake off the creeping sensation of unreality that was dogging him. "Is it indeed, ma'am?" he said only.

"Oh, yes!" replied the baroness, with majestic complacency. "I do not think it long before all the truly stylish ladies of the *ton* will be similarly attired."

"Indeed," he said again, noncommittally.

"Yes, for it has not escaped my notice that I am regarded as one of the premier leaders of society," she went on, "and that my mode of dress, even many of my mannerisms, are copied everywhere I go! As but one example, surely you must have observed how popular ostrich feathers have lately become! *I* have been wearing them for these past fifteen years and more!'' On her long, narrow countenance was stamped an expression which in a lesser personage might have been taken for preening. ''Such an elevated position naturally entails considerable responsibility, but I am not, dear Lord Reston, one to shirk from duty, and so, when my modiste suggested that I purchase a half a dozen betsies, I could not but instantly assent.''

Damien said nothing, fighting instead the urge to gaze upward again and lose himself among the vacuous-looking cherubs floating overhead. It was with some measure of relief that he looked to Miss Manderlay when she spoke in her cool, beautifully modulated voice.

''Mama, I did not ask his lordship to visit us to converse about the latest quirks of fashion.''

''No, my dear, to be sure you did not,'' rejoined the baroness. Businesslike now, she said, ''You see, Lord Reston, Helen wishes to advance the date of the wedding.''

Damien raised his eyebrows, conscious of a wary surprise. ''Is that so, Helen?''

''Yes.'' Miss Manderlay drew through her fingers a shining strand of golden hair and repeatedly twisted it in a gesture that seemed to Damien unwontedly indicative of nervousness. Her blue eyes lifted to his. ''November *does* seem rather far away, Reston, and I thought that if we were to marry sometime in August, we might hold the ceremony in London. It would be considerably more convenient for those of our family and our friends at present lodged in town.''

It occurred to Damien to fleetingly ask himself if his betrothed might be *enceinte*, the responsible party being the Earl of Audley, but he dismissed the speculation at once. Miss Manderlay was too fully entrenched as a darling of society to risk such a scandal.

So what lay behind this peculiar request? After a few moments of fruitless cogitation, mentally Damien shrugged. What did it matter to him whether he was married to Miss Manderlay in August or November?

The end result was the same.

"As you will, Helen," he told her, and saw a strange tension in her shoulders recede.

"I am glad that is settled," the baroness said briskly. "The ceremony shall be held in St. Paul's, of course, with the wedding breakfast to follow. As for the other details, Lord Reston, you may leave them to us."

"Very well," said Damien, and stood up. He had no place in particular to go to, but was more than ready to leave.

"Pray do not run away so quickly," Lady Calpurnia said with ponderous waggishness. "We must also discuss the plans for the prenuptial ball the baron and I are holding for you and Helen."

"Yes?" said Damien without interest, remaining on his feet. Vaguely he wondered if this was what Hell felt like: this same numb, leaden sensation, with its sharp pinpricks of agony interspersed relentlessly throughout.

"As to that," continued the baroness, "we had thought to have it in August, at the very end of the season, but now, of course, that will not do. This is—let me see—the last week of May. . . . If we say the third week of June, and issue the invitations next week—Will that suit you, Lord Reston?"

"Yes."

Before he could make his farewells the baroness also rose to her feet, saying archly: "Excellent. I am sure you two have much to say to each other, as affianced couples must, so I will leave you for a few minutes! It is shocking the liberty allowed today's young people, but I would not wish to be thought trailing behind the times!" With that self-satisfied pronouncement she left the room, and a heavy silence promptly descended, during which Damien let his eyes drift irresistibly up again to the ceiling.

At length Miss Manderlay said: "My dear Reston, are you quite well?"

Dispassionately he looked at her: at her cool, golden loveliness, at her exquisite pale blue morning dress of soft, sheer silk and dainty blue slippers. She was, he supposed, very beautiful. He tried again to picture holding her in his arms on their wedding night, and once again his imagination failed him utterly. "Certainly."

"You seem—"she hesitated "a trifle distracted, perhaps."

"Not at all. Is there anything further you wish to discuss with me?"

She bit her lip, and said: "I trust you are not unhappy at the advancement of both our wedding date and the ball my parents wish to hold for us?"

"No."

"Perhaps—perhaps you thought our—my—request a little odd?"

"The date does not concern me."

She lifted limpid blue eyes to his, in which he was startled to detect a trace of anxiety. Slowly she said, "There have been rumors that . . . you might wish to cry off."

What the devil? he thought. Aloud he repeated, "Rumors?"

"The—the Earl of Audley told Mama so."

Damien said stonily: "I will not cry off, Helen."

"So I informed Mama, but she—she felt it best to—to—"

"Hasten things along?" he supplied coolly.

"Yes. She and my father—they favored your suit greatly, and would not wish to see any impediments to our union."

"And what about you, Helen?" he surprised himself by asking.

She dropped her eyes to the soft white hands folded demurely in her lap. "My first object must be to please my parents."

"Of course." Damien's curiosity as to the labyrinthine inner workings of Miss Manderlay's mind faded as abruptly as it had come, and he lapsed again into lethargic silence. Apparently reassured by the conversation that had transpired between them, neither did Miss Manderlay seem to feel obliged to offer any further remarks, and she kept her gaze firmly fixed on her interlaced fingers.

This was how the baroness found them when by and bye she returned, full of coy references to the dissolute habits of the modern youth, but Damien wasted no time in bidding the Manderlays a succinct *adieu* and making good his escape.

"Oh, Thomas," Augusta said breathlessly, "how wonderful it is to see you again! I have missed you dreadfully!"

"I have been counting the minutes until we might meet again," Thomas Culpepper replied softly. "I was delighted to receive your note, Gussie."

They sat in the cool shade of the same small pavilion in which they had found both refuge and a deeper understanding of their own hearts during that torrential afternoon rainstorm. Today they were not shielded from view of the passersby by means of an opaque curtain of water pouring from the eaves, so they contented themselves by sitting rather close together on a bench, with one of Augusta's bare hands discreetly tucked into Thomas's.

"As I was to send it to you. I am sorry to be a bit late," Augusta went on. "Just as I was about to leave the house this afternoon, my aunt received a personal invitation from the Princess Sophia, inviting her and myself to a small rout she is hosting on Friday: Aunt's excitement cannot be adequately described, I assure you! It was only by dint of employing the utmost tact that I was able to extricate myself from an excursion to Piccadilly on the instant, and convince her that we did *not* require new gloves, or stockings, or ribbons for our hair!"

"I am thankful for your persuasive abilities." Thomas smiled and tightened his hand on hers.

Augusta's heart gave a gay little leap. "I would not have

forgone the pleasure of seeing you for all the world!" she told him. "Tell me, how fares your pupil, young Humphrey?"

Thomas's smile broadened into a grin. "I have set him to a translation of Cicero's *Orations Against Catiline,* and I am afraid he finds it unpleasant work."

"You must admit that Cicero can be daunting," rejoined Augusta. "His use of the Latin tongue, while masterful, is both dense and subtle! However, it must be said in his defense that he is one of the few of the great Roman thinkers with a sense of humor."

"Just so: *'Nihil tam absurde dici potest, quod non dicatur ab aliquo philosophorum.'* "

Augusta laughed delightedly. "Indeed, it is one of my favorite quotations! 'Nothing so absurd can be said, that some philosopher has not said it.' "

"It is a favorite of mine as well! I cannot tell you how many times I have read *De Divinatione!*"

"Oh, Thomas!" sighed Augusta. "We were *made* for one another, do you not think so?"

"I must own that I do," he said, smiling at her in such a way that made Augusta long for a frightful storm to strike Hyde Park at once, and send the concealing rain cascading down around the roof of the pavilion. How splendid to have found such happiness with another! How fortunate she was!

Then Augusta's radiant bliss was tempered by a sobering reminder.

If only those she cared for were equally as happy . . .

"What is it, my beloved?" inquired Thomas. "A frown has suddenly creased the noble perfection of your brow."

"Yes, I have just thought of something . . . I cannot quite put my finger on it, Thomas, but something seems to have gone terribly awry in the household."

"How do you mean, Gussie?" Thomas asked, gazing at her with such palpably tender concern that Augusta could not but feel insensibly comforted by it.

"Well, Caro—she is my companion, you know, but really she is more of a friend, a very dear friend, and she is quite one of the family by now!—has of late seemed rather pale and in low spirits, though she insists, whenever I inquire, that nothing is wrong. Recently she has met again a friend from her past, with whom she is clearly on intimate terms. His name is Captain Prescott, Thomas, and he has just returned from the Peninsula. He is a most amiable gentleman, with delightfully easy manners! A bachelor, too, and is being urged by his parents to marry and settle down to the running of his estate in Devon which is, I have gathered from Caro, a large and prosperous one. I would have thought," Augusta went on slowly, "that she and the captain would suit each other magnificently! Yet Caro, while she seems glad to have renewed her acquaintance with Captain Prescott, evidently views him as but a friend."

"I should advise against matchmaking, Gussie," Thomas said, looking grave. "There is a fine line between affectionate concern and odious interference."

"Yes, you are quite right!" she agreed. "It is just that it would have been so *tidy!* Which leaves Caro mysteriously blue-deviled, and my brother, on the rare occasions when he is to be found at home, in the blackest of moods, and so intimidatingly aloof that I positively *quail* to approach him! Why, just this morning, Thomas, I hoped to closet myself with Damien and tell him all about you, and about us! I had, in fact, brought myself to the sticking point and requested an interview with him, but—but—well, somehow it never happened, and thus, I fear, you and I remain for the moment at *point non plus.*"

Thomas was silent, his greenish-blue eyes so serious that Augusta's breath caught in her throat.

"Thomas, what—what is it?" she faltered.

"I cannot wonder at your hesitating to inform your brother about our relationship. That it is indecorous in the extreme I cannot deny, painfully though I wish it might be otherwise!

Gussie, we cannot—*must not*—continue to conduct ourselves in such a shamefully covert fashion."

Augusta hung her head. "Yes, I know," she said miserably. "I am sorry I did not press harder today with my brother."

"Are you ashamed of me?" he said, very quietly. "Is that it, Gussie?"

"No!" exclaimed Augusta, bringing her chin up sharply. "Of course I am not! Indeed, I am *exceedingly* proud of you!"

"Be that as it may, there remain many obstacles between us," he said heavily. "The differences in our backgrounds, in our stations, in our fortunes—all are formidable. I would not be astonished if your family were to believe me to be the basest of fortune hunters."

"*I* know it is not true, and that is what matters!" she flashed. "If we tell them *now* that we are in love and wish to marry, then they cannot possibly think so, for it will be *years* before I come into my inheritance!"

"And in the interim, should they disapprove of the match?" Thomas said, still in that ominously quiet voice. "Even assuming that I am able to secure for myself a modest curateship, our income would at best be humble. You would be forced to live in circumstances greatly reduced from those to which you are accustomed, and I would not care to subject you to that."

"Why do you not ask *me* if I would care for it?" she returned heatedly. "You need not *assume* that my priorities are at odds with yours!"

Carefully Thomas withdrew his hand from hers. "A man has his pride, Gussie. He would not like to see the woman he loved lowering herself so profoundly, merely because of his own selfish desires."

"*Pride?* What does that have to say to anything? Surely you are not going to let your foolish *pride* come between us?" cried Augusta, feeling cruelly abandoned at the loss of his warm fingers intertwined with her own.

He sat up even straighter, and inched away from her. "It may seem foolish to you," he answered stiffly, "but it is not foolish to me."

Augusta stared at him bleakly before murmuring, " 'Pride goeth before destruction, and a haughty spirit before a fall.' "

"The Bible, of course," he replied grimly. "Proverbs. But do not think to sway me with an apt quotation! One must live by one's lights, and I shall not abandon my scruples so frivolously, my lady!"

"My lady?" echoed Augusta incredulously. She felt hot tears flooding her eyes and furiously she batted her lashes to keep them from falling. "If *that* is how you care to address me now, sir, I can plainly see where matters stand! It is obvious there is no longer any need for me to speak with my brother about us, for there is no longer any *us!*" She shot to her feet, and, choking back a sob, said unsteadily: "Farewell, sir! I am sorry to—to have *troubled* you with my human failings! Indeed, you may rest assured I shall trouble you no longer! Good-bye!" And with that, Augusta whirled about and hurried from the little pavilion. She nearly ran home, so anxious was she to flee to the privacy of her bedchamber and bury herself in the pages of a book where she might forget about Thomas, forget about their dreadful quarrel and the abrupt severing of relations between them . . . forget that her heart had been neatly, swiftly, and irrevocably broken in two.

Chapter 16

Caroline stood in the doorway of Augusta's bedchamber, watching as Mrs. Yardley meticulously adjusted a glittering topaz and crystal brooch set in the bodice of her niece's evening gown of marigold-yellow lutestring.

"Pray do not fuss so, Aunt!" said Augusta irritably. "I am quite sure the Princess Sophia will not notice the angle of my brooch!"

Mrs. Yardley gave the offending article a final tug, and straightened. "Whatever has put you in a state of such high dudgeon, Augusta? I vow, you have been quite *picksome* these past few days!"

Augusta only shrugged, and restlessly twitched the glossy silk material of her skirt.

"In fact," her aunt pursued, "you were barely civil to poor Captain Prescott tonight! And he so kind as to have dined with us, and given us each one of those pretty shawls the Spanish ladies wear—whatever are they called, Caroline dear? I have wholly forgotten the word for it!"

"Mantillas, ma'am," Caroline told her.

"Yes: thank you! *Such* a charming gentleman he is, and pointedly attentive to all of us, which I am sure he need not have been, given that he is a particular friend of *yours,* Caroline—not to mention the fact that *you,* Augusta, were behaving as if you were a hundred miles away, in spirit if not in the flesh! I declare I outright *winced* when the captain had to ask you *three times* to pass him the dish of boiled potatoes!" She paused, frowning. "Did you not think the potatoes had far too much butter and parsley in them? I know I did! And the apple soufflé! How woefully flat it was! I *did* speak to Cook this morning, and told her bluntly that if she felt herself unequal to the task of preparing a soufflé I would not have caviled at a simple grape pudding or even some cream rolls. But she assured me the receipt she intended to employ had been used with great success by the pastry chefs at the prince's Pavilion in Brighton, and that she might attempt it without a qualm!" Mrs. Yardley heaved a sad, gusty sigh. "I do not know which is worse, Cook's arrogance or my own gullibility in believing her!"

"You cannot have failed to notice that the captain ate with considerable gusto, ma'am," Caroline said kindly, "and that he praised everything on his plate!"

The older woman brightened. "Yes, that is so. You are *such* a comfort to me, my dear! What a pity it is that we cannot take you with us to the princess's rout! I do wish your name had been included on the invitation, for it promises to be a most convivial evening—not above a hundred guests, I daresay, and bound to be wonderfully intimate!"

"I am sure a restful evening at home will be a welcome one, ma'am," Caroline said, with unforced sincerity. "I had thought to read for a few hours, and retire early to my bed! Do—do you think his lordship would mind if I ventured into the library to select a book? I am afraid I have not been to Hookham's this week."

"Oh, no, of course Damien would not mind," Mrs. Yardley

said airily. "He has quite a *vast* number of books in there, and I am confident you will find just the volume to occupy you! I do wish he had joined us for dinner tonight, for then the captain need not have enjoyed his brandy in solitude! No doubt he is already gone out for the evening—I believe I overheard Lady Jersey mention the other day that Lord Alvanley recently won an enormous wager (pertaining to the movement of a fly upon a wall, if you can fathom it!) and is hosting a gathering at White's for the members of the Four Horse Club. Oh, good heavens, do but look at the time! Augusta, we must be off at once!"

"I wish that *I* might stay at home too," said Augusta mutinously, as reluctantly she rose to her feet and picked up from her dressing table a pair of long gloves and a yellow silk reticule fashioned over a delicate gilt frame.

"Do not say it, child!" expostulated her aunt in horror. "It is a signal honor the princess has bestowed upon us!" As she and Augusta left the bedchamber Mrs. Yardley added, "Caroline, might I trouble you to examine my plum-colored crêpe carriage dress? The ribbons *will* not stay in place, and I fear that the stitches have given way!"

"Certainly, ma'am; shall I go into your room?"

"Of course, my dear, you ought to know you have free run of the house! And if you are tired, and do not care to sew tonight, then do, pray, leave the chore until another time which more conveniently suits you!"

"You are very good, ma'am," Caroline said, smiling. "It is little enough you or Augusta will permit me to do! I will gladly have a look at the dress, and decide then. Good night!"

When Augusta and her aunt had walked down the hallway and disappeared down the stairs, Caroline went into Mrs. Yardley's chamber and there found draped across a chair the crêpe gown.

A quick examination revealed that the miscreant ribbons would need only a cursory stitch or two to secure them, and so Caroline set at once to make the needed repairs. Ten minutes later she had finished, and carefully she restored the gown to Mrs. Yardley's commodious armoire. As she was closing the door she caught a glimpse of herself in the pier glass and halted, staring for a moment at her pale, high-cheekboned face, in which her eyes seemed far too large, and at her simple, low-necked gown of light green gauze over a deeper green satin (for she had not bothered to change her dress after the captain had departed). Was it her imagination, or did her gown now hang a trifle loosely on her? If she did not take care, she thought dismally, she would soon be reduced to the dreadful thinness of the previous winter.

With a sigh Caroline shut the armoire door and slowly made her way downstairs. The hall, she saw, was deserted and silent. The heavy paneled door to the library was very slightly ajar, and hesitantly she pushed it open and stepped inside, into a large room graced by a high ceiling and what seemed like endless shelves of books, lit by a small fire in the hearth and a single flickering candle, and—

"Good evening, Caroline," drawled the marquis, looking up from the armchair in which he sat with one long leg crossed over the other, a leather-bound volume held in his strong, elegant fingers.

"Oh!" gasped Caroline, one hand flying to her breast, where she could feel the wildly erratic thumping of her heart. "I do beg your pardon! I—I did not think you to be in! Mrs. Yardley said that—that you were at White's tonight!"

"I was invited to go to White's, but I declined." Though his handsome face was impassive, his dark eyes gleamed with some intensely powerful emotion Caroline could not identify, but which set her heart to hammering even harder.

"I—I see," was all she could think to lamely reply.

"Will you not come in?" he said, closing his book with a soft snap.

Instinctively she took a faltering step backward. "No—that is, I—I should not wish to disturb you."

He smiled, though it was not a wholly pleasant one. "That, my dear," he said, "you have already done."

Her face burning, Caroline murmured, "I'm sorry, my lord," and retreated another step.

"Close the door," he commanded, "and come in."

Torn between the desire to be with the marquis, no matter how odd his mood, and the urge to basely flee, she remained rooted to the ground, watching wide-eyed as lazily he rose to his feet, strolled past her, and shut the heavy portal, sealing them in the solitary privacy of the dimly lit chamber. She turned to face him as he moved to his big mahogany desk and casually leaned against it, then folded his arms across his muscular chest. With a little jolt she realized suddenly that he wore no coat atop his close-fitting buckskin breeches, only a fine cambric shirt, whose long full sleeves were buttoned at the wrist; the panels at his chest, however, were unfastened near the top, revealing a vivid spray of dark hair.

Wantonly her mind flashed to that afternoon at Landsdowne, when she had watched Damien remove his blue coat, and wondered at the bare flesh that lay beneath it. And here before her was a tantalizing little display, hinting at the masculine power and vitality that yet was hidden from her gaze and from her touch—

Dear God, but she was *staring* at his chest! Feeling a blush burn even more hotly on her cheeks, she lifted her eyes to his and saw that he was gazing at her too, blatantly raking her from head to toe in a way that made her half wish she had a voluminous shawl to drape round her bare arms and low décolletage.

Silence hung between them, heavy and alive with a quivering tension, until finally Damien said softly, "Did you enjoy your dinner this evening, Caroline?"

It was a simple enough question, but warily she returned: "Yes, it—it was very pleasant."

A little smile curved Damien's sensuous mouth, but there was no humor in his countenance as he continued silkily: "I understand from Uxley that your dear friend Captain Prescott dined with you."

"Y-yes. We were sorry you did not join us."

At her hesitant words the smile quickly disappeared from Damien's face. "Join you?" he repeated, his voice harsh now. "Why the devil should I wish to join you, and sit passively by as the captain plays the lover, damn him, and as every slow minute drags past I long to run him through with a sword?"

"But what are you saying?" Caroline exclaimed in bewilderment. "The captain does not pay court to Augusta!"

"Don't be coy, Caroline, it doesn't become you!" he growled. "Surely it cannot have escaped your notice that Captain Prescott is in love with you!"

"Oh, no, you are mistaken!" she said quickly.

"Now you are lying to me! Do you deny that he is the man in your dreams?"

"*What?*" She was so taken aback she hardly knew whether to laugh or to weep.

Visibly he ground his teeth. "The man for whom you cry out in your sleep! The one you search for! It would not take a fool to realize that Captain Prescott is your long-lost lover!"

"It would take a fool to believe so!" she retorted angrily. "Captain Prescott has ever been a kind and thoughtful friend to my family—nothing more!"

"Indeed?" he snarled. "Then who is it you dream of, pray?"

"My *father!*" she said tightly, her hands balling into fists at her sides. "He was killed at Cadiz! When the battle was finally over, there was such dreadful chaos that no one knew who had lived or died! After waiting half a day I could not bear it any longer and went myself to search for him. There were frightened horses running loose, trampling bodies where they lay, and everywhere soldiers looking for their injured! The ground was littered with discarded weapons, empty shells, mangled hats and torn sashes, all the various paraphernalia of war, bloodied and sadly useless now!'' Deliberately Caroline drew a deep, calming breath, and forced her hands to relax. ''I found my father underneath an olive tree. He had been shot to death. In one of his hands he still clutched the double locket which contained the miniatures of my mother and me.''

''My God,'' Damien said quietly. ''I am so sorry. I did not know.''

''You did wish to learn more about my past, that day we rode together,'' said Caroline, with an effort continuing to keep her voice steady. ''I was grateful for your kind interest, but I—I could not tell you then. It is—difficult to speak about.''

''But of course it is,'' he said. ''My darling girl.'' He uncrossed his arms, and Caroline thought he looked as if he wished to stretch out a hand to her. But he said only, still in that gentle tone: ''Will you not tell me the whole of it?''

She looked at him for a long, considering moment, then, almost without conscious effort, obeyed. ''I recall that you once asked if I had any family. As to that, my father was the only child of a poor, but genteel couple in Cumberland; they owned a small farm, and my grandfather also served as a sexton in the local parish. When my father was seventeen he traveled into Scotland and there he met at a fair my mother, the sixteen-year-old daughter of an affluent sheep-farming family whose roots were noble ones: through a tangled series of bloodlines they were related to the Stuarts, and claimed, in fact, direct descent from the tragic Arabella Stuart. In any event, it was love at first sight for Mama and Papa; they were married before the week was out, and my mother was promptly disowned. They returned to England, where my father's parents generously made her welcome, but who soon sickened and died from smallpox. I was born within a year of their marriage. It—it was a difficult birth, and my mother could bear no more children. My father carried on as best he could with the farm, but there were successive droughts and by the time I was nine or so, he was forced to sell his property and go into the army so that we might not starve. Reluctantly my mother and I went back to her family, and my father left for the Continent. Mama was made so miserable in Scotland, however, that she sold a few pieces of jewelry left to her by her grandmother and used the proceeds to take us to Portugal.'' Caroline smiled reminiscently. ''How my mother and I cried to be reunited with Papa! We clung to him so hard that I daresay we nearly broke his back, poor man!'' She looked at the marquis, her eyes misty with tears. ''You know the rest, I believe.''

''But I don't,'' he said. ''What happened after you arrived in Portugal? How did you manage?''

''Well, as I have mentioned to you, Mama and I trailed behind Papa as best we could. To be sure, it was not the most comfortable existence, but we were all together, and that was what mattered! Mama schooled me to the best of her ability, and so did Papa and his friends, so that as I grew I received an unorthodox, but surprisingly thorough education.'' Caroline paused, then went on more haltingly: ''When I was seventeen, Mama contracted dysentery. We had a little ipecacuanha to give her, but she had never really regained her strength after my birth, and the years of hard travel had further depleted her, and so after a brief illness, she . . . she was gone from us. Then, three years later, my father died as well.'' Rapidly now, anxious to complete her tale: ''I did not wish to return to England, for there was nowhere for me to go. And I certainly did not intend to retreat to my mother's family, who had made us so terribly unhappy.''

''There was a general, was there not?'' said Damien. ''He took a hand in your affairs?''

Caroline nodded. ''Yes. Papa's commanding officer, General Gage, was very kind, but told me that it was both unseemly and dangerous for me to remain. I was wretchedly upset, but could not but accede to the force of his reasoning. It was he who found for me a post as governess to his daughter's children, in Denbury."

"The daughter who fed you gruel, and whose charming son accosted you in stairwells?"

Caroline nodded again, and sarcastically Damien rejoined: "The general could not have been so kind as you seem to think him."

A faint ghost of a laugh escaped her. "I cannot blame General Gage, for because of him I was able to earn my keep, and that was no small matter, you know."

"Yes, I do know," Damien said softly. "Thank you for confiding in me, Caroline."

She bowed her head, fighting a sudden rush of tears. She heard him say, "I am sorry, too, for being jealous of Captain Prescott. I can see now that I owe him only my gratitude," and then, with a shock of tingling awareness, she felt Damien's arms slide around her.

For the merest second she melted into his embrace, luxuriously breathed in the clean, virile, manly scent of him and gloried in his longed-for nearness. Then, abruptly, her memory assailed her and violently she pushed away from him. "How— how *dare* you?" she said furiously, linking her hands together at her waist to still their shaking.

His handsome face was baffled as he looked down at her. "How dare I?" he echoed blankly. "What have I done to make you so angry?"

"Now it is *I* who must accuse *you* of being disingenuous!"

"My darling girl—"

"I am *not* your darling girl!" she cried. "Apparently you have found someone else to replace me, and swiftly too! Do you not remember, my lord, you were to meet with the lady at Carlton House? Or has *she* been summarily replaced as well?"

At once comprehension flashed in his eyes, and to her wrathful amazement he even smiled faintly. "My dearest heart, it was but a ruse," he said. "You were with Audley; I could not let you be exposed to his greedy scrutiny and, doubtless, his malicious calumnies."

Caroline stared at Damien, feeling her chest rapidly rise and fall with the tumultuous force of her emotions. She *wanted* to believe him, she *wished* to believe she was his dearest heart, his darling girl, but what if she was only once again skipping along a primrose path of her own concoction, willfully engaging in self-delusion of the worst kind? She could not bear the redoubled pain that would inevitably follow; it would destroy her.

Her nerves, already ravaged by the intensity of the previous half hour with Damien, threatened to give way and hysterically she cried: "No, no, I do not believe you! I must not!" She whirled and blindly made for the door, but had taken only a few stumbling steps when Damien caught her.

Roughly he turned her to face him, and said harshly: "I will *make* you believe me, Caroline Smythe!"

Then, with a speed that took her breath away, he had crushed her against him and his mouth was on hers, hot and firm, demanding and merciless. *This* kiss began not as it had started on that bluff at Landsdowne, a soft, tender gesture of comfort; instead it was a raw assault on her senses, as with his lips and tongue and teeth he skillfully plundered her own mouth, drawing from her a dazed murmur low in her throat.

Her eyes drifted shut and involuntarily she shuddered with pleasure when Damien gripped the back of her head and held her thus as he kissed her yet more deeply, until she felt as if the whole world had magically shrunk to this one place, this singular moment in time, when there was nothing but pure sensation, and no one but themselves in a Paradise of their own creation.

Oh, but she believed him, she believed him now! Her arms crept up to his broad shoulders, her fingers burying themselves in the fine material of his shirt, and Damien groaned as she pressed herself even more closely to him, reveling boldly in the provocative feel of her breasts against him. There were only a few insubstantial layers of fabric separating her tingling nipples from the warm bare flesh of his chest, and even they seemed bulky and obtrusive, so terribly in the way of the untrammeled contact she desired . . .

"You are mine, Caroline," Damien whispered fiercely. "You are *mine!*" His lips went to the side of her throat, where the skin was soft and vulnerable, and he kissed her again and again, lower and lower, until at last his mouth had found a firm swell of breast rising above the neckline of her gown. Slowly he drew his tongue, like a tantalizing trail of fire, across that curve, dipping into the valley between her breasts and sending a dizzying spiral of molten bliss coursing down through her until her very toes curled in her slippers.

"Yes," she murmured, "oh, please," hardly knowing what she was saying, hardly knowing what she was doing as she brought her hands down to cup her bodice, offering herself to him—no, pleading with him, *begging* him to touch her, to taste her.

"My God, but you are beautiful," Damien muttered heatedly in response, and then his own hands came round, capturing her fingers in his and drawing them down to her sides, leaving her utterly defenseless as with his lips and teeth he deliberately worked at the ribbon-hemmed top of her gown, licking and nuzzling at her, wetting the gauze and silk so that her skin seemed to burn and radiate with the heat of their contact, taking his time with such leisurely enjoyment that Caroline thought she might scream from both the rapture of it and the impatience he was building in her . . . and finally, finally, when she thought she could bear it no longer, the flimsy material of her bodice gave way to his quest and he had closed his mouth upon a pink nipple, erect and quivering.

Then she did cry out as he suckled upon her, and only after

some delirious span of time had passed did she dimly realize that he had released her hands to bare her other breast to his view and knowing caress as well. Her fingers went to his dark head, and to grasp at the thick shining hair, urging him to continue in his course as he stroked her soft responsive mounds, kneaded and sucked and lightly bit at her.

"M'm," she murmured, "yes," over and over, and then a delicious warmth suffused her limbs, heavy and languorous, and between her legs, at the juncture of her thighs, a new and insistent ache made itself known. Oh, but now that one craving need was being met, avariciously did another one grow. She wanted Damien to touch her there, in her woman's secret place . . . She *needed* him to touch her there, for it was a hunger that wholly enveloped her, and it was one that instinctively she knew only Damien could satisfy.

At length Damien lifted his head, and straightened, and smiled down at her, his dark eyes alight. "I love you," he said simply, in his deep, cultured voice. "Will you believe that as well, my darling?"

"Yes," she whispered joyfully, and reached up to wonderingly stroke her fingers across his cheek, creased now with his brilliant smile. "Oh, yes, Damien, just as I believe you must know that I love you too!"

He grasped her hand and kissed it fervently. "Thank you," he said quietly. "I am grateful for your love, for I do not deserve it—"

"Hush," Caroline interrupted. "You deserve all the love that overflows my heart, and more!" As she gazed up at him, she observed a flicker of self-doubt, of refutation, in those deepset eyes, and quickly she drew his free hand again to her bare breast and at once saw his uncertainty replaced by fiery passion, heard his breath come more quickly between parted lips. "There is only one way I can show you how much I love you," she whispered, and turned her back, presenting to him a long row of tiny pearl buttons. "Unfasten them, please," she told him over her shoulder, and felt her knees shake at her own boldness.

"Caroline . . ." he said, very low. "Are you sure?"

"Quite sure," she replied unhesitatingly, and shivered to feel his fingers sliding along a curl at the sensitive nape of her neck.

Damien paused for only a moment longer before he began to unbutton her gown. He saw that his hands were shaking a little in his eagerness, was vividly aware of his own hardness and the feverish urgency pulsing in what seemed like all the veins of his body, and it took every ounce of self-control he possessed to keep from ripping the delicate silk and gauze from her back and taking her then and there as they stood together on the Aubusson carpet.

As mechanically he separated button from slit, over and over, it seemed it would take him forever to complete his task, in what was at once agonizingly slow torture and anticipation of the keenest sort. His reward was that each button freed, then bared, more of Caroline's sweet flesh to his avid stare, until at last he was done and was able to slip her gown from her shoulders to the floor. Stepping free of the dress puddled at her feet, she turned to face him once more, clad only in her sheer chemise and a single thin petticoat, stockings and dainty kid slippers. In the dancing light cast by the room's solitary candle her bared skin glowed a soft clear olive, and her lovely eyes shone a deep forest green as she tilted her face to him, on it a vulnerable expression of questioning shyness.

"You are so very beautiful," he said, his voice a little hoarse as he answered her unspoken question, "and I want you so badly, Caroline, I think I could die from the wanting!"

She smiled at his earnest words, the anxiety gone from her countenance, and whispered, "I do not wish you to die, my love, but . . . can you not hurry?"

Damien groaned and reached for her, kissing her long and lingeringly, his hands stroking the womanly swells of round breasts and flaring hips, the long, slender line of her waist; then quickly, impatiently, he unfastened the cambric tapes of her petticoat and let it drop to the carpet. Her chemise soon followed, and then Damien knelt before her, stroking the soft, firm flesh of her legs and exulting in their trembling at his every caress, before he tugged off her slippers and pulled down her stockings.

He looked up and his breath caught in his throat. She stood before him entirely nude, and Damien thought, awed, he had never seen anything so magnificent in all his life. Slowly he rose again to his feet and took her hand in his, and led her to the big round carpet set before the small cozy fire. "I am afraid it is not much of a bed," he told her wryly.

"It is as soft as velvet," she replied, and sank down upon it, her ankles tucked under her knees, and looked up at him expectantly.

Damien needed no further invitation. Swiftly he divested himself of his clothing and boots, heaping them in a careless pile beside him, and when he, too, was naked, he joined her upon the carpet, stretching out upon it at full length and drawing her eagerly against him.

She gave a breathy sigh, and said with purring satisfaction: "Oh, Damien, you feel just as I dreamed you would . . . hard and soft, rough and tender all at once . . . Only dreams could never compare to the—the incredible reality of you!"

"I feel quite the same way," he murmured in her ear, "for you are exquisite, my little goddess," and then he traced its delicate outline with his tongue and felt his own excitement increase at hearing her tiny moan. One of his hands curved underneath her shoulders; the other traced a lazy path across her breasts, her flat stomach, toyed with her hips, then with the soft hair below them. She gasped, and shut her eyes, and her fingers came up to grasp at his where they curved around her upper arm. He linked their hands together as he continued his exploration between long, feminine legs which to his joy had timidly parted to permit him yet greater access.

He stroked the soft, damp folds there, thrilling to hear her whisper, "Oh, Damien . . . oh, Damien . . . oh, yes, my love!" Slowly, gently, he slid one finger, then two, inside her warm sheath even as he bent his head to hers and kissed her, his tongue provocatively mimicking the motion and the leisurely pace of his hand. She moaned again, more urgently now, and then his fingers went to the hard little pebble of flesh sweetly nestled further up her woman's mound and he began a steady, rhythmic caress.

As he touched her, circled that taut pebble, worshipped her with every deliberate stroke, Damien delighted in the new tension he sensed in her body pressed against his, the unconscious tightening of the muscles of her legs and arms. Her neck arched, and she lifted her head for his kiss, murmuring needfully, "Please . . . oh, Damien . . . please . . ."

"Yes, my darling girl, yes," he whispered back, and brought his lips down to hers. She kissed him ardently and without restraint, and when a few moments later she reached her peak she cried out against his mouth, shuddering in convulsive ecstasy.

When her body stilled, and relaxed, she opened her eyes and gazed up at him as if dazzled. "Oh, my God," she said slowly, "I never knew I could feel that way," and Damien laughed, more than a little proud to have given her such pleasure.

She propped herself up on one elbow, her auburn curls tumbling free from her coiffure to spill becomingly about her face and neck. "I," she announced with a determination that both amused and aroused him, "would like to do for *you* what you have just done for me!"

"Can't," he replied promptly, and pointedly glanced down at his shaft, firm and erect. "We lack the same—er, equipment, you see."

"I do see," she murmured. "How—how splendid you are!"

She reached out and grasped him in one small hand, her fingers sliding instinctively around the intensely sensitive tip.

Damien jerked at the bolt of voluptuous gratification he felt, and for a short, bewitched interlude he lay back upon the carpet and allowed her to work her magic upon him, as with increasing boldness and finesse she stroked him and with her other hand she cupped the heavy globes at the base of his manhood. All too soon, however, he felt himself approaching that tempting edge, and gently he covered her hands with his own and drew them away.

"No," she protested, but did not resist when he rolled her to her back and he positioned himself atop her, spreading her legs wide between his knees. He was so hard now, so desperately hard that he could feel himself trembling from the desire raging through him, but he would not go any further unless and until she gave her consent.

"Are you ready for me, Caroline?" he asked her softly, gazing down into her big, luminescent green eyes. "Do you truly wish for this?"

"Yes," she said. "Oh, yes, please!" and eagerly she brought her hips up to meet him.

"Oh, my darling girl," he whispered, and then his shaft was at the hot, wet gate of her womanhood. With slow, careful movements he slid inside her, vividly attuned to her every subtle reaction, determined to keep his own fiery urgency in check, for it was her pleasure that must come first.

To Caroline it seemed that she had entered into a haze of wild sensation and delight she had never imagined possible. Damien surrounded her, filled her, subsumed her; in her nostrils was the heady scent of him, above her she saw his beloved face, focused and alight as he gazed into her eyes, and between her legs was the long, hard totem of his potent masculinity, with every gentle little stroke assuaging the hunger he had created in her . . . yet somehow building it too.

Just then he slid deeper, and she felt a brief stab of pain and clutched at the muscled forearms braced on either side of her.

Damien paused, and whispered with obvious concern: "Have I hurt you?"

"It is nothing," she assured him with perfect truthfulness, and, aware again of the delicious need throbbing at her core, she pleaded, "Pray, my love, do not stop!"

With a groan he obeyed her soft request, his strokes becoming long, deliberate, and rhythmic as he moved above her and inside her, each slide of his flesh within hers yielding a sensuous surge of hot pleasure, as she felt herself lifted higher and higher on dazzling waves of pure sensation, drifting inexorably toward some beckoning destination she at once longed to attain and yet never wished to reach . . . for she never wanted to end the mindless glory of these moments when their bodies moved gracefully together as one.

In some far distant reaches of her consciousness Caroline knew she was panting, had her hand's fingers gripped around his strong broad shoulders, was meeting him thrust for thrust as they stared at each other in the semidarkness and the warm perspiration dripped salty drop by drop from his face onto hers and she licked at them in an uncaring abandonment.

"I love you," she gasped, "oh, Damien, I love you so!"

"I love *you*," he whispered, plunging into her once more, and then she had sailed into a storm of swirling, shattering bliss as she cried out, helpless in the sweet paroxysm that took her over, body and soul, sucking her into a mighty vortex of unparalleled euphoria where there was no past, no future, only this perfect, crystallized moment.

And then, just as her own tremors began to fade, the tempo of Damien's movements increased and he leaned down to kiss her hard, and nuzzle roughly at her tingling breasts. More than anything wanting him to share with her what she had just experienced, Caroline stroked her hands along the pumping rock-hard muscles of his buttocks, stretching to reach those heavy, warm globes she had fondled before. Her searching fingers closed gently round them, caressing them, and then

Damien groaned, "Oh, God, Caroline!" and his long, powerful body went rigid as he threw back his head, his eyes tightly shut as the cords in his throat stood out in sharp relief, and joyfully she felt his hot, wet seed spilling into her.

Some long moments later he opened his eyes and smiled down at her, so brilliantly and with such unabashed tenderness that she felt the breath leave her lungs in a gratified rush of female satisfaction.

"My lord, I have pleased you?" she inquired demurely.

"Pleased me?" he growled. "You have nearly killed me, wench!"

"I am so glad," she murmured, and then he had kissed her, reluctantly pulled himself free of her, and rolled over onto his side, bringing her securely against him.

"You are the most beautiful woman in the world," he told her, "the most desirable, delicious woman this poor earth has ever known."

Caroline smiled. "I doubt it," she responded, stroking his lean jaw lovingly, "but it is very pleasant to know that *you* think so!"

At some point the little fire had died away in the hearth, but the room was still warm. A comfortable drowsiness enveloped Caroline as she rested within the circle of Damien's strong arms, her cheek nestled against his chest, her entire body cushioned by the plush carpet upon which they lay. Her eyelids slowly drifted shut and lazily she murmured: "I should never need a blanket could I but sleep every night like this . . ."

She felt Damien's warm lips at her temple as he replied quietly, his breath lightly stirring at the curls there, "I have never felt such rightness, such a sense of belonging . . . of completion."

"I am so glad, my love," she repeated, and then, happier than she had ever been in her life, Caroline smiled again and fell deeply and profoundly asleep.

Chapter 17

Somewhere a door snicked shut, and out in the hall a voice said, loudly and shrilly, "I am sorry to disappoint you once again, Aunt, but I *cannot* share your delight in such a wretchedly insipid evening!"

Caroline awoke with a start, and saw that Damien, too, had stirred and opened his eyes. Vividly aware now of her nakedness, and how dreadful it would be if they were to be discovered this way, urgently she made as if to rise. But Damien's arms tightened around her, and silently he shook his head, in his gaze a warning for her to remain still.

"I do not know what bedevils you, Augusta, I swear that I do not!" came Mrs. Yardley's exasperated reply. "Thank you, Uxley, that will be all! I am sorry to have roused you from your bed at this late hour! You may return to your quarters at once! Come, Augusta, I wish to hear no more of your pettish complaints! The Princess Sophia was kindness and condescension itself, and I am sure *everyone* there exerted themselves to please you!"

"Hah!" said Augusta sarcastically. "A greater bunch of simpering fools I hope never to meet! If I heard a dozen remarks upon the weather I heard a thousand of them!"

"Oh, child, you have worn me out this night," sighed Mrs. Yardley. "I *distinctly* feel a horrid headache coming on, and I should not be surprised if I am laid low with it all day tomorrow!"

"Good! Then we need not make calls nor receive callers!" Augusta said callously. "*I* shall sleep till noon!"

There were sounds of her sulky footfalls going methodically up the stairs, followed by the muted whisper of Mrs. Yardley's slippers and trailing shawls, until finally all the noises of their ascent had faded into the heavy silence of deep night.

"We must rise, Damien," Caroline said quietly, and forced herself to break away from the warm encirclement of his arms and stand up. Swiftly and efficiently she dressed in the guttering light of the candle, turned and waited while he buttoned her gown, then watched as he too donned his garments, hating to see his strong, powerful masculinity masked by clothing but acknowledging there was no help for it. No matter how fiercely she might wish it to be otherwise, this magical interlude between them had to come to an end. When he had pulled on his boots and straightened again, she drew close to him, stretching out her hand.

"Thank you, my love," she said, relishing the feel of her fingers in his grasp. "For—for *everything,* including"—faintly she smiled—"the most delightfully peaceful sleep I have enjoyed in many years."

Damien's dark brows came together as he looked down at her and frowned. "Do not thank me as if this is some sort of good-bye."

She gave her head a tiny shake. "It *must* be; we both know that we might not with impunity enjoy such—such closeness again."

"No!" He took her other hand in his and held it tightly.

"Marry me, Caroline," he said impetuously, "and be with me for always!"

"I wish I could!" Earnestly she gazed up at him, knowing that her heart was in her eyes, revealing all her love and longing. "Oh, how I wish I could! But but you must marry Miss Manderlay, Damien!"

"*Hang* Miss Manderlay! It's you I love!"

"You have made a solemn promise," Caroline replied, hearing the painful wobble in her voice. "You are too much a man of honor not to fulfill your commitment."

He laughed without amusement. "I am what you have made me! I daresay before I met you I might have been willing to overthrow my honor, my pride, my reputation, but now . . . why, I am as neatly trapped by them as any animal in a noose! It is a fine piece of irony, is it not?"

"You are too harsh to yourself," she said softly. "*I* have done nothing. It did not take me long after our becoming acquainted to realize your worth, despite the fact that you took great pains to conceal it from me—conceal it from the world. I only wonder I did not fall in love with you the moment I opened my eyes and beheld you by my bed in that little inn in Baldock."

"I was a different man then. I can only be glad you were not swayed by my dubious charms."

"Never dubious," she said, and smiled up at him with all the bravery she could summon. "Only wondrous!"

But he did not return her smile; he only gripped her hands more tightly. "Caroline, do not turn me away! Even now you might be with child—with *my* child!"

Her smile faced, and died. "I cannot be," she told him. "It is too close to the time of my monthly courses."

His brows went up, and swiftly she explained: "My mother, you see, was kind to the—the camp followers who went along behind the soldiers, providing their—their services to the men, and as I grew older I often went with Mama when she visited the women during times of illness or distress. I could not help but learn a great deal about the functions of the female body— among them being the women's methods for protecting themselves against conceiving a baby.''

Damien's chest was tight. ''My wise Caroline,'' he said softly. ''How much you have learned of this world in your short life.''

''Too much to be a proper lady, I fear,'' she returned, with a little self-deprecating smile.

''On the contrary. You are the truest lady I have ever known.''

''Thank you for saying so. I shall treasure those kind words.'' She looked up at him, and he saw great tears shimmering in her eyes. She squeezed his hands and, stretching up high on her tiptoes, kissed him once, twice, a third time, then stepped back, blinking hard. ''Good night, my love,'' she whispered brokenly.

''Good night, dearest heart,'' Damien said, his own voice a little unsteady, and with his empty hands clenched into tight fists, he watched her turn and swiftly leave the library, closing the door quietly behind her.

Alone again, Damien gazed around the room as if he had never seen it before, blankly eyeing the many rows of books, his big mahogany desk, the heavy velvet curtains shielding the tall windows. Then, his movements slow, he went to the armchair in which he had been sitting when Caroline had come to him earlier that evening. He lowered himself into it, and with the lightest puff of breath he blew out the flickering candle on the little table next to him, and sat very still in the welcome shroud of darkness.

Augusta watched disinterestedly as her aunt plucked a plump peach-filled pastry from the platter in front of her and bit into it with obvious enjoyment. She poured herself another cup of tea and glanced at her untouched plate, then looked across the table to where Caroline sat with her fingers wrapped around her teacup, staring into the steaming brew in front of her as if it might contain the answers to some questions that urgently plagued her.

At last Aunt Violet swallowed, patted her lips with her damask napkin, and said animatedly: "I am most heartily sorry neither of you cared to accompany me to Almack's last night, my dears, for the place was veritably *abuzz!*"

As Augusta did not feel inclined to respond, it was left to Caroline to raise her eyes from her cup and say politely, "Indeed, ma'am?"

"Oh, yes! I had it all from Caecilia Russell! Mr. Brummell and Lord Alvanley, together with Sir Henry Mildmay and Henry Pierrepoint, gave a ball a few evenings ago at the Argyle Rooms—though perhaps you knew that already?"

"No, ma'am. I—I have not looked at the papers recently."

"Yes, it took place on Monday night. Even though Mr. Brummell and the regent had recently quarreled, and despite the regent's sudden hostility toward Sir Henry, they decided to invite him anyway. Well! When the prince arrived and approached the four hosts, he shook hands with Lord Alvanley and Mr. Pierrepoint, but then moved forward, *ignoring* Mr. Brummell and Sir Henry! The snub could not have been more calculated! And then Mr. Brummell said—oh, my dears, you will scarcely believe this! I vow I nearly toppled from my chair when Caecilia repeated it to me!—Mr. Brummell said, very clearly and distinctly, in a wonderfully carrying tone, 'Alvanley! Who's your fat friend?' "

"Good heavens," Caroline murmured.

"That is precisely what *I* said! There can be no doubt that the regent and Mr. Brummell have broken irrevocably, of course. It is the end of an era, you may be sure of that." Aunt Violet nodded sagaciously.

"But what shall become of Mr. Brummell, ma'am?" inquired Caroline, an expression of concern on her rather pale countenance. "Has he not been one of the prince's intimates for some time now? One of the—the Unique Four, as I understand they are termed?"

"Oh, yes! As to what shall become of Mr. Brummell, doubtless he will go on as before, as amusing as ever! In fact, he was at Almack's last night, entertaining Lady Jersey with all sorts of *wicked* anecdotes about Madame de Staël! Caecilia had gone to secure for herself a claret cup, and could not help but overhear them as they stood near one of the refreshment tables!"

"I am glad to hear Mr. Brummell has not felt obliged to abandon his place in society, then," said Caroline. "But who is Madame de Staël, ma'am?"

Aunt Violet opened her eyes wide at this naive question. "My dear, surely you have heard of the famous Germaine de Staël! Her Paris salon was known round the world, until her resistance to that dreadful monster Napoleon grew so obvious that she was forced to flee to her estate on Lake Geneva! Now she is come to visit London, and apparently even the regent wishes to meet her! Caecilia says she is to be presented to him at the end of the month."

Augusta bestirred herself sufficiently to add, "She is a brilliant woman of letters, Caroline. Three years ago she published a remarkable book called *On Germany;* its unabashed enthusiasm for German Romanticism is already exerting a tremendous influence on European thought."

"Indeed, they say she is a formidable bluestocking," agreed her aunt, "and that she talks everywhere, to anyone, at great length. According to Caecilia, Lady Holland is reported to have said to Mrs. Creevey, 'The great wonder of the time is Madame de Staël. She is surrounded by all the curious, and every sentence she utters is caught and repeated with various commentaries.' "

"She sounds like a most learned and interesting personage,"

remarked Caroline. "I am sorry I have not had the opportunity to meet her."

"Well, I, for one, am not in the least bit sorry to have failed to make her acquaintance!" Aunt Violet returned frankly. "I daresay I should not be able to comprehend half the things she says! Too, apparently she is no treat for the eyes, for she is nigh on fifty years of age, coarsened and *quite* thick in the waist, and has somehow acquired for herself a comely young husband, whose hand she has accepted but not, curiously enough, his name! Caecilia says he is nearly as good-looking as Byron."

"Oh, Aunt, must you dwell on appearances when it is *accomplishments* that matter?" Augusta put in impatiently.

"My dear Augusta, what *has* been troubling you these past few days? If I did not know your powers of digestion to be robust, I would say that you suffer from dyspepsia, for I know that when *I* do the pain is excruciating, and I can hardly say a pleasant word to anyone! Indeed, I have observed that your appetite has remarkably diminished, and that you merely push your food about your plate as if it has become repulsive to you!"

"It is *not* dyspepsia," muttered Augusta. "I have not been hungry, that is all."

"That is all?" echoed her aunt disbelievingly. "Lord, that is akin to saying that—that Damien no longer cares for the cut of his coat!"

Augusta only shrugged, and sipped moodily at her tea.

"Caroline," Aunt Violet said portentously, "do have a good look at Augusta, I pray you! Do you detect a conspicuous glitter to her eyes, or skin shrunken around her bones?"

"No, ma'am," came the careful reply.

"Well, I am not at all sure that I do not! If it is not dyspepsia, then you may have consumption, Augusta! I shall send for the doctor directly breakfast is over!"

"You will do no such thing!" Augusta snapped, rising tem-

pestuously to her feet and flinging her napkin on the tablecloth.
"What you shall do is to *leave me alone!*" She turned and
hurried from the breakfast room, and ran up the stairs to her
bedchamber, where she slammed the door behind her and threw
herself onto her bed, and gave vent to a hearty bout of tears.

God in heaven, but these last days had been wretched ones!
Two times had she had sent Thomas a note, begging to hear
from him, but there had been no word of response. Every day
her hope of a reply grew dimmer, but the misery she was
experiencing did not fade also; instead it only seemed to inten-
sify.

Augusta rolled onto her back and stared sightlessly at the
embroidered damask of the canopy overhead. If *this* was what
love was all about—this unrelieved agony, this hideous pining
for another, this bizarre inability to enjoy her food as she was
accustomed to—well, she had been infinitely better off before
she had met Thomas Culpepper and rashly fallen in love with
him!

But . . . she could not help feeling the way she did, for she
had come to discover that her heart was a wayward organ, and
stubbornly refused to obey her stern commands to care less,
to miss him less, to want him less.

Augusta gave a mighty sniff, then stood and went to her
dressing table, where she rooted among the reticules there carelessly strewn about until she found a handkerchief, with which
she promptly blew her nose.

"It is much better this way," she told her red-eyed, pink-
nosed reflection in the mirror. "It would have been an impossible situation, after all, for—for our stations in life *are* very
different, and no doubt Damien would have forbidden us to
wed in any event! So it is best to have terminated it now, before
we became even more deeply entangled!" She concluded her
courageous little speech with a decisive nod, though secretly
she was forced to admit that the Augusta gazing back at her
in the mirror did not look the slightest bit convinced.

* * *

Damien had just emerged from the changing room at Jackson's Saloon, his hat and gloves in hand, when he heard a cheerful voice hailing him and turned. Charles Highcombe was bearing down upon him, a wide grin on his round, amiable face.

"My dear fellow! It is an age since I have seen you! Are you on your way out? Have you finished your sparring exercise, then?"

"As you perceive, Charles," answered Damien.

"If only I had your science!" said his friend enviously. "You've excellent bottom, and are *never* glaringly abroad! How the devil do you contrive to look so cool after an hour in the ring? Yes, yes, Max, I see you! I'll be over presently! Keep at that singlestick! Shall you be at White's tonight, Damien? Do let us share a bottle of port together!"

"I am afraid not; this afternoon I am going out of town for a week or two."

"For a week or two?" said Charles, then nudged him slyly with his ebony walking cane. "Not going to miss the ball the Manderlays are throwing for you on the twentieth, are you?"

"You have received the invitation, I conclude."

"Yes, and on the thickest paper I swear I've ever seen! My mother says it's going to positively be the most lavish entertainment of the season!"

"It may well be," Damien said, "but I cannot speak on the subject with any authority. I am not involved in the preparations."

"No, and why should you be? It's all for the females to flutter over, ain't it? And knowing the Manderlays and their freedom with their blunt, it's going to shine everyone else down! But—but—" Charles' gray eyes narrowed suspiciously. "Damn it, you haven't answered my question! You *are* going to be there?"

"Charles! Are you suggesting that I might fail in my duties to my betrothed?" Damien drawled. "You quite shock me."

"I'm not suggesting anything! Only—only—you've been acting dashed peculiar of late, my dear fellow! Never see you anymore at White's, or Watier's, or the Alfred, or the hells in St. James', or Vauxhall, or—or any of the parties my mother bullies me into attending! What the devil are you *doing* with yourself?"

Damien looked at his friend for a long moment. "Would you believe me if I said I was reforming?"

"Reforming?" echoed Charles, incredulous. "Never say you've fallen under the sway of that—that preacher who walks like a monkey? What's his name? Wilbur Willenforce? The old fellow who's agitated half the M.P.s in Parliament into pushing through an act to abolish the slave trade, or some arrant nonsense like that?"

"His name is William Wilberforce, and no, I have not become a follower of his."

"Thank God!" Charles exclaimed, but his relief was short-lived as pensively Damien spoke.

"Though I cannot like Wilberforce's methods, equally can I not condemn his principles. The traffic in human beings is reprehensible, and should be abhorrent to all thinking, moral people."

"Yes, yes, to be sure!" rejoined Charles hastily. "But why must you avoid your usual haunts? What *do* you mean when you say you're reforming?"

Damien's mouth twisted into a simulacrum of a smile. "I have been reading a great deal on the topic of agriculture."

"*Agriculture!* Good God! What the devil for?"

"So that when I go to Windemere this afternoon, and throw myself upon the mercy of my estate manager, he may not think me quite utterly an ignorant fool. I observe that your friend Max is gesticulating at you with an impatience bordering on an apparent desire to club you on the head with that singlestick.

Therefore I shall not detain you any longer, Charles. Try to keep your guard up, and don't rattle in too hard, as you are wont to do! Good day!'' With that same faint, twisted smile, Damien nodded, and left the Saloon.

"I'm happy to see you at last, my girl!'' said Captain Harry Prescott, having been ushered into the drawing room by a visibly disapproving Uxley. "Yes, I know I'm unfashionably early, and have no doubt scandalized your butler, but I've called several times in the past week, all during the proper hours, and have never once found you at home!'' He seated himself on the long flower-patterned sofa where Caroline sat with her ever-present needlework in her lap; this morning she was repairing the torn silk lining of one of Mrs. Yardley's bonnets. "And if I may be perfectly frank,'' the captain added, "I'm not sorry to see you alone, for I've been hoping to enjoy a solitary conversation with you! Might we expect to be undisturbed for a bit?''

"I think so, Harry,'' Caroline replied. "Lady Augusta has lately taken to having breakfast sent up to her on a tray, and does not now emerge from her room before noon, and Mrs. Yardley has gone out shopping, and informed me she does not expect to return in time for luncheon.''

He looked at her from underneath bushy red eyebrows. "Good! Although I suppose I ought to ask: I trust I'm not getting you into any kind of trouble with your employers, visiting alone with you like this?''

"Oh, no! I am treated with the utmost liberality, Harry! The Restons have been nothing but kindness itself to me!''

"Indeed, so I have thought. And yet . . . you appear a little paler, and thinner, than when I last saw you a week ago, my girl. It occurs to me to wonder if something in your situation here has altered—and for the worse.''

Touched by his concern, Caroline summoned up as sincere

a smile as she could manage. "As to that, I shall only say to you—in the strictest confidence, mind!—that I have deduced that her ladyship has recently experienced a disappointment in love, and because of that her spirits have been very low. As her friend and companion, I cannot help but feel the greatest sympathy for her."

"Yes, certainly, and I'm dreadfully sorry to hear about Lady Augusta's sufferings, for she's a splendid girl," the captain rejoined. "But that's no reason why *you* should be wasting away!"

"I am hardly wasting away, Harry," she said. "But do let us speak of something more interesting than myself! Tell me how you have spent these past days! Have you found a carriage at Tattersall's? As well as the horses that you mentioned you were considering?"

"Oh, aye, I've a new carriage, and I've bought the horses, too! A finer pair of sweet-goers you'd be hard-pressed to find anywhere!"

"I am glad to hear it! What else?"

"Ah, so you wish for the full accounting, then?" At her nod he continued: "I've been to Stultz for some new coats, and to some of the other tailors whose names I can't remember! A fellow at my bankers' recommended half a dozen of 'em along Bond Street, and now I suppose I owe them all a king's ransom for the fine clothes they've made me! What a dash I shall cut in the countryside, shan't I, in my fine London garb!"

"As you yourself said, Harry, you needed something besides your uniforms to wear," Caroline pointed out.

"Yes, of course you are right. It is just that . . ." Restively he shifted his shoulders beneath his new superfine coat of dark blue. "Well, after you've spent ten years as a military man, never knowing if the next day will see you alive or dead, it does seem peculiar to be strolling about the streets of London without a blessed care in the world!"

"I imagine it would. But Harry, you have certainly earned your leisure, and your freedom from care."

"You are good to reassure me," he said. "I confess I have felt more than a little guilty!"

"After you have risked your life many times over for your country? Perish the thought!"

"So I shall then, and freely divulge to you that I have *thoroughly* been the idle man about town!" He grinned at her. "I have several times gone riding, and have seen a balloon ascension *and* a cockfight; I've also visited a few of the picture galleries, as well as Astley's Amphitheater and the Royal Menagerie at the Tower, *and* Madame Tussaud's Waxworks. In short, I have been gay to dissipation!"

"I can see that you have!" Affectionately Caroline returned Harry's smile; she was not too overcome by her own secret grief to recognize the pleasure she took in his easygoing company.

"In between all this frivolity, I've also managed to execute a few commissions for my father, spend several useful hours with my bankers, and make some purchases on behalf of my mother and sisters. By the bye! I had a note from Lucy—she's my sister who's next to me in age, you know—saying that she has just become engaged to that barrister who's been courting her these two years and more, and so I wanted to find her an especially nice bride-gift! Do you think a necklet of pearls from Rundell and Bridge will do?"

"I am sure it shall," Caroline said warmly. "You are a most thoughtful and generous brother, Harry!"

"Well, even though we've long been separated, Lucy means a great deal to me—they all do," he replied, his freckled face growing more serious. "Which brings me back to the reason why I wished to speak with you privately, my girl! You have yet to tell me what happened to you after you left the employ of General Gage's daughter. *He* only knew that she had some kind of hysterical report from her sister, a Mrs. Ashby, I believe, who said that you arrived late and in a deplorable condition!"

Looking down into her lap, Caroline picked up her needle and carefully resumed stitching at the silk lining. "On my way to meet Mrs. Ashby, I—I met with an accident and so was delayed."

"What sort of accident?"

"It will sound dreadful, I know, but . . . well, I am afraid I threw myself into the path of Lord Reston's curricle."

"What?" the captain ejaculated in horror. "In God's name, why?"

"I was attempting to rescue a puppy who had been thrown into the street."

"That's just like you!" he said. "You were always saving every abandoned or injured animal to cross our path! How badly were you hurt?"

"I broke my arm, and suffered a few bruises, but it could have gone *considerably* much the worse for me had it not been for the skillful driving of the marquis! In any event," Caroline went on, "his lordship rescued *me* and saw to it that I promptly received the attention of the local doctor. When he discovered that I had lost my situation with Mrs. Ashby as a consequence of my mishap, he offered me a position as a companion to his sister Lady Augusta."

"I see," Harry said slowly. "And it has been, I take it, a congenial role for you."

"Yes," she said simply, but kept her eyes fixed on the bonnet she held.

"You will forgive my speaking candidly, my girl, but I believe I may claim the privilege as an old friend! For how long do you plan to remain with the Reston family?"

Startled, Caroline glanced up. "How—how long?" she repeated stupidly, feeling the fresh pain tear anew at her heart at the captain's blunt words.

"Yes. I do not suppose that the position of a companion or governess can ever be considered a permanent one."

"That is so."

"I am asking, then, if you have given much thought as to your future."

Desperately Caroline tried to conceal her sadness as she replied: "Your timing is uncanny, Harry! I have recently been making discreet inquiries amongst the ladies of Mrs. Yardley's acquaintance, in an effort to discern if they, or someone whom they know, might require the services of one such as myself."

"Even while your position here is a stable one?" he asked, looking at her keenly.

"Yes. As you say, there can be little security in my profession."

"Do you enjoy it?"

"It is not a question of enjoyment, Harry. I must earn my keep, and rejoice in the situations, such as this one, which pay me well and permit me the luxury of associating with—with genteel families like the Restons."

"Well!" the captain said briskly. "I can see there is no use in beating around the bush, my girl! My business here in London is complete, and I depart for Devon within the next day or so. I have come here today to inquire more particularly into your circumstances, and having satisfied myself on several counts, I may now comfortably ask you: would you care to marry me?"

"*Harry!*" exclaimed Caroline, wholly taken aback. "What on earth are you saying?"

"I should think it perfectly clear," he replied with unimpaired calm. "You are an old friend, alone in the world. In order to gratify the wishes of my sire, I am desirous of marrying and starting a family, and having a helpmeet to assist me in the running of my estate."

Mrs. Yardley's bonnet dropped unheeded to the floor as Caroline stared at the captain. It was not a romantic offer, to be sure, but one plainly and honestly couched; there would be no pretensions of love or passion between them, only a fond alliance between two partners linked by the mutual interests of offspring and commerce. It would be an easy way out of her dilemma: a comfortable marriage and a swift escape from the Restons.

Caroline swallowed hard. Perhaps, if she had never known Damien, had never loved him and found such ecstasy in his arms, it *would* have been easy to assent to the captain's business-like proposal.

But it was impossible now to imagine herself another gentleman's wife. Oh, she knew full well that Damien was unattainable, that he belonged to Miss Manderlay . . . but she could not, before God and man, take her vows to marry Harry Prescott, to love and obey him, and feel herself to be anything other than the basest hypocrite.

Caroline reached out and patted one of the captain's strong, freckled hands. "You are very kind, Harry," she said, as steadily as she was able, "but I must decline your very obliging offer. You must go home to Devon, and there find yourself some pretty young miss with whom to fall madly in love and produce an entire flock of little Prescotts for your father to spoil!"

"I should not like to think that I am leaving you in the lurch, my girl," he said earnestly. "Indeed I should not!"

"In the lurch?" Caroline said, rallying. "Whyever should you think so, my dear old friend? I am doing very well for myself—I should blush to divulge to you both how light my duties are and how handsome a salary I am receiving!—and have every expectation of shortly securing another position just as agreeable!"

"If you are sure . . ."

"Quite sure!"

"Well, if that is the case," he said, looking a little sheepish, "I may as well tell you that there *was* a young lady I met in Devon, a friend of Lucy's. Penelope! With eyes as blue as the sea, and a complexion like good Devon cream! No promises were made between us," he added hastily, "otherwise I would never have offered for you, my girl! But now . . ."

"Now you may feel yourself perfectly free to declare yourself," said Caroline, more than a little relieved to learn that the captain's heart was not in the least injured by her refusal. She patted his hand once again, picked up Mrs. Yardley's bonnet, and said, as she bent her head over her sewing once more: "She sounds like a most delightful girl, your Penelope! Now do, pray, tell me all about her!"

Chapter 18

Caroline watched as Augusta listlessly danced a quadrille, occasionally nodding her head in indifferent reply to her partner's sprightly attempts at conversation. She herself had politely turned down all requests to dance, and was cravenly waiting until the end of the set to make her way over to the long row of chairs where the dowagers sat.

Neither she nor Augusta, for their own undisclosed reasons, had wished to attend this soiree in the stately, if faintly shabby, town house owned by the Highcombes, but Mr. Charles Highcombe was this evening to announce his betrothal to a Miss Aldora Kimball, and Mrs. Yardley had firmly stated that, no matter how objectionable the young lady's background might be (for her father was a rich India merchant, and *his* father a lowly proprietor of a coffeehouse near Paternoster Row), given the longstanding connection between their two families, the Restons ought certainly to be there.

"But *Damien* won't even be present!" Augusta had protested. "He's left London again!"

"All the more reason why *we* should go!" Mrs. Yardley had said. "When I called on Mrs. Highcombe yesterday she informed me that the engagement was quite a sudden one—I gather that Mr. Highcombe only spoke to Mr. Kimball on Sunday—but that both she and the Kimballs are anxious to formally make known the engagement to society."

"So that the bargain might well and properly be sealed," Augusta had commented waspishly.

"One might choose to look down one's nose upon such a match," her aunt had rejoined pragmatically, "but *her* wealth shall repair the shattered fortunes of the Highcombes, and *his* lineage shall vastly enhance the status of the Kimballs. It shall not be the most *illustrious* union, of course, but I am sure we ought to join in the Highcombes' rejoicing."

"I do not want to *rejoice!*" Augusta's voice had been petulant and rather shrill. "I do not care to hear announcements of engagements! I want to stay *home!*"

Deeply shocked, Mrs. Yardley could only say "Augusta!" in a tone so permeated with outrage that after a moment her niece hung her head and sulkily consented to attend the soiree.

As for Caroline herself, she too would have preferred to remain at home, but as she did not like to disappoint Mrs. Yardley, she had quietly acquiesced to that lady's plans. Besides, she reminded herself, she might make good use of this opportunity to tactfully ask after a new position, and as the orchestra had just concluded its piece, determinedly she approached the row of dowagers who sat against the wall, either watching the proceedings or talking animatedly amongst themselves.

"Good evening, Mrs. Samuelson," she said to one of Mrs. Yardley's acquaintances whom she had met once or twice before, with a cheerfulness she did not feel. "I trust I find you well?"

"How do you do, Miss Smythe?" the old lady replied civilly. "Do you care to join me?"

"Thank you; I should like that." Caroline sat on the vacant chair adjacent to that of Mrs. Samuelson. "It is—it is quite a lovely party Mrs. Highcombe has arranged, is it not?"

"Yes, and on such short notice, too! But all the *ton* is here tonight, for Charles Highcombe is a universal favorite, you know!"

"Indeed, he is a most good-natured gentleman," Caroline agreed. They chatted for a few minutes on inconsequential topics; then she nervously unfurled her fan and, a little doubtfully, glanced over at her companion. In truth, she knew very little about Mrs. Samuelson: only that she was a widow whose circumstances were affluent, and that she had several grown children. Caroline took a deep, steadying breath. "Mrs. Samuelson," she began hesitantly, "I wonder if I might inquire . . ."

"Yes, my dear?"

"I hope you will not think me forward, but . . . As you know, I am a companion to Lady Augusta Reston, and I—I am searching for another situation."

"Indeed? Are you being let go, Miss Smythe?"

"Oh, no! That is, not precisely! But—but her ladyship's age is such that—and—and there is Mrs. Yardley, of course— well, I am not at all confident that I am truly needed there, ma'am!"

"Your sentiments do you honor, Miss Smythe! It is not every companion who would scruple to so conscientiously analyze her situation, and feel herself obliged to seek another."

"Thank you, ma'am. I was wondering, then, if—if perhaps you . . ."

"Oh, no, my dear, thank you! I am far too set in my ways to consider taking a young person into my household! But why do you not marry one of the gentlemen I have frequently seen dangling after you?"

"That, ma'am, is out of the question (and I do hope I have encouraged no one to *dangle* after me!). But—but might any of your sons or daughters perhaps need a governess for their children?''

''No, I believe not. But I should be glad to write to them and ask, if you wish.''

''Thank you, ma'am; I would be grateful.'' Caroline knew her smile was a little wan. Another fruitless query; she was, she admitted, becoming increasingly discouraged. She tried to disguise her disappointment by changing the topic, and shortly a chance remark of Mrs. Samuelson's revealed that she was inordinately attached to her pet bird, and gamely Caroline encouraged her to discourse at length upon that animal's many winsome habits.

''Waldo will climb upon my shoulder, Miss Smythe, and entertain me with his chatter, and peck jealously at the book I am attempting to read, until finally I put it down and allow him to kiss me! He is the most delightful little creature! Oh! Mr. Highcombe! How do you do? Pray accept my warmest felicitations! Have you brought your fiancée for us to meet?''

''Indeed I have, ma'am! 'Servant, Miss Smythe! May I introduce to you Miss Kimball? My dear, this is Mrs. Samuelson, and Miss Caroline Smythe!''

The plain-featured, richly dressed young lady at Charles Highcombe's side dipped a slight curtsy and said in a timid little voice: ''How do you do?''

''Is this your first opportunity to meet Mr. Highcombe's friends and acquaintances, Miss Kimball?'' Mrs. Samuelson asked kindly.

''Yes, ma'am.''

''No wonder you look a trifle overwhelmed, my dear! I am sure *I* would be, if I had to say how-do-you-do to so many people all at once!''

''Yes! It is—it is just that there are so *many!*'' Miss Kimball confided. ''I do not think I shall be able to remember above ten or twelve names in total!''

''Well, I daresay you shall soon become accustomed to it

all,'' said Mrs. Samuelson in her comfortable way. "Strange faces will turn into familiar ones before you even are aware of it! Oh, hello, Olive!''

Mrs. Highcombe swept up to them, on her gaunt countenance an expression approaching actual geniality. "Good evening, Rowena. How do you do, Miss Smythe? Charles," she announced, "I have come to take Miss Kimball from you for a short time. Lady Sefton wishes to meet her.''

"Then you must do so at once!" promptly answered Mr. Highcombe. "Go along then, Aldora, and I'll join you by and bye!''

Miss Kimball glanced shyly up at him, murmured "Very well," then withdrew her hand from the forearm she had been clutching, and obediently accompanied Mrs. Highcombe across the ballroom.

"She's a nice gel, Mr. Highcombe!" said Mrs. Samuelson approvingly. "You've done well for yourself!''

"Thank you, ma'am: I know it!" replied Charles with his easy grin. "Miss Smythe, would you care to take a turn about the room?''

Caroline assented, and rose to her feet with alacrity. After bidding a polite farewell to Mrs. Samuelson, she slipped her arm through his and as they began slowly pacing along the perimeter of the ballroom she said, "I wish you very happy, Mr. Highcombe!''

"Thank you, Miss Smythe, I believe I shall be," he said. "I have found my heiress at last, and the Highcombes may together breathe a collective sigh of relief!''

"Mrs. Yardley mentioned that it was all rather—rather sudden," ventured Caroline.

"Yes, I had only got wind of the Kimballs' recent return from India and their desire to marry Aldora into the Upper Ten Thousand a week ago, and had my man of business hasten to Mr. Kimball's offices in the City upon the instant. There were numerous other aspirants for Aldora's hand, of course, but

Mr. Kimball liked my bloodlines and, happily, found my own personage to be unexceptionable. And, when Aldora and I met, *I* found nothing offensive in *her.*''

"I see," was all Caroline could think to reply to Mr. Highcombe's cheerfully cold-blooded description of his courtship.

"Yes, so we placed the announcement in the *Gazette* on Monday, and my mother sent out cards of invitation on Tuesday, and here we are!" Mr. Highcombe looked about the crowded ballroom with transparent gratification. "I only wish Damien could be here! If I had known I was going to be betrothed I would have dropped a hint in his ear before he left town, but it was only later after he left that I heard the news about the Kimballs.''

"Do—do you know where his lordship went?" Caroline said, as offhandedly as she could. "Neither Mrs. Yardley nor Lady Augusta were informed as to his destination.''

"We encountered each other early last week at Jackson's Saloon," Mr. Highcombe answered with equal casualness, "and—let me see!—yes! He mentioned that he was going to Windemere, and that while he was there he intended to—oh, hello, Francis! I'm dashed glad you could come!''

Caroline was to learn no more, as jubilantly Mr. Highcombe accepted the congratulations of his friend Mr. Chester, who in turn greeted her cordially. They had but spoken together for a few moments when behind them came a cool, controlled voice speaking in a deliberately provocative tone.

"I felicitate you on your cleverness, my dear boy.''

Mr. Highcombe turned quickly, in the process inadvertently jostling Caroline's arm—the one she had broken—so sharply that an unaccustomed jolt of pain shot through her and involuntarily she gave a little cry of distress.

"I *do* beg your pardon, Miss Smythe!" Mr. Highcombe said with swift concern. "I did not realize your arm was tender still!''

Caroline glanced up into the intent, pale blue eyes of the Earl of Audley and hurriedly murmured, "No—no, it is nothing, Mr. Highcombe! It is merely—merely that you startled me!"

Mr. Highcombe glared at the earl. "Well, if Audley here hadn't startled *me,* with his presumptuous remark," he said indignantly, "I daresay I wouldn't have whipped around like that!"

The earl bowed unctuously. "My apologies, dear boy," he said. "In my haste to tender my warm good wishes I fear I rushed my fences."

"Yes, yes, thank you and all that," grumbled Mr. Highcombe.

His lordship turned his gaze back to Caroline. "You have recently injured your arm, Miss Smythe?"

"As I said, my lord, it is nothing," she returned, careful to resist the impulse to rub with her other hand at the throbbing spot. At the same time she was surprised to see on the earl's countenance an unusual look of strain. He gave a little shrug, and answered with something less than his usual urbanity.

"So you say, Miss Smythe, so you say. What is insignificant to one person may be of supreme importance to another. Once again, Mr. Highcombe, my felicitations on your propitious match. Would that we all might be so fortunate!" The earl bowed again, and turned on his delicate painted heel and strode off, leaving the little group behind him speechless for a short time.

It was Mr. Highcombe who broke the silence. "A damned mysterious fellow!" he complained, adding punctiliously, "Begging your pardon, Miss Smythe!"

Caroline only nodded absently, staring after the earl as he made his way through the crowd. What *had* he meant by his oblique observations?

"I say, Charles, your mother's waving at you," Mr. Chester said suddenly. "Don't think she merely means to say hello, either."

"No, you're quite right: I recognize that particular gesture very well. Note you the lopsided tilt of her head and the circular twirling of her fan? I am being summoned, you know! Excuse me, won't you? Francis, do offer Miss Smythe something cool to drink! She looks as if she could use it!'' And with that blunt comment, compliantly he hastened away toward Mrs. Highcombe and his fiancée.

Gallantly Mr. Chester invited Caroline to partake of some lemonade, and together they made their way toward the refreshments. He himself indulged in a stronger beverage and soon became quite loquacious on any number of subjects, including the remarkable new steam engines (he had actually witnessed the first public trial of the *Prince Regent* in West Riding the previous August), Wellington's movements through Spain, the horses he was particularly likely to wager upon at Ascot this year, and his hopes to attend the Henley Regatta, having rowed himself while at university. In brief intervals amidst this unceasing spate of eloquence Mr. Chester several times asked Caroline to dance, twice invited her to stroll with him on the terrace, and once begged her to marry him.

Caroline refused him on all counts, and though she was unsuccessful in detaching him from her side, he was, at least, an undemanding companion, requiring only the occasional nod or diplomatic smile to maintain his voluble flow of conversation. She caught an occasional glimpse of Augusta, plodding through a variety of dances, and of Mrs. Yardley flitting hither and yon, and of Mrs. Highcombe leading Miss Kimball about like some prize heifer she was pleased to display. Then Caroline was astonished to see Mr. Highcombe with the Earl of Audley, each holding a tall crystal flute of champagne. It was evidently not Mr. Highcombe's first toast of the evening, for he had begun to look rather rumpled and red-cheeked, and his gray eyes were sparkling glassily. The earl, on the other hand, never once, at least during the period of time in which Caroline was able to observe them, took a sip of his champagne, and on his countenance remained that same odd, alert tension she had noted before.

"Cricket!" abruptly said Mr. Chester.

Blankly Caroline turned to look at him. "Is there, sir? Where?"

"No, no, not *that* sort of cricket, Miss Smythe! I meant the *game* of cricket!"

"Oh! What of it, Mr. Chester?"

"Do you follow the sport, by any chance?"

"No, I am afraid not. I must confess I find its rules rather difficult to comprehend."

Mr. Chester heaved a theatrical sigh. "That's what all the ladies say! It's not so complicated, really, once you've grasped a few of the fundamentals ..." And before Caroline could even begin to make the attempt to forestall him, he had launched into a lengthy exposition, complete with animated swings of his arms intended to pictorially represent the movements of the players across the field.

Resignedly Caroline waited for Mr. Chester to strike an unwary guest straying too near, but hardly had a quarter of an hour without violence elapsed before, she was delighted to perceive, Mrs. Yardley and Augusta were coming her way.

"—therefore, if a batsman hits the ball far enough so that he and his partner can run to exchange places, a run is scored. It's perfectly simple, isn't it? But batsmen are out if the ball is caught in the air, or if—"

"I beg your pardon, Mr. Chester," said Caroline, ruthlessly interrupting him, "but I have just this moment realized that I must rejoin my party! Thank you for the lemonade! Good night, sir!" And rapidly she went to meet Augusta and Mrs. Yardley halfway in their progress toward her.

"Augusta," Mrs. Yardley said without preamble, "claims she is unwell! I am sorry, Caroline, but we must depart at once. Of course it is hardly proper to steal away before the actual announcement of the betrothal is made, and even though I daresay Mrs. Highcombe intends to call for a halt in the dancing within the next hour or two, I should not wish to inconvenience her by having Augusta faint dead away in the middle of it, and stealing poor Miss Kimball's thunder! She is a sweet, mannerly girl, by the bye: I have met her, and talked with her for some five or ten minutes! However, I cannot like her gown, I own, for the material seems rather too heavy for the season, and I did think the sapphires sewn onto the ribbon beneath her bodice and at her hem somewhat *loud!* As were, I might add, the diamonds in her ears and about her throat! Of the first water, of course! And Miss Kimball's skin is decidedly brown; there is no other word for it. The Indian sun, I must suppose, is dreadfully fierce! Though one *could* use a parasol at all times to shield one's face from exposure, and strictly limit one's excursions outdoors during the daylight hours! I can only wonder at Mrs. Kimball's permitting her daughter to subject her complexion to such rigors! Oh! I have met Mrs. Kimball as well, Caroline, and Mr. Kimball too! A pleasant enough couple, if a little quiet—they did not in the least attempt to put themselves forward, and I cannot but think the better of them for it! I do not doubt it will seem a little odd for Mr. Highcombe to welcome into his family such an *off* set of in-laws—*his* ancestors, after all, came over with the Conqueror!—but I am sure they will contrive somehow. Will he and the new Mrs. Highcombe feel obliged to invite them to dine very often, do you think?''

"I," said Augusta through clenched teeth, "am leaving! If you do not care to come with me, Aunt, you may call for a hackney when you *are* ready to depart!" An awful scowl on her face, she turned and began pushing her way through the crowd.

Caroline, glancing helplessly at Mrs. Yardley, followed. She had taken only a few paces when the older woman caught up with her, speaking resignedly.

"It is but eleven o'clock! Lord, Caroline! How on earth shall we occupy ourselves until it is time to retire?"

The carriage ride back to Grosvenor Square was a silent one, punctuated only by Mrs. Yardley's occasional disgruntled remarks. However, as they were issued in a low, muttered undervoice, Caroline felt herself free to assume that the older woman did not feel in need of a reply, and so she, like Augusta, remained mute.

Uxley was still at his post when the ladies came to the door of the town house; indeed, he presented every appearance of a sentry anxiously awaiting the arrival of reinforcement troops, for no sooner had they entered the hall than he spoke.

"I am terribly sorry, my lady, ma'am, but—but there is a gentlemen here, awaiting you!"

Mrs. Yardley's eyebrows rose so high they threatened to disappear underneath her fringe of gray-blonde curls. "A gentleman, Uxley? At this hour? Who is it?"

"He would not give his name, ma'am. He only said that he would wait for your party to return, and then he—he pushed his way past me into the drawing room!" Distressfully the butler wrung his hands. "I have for the last hour been debating within myself whether I ought not to have summoned the watch!"

Mrs. Yardley looked doubtfully to Caroline. "Could it be another of your friends, my dear?"

"I—I hardly know, ma'am. I should like to think that none of *my* friends would rudely force themselves into someone's house at this late hour of the evening!" A terrible thought occurred to Caroline and she added anxiously: "Do you suppose this gentleman brings word of—of the marquis, ma'am? Perhaps his lordship has met with some kind of mishap!"

"Good heavens, I do hope not! Well, I daresay the only thing to do is to go upstairs and see who it is. Uxley," Mrs. Yardley instructed solemnly, "if you should hear us scream, then you *will* want to call for the watch at once!"

His eyes as round as saucers, Uxley nodded. "Yes, ma'am!"

The three ladies went upstairs and paused before the closed door of the drawing room. Silently they exchanged irresolute glances, and in the end it was Caroline, her heart pounding hard, who pulled open the door and stepped inside.

She saw a tall, thin young man leap up from his chair. Dressed respectably in modest nankeen trousers of a pale yellow, a short white waistcoat, and a coat of blue merino, he had a mane of shaggy, light brown hair, and a thin, appealingly sensitive countenance in which blue-green eyes flashed to hers with a look of eager hope which swiftly faded.

"Sir?" said Caroline inquiringly. "How is it that I may be of service to you?"

The young man bowed. "I—I am heartily sorry to intrude, ma'am! It is only that I—I *must* see the Marquis of Reston at once!"

There was a shriek from behind Caroline. *"Thomas!"* cried Augusta, and burst into the drawing room, nearly toppling Caroline in her haste to reach the young man. Righting herself, Caroline watched, openmouthed, as Augusta flung herself into the arms of their guest—doubtless none other than Mr. Thomas Culpepper—and sobbed incomprehensibly against his shoulder.

"Gussie, Gussie," the young man murmured, patting her.

"Augusta!" ejaculated Mrs. Yardley, scandalized. "What on *earth* is the meaning of this? Detach yourself *at once!"*

"I won't, I won't!" her niece sobbed, and only wormed herself more tightly into Mr. Culpepper's embrace. "Oh, Thomas, I have missed you so wretchedly! When I did not hear from you, I thought—I thought that you did not care for me any longer!"

"Never that, Gussie!" he whispered tenderly. "Never that! Only my absurd, misbegotten pride stood between us!"

"Augusta, I *command* you to come here immediately!" Mrs. Yardley cried.

"No!" returned Augusta with equal determination. "I shall never be separated from Thomas again!"

Mrs. Yardley moaned "Oh, my *Lord!*" and sank into the nearest chair, where she frantically began fumbling in her reticule.

Quickly Caroline stepped forward and pulled from her own reticule a little vinaigrette, which she held underneath the older woman's nose. Mrs. Yardley closed her eyes, breathed deeply, then said faintly, "Thank you, my dear! On *you,* at least, I may rely!"

There came the sound of hasty, heavy footsteps pounding up the stairs, and a few moments later two of the burliest Reston footmen appeared in the doorway, their clothing comically askew but each clutching a deadly looking club. Behind them trotted Uxley, who breathlessly spoke.

"Ma'am! I heard a scream!"

Mrs. Yardley opened her eyes and gave a little yelp. "Oh! It is—it is only William and John! I hardly recognized them with those frightening implements! Caroline, my dear—the vinaigrette, please! Yes! Thank you! That is better!"

Uncertainly Uxley glanced about the room, his glance lingering unavoidably on the amazing spectacle of a weeping Lady Augusta Reston tightly clasped in the arms of a personage *inconnu.* "Is—is our presence here required, ma'am?" he said uncomfortably.

"Yes!" stridently declared Mrs. Yardley. "You may instruct William and John to remove this—this interloper at once, and throw him into the street! *Then* you may summon the watch, and have him taken away!"

"You will do no such thing, Uxley!" Augusta screeched, turning to glare at the harassed butler.

"No, my lady," he said promptly, plainly relieved at being released from so unusual and onerous a duty, and next to him the hulking footmen immediately lowered their clubs.

All at once an awkward silence descended upon the curiously

disparate group assembled in the drawing room, with everyone, Caroline thought, at a loss as to what to say or do next. It was hardly *her* place to dismiss either the butler or the footmen, who obviously longed devoutly to flee, or to suggest such a course to the distraught Mrs. Yardley, who had rested an elbow upon the arm of her chair and propped her brow upon her palm as if her neck could no longer support the weight of her head. Meanwhile, Augusta was fully occupied in having her face gently patted dry by Mr. Culpepper and was evidently oblivious to anything or anyone else.

It was at this precise moment that a voice spoke, with remarkably cool aplomb given the bizarre tableau which had formed before him.

"What the devil is going on here?"

Caroline whirled about, just as Augusta gasped, *"Damien!"* and the three servants obsequiously stepped aside *(scuttling* was more like it! thought Caroline) to permit the Marquis of Reston himself to enter the drawing room. Leisurely he did so, and surveyed them all with only his dark eyebrows minutely raised to indicate that he found in his drawing room anything at all out of the ordinary.

"Damien, you have come back!" said Augusta breathlessly.

"Yes, and apparently in the nick of time," he replied. "Uxley, may I inquire as to the reason why your footmen are so haphazardly dressed and bear arms?"

"As to that, my lord, I—this young man, and —I had thought about the watch, of course, but—well, Mrs. Yardley—that is to say, she told me—and there was a scream, my lord, and . . ." The normally unflappable Uxley trailed off, and looked hopelessly up at his master.

"You and your men may go, Uxley," Damien said, not unkindly.

"Thank you, my lord!" the butler said in accents of profound gratitude. He bowed deeply, then lost no time in ushering John

and William out of the room before him, bowing again, and closing the door with the utmost exactitude behind him.

Caroline watched bemusedly as Damien turned to his sister and spoke, with such dispassionate understatement that she might have laughed had her nerves not been so overset.

"Doubtless you shall at some point enlighten me as to the identity of this young man whose hand you are clutching in a death-grip."

"I most certainly shall!" returned Augusta, tilting her chin proudly. "It is my pleasure—no, it is my *honor* to present to you—"

"My lord!" interposed a pale, but resolute Mr. Culpepper, firmly disengaging his hand from Augusta's, stepping forward, and bowing to Damien. "I am Thomas Culpepper, of Norwich, presently attached to the family of Sir Everard Richmont as a tutor, and am in search of a curateship appropriate to my education and ambition. I briefly encountered your sister, Lady Augusta, at Christie's some weeks ago, at a book auction, and when chance thereafter brought us together again I improperly took advantage of this unforeseen but welcome opportunity to further my acquaintance with her. After that, my lord, I must inform you that we—we met clandestinely, and while I cannot but be sorry for the lack of decorum attached to my behavior, there can be no tinge of regret on my part, for I fell very deeply in love with Lady Augusta!"

Damien regarded Mr. Culpepper without expression, then seated himself upon the flowered sofa and crossed one long, booted leg over the other. "Indeed?"

"Yes! And—and I have these many days past come to this house, my lord, asking to be admitted into your presence, only to be repeatedly told that you were not at home."

"I *wasn't* at home," said Damien. "I was, in fact, away."

"Thomas!" interrupted Augusta impetuously. "I did not know you had come here!"

Mr. Culpepper glanced at her. "I did not wish you to know,"

he said quietly. "I wanted to do my duty as a man, and lay my case honestly before your brother."

"Very proper," approved Damien. For the first time he bent his gaze fully upon Caroline, and said, "Did you know about this?"

"Y-yes, my lord," she admitted. "A little. I know it was very wrong of me to say nothing, but—"

"But you wished to respect Augusta's confidence," he finished calmly. "It is wholly understandable; you may be assured that no blame attaches to you."

"Thank you, my lord." Caroline knew her heart was in her eyes as she looked unguardedly at Damien, and felt warm relief and gladness rush through her as she glimpsed for a moment an answering flicker in the dark depths of his own eyes before he turned back to Mr. Culpepper, who squared his thin shoulders and went on determinedly.

"There is more, my lord! Not only do I love your sister, but I wish to marry her! I am all too aware that ours would be an unequal match in terms of birth and fortune; in intellect, however, and, most importantly, in the depth and duration of our mutual affection we should be most brilliantly paired!"

"Oh, Thomas!" sighed Augusta, and came forward to once more slip her hand into his, and stare defiantly at her brother.

"Mr. Culpepper," began Damien, "I—"

"We are prepared to wait, my lord!" the other, younger man said. "Years if we must, and to live frugally upon my income as best we may. We are not afraid of hardship!"

"No, we are not!" agreed Augusta, adding with considerable pride, "Thomas attended Cambridge, Damien! I am confident that it shall not be long before he secures a splendid curateship, and begins to distinguish himself in the church!"

Damien said: "I—"

"While I hope that the aspirations Lady Augusta—Gussie—cherishes for me may someday be realized," Mr. Culpepper said, "my chief concern, my lord, is to vow to you that she will be treated as tenderly, as lovingly as any wife ever was! I am cognizant of the fact that your disapproval of our marriage may be such that you will feel obliged to disown Augusta, and cast her from the bosom of her family, and to disavow all further intercourse between yourselves. Much as I should be devastatingly sorry to be the cause of the severing of these sacred ties between you, my lord, I shall not scruple to inform you that Gussie and I are fixed in our intentions!''

His expression fathomless, Damien looked from Mr. Culpepper to his sister. He opened his mouth once more to speak, but then, for the first time since Damien had entered the drawing room, Mrs. Yardley threw herself into the fray. In a weak, desperate tone she entreated.

''For the love of God, nephew, tell them you forbid this dreadful marriage!''

Damien glanced at her and said, ''I shall do nothing of the sort.''

''What?'' squeaked Mrs. Yardley in disbelief, as Augusta gave an ecstatic whoop and threw herself upon her brother, hugging him rapturously.

''Oh, thank you, Damien, *thank* you! We did not expect such leniency! Oh, how utterly happy you have made us! *Thank* you, my dear brother!'' Radiant with joy, she sprang to her feet and rushed into the arms of Mr. Culpepper, who spoke quietly, but just as fervently.

''Thank you, my lord! You may have no qualms in entrusting your sister to me!''

Damien straightened his rumpled cravat and said, with a faint smile, ''I know that, Mr. Culpepper.''

''But—but—all the young men of the *ton!*'' sputtered Mrs. Yardley. ''The dozens of gentlemen who have danced attendance upon Augusta all these weeks! Surely any one of them would be preferable to—''

''Not another word, Aunt!'' cried Augusta hotly. ''My

Thomas is worth a *dozen* of those silly fops, and if you dare to disparage his character I shall never speak to you again!''

"Hush, Gussie," Mr. Culpepper said soothingly. "You must see that your aunt is greatly shocked; it is only to be expected, after all. As is her duty, she has exerted her utmost to see you wed to a gentleman of your own circle, and you cannot fault her for that! We can only hope that in time, she will be reconciled to the fact of our betrothal and subsequent marriage and may, someday, come to regard me as a loving and loyal nephew."

Augusta's fierce expression softened. "You are right, Thomas," she said, and turned to Mrs. Yardley and continued penitently, "Pray forgive me, Aunt! For my harsh words just now, and for my churlish behavior of these past days! It was only because I thought that Thomas no longer loved me, and my heart was quite thoroughly rent in two!"

Her own countenance rigid, Mrs. Yardley looked frostily up at her niece. "Humph," she said only. "Humph." Then, unexpectedly, her lips began to tremble and blindly she reached into her reticule, produced a tiny scrap of lacy linen, and dabbed with it at her eyes, saying tremulously, "How much you remind me of myself, Augusta, when I knew that I was well and truly enamored of my own poor Crayton!" She gave a pathetic little sob and added unsteadily: "Far, far be it from me to stand in the way of true love! You have my blessing, children!"

"Oh, *Aunt!*" said Augusta, and, swiftly crossing to the chair in which Mrs. Yardley sat, she cast herself upon her knees and enfolded her tearful aunt in her arms, at the same time herself giving way to a fresh outburst of weeping. Mr. Culpepper followed, and silently stood with his hand upon Augusta's shoulder, his thin countenance at once solemn and glowing.

Caroline looked to Damien and found, with a secret little thrill of pleasure, that his dark eyes were fixed upon her. She returned his smile with one of her own, and then the wry amusement on his face faded, to be replaced by an expression of raw, yearning wistfulness and a naked agony. That same longing, that same anguish at once was mirrored in her own soul and quickly she took a hasty step toward him, but checked further movement when she forcefully reminded herself that she and Damien were not alone. Instead she cleared a throat gone suddenly tight and said shakily:

"My lord, I shall intrude on this family scene no longer! If—if you will excuse me?"

"Of course," Damien replied, coolly impassive once again; only the subtle clenching of his jaw betrayed him. "Good night."

"Good night, my lord," she murmured, and, tears rising hot and fast, she turned and swiftly left the room.

Chapter 19

Caroline sat with her hands tightly folded in her lap, trying not to reveal her inner agitation and nervousness as Mrs. Dent, proprietess of the Dent Employment Registry, sat behind her desk reviewing Caroline's carefully annotated application. This was the seventh such agency she had visited, and her third so far today. Each time she had met with rejection, couched in terms ranging from the disdainful to the openly rude. And now, her time was running out, for shortly she must hurry back to the Reston town house and prepare for Damien and Miss Manderlay's prenuptial ball, which was to commence this evening promptly at ten o'clock. She had not been invited to the dinner party the Manderlays were hosting in St. James' Place prior to the ball itself, but Augusta and Mrs. Yardley had been, of course; they had declared themselves in urgent need of her assistance as they always did prior to going out for the evening, and Caroline did not wish to fail them. Nor did she wish to attend the ball—every feeling revolted painfully at the very idea—but again, the ladies were insistent that she join them,

and in her bleak despair she had been unable to manufacture
a convincing excuse to cry off.

"Miss Smythe," came Mrs. Dent's flat, precise voice, and
Caroline, suppressing a start of surprise as she was abruptly
roused from her dismal reverie, looked up and met the older
woman's measuring gaze.

"You say here that you are qualified to teach young ladies
grammar, elocution, and deportment; French, Latin, Spanish,
and the rudiments of Greek; history and some mathematics;
geography and the elements of the natural sciences; and that
you are proficient in the use of the globes, both terrestrial and
celestial. Furthermore, you state that you are capable of teaching
singing and dancing, without the aid of a master."

"Yes, ma'am."

Mrs. Dent lowered the sheaves of paper she had been studying onto the spotlessly clean surface of her desk, and punctiliously she aligned them. "These are impressive abilities, Miss
Smythe."

"Thank you, ma'am."

"Yet you list here only one situation as a governess, to the
Tintham family of Denbury Manor."

"Yes, ma'am." Caroline's spirits, which had risen at Mrs.
Dent's words of praise, swiftly plummeted.

"You have no character reference from Mrs. Tintham?"

"No, ma'am."

Mrs. Dent pursed her lips and glanced down at the papers
in front of her. "I note that you are at present a companion to the
Lady Augusta Reston, of Grosvenor Place and Windemere."

"Yes, ma'am."

"Have you a character reference from her ladyship?"

Caroline gripped her fingers together still more tightly. A
radiant Augusta had been bubbling with plans for her wedding
at Windemere in September, as well as for the school she and
Mr. Culpepper were set on establishing as soon as possible
following their marriage. Exuberantly she had reminded Caro-

line of her desire to include her as a high-ranking member of the staff, and several times had besought her advice concerning issues such as the curriculum, meals, quantity and variety of exercise appropriate to their young pupils, furnishing of the bedchambers, and the ideal number of maidservants. Caroline had not had the heart to thwart Augusta's glowing enjoyment by informing her that she intended to leave the Reston household as soon as possible and then asking her for a reference; furthermore, as much as she might condemn her own weakness, she knew that she could not endure the thousand questions (no matter how kind and concerned) that were sure to be precipitated by such an announcement.

Now she said only to Mrs. Dent: "No, ma'am, I am afraid that I do not."

"H'm." Frowning, Mrs. Dent tapped her fingers upon her desk, then said bluntly: "Miss Smythe, as impeccable as your qualifications are, and as unimpeachable as I believe your own morals and integrity to be (for I am, I assure you, an excellent judge of these matters!), without character references I do not see how I may in good conscience recommend you to prospective employers."

"Yes. I—I understand, ma'am." Caroline's heart sank as both terrible disappointment and a haunting fear for the future flooded her like a cold dam bursting its bounds. Mrs. Dent's was the final registry on her list; the others, she had gathered from a discreet conversation with the surprisingly sympathetic Uxley, were less respectable, and they had earned a reputation for insisting that applicants such as herself pay a fee in advance, then failed to find them positions or even to arrange for a single interview.

Dear God, what would she do now? She simply *had* to go— had to leave Damien forever, for this excruciating torture of being so near to him and yet so impossibly separated at the same time was daily more intolerable, and she knew that she couldn't bear it for much longer.

Perhaps, Caroline thought desperately, she might take a post as a seamstress. The hours were long and the wages low, but her skills were such that there might be a reasonably good chance some respectable, established modiste would be willing to hire her on at once. In fact, she could approach Madame Huppert the first thing tomorrow morning . . .

But then her heart seemed to plunge to the floor as she recalled that the season, with its manifold demands for gowns and accouterments of the latest mode, was drawing to a close. If anything, modistes such as Madame Huppert would be letting go some of their seamstresses, rather than taking on new ones.

"Miss Smythe." It was Mrs. Dent speaking, her tone remarkably forbearing as once again she regained Caroline's wayward attention. "As much as I would like to help you . . . well, I *am* sorry."

"Y-yes," murmured Caroline drearily. "Thank you, Mrs. Dent. Pray forgive me for—for having proved to be a waste of your time." She gathered up her reticule and made as if to stand, then halted in surprise when there came from the vestibule outside Mrs. Dent's office a sudden loud commotion.

"I shall *not* wait outside!" exclaimed a sharp, indignant female voice. "Do you have the temerity to suppose that I have all day to stand idly about, young lady? *You,* no doubt, do so, if the general disorder of this anteroom is any sort of evidence! And I daresay Mrs. Dent likely does so as well, given the quality of the individuals *she* has the audacity to thrust my way! *Excuse* me, young lady! Step aside! I am going into that office you are misguidedly attempting to shield with your person! I give you fair warning, if you do *not* remove yourself from that doorway I shall without a qualm strike you with my parasol! *Thank* you!"

Caroline looked around in alarm as the door slammed open and a sticklike old lady strode in, dressed in a full-skirted, white lingerie gown, a frothy lace-edged petticoat, and a blue velvet spencer whose lapels were edged in red lingerie. She also wore brown kid gloves and on her head was set a towering black velvet hat trimmed in dotted yellow lawn and a yellow and black ribbon. Altogether it was, Caroline perceived in astonishment, an ensemble which had been the height of fashion some twenty years ago.

"*There* you are, Mrs. Dent! I have this past fortnight been in daily expectation of hearing from you, for, as I wrote to you in my letter, that—that creature, Miss Tristam, was *utterly* and *completely* unacceptable, and I have in the interim been waiting with what I can only describe as inhuman patience for her replacement!"

"Good afternoon, Miss Rutledge," Mrs. Dent said, a subtly pained note in her voice. "As you can see, I am currently occupied. If you would be so good as to return to the vestibule and—"

"*More* waiting?" retorted the old lady acidly. "I think not! All I have done, Mrs. Dent, is *wait* for six months for you to adequately do your job!"

"I have sent you no fewer than ten of my most qualified applicants," said Mrs. Dent, "each of whom has apparently dissatisfied you within a period of four weeks or less. As I explained to you in *my* letter following Miss Tristam's summary dismissal from your employ, I do not feel that there is anything further I might do for you, Miss Rutledge."

"I'll not let you off so lightly, Mrs. Dent! Do not think to fob me off with your paltry excuses! I engaged you to perform a service for me, and a service *you will perform!*" The old lady punctuated this declaration with decisive thumps of the tip of her parasol on the floorboards.

Caroline cleared her throat. "Pray excuse me, ma'am," she said to Miss Rutledge, "but might I inquire as to the type of employee you are looking to engage?"

Watery eyes of faded gray, swimming in a sea of wrinkles, glared at her. "Not that it's any of your business, missy," came the tart reply, "but I am attempting to find a companion!"

"I," said Caroline, "am a companion attempting to find an employer."

"Indeed?" Miss Rutledge turned to glare even more unpleasantly at Mrs. Dent. "Holding out on me, are you? I'm sure I don't know why I should be surprised to discover your arrant, bare-faced deceit!"

Mrs. Dent seemed to suppress a sigh as she folded her hands neatly on the desktop. "Miss Smythe has for the first time come to me this afternoon, Miss Rutledge, and—"

"Smythe?" interrupted the old lady. "What sort of name is that? In *my* day, people would call themselves 'Smith' and that would be the end of it! None of this pretentious 'Smythe' business! I suppose you've one of those absurd hyphenated surnames as well?" she asked, rounding abruptly on Caroline.

"No, ma'am."

"There's something to be grateful for, I suppose!"

"As I was saying," resumed Mrs. Dent, "I have only met Miss Smythe for the first time this afternoon, and though her personal qualifications are excellent, she lacks character references from her prior employers."

"Why?" demanded Miss Rutledge, peering sharply at Caroline. "Caught absconding with the plate, or with the eldest son?"

"No, ma'am."

The old lady seemed a trifle taken aback by Caroline's calm reserve. Caroline, observing this, could not but be thankful that she had evidently managed to conceal the intense strain under which she was laboring. With a renewed sense of hope she watched as Miss Rutledge, beetling her brows, seemed to be mulling something over, then, finally, spoke.

"You appear to be a lady, and your speech is, thankfully, genteel. You'll have to do some mending, you know! The shopping as well, for I can't entrust that simple chore to that devious cook of mine! Furthermore, you will be required to oversee the maids—a more shiftless lot was never born, I dare swear!—and to keep track of the household accounts, *and* ensure that the gardener doesn't make off with my roses and attempt to sell them at the marketplace in town! In addition, I expect you to read to me in the morning and assist me with my correspondence in the early evening, and have my tea served *exactly* at four!" Scowling, she added: "The salary is twenty pounds per annum."

"Very well," said Caroline, her heart beating quickly. It was a fraction of the sum she was currently receiving, and certainly Miss Rutledge would hardly be an easy mistress, but nonetheless, here was her chance to escape! "When you are not in residence in London, ma'am, where is your home, and when would the position be available?"

"I live just outside Shrewsbury, missy, and you ought to know at the outset of our arrangement that I do *not* in the least care for London, and go there as little as possible! So if you are thinking that we shall be spending the season here each year, participating in all sorts of frivolous jollifications of which I do not approve, you may disabuse yourself of *that* notion upon the instant!"

"Very well," Caroline repeated, feeling a curious mix of emotions at Miss Rutledge's acerbic words. Shrewsbury was far to the northwest of both London and Windemere; this distance, combined with her employer's patent distaste for the city, would ensure that the likelihood of ever encountering Damien again would be well nigh impossible. This suited her purposes admirably, and yet . . . Her heart twisted in her breast at the thought of never again gazing upon a face and form that had become familiar and beloved, and more precious to her than her own life. *Oh, Damien!* she silently cried out, as meanwhile she strove to give the appearance of listening attentively as Miss Rutledge continued.

"The position, missy, is available at once, as you might perhaps have surmised from my earlier conversation with Mrs. Dent here had you been a trifle cleverer! Now that I have engaged your services, I shall depart from this wretched metropolis at first light tomorrow.''

"T-tomorrow, ma'am?" exclaimed Caroline, aghast. "So—so soon?"

"Have you any objections?" snapped the old lady.

Fiercely Caroline suppressed an ardent desire to burst into tears. "I—I—suppose not."

"How very kind of you!" sarcastically replied Miss Rutledge. "Present yourself at Lothian's Hotel at no later than five-thirty tomorrow morning, and without a mountain of baggage, pray!" She turned to Mrs. Dent and said: "I shall have your fee forwarded to you before I leave Lothian's, though why I am paying you at all (when it was because of my own enterprise in coming here this afternoon, no matter the horrid inconvenience to myself, that I have succeeded in achieving my modest aim) I am at a loss to understand! But as usual, I am more generous to people than they deserve! Good day!" With that irascible valediction, Miss Rutledge turned and stumped out of Mrs. Dent's office, loudly pointing out to the assistant as she passed through the anteroom the egregious layer of dust that conspicuously swathed the furniture.

Then Caroline rose to her feet, feeling more than a little stunned, and said: "Thank you, Mrs. Dent."

"I believe it is I who should be thanking you," dryly replied the other woman. She hesitated for a few moments, then went on carefully: "Far be it from me to interfere, Miss Smythe, but are you quite certain you wish to enter into this particular situation?"

"Yes, ma'am," Caroline said, with all the assumption of firmness she could manage. "Indeed, I consider myself most fortunate to have met Miss Rutledge."

Mrs. Dent regarded her closely, then held out her hand and said: "I wish you well, Miss Smythe."

"Thank you, ma'am," Caroline answered, surprised by the warmth of the gesture, and after clasping Mrs. Dent's hand, quickly left the employment registry and made her way to the street, where she hailed a hackney cab and directed the driver to take her to Grosvenor Square. She feared she was going to be a little late and, worse, she dreaded having to inform Augusta that she would be leaving the Reston household as of tomorrow. And Damien! she thought, anguished. How on earth would she tell him? Would she even have a moment alone with him tonight?

The streets were congested with late-afternoon traffic, and she was in fact some half an hour late returning to the town house. In the flurry of dressing, crimping of hair, last-minute repairs to a ripped sleeve, the scrutinizing of gloves, the search for and discovery of a waylaid kid slipper, and the painstaking selection of jewelry, Caroline found it impossible to privately divulge to Augusta her shocking news, and as a few hours later she stood on the step watching the Reston carriage clatter away into the twilight with Augusta and Mrs. Yardley, she knew a cowardly moment of relief that she was able to—if only briefly—postpone the inevitable.

As Damien moved through the stately paces of the quadrille with Miss Manderlay, dispassionately he observed that his fiancée looked pale, and that her lovely, normally serene countenance could even be said to appear a trifle pinched. She uttered all that was proper in response to his own polite remarks, but otherwise was notably mute.

As he was himself suffering under the brutal lash of his own particular demons, Damien did not introduce the topic of Miss Manderlay's untoward reticence on what should have been for her an evening of triumphant happiness. Instead they continued through the figures of the quadrille in a ponderous silence broken only by the occasional stilted exchange of meaningless comments: two people, he thought bleakly, as remote from each other as if they were at opposite ends of the earth.

At last the music ended, and with a polite bow Damien led Miss Manderlay from the floor, only to be intercepted by the Baroness Manderlay, who wholly made up for in overflowing good cheer what her daughter so pointedly lacked.

"How beautifully you dance together, my dears!" Lady Calpurnia said archly. "I do hope that will not be the only time tonight you favor us with such a charming display of grace!"

"Should Reston solicit my hand again, Mama, naturally I would be delighted to accede to his request," Miss Manderlay replied colorlessly.

"His lordship, I am sure, will do his duty," said the baroness, her voice laden with an undisguised significance that was not lost on Damien. He inclined his head with a slight, ironic smile, and Lady Calpurnia continued brightly: "I do believe the orchestra is about to commence a waltz! Come, Helen! Sir John Maccabee has confided to me that he wishes more than anything for a last waltz with you before you enter into the married state"—she simpered, in a highly unbecoming manner that contorted her elongated features into an expression of equine glee—"and I know you would not care to disappoint such a faithful friend!"

"No, Mama," said Miss Manderlay, and docilely allowed her beaming parent to lead her over to the immense potted palm underneath whose arching branches Sir John had hopefully positioned himself, like some shipwrecked castaway awaiting the arrival of the rescuing vessel.

Damien turned away and, for the first time since the ball had begun, caught sight of Caroline, standing next to his Aunt Violet who was discoursing vivaciously with two or three of her friends.

Dear God, Damien thought, his chest tightening, but Caroline was stunningly beautiful, ethereal and devastatingly feminine in a delicate gown of the softest, palest green and her gleaming auburn curls caught up in a simple classical knot atop her head.

Across the overwarm, overcrowded ballroom their eyes met.

Behind him the musicians began playing a waltz, its cadence lyrical and sweeping, and hardly knowing what he was doing, Damien walked directly to Caroline, his gaze focused as steadfastly on her as if they were the only two guests in the room, and when he reached her he spoke quietly.

"Will you dance with me, Caroline?"

"Yes," she whispered unhesitatingly, and moments later they were whirling together across the floor, their steps perfectly matched, their bodies moving together in effortless synchronization. Nothing was said between them, yet to Damien this was an entirely different sort of silence from that which he had just endured with Miss Manderlay. *This* silence was quivering with unspoken words of love, and longing, and despair, and as Caroline gazed up at him, in her huge green eyes, so sweetly and lushly framed by thick black lashes, was such eloquent yearning and sorrow that Damien ached to crush her against him and kiss her sadness away, caress her until she smiled at him, make love to her until she cried out with unfettered bliss.

But he could not. He could only dance with her, and merely that, he supposed bitterly, was a dangerous act, for even now he glimpsed the Earl of Audley, distinctive amongst the crowd by his height and the glittering splendor of his attire, watching them with pale blue eyes that were alert and, surprisingly, sanguine.

All too soon the dance came to an end, and he had no choice but to escort Caroline back to his aunt. He offered her his arm, and felt an irrepressible thrill of heated pleasure at the contact of her gloved hand upon his forearm. They had but gone a short distance before Charles Highcombe came hastily to meet them and spoke with a smile that seemed preternaturally bright.

" 'Servant, Miss Smythe! Hello, Damien! My heartiest felicitations to you!"

"Thank you, Charles," Damien replied. "Might I also tender mine to you?"

"Yes. Yes, I thank you!"

"Where is your betrothed?" he inquired. "I should like to meet her."

Charles gestured vaguely. "Oh, she's somewhere about, I suppose. The last I saw my mother had her in tow."

Damien exchanged a speaking glance with Caroline, but responded politely to his friend: "If the opportunity should arise, I hope you will present me to her."

"Certainly, certainly!" Charles fidgeted with one of the buttons on his waistcoat, then said, with noticeable awkwardness, "I—I wonder if I might have a word with you, dear fellow? Nothing *truly* urgent, I daresay, just—just something I thought I ought to mention!"

"Of course. What is it?"

A wave of crimson flooding his round face, Charles looked quickly at Caroline before returning his gaze to Damien. "The thing of it is—well, I'm sure it's nothing, you know, but . . . At that party of my mother's which you were unable to attend, I'm very much afraid that I—not that I precisely remember— the champagne—" Suddenly his gray eyes widened and he stammered, "Must be going, old fellow! I'll bend your ear another time!" He wheeled about and without another word beat a hasty retreat through the crowd.

Damien barely had time to murmur "What the devil?" to Caroline before he heard from behind them a cool voice speak, with purring satisfaction.

"The very two people with whom I wish to speak! How wonderfully convenient!"

He and Caroline turned, and found that the Earl of Audley had approached, and was smiling benignly upon them.

"Sir," said Damien just as coolly, though he was aware of a familiar, uneasy prickling at the back of his neck. The earl, he sensed with an uncanny certainty, believed himself to be in possession of some sort of trump card in whatever covert game he was conducting.

Audley gave a graceful bow. "If you and Miss Smythe would

accompany me to a little saloon I know, Reston, I should be grateful. There are a few things I should like to say to you both.''

Though his request was couched in a tone of the silkiest courtesy, Damien was not deceived; there was a distinct threat underlying the earl's urbane speech. Well, whatever it was, it might as well be confronted, for he was weary unto death of playing, however unwittingly, mouse to Audley's cat. "As you will, sir,'' he replied, once again offering his arm to Caroline, who, wide-eyed with apprehension, slipped her hand around his forearm and clutched it as if for ballast in a world gone suddenly awry.

The earl bowed again and with studied deliberation preceded them from the ballroom and thence to a chamber which evidently had been at one time a library, to judge by the many rows of shelves lining its walls, but which were largely empty of books and instead were cluttered with a remarkably disparate collection of *bric-à-brac* including a variety of china figurines (though most seemed to be of coy, improbably pink-checked shepherdesses), an old Rococo clock, several badly painted miniatures, a handful of low Chinese bowls, and two elaborate vases constructed entirely of seashells.

The earl closed the door behind them and with a wave of his hand invited Caroline and Damien to be seated. "Thank you, I shall stand,'' answered Damien curtly, but Caroline, as if her knees were weak, swiftly sank onto the nearest chair.

Audley followed suit and lowered himself onto a brocaded love seat, then smilingly gazed up at Damien as if he were taking a moment to relish the scene he was about to orchestrate.

"Well, sir?'' said Damien impatiently. "What is it you wish to say?''

The earl's smile broadened, and he returned simply: "Why, only that I can ruin you, Reston, if I choose to do so.''

"What?" Caroline cried in horror, half starting up from her chair.

Calmly Damien gestured for her to resume her seat and said to Audley, "Perhaps you might explain yourself."

"With the greatest pleasure in the world, my dear Reston! To begin at the beginning: I have from the moment of Miss Smythe's appearance been interested—*profoundly* interested—in her connection to your family. While she herself has been pointedly evasive as to how she came to be one of the Reston *ménage,* I could not fail to mark the comfortable terms on which she seemed instantly to be with your friend Charles Highcombe who, I had no trouble recalling, accompanied you on your less than successful race to Cambridge. As to *why* it was abortive—curiously enough, no one beside myself seemed to wonder why such a notable whip as yourself failed to easily overcome Lord Essex and his showy, but dubious grays. Later, it did not escape my notice that you looked upon Miss Smythe with a decided, if subtle, partiality. Oh, I doubt that anyone else would have noticed, Reston: it is just that I pride myself on the keenness of my powers of observation."

"As well you might," grimly rejoined Damien.

The earl smiled. "Thank you! To continue: as time passed, the mystery only deepened, but it was not until the evening of the Highcombes' ball, at which Charles Highcombe announced his betrothal, that I was able to put together a few more pieces of the puzzle. Mr. Highcombe's inadvertent jostling of your arm, Miss Smythe, and his own willingness to overimbibe which fortuitously loosened his tongue—"

"I suppose that explains Charles's desire to confide something to me a few minutes ago," Damien remarked. "A guilty conscience, no doubt! He was ever the hopeless rattlepate."

Very pale, Caroline asked the earl, "But—but what did Mr. Highcombe tell you, my lord?"

"He described to me the incident with Reston's curricle in Baldock, Miss Smythe, after which I myself ventured there (what a dreadful little town, I might add!) and made a few inquiries. Apparently the whole of the population believes you to have there been made his mistress.''

''An injured woman with a broken arm?'' said Damien scornfully.

''Indeed! One can only admire the vividness and creativity of the townspeople's imaginations! Nonetheless, the die, so to speak, had been cast. It would take very little for *our* set, my dear Reston, to not only arrive at the same conclusion but to believe that for these many months you have been sheltering under your very roof your paramour from Baldock.''

Anger roaring through him, Damien clenched his fists and took an ominous step toward the earl. ''Sir, you have gone too far!''

Audley held up a thin white hand. ''*I* am not accusing you of such unworthy behavior,'' he said placidly. ''I am merely stating what could, with a few judiciously phrased innuendoes on my part, be bruited about the *ton*—and which would, in a matter of days, be transformed from the gossamer substance of rumor and assume the wholly solid appearance of the truth.''

''The damage to the Reston family would be incalculable!'' Caroline interposed, her voice shaking. ''You must not disseminate such a false, wicked tale, my lord, I beseech you!''

The earl smiled at her. ''As much as I should like to accommodate your wishes, Miss Smythe, I fear that my own must here take precedence.''

''What is it that you desire me to do, Audley,'' said Damien, ''in exchange for your silence?''

''Why, have you not guessed? You are to end your betrothal to Miss Manderlay.''

''He—he cannot do so with honor!'' Caroline exclaimed, aghast. ''How could you ask such a thing of him?''

''Hush, Caroline,'' Damien said gently to her, then looked again at the earl. ''To what purpose am I to cry off, Audley?''

''I confess that I am astonished that you find my motives so opaque,'' commented the other man. ''It is my intention, of course, to marry Miss Manderlay myself. I am a little sorry that it must be at the cost of your honor and reputation, Reston, but, as the old platitude goes, all is fair in love and war.''

"I see," said Damien, his mind racing. Of course: it all made sense now. Having had his suit thwarted when his, Damien's, offer was accepted by the Manderlays, the earl had been only too pleased to intuit the esoteric circumstances of Caroline's admittance into the Reston family fold, and to ferret out some small portion of the truth . . . just enough to cleverly deploy in a way that would not only basely injure himself but Caroline as well. She would inevitably be embroiled in the scandal that would rock London, and as little as Damien cared for his own standing in society, he would not wish to see the woman he loved come to such grievous harm.

"Yes, it's all rather simple, isn't it?" responded the earl affably. "Because of your noble principles, Reston, you will be forced to do as I say. But you must agree it is better, after all, to have things fall out in this fashion. Helen and I are far better suited to one another, you know! Some have deemed her an ice goddess, but her temperament is one which I admire and esteem, and is perfectly matched to my own. At the risk of sounding foolishly sentimental, I think it might not be going too far as to say that I love her. And, like Mr. Highcombe's happy arrangement with Miss Kimball, what Helen's background might lack in aristocratic connections, I can certainly provide; and whatever my own situation might lack in financial substance, the Manderlays have in ample supply. So you see, until *you* happened onto the scene and overawed her parents with both your impressive lineage and your prodigious fortune, Helen and I were in a fair way to coming to mutually satisfactory terms.''

"It is," said Damien dryly, "quite a romantic tale, Audley."

"I own that I think so myself," the earl returned complacently.

A little wildly, Caroline looked from Damien to the Earl of

Audley. "Damien," she said urgently, "you must not agree to the earl's demands! I shall not permit such a sacrifice!"

Damien went to her, and placed a hand on her shoulder. "Do not worry yourself so, my darling girl," he said softly.

She covered his hand with her own and whispered back, very low, "How can I not? I love you!"

All at once a new voice trumpeted indignantly into the room: "Well! I believe I have seen *quite* enough!"

Quickly Damien turned.

There on the threshold stood a visibly enraged Lady Calpurnia, and at her side was his fiancée, a very pale, very strained Miss Helen Manderlay.

Chapter 20

Caroline flashed Damien a look of frantic dread, then, before he could stop her, shot to her feet and, her head lowered, hurried past the baroness and Miss Manderlay and disappeared.

He would have followed her, only to have his path blocked by Lady Calpurnia who, with a speed that was astonishing in one usually so magisterially slow in her movements, slammed the door shut and stepped in front of it. "You will go nowhere, Lord Reston, until this matter between us is firmly settled!"

Damien gritted his teeth and withdrew a few paces. Caroline was obviously distraught and he wanted nothing more than to go to her and comfort her, but short of physically dislodging Lady Calpurnia he had no choice but to remain.

"I was never so shocked," began the baroness in a voice of high, quivering outrage, "to see you *caressing* that female, Lord Reston, and to hear her say that she loves you! No doubt *she* is the reason Lord Audley intimated to me that you might have intended to break off your betrothal with Helen! Well, I won't have it! Helen's dress is very nearly complete, and we have just yesterday received the invitations from the print shop! You will marry Helen if I have to—to *drag* you down the aisle of St. Paul's!''

Sweetly and maliciously, the earl smiled at Damien. ''It is a charming image, is it not, my dear Reston?''

Lady Calpurnia turned to Lord Audley, a somewhat softer note in her voice as she said: ''I am terribly sorry that you feel yourself to have been slighted by the baron and me, my lord, but you cannot deny that Lord Reston makes a greatly superior matrimonial prospect to yourself.''

To Damien's surprise the earl actually winced, then wryly replied, ''One cannot but marvel at your frankness, Lady Calpurnia.''

Preening, the baroness smugly said, ''Indeed, I believe I may say without false modesty that I am well-known for prizing candor above all other attributes, my lord!''

''Truly, it is a very admirable quality,'' murmured Lord Audley blandly. ''I myself am occasionally prone to employ it, for—''

''*Candor!*'' Miss Manderlay interrupted, her eyes glittering with more fire than Damien had ever before witnessed in their blue depths. ''Is it *candor* you wish for, Mama? Very well! Then I shall take leave to *candidly* inform you that I do not want to marry Lord Reston! I have *never* wanted to marry him, and only gave way to your repeated urgings to do so because all I have ever striven to do is be a dutiful child to you and Papa!''

''I *beg* your pardon?'' gasped her mother, stunned.

Miss Manderlay turned to the earl. ''Is it true, Clifton?'' she said. ''Do you truly love me?''

Slowly Lord Audley rose to his feet, and took a few steps toward her. ''Helen, I—'' He hesitated, then said, with rare simplicity: ''Yes.''

''And do you truly wish to marry me?''

''Yes.''

"I am glad, for it has long been my desire to do so." She went to him, and gave him her hand, then turned to Lady Calpurnia, in her lovely face once more her usual cool serenity. "It is Clifton I shall marry, Mama."

"But Helen!" protested the baroness desperately. "We *both* heard Lord Audley speak of the worldly advantages of such a match! I daresay he is as much interested in your fortune as in yourself!"

"Perhaps," said Miss Manderlay calmly. "Yet let us not be disingenuous, Mama: we cannot permit ourselves to be blinded to the status to be acquired by association with *his* noble bloodlines. It is true that they lack the ancient prestige attached to Reston's, but if Clifton is willing to overlook my plebeian background, I am sure I am happy to disregard the fact that his fortune does not compare to my own."

To Damien she added, "I must apologize, Reston, for terminating our betrothal, but I am not so certain that such an action will not suit your own purposes admirably."

Feeling perhaps as stunned as the baroness herself, Damien only bowed, then watched as that lady tottered to a chair and collapsed into it.

"But—but—" she said feebly. "Your father and I have only wished what is best for you, Helen."

"Yes, Mama, I know that," answered Miss Manderlay. "You may achieve that end by consenting to my marriage to Clifton."

"Yes, to be sure," murmured her mother dazedly, then lifted her eyes to Damien. "My lord, I do not know what to say to you."

Well, this is a first! thought Damien, repressing a grin. Aloud he replied gravely: "Ma'am, I strongly doubt that there is, in fact, anything more to be said. Now, if you will excuse me?" He bowed again, and with a light step and an equally light heart he promptly quit the room.

* * *

Urgently Caroline rapped on the door to the Reston town house. Fortunately she had managed both to see Charles Highcombe as she hurried back into the ballroom and beg him to inform Augusta that she was leaving the Manderlays' ball, and to quickly summon a hackney cab to drive her to Grosvenor Square. The driver and horse now patiently awaited her return, which she had promised would be swift.

The door opened, and with a faint look of surprise on his countenance Uxley admitted her into the house. "Good evening, Miss Smythe!" he said. "I take it that her ladyship and Mrs. Yardley have remained at the Manderlays' ball? I do hope that you are not unwell, miss."

"Yes—no!" Caroline said. "I—I cannot explain it to you now, Uxley, but—but I shall be downstairs again in a trice, with some letters for you to deliver to his lordship and her ladyship. If—if you would be so kind as to wait for me here?"

"Certainly, miss," the butler said, and with a nod of thanks Caroline ran upstairs and to her bedchamber, where in a matter of minutes she had changed her gown into a serviceable dress suitable for traveling, hastily scrawled two notes, and, mindful of Miss Rutledge's cross admonition, packed only two small bandboxes.

As she hastened down the stairs she was conscious only of the crucial need to be gone before the others returned. Not for the world would she wish Damien to allow himself be led to society's sacrificial altar and slaughtered there. Once she was gone, the Earl of Audley could no longer threaten Damien, and he would be safe again. She was glad, now, that Miss Rutledge planned to leave London within a matter of hours. There would be plenty of time later—days, months, all the years of her life—to miss Damien, and to mourn, and, at least, to derive some small shred of satisfaction from the knowledge that by her leaving in this abrupt, secretive fashion she had, this one time, rescued *him*.

The Manderlays' ballroom was densely packed, and it seemed to Damien that at least an hour of diligent searching passed before he could be sure that Caroline was nowhere to be found within it. Twice he caught a glimpse of Charles Highcombe gesticulating wildly at him, but, assuming that his friend wished only to confess his indiscreet behavior in the company of the Earl of Audley, Damien did not press forward through the crowd to meet Charles, and instead continued in his quest for Caroline.

Finally, having circled the ballroom for what seemed like the tenth time, he came to a halt and eyed his surroundings in considerable frustration. It was then that Augusta pushed her way through a knot of people and hailed him, saying with remarkable cheerfulness, *"What* a hideous crush! I cannot blame Caro in the least for having gone home!"

"Gone home?" repeated Damien. "Are you sure?"

Augusta looked at him in surprise. "Why, yes, for Charles Highcombe said she had charged him with a message for me. Poor Caro! I daresay the heat overcame her. Why will no one ever open a window at these wretched affairs?"

"I must go," Damien said abruptly. He had to see Caroline, be with her, hold her and kiss her and tell her of their amazing good fortune!

"Go? Go where, my dear brother?"

"Home."

"And leave your own ball?" asked Augusta, her dark eyes round with astonishment.

"Yes." He half-turned away, but she caught at his arm, saying: "If *you* are going, then I believe that I might safely do so too! Will you give me ten minutes in which to find our aunt, and inform her as to our actions?"

"Yes—but only ten," he warned her. "After that I am afraid I must depart without you."

"Oh, I have become quite efficient at negotiating these ballrooms!" she said with a saucy smile. "I shall meet you shortly at the front entrance!" She waggled her fingers at him, turned on her heel, and was gone.

Damien's own progress toward his destination was slowed by the congratulations and wishes for his happiness offered by several of the guests. He accepted them blandly, leaving without a twinge of conscience to Miss Manderlay the task of disseminating the news of their broken betrothal, and so in the end it was Augusta who waited for *him* by the front door.

She did not twit him about it, but only said: "As you might expect, Aunt wishes to remain, so I have called for your carriage, and she will follow us home in the other at her leisure."

Since Damien and Augusta were the first guests to depart, his carriage was quickly brought round, and no more than five minutes of waiting had elapsed before they were seated upon its elegant velvet seats and the horses were clattering away at a smart trot.

Augusta leaned forward. "My dear brother, now that we are alone, will you not tell me why you are leaving the Manderlays' ball? Has there been trouble of some kind?"

Damien looked into his sister's face; her expression was one of sincere and frank concern. He was moved by it, and said with equal candor: "As to that, Gussie, I shall not prevaricate: Miss Manderlay has terminated our engagement."

"Oh, I am so glad!" Augusta exclaimed with unabashed delight, reaching impulsively across the distance between them to squeeze his hand. Then she drew back, adding more hesitantly: "That is—that is, I believe this to be *good* news, Damien?"

He smiled at her. "Yes, Gussie, it is *very* good news indeed."

She relaxed, and brightly returned his smile. "Indeed, so I thought, but I should not have betrayed my own joy until I had ascertained that your own reaction was akin to mine. I may tell you now, dear brother, with *considerable* relief, that as assiduously as I tried, I have never felt for Miss Manderlay the—the warmth one ought to feel for one's sister-in-law!''

''No,'' he said, ''I imagine you did not. Do you know if Audley has any sisters?''

''The Earl of Audley?'' Augusta echoed, nonplused. ''No, I do not know. Why?''

''I was merely wondering if *his* sisters share his rather glacial temperament, and will rejoice in Miss Manderlay's entrance into their family.''

''What? Oh, Damien, do you mean it?''

Gravely he replied, ''Alas, Gussie, it is all too true. I fear that I have been jilted in favor of the earl.''

''Much you care!'' she retorted shrewdly. ''Well, I am sure I wish them very happy, for a pair more suited to each other I never knew! (Unless it were Thomas and me, of course, but *that* is a very different story!) But Damien, how did this miracle come to pass, and at this very late date? Oh, my Lord! I can only imagine the dismay of the baroness at having let slip between her fingers the greatest prize of the Marriage Mart!'' Augusta burst into a hearty peal of laughter.

Damien grinned. ''I suspect that Lady Calpurnia will soon be reconciled to the prospect of having an earl for a son-in-law.''

''Yes, how vastly superior to a mere marquis!'' Augusta laughed again. ''Oh, but this is rich! I can hardly wait to tell Caro, for I am sure she will enjoy the joke tremendously!''

''Will she?'' said Damien.

''Why, yes, I would think so, for I cannot imagine she holds either Miss Manderlay or her mother in any particular esteem, given the extraordinary lack of civility they have displayed toward her!''

''Gussie,'' Damien said slowly, ''you have mentioned a

certain warmth you would wish to feel for your sister-in-law."
He paused, and Augusta tilted her head inquiringly at him.

"Yes?"

"Would it be the same sort of affection that you feel for
Caroline?"

Instant comprehension lit Augusta's dark eyes and she
gasped, "Oh, *Damien!* Are you going to offer for Caro?"

"Yes," said Damien. "Would that please you, Gussie?"

"Please me? *Nothing* would make me happier than to have
Caro for my sister! She is the dearest, sweetest girl in the
world!"

"I own that I think so too. I am glad that you share my
sentiments."

"But of course!" Augusta said warmly. "Who would not,
after having known Caro for a bare half hour!" She leaned
back against the squabs, and after a few moments of reflective
silence she asked, "Is *that* why you have seemed so beset by
the blue devils of late, Damien? Because you felt yourself to
be trapped in a betrothal to a lady you did not care for, while
at the same time you found that you loved another?"

"Just so," answered Damien. "Now, perhaps, you will
understand why I so readily gave my consent to your own
betrothal to Thomas Culpepper. Even if I could not escape the
torment of a marriage like the one our parents had, you, at
least, might be spared."

"And now, thank goodness, you too are to be spared, and
may marry for love like myself!"

"If Caroline will have me," he rejoined soberly.

"If? Do you mean that she does not return your affections?"

"No, I believe she does. It is just that—" He hesitated. "As
you know, Gussie, ever since our parents died I have led a life
of—of dissolution and frivolity, indifferent to all but my own
pleasures. In the meantime I am ashamed to say that I have
nearly let Windemere go to wrack and ruin, and all in all have
so little to be proud of that I hardly know if I am worthy to

kiss the hem of Caroline's gown, let alone ask for her hand in marriage.''

"Come, it is not so bad as all that!" Augusta said loyally. "Windemere has survived, and so, I am happy to say, have you! A man may change, Damien, it is never too late!"

He looked at his sister in the semidarkness of the carriage. "Do you think so?"

"Yes, indeed I do! As to your past exploits, I am sure it is not to be wondered at that in the aftermath of our parents' deaths you became—became rather wild! Only consider the example *they* provided! They might hardly be termed paragons of virtue! Nor, I might add, did they betray the slightest interest in either the upbringing or the eventual destinies of their offspring! Highly unnatural, *I* call it!''

"I suppose it was," Damien said thoughtfully. "Until I met Caroline, and learned of the closeness and intimacy of her own family, I never thought to question how *we* were raised.''

"Though we never lacked for material possessions, it was a *shabby* existence!" Augusta declared roundly. "I can assure you, my dear brother, that *my* children shall receive a surfeit of love and attention, and I daresay yours shall as well!''

Damien's breath caught in his throat as a vision of Caroline, mother to their sons and daughters, rose in his mind. "Yes," he said. "Yes, they will know a very different sort of parents, Gussie!''

"It is a wonderful thought, is it not?" she remarked cheerfully. "I pray that Thomas may secure his curateship near Windemere, so that our children will come to know each other!''

"We must exert all our influence to ensure that he does," Damien said with a smile. After a moment he added, "Gussie, it is very pleasant to be speaking to you with such openness. I own that I should be loath to see you settled far from Windemere for yet another reason: I would not wish to see this new rapport between us denied the further opportunity to grow.''

He held out his hand and swiftly she reached out to clasp it in her own, saying with the sparkle of tears in her eyes: "Nor would I, my dear brother, nor would I."

The rest of their journey passed in a comfortable silence. When they reached the Reston town house some ten or fifteen minutes later, Uxley opened the door, and began to greet them but was summarily interrupted by Damien, who inquired: "Is Miss Smythe already abed, Uxley?"

"Abed, my lord? Why—why, no, she is not!"

"Good!" Damien said with an eagerness he did not trouble to conceal. "Where is she, then? In the drawing room, or one of the other saloons?"

"No, my lord," returned Uxley, looking baffled, "for Miss Smythe has gone."

"Gone?" Damien said, stupefied. "Do you mean to tell me she has left the house?"

"Yes, my lord, with two bandboxes. A hackney drove away with her perhaps forty-five minutes ago."

Feeling as if he had just been broadsided, Damien but dimly perceived Augusta's steadying hand on his arm. "Where did Miss Smythe go, Uxley?" she asked.

"I do not know, my lady. But she left you each a letter." The butler went to one of the side tables and retrieved two missives from a gold-rimmed salver, one of which he handed to Damien, and the other to Augusta.

With a sense of burgeoning unreality Damien broke the wafer and quickly read:

My beloved Damien:

I must leave you, to save you from the dreadful malefactions of the Earl of Audley. Do not worry for my safety or well-being, for I have taken a perfectly respectable position, far from London where the earl's evil influence will never penetrate. I am so very sorry to go from you this way, without the chance to see you once more, but perhaps it is better as it is, for I do not know that I should be able to tear myself away if we had.

Know that I shall always think of you, and that you will always be my dearest love, for as long as l draw breath and perhaps, if God is kind and wills it, throughout eternity as well.

C.

Damien stared at the neat feminine script which seemed to waver before his incredulous gaze. He wanted to thrust his fist through a wall, he wanted to jump on a horse and wildly ride in all directions in search of Caroline, he wanted to throw back his head and shout at the top of his lungs his anguish to the high heavens ... Instead he stood very still, and for a brief moment closed his eyes against the torrent of powerful emotions which threatened to swamp him, and take him under so deeply he felt as if he might drown in them.

My God, he thought, the irony! To have miraculously been released from his betrothal, and then to have lost his darling girl, his dearest heart, both within the sickeningly short span of an hour or two! He had returned home this evening thinking himself the most fortunate man alive—a free man once more, able to joyfully offer his heart and his hand, his wealth and all his possessions, his body and his soul—*everything!*—to Caroline, only to discover that she had crept away in the night.

And how like her, he reflected, to have done so to protect *him!* She was the most gallant woman he knew, the bravest, the sweetest, the most adorable and desirable—and he loved her with an intensity and a conviction that, just a few months before, he had never known was possible. He *had* to find her, he *would* find her, he vowed, if it was the last thing he accomplished in this life!

Finally Damien looked up from Caroline's letter. "Well?" he said, gazing bleakly at his sister, whose own expression was deeply troubled as she replied: "Caro has gone, having found, she says, a situation which will better suit *our* purposes! Whatever can she mean by it?"

"It is a long story," he responded. "Does she say where this new situation is located?"

"No, only that she is wretchedly sorry for leaving us in such a hurly-burly manner, and that she hopes we will forgive her. Oh, Damien, why would Caro have fled like this?"

All at once aware of the butler's presence in the entrance hall, Damien said, "I shall tell you all, but come with me into the library, Gussie. That will be all, Uxley: thank you."

"Yes, my lord," Uxley answered, but did not move.

Damien had already begun to turn away, his mind whirling with frantic thoughts of Bow Street Runners and carefully phrased notices in newspapers throughout the country, but then he perceived Uxley's peculiar immobility and firmly repeated, "You may go, Uxley." Anxious to be closeted with Augusta, so that he might privately converse with her and discuss the few options they had for the recovery of Caroline, Damien only vaguely registered the fleeting expression of uncertainty that crossed his butler's countenance; then Uxley had bowed, impassively murmured "Yes, my lord," and left the hall.

It was an oversight Damien was later to greatly regret.

Chapter 21

Caroline glanced wistfully out the window at the glorious autumn vista that beckoned so enticingly. A brisk, playful gust of wind danced through the trees clustered outside, fluttering vivid green and gold, crimson and copper-colored leaves determined yet to cling to their branches, and sending others flying gaily through the air.

It was September now, and Caroline could hardly believe it, for though the days since her arrival in Shrewsbury had been busy ones, they had nonetheless dragged with agonizing slowness. Even as she attempted to occupy her mind with the exact and thorough fulfillment of her duties—which were, to be sure, numerous—her heart could not forget what she had left behind in London. She missed Damien, ached for him as he haunted her thoughts during the long days and her dreams during the even longer nights. Again and again she reminded herself that she had done the right thing by taking this position as Miss Rutledge's companion; it was a thin enough blanket to draw round her shoulders on the increasingly colder evenings, but it was all she had left. That, and her memories of him, which made her smile, and laugh; shiver, and burn.

As she had so many times before, she wondered where Damien was at this moment: had he and his new marchioness, the Lady Helen, gone off to the country estates of friends, on a lengthy round of visits coinciding with the opening of pheasant season? Or would they have stopped at Windemere for Augusta's wedding to Thomas Culpepper? She did not know the date of this event, for Miss Rutledge, with her virulent scorn of all matters pertaining to the city and to the *ton,* did not care to receive any of the London newspapers; nor had she thus been able to read the accounts of Damien's wedding to the former Honorable Helen Manderlay, which were certain to have included fulsome descriptions of the ceremony, the lofty personages who attended, the magnificent attire of the bride, where the breakfast following the service was held and the type and quantity of refreshments that were served, what the bride wore for her traveling dress, and whence the noble couple sojourned on their honeymoon.

She was, Caroline admitted to herself, at once half sorry and half glad she had not had access to the town periodicals. She supposed there might have been some useful feeling of finality in reading about Damien's marriage, however unhappy that feeling might be, and she could not deny she would have eagerly grasped the opportunity to learn of *any* news that had to do with him. But each word of such an account would certainly have been a cruel knife-stab in her breast, and *that,* she thought sorrowfully, she could just as well do without.

"Miss *Smythe!*" came a sharp voice, causing Caroline to jump a little in her seat. Across from her, sitting bolt upright on an uncomfortable straight-backed chair, Miss Rutledge was glaring, her lace-capped head lowered like an angry old bull's about to charge.

"I—I beg your pardon, ma'am," Caroline apologized at once.

"That is the *second* time this hour you have been distracted by the view!" her employer chided her irritably. "I do not pay you to admire the landscape, missy!"

"No, ma'am," murmured Caroline.

"What *is* it that you stare at so longingly? It is merely a withering clutch of trees out there, shivering in the wind, and great ugly heaps of desiccated leaves which will have to be raked by that slothful gardener of mine!"

"I—I have always liked the autumn, ma'am."

"What nonsense! *I* have always considered it to be a dreary season, its only purpose to serve as the melancholy harbinger of winter!" The old lady snorted. "I suppose you will wish to go for a walk this afternoon, too!"

"Yes, ma'am, if—if there should be the time to do so."

"Well, I do not know that there will be," Miss Rutledge returned crossly. "There is the tablecloth whose embroidery requires repair—mind that you keep your stitches small and neat!—and you must ensure that Cook doesn't overbeat the muffin dough today, for I thought yesterday's horridly tough! I do not know how I managed to consume three of them! I suppose I only wished to spare Cook's feelings, though the wretched creature is hardly deserving of such sensitivity! And, might I add, we have scarcely made a dent in today's selection from *Of the Laws of Ecclesiastical Polity* because of your woeful inability to concentrate!"

"Yes, ma'am; I *am* sorry," Caroline said, and again picked up the heavy volume, one of Mr. Hooker's eight that comprised his Elizabethan masterpiece on the subject of church government. She herself considered it dreadfully dull, but Miss Rutledge evidently took great enjoyment in the scholarly minister's pious, long-winded treatise.

Caroline cleared her throat and turned once more to the section entitled "Nature, Righteousness, and Sin." Aloud she said, "To continue with Book One, Chapter Nine:

" 'Now the due observation of this law which reason teacheth us cannot but be effectual unto their great good that observe the same. For we see the world and each part thereof so compacted that—' ''

She was interrupted by a little scream from Miss Rutledge. "There he is again!"

"Who, ma'am?" Caroline inquired, dutifully glancing round the dingy, ill-heated little saloon and wondering, not for the first time, whether her employer was wholly in command of her mental faculties.

"No, no, do you look out the window! That man! I saw him again, skulking round the trees!"

Caroline obeyed, but saw nothing that she had not before perceived. "I am afraid that I do not see anyone outside at present, ma'am."

"It is the same one I saw yesterday, just outside the garden gate!" declared Miss Rutledge, vehemently nodding her head. "*Entirely* dressed in black, and obviously engaged in some sort of unwholesome activity, for no sooner had he caught my eye than he hurried off down the road!"

Politely Caroline said (for she had heard it was best to humor the insane): "Is it also the gentleman whom you thought you saw addressing one of the maids earlier in the week, ma'am?"

The old lady drew herself even more upright, if such a thing was possible, and indignantly snapped, "*Thought* I saw? Do you dare to impugn my eyesight *and* my veracity, Miss Smythe?"

"No, ma'am."

"I should hope not! Perhaps you may then be accounted to be of marginally more substantial intelligence than that simpering dolt of a maid—she's got more hair than wit, *I* say!—who upon being interrogated would only reply that he told her he understood this house was to let, and was hopeful of making further inquiries! A greater bag of moonshine I have never heard in my life! Only let him approach *me* and be so brass-faced as to ask whether my house is to be rented out! I should soon show him his place, the arrant knave! Hovering round helpless women's homes, indeed! I should not be amazed, Miss Smythe, if we are all murdered in our beds one night!''

As some sort of reply seemed to be expected of her, meekly Caroline said: "I hope that we are not, ma'am."

Miss Rutledge only sniffed and stared fiercely out the window. After some considerable time had passed, she apparently had not caught another glimpse of the mysterious gentleman in black, for she brought her gaze back to Caroline and said with palpable annoyance, "Well, what are you waiting for, missy? Continue reading!"

Obediently Caroline looked to the book in her lap. " 'For we see the world and each part thereof so compacted that as long as each thing performeth only that work which is natural unto it, it thereby preserveth both other things and also itself.' "

"Very true, very true!" interpolated Miss Rutledge, nodding wisely.

" 'Contrariwise, let any principal thing, as the sun or moon, or any one of the heavens or elements, but once cease or fail, or swerve, and who does not easily conceive that the sequel thereof would be ruin both to itself and whatsoever dependeth upon it?' "

"Have I not frequently said so?" was the complacent rejoinder.

Lord help me, Caroline thought dismally, but it was going to be a long morning! On and on she read, and it was not until she reached the section called "The Foundations of Society" did Miss Rutledge pronounce herself sufficiently elevated, morally and intellectually, for one day. She then dismissed Caroline with an abrupt wave of her hand, and Caroline with a rapid step proceeded to the kitchen to confer with the long-suffering cook and thence to the dining room to survey the bedraggled tablecloth, the repair of which took her nearly two hours, so that it was nearly three o'clock before she was able to don her old brown cloak and a drab but sturdy bonnet and slip out of the house while Miss Rutledge partook of her customary afternoon nap.

Caroline breathed deeply of the cool, crisp air, and gratefully lifted her face to the soft rays of the autumnal sun. Heavens, but it felt wonderful to be striding along the quiet road, swinging her arms and relishing a rare moment of freedom! She did not think ahead to the ordeal of teatime that shortly loomed (for she had yet to serve to Miss Rutledge a cup of tea that had been prepared to her satisfaction), or the tasks that must be performed and the tedium endured before she might retire to her bedchamber for the evening. She only looked at the trees, and the blue sky scudding with plump white clouds, and the little stream that meandered alongside the road, wondering idly if it would freeze in the winter. She was some fifty paces from Miss Rutledge's house when gradually she became aware of the sounds of hoofbeats and carriage wheels behind her, and swiftly she moved aside so that the conveyance might conveniently pass.

But the hoofbeats only slowed, and then stopped, and then Caroline heard a familiar voice, deep and cultured and aristocratic and entirely beloved, a voice she had never again thought to hear in this lifetime.

"Caroline! Caroline, my love! Will you not turn and greet me?"

With a gasp she whirled, and for a giddy moment thought she might faint from the shock of seeing Damien, clad in a many-caped greatcoat and tall beaver hat, driving a trim, sleek closed carriage drawn by his handsome chestnuts. Her lips parted but no sound issued from them; she could only stretch out a shaking hand to him in utter wonderment.

"My dearest heart!" Damien said, and then he had lightly leaped to the ground and come to her, and enfolded her in his embrace, holding her so tightly it was as if he never, ever meant to let her go.

Dazedly Caroline breathed in the richly masculine scents of

wool and horse and soap, rested her cheek against his broad chest, stood on tiptoe and luxuriously slid her arms about his neck. Surely this was a dream, and one from which she never wished to awaken! "Oh, Damien, Damien," she murmured. "Is it truly you?"

With a laugh Damien drew back, but only to assure her, "Yes, my darling girl, but of a certainty it is I!" and in the next moment he had gathered her still more closely to him and kissed her, long and hungrily, with all the intensity and fervor of a man who had been wandering in the desert and come across a desperately sought spring of sweet water.

With the same passion Caroline returned his kiss, closing her eyes and surrendering to the fiery excitement he never failed to arouse in her. Blissfully she gripped the thick silky hair at his nape and sighed with unabashed pleasure, only dimly aware of the fact that her bonnet had tumbled from her head and was very likely being ushered toward the stream by a mischievous gust of wind. She could not have said how long she and Damien stood thusly, only that she uttered a soft sound of protest when finally he straightened, stepped back, and gripped both her hands in his own.

"You are thin again," he said. "I perceive that it shall be my first priority to feed you until you have regained your former bloom, my dearest girl!"

"Never mind that!" she replied, gazing up into his handsome countenance, taking in with acute delight his dark, deep-set eyes, the sleek dark brows, the straight nose and sensuous mouth, the firm jaw. "Only tell me—oh, pray tell me *everything!*" A dreadful thought occurred to her and convulsively she clenched her fingers around his. "Damien! Are you—are you married?"

His smile was dazzling. "No, I am not."

Stunned, her thoughts scattering, Caroline could only whisper, "Not married, Damien?"

"No. Miss Manderlay released me from our betrothal, and

so for these three months I have been an honorably unencumbered man, but I could not find you, Caroline, to tell you so! They have been, I assure you, the longest three months of my life!''

''How—how *did* you find me?''

''There was so little that I could do,'' he replied. ''I hired Bow Street Runners to canvass the countryside, and placed discreet notices in dozens of newspapers. But as the weeks went by, and there was no word of your whereabouts, my anxiety grew so great I thought I might go mad!''

''I am so sorry to have caused you such distress,'' she said, freeing one of her hands to lovingly stroke at one of the fine wool capes of his greatcoat. ''You are not—not angry with me for having left you so?''

''I could never be angry with you, Caroline,'' returned Damien. ''I understood very well why you felt you had to go, and I am humbled to think that you would have made such a sacrifice for me.''

''I would do anything for you,'' she told him softly. ''You must know that.''

''Thank you, my darling.'' He reached for the hand that rested upon his greatcoat, and raised it tenderly to his lips. ''So, while the Runners did their work and the newspapers theirs, in a feeble attempt to distract myself I went home to Windemere and, much to the amazement of my poor bailiff and the entire staff, vigorously threw myself into estate affairs. Then, just when I began to succumb to despair, believing that you truly had vanished without a trace, Uxley stepped forward.''

''Uxley?'' repeated Caroline, puzzled.

''Yes. I had gone again to London, to confer with the head of the Runners, and when I returned to Grosvenor Square I found Uxley waiting for me, in his grasp one of the many newspapers in which a notice had been placed. He had recognized you at once from the description, and confided that he might have the barest clue as to your location.''

"He guessed that I had gone to the employment registries he had recommended!" exclaimed Caroline.

"Exactly. He could not have been more apologetic for withholding such crucial information, but, as I told him, he *had* tried to make it known to me the night of your disappearance, and in my haste to begin formulating strategies for your discovery I misguidedly ignored his tentative attempt to do so, and thereafter failed to convey to him the utter gravity of the situation."

"Oh, I am so glad that Uxley came forward!" Caroline said, and thought that never in her life had she made a statement with such heartfelt conviction.

"Indeed, I do not believe I can ever repay such a monumental debt," Damien agreed. "It was but an afternoon's work, then, to locate the very helpful Mrs. Dent, who promptly provided me with the name and direction of a certain Miss Edwina Rutledge. Mrs. Dent sends you her regards, by the bye, and wishes us very happy."

"How—how kind of her!" said Caroline, gazing wide-eyed up into Damien's face. "Are we to—to be wished happy?"

"I trust you do not think I came here to offer you *carte blanche?*" he replied with a mock frown. "Naturally we are to be felicitated, Caroline, for we are very shortly to be wed."

"Are—are we?" she said, a little breathlessly, feeling a smile that she knew to be uninhibitedly radiant lighting up her face, and widening still further when she saw his own answering smile.

"Yes, I would have arrived here some days prior to this, but I required a little time to secure for us a special license. Should you like to be married next week at Windermere, alongside Gussie and her Thomas? While I was waiting for the license I rode there to ascertain their willingness to participate in such a plan, and they several times pressed me to tell you that they would like it above all things. In point of fact, I would not deem it an exaggeration to describe Gussie as being absolutely wild with delight.''

"We can be married next week? Oh, I *am* dreaming!" Caroline said dazedly. "Oh, yes, Damien, if you are quite sure Gussie and Mr. Culpepper are convenable!"

"I have not the least doubt of their sincerity," he replied. "Of course, I fear you will have no time in which to assemble a proper trousseau."

"*That* hardly matters!" she said, but then she paused thoughtfully. "However, I daresay it *is* foolish of me, Damien, but— "

"The dress," he said instantly. At her hesitant nod he went on, "As to that, I hope that you will not mind, but Gussie and I have charged Aunt Violet with that task—one upon which she embarked with marvelous enthusiasm."

"How could I mind? Indeed, I think it is very kind of Mrs. Yardley to permit herself to be burdened with such a responsibility."

"You and I know that it is hardly a burden to Aunt Violet: it is more in the nature of manna from Heaven to her."

Caroline laughed. "I must admit that you are correct!"

"Fortunately, she is blessed with excellent taste, and I am confident that your gown will be nothing short of exquisite. When I took my leave of her she could speak of nothing but white net, clouds of tulle, and silver spangles!"

"Oh, it does sound lovely!" said Caroline admiringly. A little shyly she added: "Will you forgive my silly vanity, my love, in inquiring about something so trivial as a dress? It is— it is only that I would wish you to think me beautiful upon our wedding day!"

"You," Damien said a little raggedly, "are *always* beautiful to me, Caroline!" And with that he caught her up in his arms again and kissed her with such dizzyingly satisfying conviction that Caroline could almost, *almost* begin to believe that it was true.

An unpleasantly penetrating screech caused them to abruptly

step apart, and to turn instinctively toward the source of the noise. It was none other than Miss Rutledge herself, advancing toward them along the road, gripping in one scrawny fist an ancient parasol which she threateningly raised when she drew near.

"*What* is the meaning of this?" she demanded furiously. "Never have I been forced to witness such blatant immorality on my very doorstep! Miss Smythe, you will return to the house at once, while I dispatch this—this *loose fish* upon the instant!"

Unhurriedly Damien took in the old-fashioned blue-and-white-striped cotton gown, the long swansdown-edged velvet stole haphazardly flung about skinny shoulders, and the striped silk bonnet elaborately festooned with several grandiose bunches of ribbons; he raised his eyebrows, and murmured blandly to Caroline, "Your employer, I take it?"

"Yes," she replied in an unsteady undervoice, repressing a powerful urge to giggle at the cool *sang-froid* with which he encountered the remarkable Miss Rutledge, then she said to that lady: "I—I fear you are laboring under a misapprehension, ma'am, for this gentleman is by no means a—a loose fish, but—"

"But a scoundrel in league with that *other* miscreant!" rudely interrupted the old lady, bending a fierce scowl upon Damien who, apparently to her even more heightened affront, evidenced no particular tendency to quake in his elegantly gleaming boots at this ocular onslaught.

Instead he offered a bow so slight as to be vaguely contemptuous, and replied calmly: "I should not be honest with you, ma'am, were I to say that I am sorry to be this day depriving you of the presence of your companion, for having had the dubious pleasure of your acquaintance for all of some sixty seconds, I readily perceive that you have signally failed to treat Miss Smythe, my betrothed, with the barest modicum of the respect and courtesy which she deserves." He ignored Miss Rutledge's flabbergasted puff of outrage and to Caroline he said with a tender smile, "Shall I wait with the horses whilst you go retrieve your belongings, my dearest girl, or shall you require my escort into the house?''

"No, I thank you; do wait with those patient creatures, if you will; I shall return to you in a twinkling," she promised blithely and, true to her word, having hastily packed her two small bandboxes once more (only with a markedly lighter spirit this time), veritably flew down the steps and the short walkway that led to the road where Damien stood with the reins of his mounts in his hand, speaking gently to them. Miss Rutledge still hovered nearby, casting fulminating glances at him and impotently clutching her parasol, giving every appearance of heartily desiring to strike him one or two (or several) resounding blows with it.

"Good-bye, Miss Rutledge," Caroline called politely, "and thank you! You need not worry about payment of this month's wages!"

She received no reply other than a dreadful glare, and as Damien opened the door of the carriage and took from her the pair of bandboxes to toss inside he murmured, "If looks could kill, I daresay we should at this very moment be stretched lifeless in the dirt.''

Caroline laughed, receiving from him her bonnet which he had retrieved from wherever it had tumbled to (apparently not the stream after all, for it was not damp, but only a trifle dusty) and placed on one of the seats, and with murmured thanks she set it atop her curls and tied the gray ribbon in a jaunty bow underneath her chin.

"I do not care for that hat," Damien remarked. "You ought never to wear again anything so patently practical! Fortunately, Aunt Violet had prepared for you two large trunks of your London clothes to be brought along with me, and I daresay she included amongst them some more becoming headgear. Promise me you will discard that sad excuse for a bonnet at the earliest opportunity."

She laughed again and agreed, then, as he extended a hand

to help her into the carriage, she said, "May I not ride outside with you, my love? It is too soon to be parted from you, even though we should be but a few handsbreadths apart!"

"You may," he said, suiting words to action, and as soon as she was comfortably settled next to him on the seat he urged the horses into motion and added, "But only during the short distance to Shrewsbury, where I have bespoken for us an early dinner at the town's best inn, as well as their two finest bed-chambers and a private parlor. You will recall little Martha, the maidservant who attended you at Windemere? She and one of my grooms await us there, along with the horse I shall ride on our journey home. Tomorrow, when you are well rested and we have breakfasted, we will set out and proceed in easy stages, with Martha to lend you both the consequence and the propriety due to my future marchioness."

Issuing a soft little sigh of delight, Caroline surrendered herself up to Damien's masterful care. She would likely, she thought, need to pinch herself several times a day, in order to convince herself that this was all really happening, that it was not some fantastical daydream spun in her head. Very soon, over their dinner, perhaps, she would ask Damien to tell her the manner in which he came to be freed of his entanglement with Miss Manderlay, and how everyone at Windemere fared, and what sort of wedding Augusta and Mrs. Yardley were planning, and—oh, a thousand other questions, but for now, she wanted only to sit beside him and bask in his closeness, and let all the cares and woes of these past difficult months slip away.

She snuggled a little closer to him and gave another contented sigh. They rode for some time in a companionable silence, which by and bye Damien broke by speaking thoughtfully.

"I believe you shall find Windemere quite a changed place from how you first encountered it."

Caroline peeped at him from underneath her lashes. "Yes? How so?"

"Why, with Goodsall's assistance, I am well on the way toward becoming a gentleman farmer, not unlike the famous Mr. Coke! We are full of plans, Goodsall and I, for new crops to be planted in the spring, the purchase of modern equipment for the farms, repairs to the tenants' cottages, drainage and improvement of the roads, and all sorts of fascinating schemes. I daresay I shall be boring you outrageously with my endless talk of Tullian drills, stickleback manure, and sheep-hurdling!"

"On the contrary, I should be delighted to be included in such conversations," Caroline told him. "I shall be proud to be a knowledgeable farmer's wife!"

Damien smiled and, transferring one of the reins to join its mate in his left hand, slid his right arm around her shoulder. "I do believe you will," he said, and went on: "You will see a considerable change to the house as well. Mrs. Dawkins and Milton, and their vast crew of minions, have been quite busy restoring all the rooms to their former grandeur, cleaning and dusting and polishing and mending with what I can only describe as the fanatical vigor of the newly converted. The other day I came across Mrs. Dawkins weeping into her apron, and when I inquired in some alarm as to what had happened to make her cry, she only grinned at me through her tears and said that Windemere was beginning to look as it had in my grandfather's day."

"How happy she must be!" said Caroline. "She loves Windemere so very much, I know."

"As I am coming to," Damien replied. "After all these years of disaffection and neglect, it has begun, slowly but surely, to seem to me like home. Only it lacked *your* presence, Caroline, to truly make it so!"

Softly she said, "I have never really had a home . . . where one might live forever, surrounded by family and familiar comforts. It is a fantastical prospect, I must confess."

His arm tightened about her. "Not fantastical, but soon to be a reality, I assure you."

Caroline smiled, thinking of the future, filled with promise, that stretched invitingly out ahead of her and Damien. She was imagining a dark-haired, dark-eyed little boy, the image of his handsome father, and a little girl, possibly with her own auburn ringlets and green eyes, when all at once Damien spoke.

"The miscreant to whom the redoubtable Miss Rutledge referred—was he by any chance a fellow clad wholly in black garments?"

"Why, yes, so Miss Rutledge claimed," said Caroline in some surprise. "I never saw him myself, but *she* was convinced he existed, and that he had come to menace the occupants of the house. How did you happen to know of him, my love?"

Damien threw back his head and laughed. "I sent him there."

"Sent him? What do you mean?"

"Not to torment your Miss Rutledge—which, having met her, now strikes me as an excellent notion—but to ascertain that you remained in residence there while I was forced to linger in London, awaiting the special license. I wanted to take no chances that you might slip away again, my dearest heart! The fellow was a Bow Street Runner and, evidently, not one of their subtlest."

Caroline laughed too, saying, "The mystery explained! I own I several times doubted Miss Rutledge's sanity, and now I perceive that I have failed to do her justice."

"Next you will be telling me we should immediately return to her abode, and inform her that he was *not* a villain who only awaited his chance to commit some fell deed to her person."

"Well . . ." Caroline said doubtfully.

Firmly Damien replied: "I do not mind rescuing puppies and donkeys, my darling girl, but I draw the line at easing the troubled minds of bracket-faced old harridans who have caused you to suffer. Indeed, I can only term it a just recompense."

Caroline smiled at him, murmured "Yes, my love," and cheerfully she consigned all further thoughts of her former employer quite utterly and permanently to oblivion.

ABOUT THE AUTHOR

Martine Berne has worked as an English teacher, a public relations assistant, an investment banker, a bartender, and a children's book editor. She has lived in Southern and Northern California, Mexico, New England, New York City, and, most recently, in South Florida. She and her husband have welcomed into their "pack" a ninety-five-pound yellow Lab adopted from the Humane Society of Broward County—Simba—and, more recently, a baby boy, named Max.